THE INHERITORS

books by

HAROLD ROBBINS

Never Love a Stranger
The Dream Merchants
A Stone For Danny Fisher
Never Leave Me
79 Park Avenue
Stiletto
The Carpetbaggers
Where Love Has Gone
The Adventurers
The Inheritors
The Betsy
The Pirate
The Lonely Lady
Dreams Die First
Memories of Another Day
Goodbye, Janette
The Storyteller
Spellbinder
Descent from Xanadu
The Piranhas
The Raiders
The Stallion
Tycoon
The Predators
The Secret
Never Enough
Sin City
Heat of Passion

with

JUNIUS PODRUG

The Betrayers
Blood Royal
The Devil to Pay
The Looters
The Deceivers
The Shroud
The Curse

THE INHERITORS

HAROLD
ROBBINS

IRIDIUM PRESS
an imprint of
OGHMA CREATIVE MEDIA

OGHMA

CREATIVE MEDIA

Iridium Press
An imprint of Oghma Creative Media, Inc.
2401 Beth Lane, Bentonville, Arkansas 72712

Identifiers: ISBN: 978-1-63373-550-7 (hardcover) |
ISBN: 978-1-63373-551-4 (trade paperback)
Subjects: | BISAC: FICTION/Thrillers/Historical. | FICTION/Thriller/Suspense. |
FICTION/Romance/Historical/American

Iridium Press trade paperback edition, December, 2019

Jacket Design by Theresa Fajardo
Interior Design by Casey W. Cowan
Editing by Michael L. Frizell

This book is for Paul Gitlin

With Love

And many thanks to the man who wears the hat, Bradley Yonover.

CONTENTS

FOREWORD

BY MICHAEL L. FRIZELL

JUST TALK TO THE READER:
Writing Advice from Harold Robbins

HERE'S AN 89-DEGREE ANGLE.

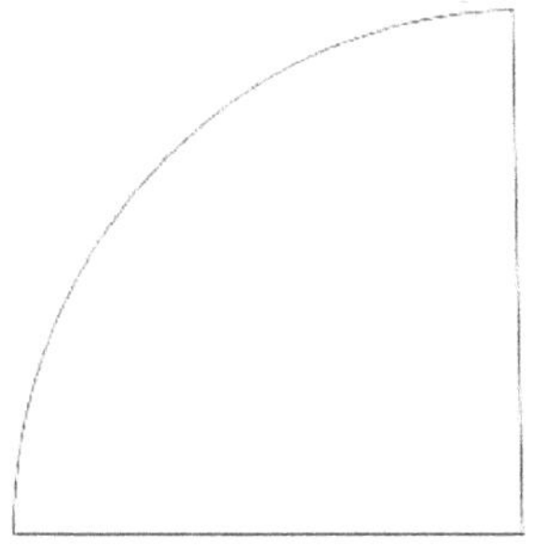

Mildly infuriating, isn't it?

It's like an itch on the bottom of your foot that manifested only after you finished lacing up your boot. Or a bug who met an untimely end on your windshield moments after you washed it. The gas pump stopping at $30.01. A politician making a promise. The blacks in your pants and shirt matching until you step outside. Human pop-up ads vying for your attention to sell you lotion in the mall when you just don't. Want. To. Talk.

Crocs.

This is how I feel whenever I write. The work is never perfect. It's always missing... something. I second-guess every word, every turn of phrase, and every comma.

Did DaVinci not say that art is never finished, only abandoned?

Should I ever view my work as a 90-degree angle, I'll quit writing. It won't be worth the pursuit.

In fact, I'm considering calling my memoir *The 89 Degree Angle.* The 90-degree angle infers perfection. Greatness. Achievement. I always feel like I'm that close.

One correct word. One inch to the right. One breakthrough. One win.

One degree closer.

I'm determined to push through imposter syndrome or any niggling little kernels of doubt to tell the stories I dream of telling.

A graduate student once told me through gritted teeth and a quivering lip that the first draft of the statistical results chapter of her thesis was an 89-degree angle. She had no idea how to make it interesting or readable. After multiple drafts, she remembered a story I told during orientation. The chair of my first thesis listened with little sympathy as I extolled the horrors of the worst writer's block I'd ever experienced. I just couldn't get started. I sat at my manual typewriter (yeah, I'm that old) and just… stared.

"Writer's block is bullshit. You're just not writing." He grumbled when he said it, locking eyes with me, almost daring me to contradict him. "Get a piece of poster board and write, in big letters, 'I'm not writing the great American novel!' and hang it above your desk. That way, whenever you sigh and throw your head back, you'll be reminded to just get it written." He then dismissed me with a wave.

I did. I finished the 110-page thesis in three weeks.

"It doesn't have to be perfect," I told her. "Just get it written."

So the graduate assistant followed my advice. She also got her own poster board. Several tortured drafts later, she clicked *SEND* and waited.

Her advisor sent it back to her. The email read:

`What is this? Rewrite the whole thing.`

More tears led to a draft that her chair deemed "Kinda readable." I told her to take that as a win.

Look, even the best writers have editors who serve as a second set of eyes and can shepherd their work to the next level. Sometimes, though, it takes a bottle of scotch and the balls to tell the truth. That's why Harold's work is appealing years after his death.

Harold liked Glenmorangie. I must admit that I like it, too, but not as much as Edradour. Jann Robbins writes, "He (Harold) discovered (Glenmorangie) while doing research for *The Inheritors*. His main character was a Scotch drinker who always requested, eighteen-year-old Glenmorangie" (p. 149). After the publication of the book, the product became so well-known that the distillery thanked him by sending him a case of single malt. For the next twenty years, the distillery sent him a case for Christmas.

Did a case of scotch make Harold inspired to write more? I can't answer that. Two shots and I can't even type. I'm a lightweight. You should ask Hunter Thompson, Raymond Chandler, Dorothy Parker, or Ernest Hemingway.

Perhaps it was the million-dollar advance for the film rights paid by Joseph Levine, a film producer responsible for the production of almost 500 movies during his prolific career, that inspired him to write. Harold credits Levine for making the movie versions of his books successful. Harold told Jann, "Joe paid me a million for the movie rights of *The Inheritors* before I had ever written a word.... He also thought I was writing the book about him and he didn't want any other producer to get his hands on it" (Robbins, p. 241-242). *The Inheritors* isn't about Levine. Harold stated it's about "Jim Aubrey, who ran CBS and got screwed" (p. 242). Aubrey was responsible for such perennial favorites as *Gilligan's Island* and *The Beverly Hillbillies* (Wallace, n.p.). Aubrey was dismissed on February 27, 1965 for taking kickbacks, an abrasive attitude, and, as he put it, "I don't pretend to be any saint. If anyone wants to indict me for liking pretty girls, I'm guilty" ("The Return," n.p.). I'd imagine this is one of the many reasons Harold liked him.

At the time, the publicity for *The Inheritors*, driven by the notoriety of Harold and Levine, no doubt, was the most expensive and elaborate push for a book in publishing history. Over $50,000 was spent in 1969 on one billboard that spanned an entire block overlooking Times Square (Robbins, p. 243). Harold states, "Seven sexy covers faced the subway and every time they looked up they saw one of my covers. Sales went up. It cost a lot of money, but it worked. I went on a book tour that hit every major city in the US. We had an entourage of go-go girls, a rock band with a kickoff party at the Nepenthe Club in New York."

The Inheritors completed "The Trilogy of Greed" that started with *Dream Merchants* and followed by *Carpetbaggers.* This trilogy was Harold at his best, ripping scandals from the headlines and amplifying them in a world where sexy femme fatales and power brokers clashed. He was ahead of his time when it came to crafting stories about business moguls enjoying rock-star status (see also *Dreams Die First* and *Descent from Xanadu*). As Jann writes, "Today, moguls have hit television shows, movies portraying their lives" (p. 118). Million-dollar advances on their memoirs and popular social media feeds, moguls are the embodiment of the success—and excess—of the American Dream. Harold made us see beyond the glossy façades and neatly pressed suits. He showed us the rampant narcissism and the abuse of power.

Of course, we need only turn on the news the last three years to see a mogul who flaunts power, sleeps with porn stars, and thinks highly of himself. But I digress. As Jann writes, "Harold Robbins gave his reader familiarity with the world of the rich and famous. His goal was to erase the page and talk with his reader and tell them of the people he had known, met and dealt with in his life. He had an intensity in his writing that helped the reader experience between the lines" (p. 118).

So that's Harold's secret to writing: erase the page and talk directly to the reader.

Thanks, Harold. I'll try to keep that in mind. I'm still going to leave the poster board up above my desk.

Works Cited

Robbins, J. (n.d.). *Harold and Me.* Bentonville, AR: Oghma Creative Media.

Robinson, Leonard Wallace. "After the Yankees What?: A TV Drama." *The New York Times* Magazine. November 15, 1964.

"The Return of Smiling Jim." *Time* Magazine. October 31, 1969. 80. Retrieved on January 24, 2008.

THAT DAY LAST SPRING

MORNING

I WAS ON MY THIRD cup of coffee when the telephone began to ring. I let it ring. You wait three years for a phone call, you can wait thirty seconds more.

I refilled the coffee cup. I checked the angle of the sun, the window of the blonde who lived in the house just below me on the hill, the traffic on the Strip.

The sun hadn't crested the hill, the blonde was still asleep, her shades drawn, and the only car on the Strip was a lonely police car crawling along. Then I reached for the phone.

"Good morning, Sam," I said.

There was a moment's silence. I could hear the sound of his harsh breathing in the phone. *"How'd you know it was me?"*

"This is a late-morning town," I said. "Nobody gets up before ten o'clock."

"I couldn't sleep," he grumbled. *"I got in last night but I don't know it yet. I'm still on New York time."*

"I know."

"What are you doin'?" he asked.

"Sitting. Drinking coffee."

"How about coming over and having breakfast with me?"

"I don't eat breakfast, Sam. You know that."

"Neither do I. You know that, too. But I can't sleep. And I want to talk to you."

"I'm on the phone."

"I spend half my life on the phone. I want to talk to your face." He paused. Again I could hear the harsh sound of his breath in the phone. *"Tell you what. Come on over and we'll take a ride someplace. I'll even risk my neck in that new car I read you got that goes two-twenty miles per."*

"Why don't you just take a drive by yourself?"

"Two reasons. One, California drivers are all crazy and I'm afraid of them. Two, I said I want to see you."

I hesitated a moment, "Okay. I'll pick you up in front of the hotel."

"Fifteen minutes," he said. *"I got one call to make to New York."*

I put down the phone and went upstairs to the bedroom. I opened the door softly and stepped inside. The drapes were drawn tightly and in the dim spill of light I could see Chinese Girl was still asleep. She was naked on top of the sheets, her hands stretched out over her head as if she were about to dive from the high board, her long hair cascading down her back covering her like a blanket.

I walked over to the bed and looked down at her. She was absolutely motionless, I could scarcely see her breathe. The room was filled with the smell of last night's love that hung in the air like old wine. I cupped my hand gently across her small ivory-tinted marble-hard buttocks. She dug herself into the mattress and I could feel the heat of her coming into my fingers.

She spoke into the pillow without turning her head, her voice muffled and heavy. "What is it that you do to me, Steve? The minute you touch me I drown in my own juices."

I took back my hand and went into the bathroom. When I came out fifteen minutes later, she was sitting up in bed, her fingers playing between her legs.

"You're dressed," she said. "That's not fair. I was keeping it warm for you."

"Sorry, Chinese Girl," I answered. "I have an appointment."

"You can be late," she said. "Come back to bed and fuck me."

I didn't answer. I crossed the room and took a sweater from the closet and slipped into it.

"There's an old Chinese proverb," she said. "Any day that starts with a fuck can't be all bad."

I laughed.

"I'm not being funny. That's the first time you've said 'No' to me."

"It had to happen sometime, Chinese Girl," I said.

"And stop calling me 'Chinese Girl.' I have a name and you know it."

I looked at her. There was a hint of anger in her face that wasn't there a moment ago. "Cool it, Chinese Girl," I said. "Even I don't believe a name like Mary Applegate."

"But that's my name."

"Maybe so. But you look like Chinese Girl to me."

She pulled the sheet up over her. "I think it's time for me to go."

I didn't answer.

"How long will you be?" she asked.

"I don't know. Maybe a couple hours."

"I'll be gone by then."

I looked at her. "You got enough bread?"

"I can manage."

I nodded. "Good-bye, then. I'll miss you." I closed the door behind me and went down the stairs.

Outside the sun had already climbed the hill and the white glare made me blink. I put on the shades and went around back of the house to the carport.

The Iso reflected the light like a black pearl in Cartier's window. Her little Volks stood next to it looking like the ridiculous bug that it was. There was something almost forlorn and lost about it.

Maybe it was just the way I felt whenever I saw one of them. All the little skivvies had them. It was wheels, it was cheap, and it took them back and forth on their little affairs. And in between times it was parked in somebody's garage while their owners rode around in Lincoln Continentals. But sooner or later, big-car time came to an end and they were back in business.

Like this morning.

I went back into the house and found some Scotch tape in the kitchen. Then I taped two one-hundred-dollar bills to the Volks dashboard where she couldn't miss them. I pulled up in front of the hotel thirty minutes late and he wasn't downstairs yet.

I sat in the car and cursed myself for being a fool. Chinese Girl was right. I blew a perfectly good fuck.

Fifteen minutes later, he came out. The doorman opened the car and he climbed in puffing. The door slammed shut and we looked at each other.

Like for a long moment. Then he leaned over and kissed me on the cheek. "I've missed you."

I put the car into gear and went down the driveway. I didn't speak until we stopped for the light at Sunset Boulevard. "I didn't think you cared."

He took it more seriously than I meant it. "You know I do. I had to do what I did."

The light turned and I headed out toward Santa Monica. "It doesn't matter now. That's three years old." I glanced at him. "Anyplace in particular?"

He shrugged. "Anyplace you say. It's your town."

I kept on going.

"I suppose you're wondering why I called," he continued.

I didn't answer.

"I felt I owed you."

"You don't owe me anything," I said quickly. "I have the stock. Yours. Sinclair's."

"You don't have to tell me you're rich," he said. "Everybody knows that. But money isn't everything."

I turned and looked at him. "Now he tells me," I smiled. "Then why did you do it?"

His dark eyes shone behind the highly polished, black-rimmed glasses. "The pressure was on. I was afraid everything was going to go."

I laughed bitterly. "And there I was. Wide open and trusting. A perfect setup."

"Remember what I told you then? Someday you would thank me for it."

I kept my eyes on the road and my mouth shut. There were a lot of things I could thank him for. But there was only one thing wrong with them. They were nothing that I wanted.

"You know the old song?" he asked. "You always hurt the one you love."

"Don't sing it. It's too early in the morning."

"It's true," he said earnestly. "Of all people, I thought you would be the one to know that."

"Okay. You told me. Now I know."

He was suddenly angry. "No, you don't. You don't know nothin'. I helped make you rich, don't you ever forget it."

"Turn off the rockets, Sam," I said dryly. "You just finished telling me money isn't everything."

He was silent for a moment. "Give me a cigarette."

"What for? You don't smoke." I grinned at him. "Besides I've seen you do that trick before. Maybe a thousand times."

He knew what I was talking about. "I want a cigarette."

I flipped open the glove compartment behind the gear box that ran between our seats. "Help yourself."

His fingers were trembling as he lit it clumsily. We began to descend the curving road past Will Rogers Memorial Park to the coast road.

The sun was up by the time I turned the car north on the coast road. He started to throw the cigarette out the window, but I stopped him by gesturing to the ashtray.

"There's got to be something crazy about a country where it don't rain for a hundred days and everything burns up, and then when it does rain, it floods and everything washes away."

I smiled. "You can't have everything. How far do you want to go?"

"Pull over. I want to stretch my legs."

I cut across the road into a parking area. We got out of the car and walked over to the edge and looked down at the beach.

The sand was white and the water was blue and sparkling, the waves coming in on long white-capped rollers. The surfers were out already, huddling over a small fire on the beach, some of them in their wet suits. The girls were there too, but the surfers weren't looking at them. They were watching the water with calculating eyes, searching out the swells and eddies.

"It's crazy," Sam said. "Those kids are going swimming in the middle of the winter."

I grinned, lighting a cigarette. I cupped my hands to shield the flame from the breeze. He tapped me on the shoulder. I turned to look at him and lost the light.

"Do you know how old I am?"

"Sure. Sixty-two."

"I'm sixty-seven," he said, staring at me.

"So, you're sixty-seven."

"I lied about my age a long time ago. I was too old even then. I took off five years."

I shrugged. "What difference does it make?"

"I'm getting tired."

"If you don't say anything, nobody'll notice it."

"My heart notices it."

I looked at him.

"I can't run like I used to."

I was silent for a moment. "Cut down on your fucking."

He grinned. "I gave that up a long time ago. I even stopped going down to give a little head. I get dizzy."

"If you're trying to tell me that you're going to die, don't bother. I never thought you were immortal."

He stared at me. His voice was genuinely shocked. "I always did."

I lit the cigarette and turned away. The surfers were already testing the water. I could hear the sounds of their voices floating back on the wind.

"I'm selling out, Steve. I wanted you to be the first to know it."

"Why me?"

"In a kind of way it's like it was three years ago. And when I turn around, you're the only one there. Only this time the shoe is on the other foot. I can't hurt you, you can hurt me."

"I don't understand," I said.

"I want you to come back."

"No." My answer hung flatly in the breeze. "I'm never going back."

He put his hand on my arm. "You have to listen to me. Hear what I have to say."

I didn't answer.

"I can get thirty-two million dollars from Palomar Plate for my share of the company."

"Take it and run," I said.

"I would if I could. But that's not all of it. They want a guarantee of continuity. And I can't give it to them. But they said they'll accept you instead of me."

I stared at him for a long silent moment. "I'm not interested."

"You got to come back," he said intensely. "You know what I been through the last few years while you been sittin' up there on the hill, countin' your money and fucking your head off?

"I been sweatin' out disaster. Three years of it. Nothing went right. Everything I tried went right into the shithouse. Right before my eyes I watched it all turn to ashes. Then I got lucky. I hit a big one. And suddenly everybody says Sam Benjamin's got his touch back.

"But I know better an' you do too. You set that one up for me an' the only reason I went through with it was because it was the only deal where I still had credit. It wasn't my touch, it was yours. I also know now that I can't do it myself any more than I can stand on my head and piss straight up."

He took a package of gum out of his pocket, pulled the wrapper off and popped a stick into his mouth. He held it out to me. "Diet gum. No sugar."

I shook my head.

He took a couple of chews. "Nothin' works anymore. Once I thought maybe the kids were the answer. Now I know better. We put too big a load on them. We expect them to give us our answers when they don't even have the answers for themselves."

"You know where Junior is?" He didn't wait for my answer. "Haight-Ashbury. Yesterday before we came here, his mother and I go up there to look for him.

"'Denise,' I say. 'You stay right here in the hotel. I'll find him and bring him here. Besides it's raining.'

"So I take the limo and the driver takes me up an' down the streets. Finally I get out and begin to walk. I walk up and down. I never seen so many kids. After a while I begin to feel like they're all mine. I'm getting mixed up. So I lay a yard on a big black cop and in twenty minutes I'm up four flights of stairs, out of breath and in this freezin' cold flat.

"Junior's in there with about a dozen other kids. He's got a Jesus beard, an' paper showin' through the holes in his shoes. He's sittin' on the floor, his back against the wall. He don't say nothin' when I come in, just looks up at me.

"'Ain't you cold?' I ask him.

"'No,' he says.

"'You look blue to me,' I say. 'Your mother's over in the hotel. I want you to come over an' see her.'

"'No,' he says.

"'Why not?' I ask.

"He don't answer.

"'I could get the cops and roust you outta here. You're nineteen a' you gotta do what I say.'

"'Maybe,' he says. 'But you can't watch me all the time. I won't stay.'

"'What you got here? Freezin' your ass off in this icebox when you got a warm clean room at home?'

"He stares at me a minute, then calls out, 'Jenny!'

"This kid comes in from the next room. You know, with the long stringy hair an' white face an' large eyes. If she's more'n fifteen I'll go off my diet an' she's got a belly way out to here. 'Yes, Samuel?' she asks.

"'Getting any action today?' he asks her.

"'Wild.' She's smiling happily. 'The baby's kicking field goals.'

"'That's the oldest trap in the world,' I said. 'I thought you were smarter than that. It's not yours, you ain't been out here long enough.'

"He stares at me for a minute, then shakes his head sadlike. 'You still don't get it.'

"'Get what?'

"'What difference does it make whose baby it is? It's a baby, isn't it? It's like every other baby in this world when it's born, it's whoever's baby it is who loves it. And this one's our baby. All of us here. Because we all love it already.'

"I look at him and I know it's another world and I can't make it. I take a couple of hundred out of my pocket and lay the two bills on the floor in front of him.

"A couple of kids go over and look. Pretty soon they're all standin' around in a circle, starin' down at the money. They haven't spoken a word.

"Junior picks it up finally and gets to his feet. He holds it out to me. 'Can you change this for two fives?'

"I shake my head. 'You know I never carry anything less than hundreds.'

"'Keep it then,' he says. 'We don't need that kind of bread.'

"Suddenly it was like all of them found their voices. In a minute there was a racket goin' on like you ain't never heard. Some wanted him to keep it, others wanted it returned.

"'Shut up!' Junior finally roared. They all fell silent, looking at him, then one by one went to wherever they had been in the room and it was quiet again.

"He came over and pushed the bills into my hand. I could feel the tightness and trembling in him. 'Get off my back, don't ever come here again. See what one little touch of your poison does. It's tough enough for us to make out without having to fight that, too.'

"For a second I thought of belting him. Then I looked into his eyes and saw the tears. I took the money. 'Okay. I'll send the chauffeur back upstairs with two fives.'

"I left without lookin' back and sat outside in the car while the chauffeur went up with the money. All the way to the hotel, I was wonderin' what to tell Denise."

I looked at him. "What did you tell her?"

"The only thing I could. I told her I didn't find him."

He stuck another piece of gum in his mouth. "Denise wants me to get out. She says we got enough time left to put things back together. That somehow being Mrs. Big Shot don't have the kicks for her no more."

He looked me right in the eyes. "Don't make me tell her I couldn't find you neither."

I turned away from him and stared out at the blue water for a long time. I wish I knew what I was thinking or what went through my head but like everything was a blank and there was nothing but the blue water.

"No," I heard myself saying. "It's too big."

"What's too big?" he asked.

I gestured to the ocean. "It's too big to filter, too expensive to heat and I'd never be able to get it all into my swimming pool. And even if I did it all and could, somehow the water would never taste as if it came out of a well. No. Sam. This time I pass."

We walked back to the car. Twice I started to speak to him, but when I looked over, I saw that he was crying.

By the time we got to the hotel, he was in charge again. He got out of the car. "Thanks for the fresh air. We'll talk some more."

"Sure."

I watched him start into the lobby, his short arms and legs pumping him along in that peculiarly aggressive walk little fat men always have. Then I put the car in gear and went home.

The Volks was gone and the telephone began to ring almost as soon as I walked into the kitchen. There was a note taped to the wall next to the phone when I went to pick it up. I let it ring while I read the note.

Dear Steve Gaunt,

Go fuck yourself.

Very truly yours,

Mary Applegate.

It was written in a small, neat, respectful hand. I read it again and suddenly began to laugh as I picked up the telephone. I glanced out the window.

The drapes in the blonde's room were open. "Hello," I said.

It was a girl. *"Steve?"*

"Yes," I didn't recognize the voice.

The blonde came to the window. She was wearing a telephone in her hand and very little else. *"I happened to be looking out when I got up and saw the Volks driving off."*

"So?"

"So how about coming over to your friendly neighbor for a little coffee and consolation?"

"I'll be right there," I said, putting down the phone.

And that was the morning.

BOOK ONE: STEPHEN GAUNT

NEW YORK, 1955-1960

ONE

IT WAS ONLY SIXTY-FIVE cents on the meter from Central Park West to Madison Avenue but it was like a thousand light-years from one end of town to the other. I felt it as soon as I walked into the building.

The cool, high, white marble foyer, the semicircular onyx reception desk with two girls and two uniformed guards behind it, and the words in bold block gold lettering on the wall behind them.

Sinclair Broadcasting Company

I stepped up to the first girl. "Spencer Sinclair, please."

The girl looked up. "Your name, please?"

"Stephen Gaunt."

She flipped a page in her book and ran her eyes down a list of names. "Mr. Gaunt, that's right. You're down for ten thirty."

Involuntarily my eyes went to the clock on the wall behind her. Ten twenty-five.

She turned to one of the guards. "Mr. Johnson, will you escort Mr. Gaunt to Mr. Sinclair's office, please?"

The guard nodded, smiling pleasantly, but all the while his eyes were coolly appraising me. Without waiting I turned toward the main bank of elevators.

"Mr. Gaunt."

I stopped, turning toward him.

He was still smiling. "This way, please."

I followed him across the corridor to a small group of elevators almost hidden in the rear of the foyer. He took a key from his pocket and placed it in a lock and turned it. The elevator doors opened.

He let me walk into the elevator in front of him, then pulling the key, followed me. As soon as the doors closed, a bell began to ring.

His voice was still pleasant. "Do you have anything metal in your pockets?"

"Only some change."

He made no move to start the elevator. "Anything else?" He saw the bewildered look on my face. "The bell you hear is an electronic metals warning system. Pocket change is not enough to set it off. You must have something else you've forgotten."

Then I remembered. "Only this. A silver cigarette case a girlfriend gave me." I took it out.

He looked at it for a moment, then took it from me. He opened a small door in the panel in front of him and placed it inside. The bell stopped ringing immediately.

He took it out and returned it with an apologetic smile. "I'm sorry, Mr. Gaunt, to have to disillusion you, but it's only silverplate over metal with a nickel base."

I put it back in my pocket with a grin. "It doesn't surprise me."

He turned back to the panel and punched a button. The elevator rose swiftly. I looked up over the door at the blinking lights. There were no numbers, only X's.

"How does Mr. Sinclair know what floor he is on?"

The guard's expression was serious. "He has a key."

The elevator slowed and stopped, the doors opened. I stepped out into an all-white reception room. The doors closed as a young woman came toward me.

She was cool and blonde and dressed in basic black. "Mr. Gaunt, this way, please."

I followed her to a small waiting room. "Mr. Sinclair will be with you in a few moments. There are papers and magazines here. Would you like me to bring you a cup of coffee?"

"Thank you," I said. "Black, with one sugar."

She left and I sat down, picking up the *Wall Street Journal.* I flipped to yesterday's closings. Greater World Broadcasting was at 18 off an eighth, Sinclair Broadcasting, SBC, was 142 up a quarter. It wasn't only a thousand light-years from Central Park West, it was seventy-two TV stations, a hundred markets, and five hundred million dollars.

She came back with the coffee. It was not only hot and black but it was also cool, served in Coalport china that Aunt Prue would have been proud to keep in her cabinet. "Only a few minutes more," she smiled.

"That's all right," I said. "I've got time."

I watched her walk away again. She had good movement, it was all there, but like everything else in this office, very contained. I wondered what she would do if I grabbed her ass.

She was back just as I finished my coffee. "Mr. Sinclair will see you now."

I followed her out of the waiting room, through the reception hall to a door. There was nothing on it, not even PRIVATE. She opened it and I walked through.

Spencer Sinclair III looked exactly like the pictures I had seen of him. Tall, slim, beautifully turned-out, thin nose, thin mouth, square chin, cold, intelligent, gray eyes. Altogether he didn't much show his years.

"Mr. Gaunt." He rose from behind his desk and we shook hands. His grip was firm and polite. Nothing more, nothing less. "Please sit down."

I took a chair in front of his desk. He pressed a button down on his intercom. "Please hold all calls, Miss Cassidy."

He returned to his seat and we looked at each other for a few moments. Then he spoke. "We finally meet. I've been hearing so many things about you. It seems you have a talent for making people talk about you."

I waited.

"Are you curious about what they're saying?"

"Not really," I answered. "It's enough that they talk."

"You're supposed to be a comer," he said.

I smiled at that. If he only knew just how right he was. I had a date to take his daughter Barbara to an abortionist right after lunch.

He picked up a sheet of paper from his desk and glanced at it. "I hope you don't mind," he said. "I've had personnel do a little rundown on you."

I shrugged. "Seems only fair. I did the same on you. Only I did it in *The New York Times* files."

"Stephen Gaunt, age twenty-eight, born New Bedford, Mass. Father, John Gaunt, bank president. Mother, former Anne Raleigh, both deceased. Attended good New England schools. Employment, Kenyon and Eckhardt, advertising one year, Metro-

Goldwyn-Mayer, films, administration and advertising two years, Greater World Broadcasting, radio and television, assistant to the president, Harry Moscowitz, for the past three years. Bachelor. Active socially."

He put down the paper and looked at me. "There's only one thing I don't understand."

"What's that?" I asked. "Maybe I can help you."

"What's a nice Gentile boy like you doing in a place like that?"

I knew just what he meant. "It's really quite simple," I said, "I'm their *Shabbos goy.*"

I could see from his face he didn't know what I was talking about. I made the explanation simple and to the point. "Saturday is the Jewish Sabbath. They won't work. So they turned Saturday over to me. And, according to the Nielsens, so did you, and CBS and NBC and ABC."

"You're pretty cocky, aren't you?"

"Yes," I said flatly.

"What makes you think we can't stop you if we want to?"

I grinned. "Mr. Sinclair, all of you have been trying for almost a year and a half now and got nowhere. You're just lucky we're in only eleven of the hundred markets or you would have been completely wiped out."

He stared at me. "I don't know whether I like you or not."

I got to my feet. "You're a busy man, Mr. Sinclair, so I won't take any more of your time than I have to. Do I get the job or not?"

"What job?" he asked. "I wasn't aware—"

"Mr. Sinclair, if you brought me over here just to see who was kissing your daughter good night, you're wasting your time and mine. I've got a network to run and I've been away from my desk long enough."

"Sit down, Mr. Gaunt," he said sharply.

I remained standing.

"I was thinking of offering you the position of vice-president in charge of programming, but now I'm not sure that I will."

I grinned at him. "Don't bother. I'm not interested. I've been there for three years now."

He stared up at me. "Exactly what job are you interested in? Mine?"

"Not quite," I smiled. "President, Sinclair Television."

"You must be joking!" He was shocked.

"I never joke about business."

"Dan Ritchie has been president of STV for ten years now and before that Sinclair Radio for fifteen years. He's one of the best executives in the industry. Do you think you can fill the shoes of a man like that?"

"I don't want to," I replied. "They're old shoes and ready to be thrown out. They're radio, not television. You haven't got a single major executive under fifty-two, but the bulk of your audience is under thirty and growing younger every year. How do you expect to reach them when they stopped listening to their parents a long time ago?

"And I don't intend to beat my brains out trying to convince a bunch of ancients that the things I want to do are right. I want to be the word, the authority. Nothing else interests me."

He was silent for a moment. "How do I know you will listen to me?"

"You don't," I smiled. "But you can be sure I'll be listening to someone."

"Who?"

"The Nielsens," I said. "Right now, STV is number four behind the other three networks. In two years we'll be number one or damn close to it."

"And if we're not?"

"You can tie a can to me. At least you won't be any worse off. You can't go below four."

He looked down at the papers on his desk for a long while. When he spoke again, it was in another voice. He was Barbara's father. "Are you going to marry my daughter?"

"Is that one of the conditions of the job?"

He hesitated. "No."

I didn't hesitate. "Then I'm not going to marry her."

His next words were forced and painful. "But what about the baby?"

I looked at him. He just went up ten points in my book. "We're taking care of that this afternoon."

"Is he a good doctor?"

"The best," I said. "It's being done in a private clinic in Scarsdale."

"You'll call me as soon as it's over?"

"Yes, sir," I said. "I will."

"Poor Barbara," he said. "She's really a good girl."

How do you tell a father that his daughter is a ding-dong and stoned out of her mind on pot half the time?

"Is it—the baby—yours?"

I looked into his eyes. "We don't know."

His eyes fell. "If the doctor thinks there will be any problem, you won't let him do it?"

"I won't," I said. "It may sound strange to you, sir, but in my own way I care for Barbara and I don't want to see her hurt."

He took a deep breath and got to his feet. He held out his hand. "You've got the job. When can you start?"

"Tomorrow, if it's okay with you. I quit there last week and just finished cleaning out my desk this morning."

He smiled for the first time. "Tomorrow's okay."

We shook hands and I started for the door. I stopped with it half open. "By the way, what floor is this?"

"Fifty-one."

"Where's Ritchie's office?"

"On forty-nine."

"I want mine on fifty," I said and closed the door behind me.

TWO

I PRESSED THE DOORBELL AGAIN. I could hear the sound of the record player blaring away. She still did not answer.

I tried the door. It opened. The heavy sweetly acrid fumes hit me as soon as I stepped inside. All you needed for a high was to cross the room. I threw open the windows leading to the terrace and turned off the stereo. My ears tingled with the sudden silence.

"Barbara!" I called out.

There was no answer. Then I could hear her giggling. I walked toward the bedroom and stopped in the open doorway.

She was sitting, naked, in the middle of the floor, the reefer hanging between her lips. Standing over her, balancing a toy pail filled with water on his erect penis, was a tall young Negro boy.

He saw me before she did. He grabbed frantically at the pail as he lost his erection. He caught it, but not before some of the water spilled over her. His face began to pale.

She turned toward me. "Steve!" There was reproach in her voice. "You frightened him."

"I'm sorry." I stepped into the room.

The boy shrank back. His voice trembled. "You her husband?"

I shook my head.

"Her boyfriend?"

"Don't be silly, Raoul," she said sharply. "He's just a friend." She turned back to me and began to giggle again. "You just saved me fifty dollars. Raoul said that if he lost his hard-on before an hour I wouldn't have to give him anything."

I took two bills out of my pocket and gave them to the boy. "Beat it."

I don't think it took him more than a minute to dress and get out of the apartment. I closed the door behind him and went back to the bedroom.

She was stretched out on her bed. "Fuck me, Steve," she said in a husky voice. "He got me all excited. He had such a beautiful big prick."

"Get dressed," I said harshly. "We've got a date."

Suddenly she was crying. She turned her face into the pillow, smothering her sobs.

I sat down on the bed and lifted her head against my shoulder. She was trembling.

"I'm frightened, Steve," she whispered. "I'm so scared I'm going out of my skull. If they hurt me, I'll die. I know it. I can't take pain."

"Nobody's going to hurt you, baby." I soothed her gently.

"I sat here all morning thinking about it and if Raoul hadn't come I would have gone out the window." She caught her breath. "I think I'm going to be sick."

I pulled her off the bed into the bathroom and held her head while she threw up into the toilet bowl. After a moment there was nothing left in her. She began to shiver. I threw a robe around her and held her until she stopped.

"I'll be all right now," she said.

I looked at her. She was pale but her eyes were clear. "You shower and get dressed. I'll have some hot coffee ready for you by the time you come out."

She stopped me in the bathroom door before I could leave. "Did you get the job, Steve? The one we talked about?"

I nodded.

"I'm glad," she said.

I stood outside the bathroom until I heard the water running in the shower. Then I went into the kitchen, found the coffeepot and plugged it in.

—

HOSPITAL WAITING ROOMS ARE THE same all over the world. By the time the doctor came down I had the sign on the wall memorized.

THIS IS AN ACCREDITED BLUE CROSS HOSPITAL.

He came into the room, still in his surgical greens. He glanced around, noting the other people waiting, and nodded to me. "Come on down to my office, Steve."

I followed him into the small oak-paneled room. He closed the door carefully and turned to me. "You can lose the worried look, Steve. She's fine."

I felt the weight lift from my shoulders. "No problems?"

"None at all," he said, lighting a cigarette. "We even put it on the books. A simple D and C for fibroids. We'll keep her overnight. She can go home in the morning."

"Can I use your phone?" He nodded and I made the call I promised.

He looked at me when I put down the phone. "Her father?"

I nodded.

"She's afraid of him," he said. "But then, she's a very frightened girl. You seem to be the only one she has any confidence in at all."

"Yeah," I said.

"You hear a lot of things up there," he said. "The Pentothal loosens them up. She said at first it made her a little high like marijuana, then she said she wasn't afraid anymore and that the only other times she wasn't afraid was when she was high or with you.

I said nothing.

"I know a good psychiatrist in town. If you can persuade her to see him, he might be able to help her."

I stared at him. I knew Bill ever since I was a kid. But this was the first time I thought of him as a doctor. I wondered what there was about doctors that made all of them think they could play God.

"The one reason she probably trusts me," I said, "is because I mind my own business. I never try to tell her what she should do."

He shrugged. "I'm sorry. I thought you were her friend."

"I am. And my idea of being a friend is to be there. No matter what. Not to carp, not criticize, not to direct. Just be there."

"But she's just a child."

"She's twenty-two," I said. "And her mind was made up long before I knew her. And like everyone else, she has the right to choose her own road."

"Even if it's the road to self-destruction?"

"Even that." I hesitated a moment. "Don't you see, Bill, that the only way I can help her is if she asked me? Otherwise I'll be just like everyone else she's known in her life."

He was silent while he thought that one over. Then he nodded. "Maybe you're right."

"Can I see her?"

"Of course. She's in room twenty on the second floor. But don't stay too long, she needs rest."

"I won't."

"By the way," he added. "Now that we're legitimate, does she have Blue Cross?"

I laughed. "I don't know, but I doubt it. Just send the bill to me. I'll see that you get paid."

He laughed too.

"Thank you, Bill," I said and went upstairs.

She seemed to be sleeping when I entered the semi-darkened room. Her jet-black hair framed her pale thin face. I could see the childlike shadows under her closed eyes. I stood there looking down at her.

Her eyes opened and the blue of them was startling in the white face. She moved her hand gently toward me. "Hello, Steve. You waited. I'm glad."

I took her hand. It was cool and fragile. "I said I would." I sat down in the chair next to the bed. "How do you feel?"

"I hurt a little bit," she said. "But it's not too bad. They gave me something and I'm just beginning to come down." She turned her lips to my hand. "Do you think I'll ever be able to fuck again—after this?"

"Do you want an appointment?" I laughed. "I think I'll be able to fit you in sometime next week."

"I'm not joking, Steve," she said intensely.

"Neither am I," I said.

Suddenly I felt the hot tears against my hand. "I want a baby the next time, Steve. This is such a terrible waste. I don't want to go through it again, ever."

I was silent.

Her voice was almost muffled by the pillow. "Will you marry me, Steve? I'll be a good wife to you, I promise."

I put both hands on her face and turned it to me. Her eyes were wide and a little bit frightened. "This is no time to talk about it," I said gently. "You've just been through a bad scene. Let's talk about it when you're better."

Her eyes searched mine. "I won't change my mind."

I smiled at her. "I hope not," I said. Then I bent and kissed her lips. "Now try to get some rest."

THREE

I WENT DOWN THE STEPS between the jockeys and into Twenty-One. Chuck was waiting at the door for me. He put an arm around my shoulder. "I got your table set up in the back corner of the bar," he said. "Jack Savitt's there waiting. He's two martinis up on you."

"Thanks, Chuck," I said.

"Anytime, buddy," he smiled, his eyes already going over my shoulder to the new people coming in behind me.

I walked through the bar, which was packed three deep. The captain came rushing up to pull out the table.

Jack looked up, his gray crew cut somehow matching his tweed jacket. His voice was edgy. "Well?"

I sat down. "Relax," I said. "We did it."

"The whole thing?" His voice was soft and had a kind of wonder. "The way we talked about it?"

I nodded. "President, Sinclair TV."

"My God!" he said. "Just like that?"

The waiter put two martinis down on the table in front of us. Jack held up his hand. "Double it," he said. He grinned at me. "Was I right about how to handle him or what?"

I held the martini toward him. "You were right." Let him feel good about it. He didn't have to know I had an extra ace up my sleeve. But I was under no illusions. Barbara got me that job as much as anything else. I swallowed the drink. It felt good going down.

"You talk money, contract, terms?"

I shook my head. "What for? That's your job."

"Good boy," he smiled. "Don't you worry. We'll make a good deal for you."

"I'm sure you will," I smiled back at him. More than anything else he was an agent. And like every agent once you got the job, he was going to get it for you.

"Where the hell were you all afternoon?" he asked. "All I got was the message to meet you here and then you dropped out of sight. This was no time to shack up with a broad. My ulcers were developing ulcers."

I laughed. "No broad. I had some personal business that couldn't keep." Another martini appeared in front of me as if by magic. I picked it up and looked at him. "Now I want you to turn your staff loose and put some information together for me. I want a complete rundown on network personnel. Programming, sales, research, advertising and engineering, both coasts. Then the same thing station by station across the country. After that, I want a program breakdown, production and rating, program by program nationally and by market. On top of that I want a list of all pilots, planned and in work, and I want it complete, Sinclair and all other networks."

It was his turn to crow. He reached down to the seat beside him and came up with a black leather-bound loose-leaf book almost three inches thick. I looked down at the gold lettering on the cover. It was the first time I saw it in print and it was a real charge.

Confidential for
MR. STEPHEN GAUNT
President, Sinclair Television

"I'm way ahead of you, boy," he grinned. "It's all there, everything you asked for. That's the kind of service you get from World Artists Management. I've had our whole research department on it ever since you told me last week about the appointment with Sinclair. Now I've got all my boys standing by and we're ready to spend the night with you going over the whole thing, point by point."

I smiled at him. "I should've known better than to think you wouldn't be ready."

"Not only that," he said. "I've red-flagged the shows that I think will be big winners that we can get on for next season."

"Good," I said. "But what about the rest of this season?"

His voice took on a pontifical tone. "Come on now, it's October. There's not enough time to get anything good ready before next season. You can't do anything about it."

"Why not?"

"You're putting me on," he said. "You know as well as I do that the season has been all locked up for months."

"I don't know nothing," I said. "All I know is that I'm going in there and I'll be on the firing line, a target for every guy that resents my walking in. And you know Sinclair better than I do. He expects me to do something."

"He doesn't expect miracles."

"What do you want to bet?"

He said nothing.

"Why do you think I got the job?" I asked. "I'm supposed to be a miracle man. Look what I did for Greater World."

He swallowed his martini, still silent.

"Which movie company is in trouble right now?" I asked.

He stared glumly down into his drink. "They're all in trouble. Not one of them has a smell of real profits this year. They're all going crazy trying to figure out a way to rearrange their bookkeeping so they don't look sick."

"Okay," I said. "I want you to go out tomorrow morning and buy as many top features for me as you can get your hands on. The only condition is that they're all post-48's."

"You're joking," he said flatly.

I knew what he meant. Up to now the film companies had not released to television any movies produced after 1948. I let my voice grow cool. It was time he learned who was boss. "The one thing I don't joke about is my business."

It worked as well for him as it had for Sinclair. There was a subtle change in his voice. "It'll take a fortune."

"That's unimportant. Have you seen Sinclair's latest statement? Over one hundred million in cash."

"Then what will you do with them when you get them?"

"I'll blow Saturday night from nine to eleven and put them in." I noticed he said "when," not "if."

His voice was shocked. "But that's going back on everything TV has done up to now. They've been creaming the picture business on their own."

"You mean the other networks have," I pointed out. "Sinclair is in the shithouse. The only thing they got is money and I intend to use a little of it to get them a share of the market."

"But it's all wrong," he protested. "We can develop our own shows."

I knew what was bugging him. Pictures didn't deliver a ten percent packaging fee and he didn't like to give up that juicy money coming in every week. "That's right," I said. "But next year. You said yourself there's no time this year."

"The whole industry will be laughing at you."

"Let them. I couldn't care less. The name of the game is ratings. They won't be laughing when the Nielsens come in."

"When do you want to go with them?" he asked.

I could see his mind ticking over. The greater the pressure, the bigger the price, and he was going to get his cut on the other end. That was his business and it didn't matter to me as long as he delivered. "January," I said.

"That's not much time. It'll be expensive."

"You said that before." I picked up my martini. "You know that slogan the movie companies use? 'Movies are your best entertainment.' Well, I believe them."

"I hope you're right," he said glumly, swallowing his drink.

"I know I'm right. Now let's order dinner and you call your boys and tell them to meet us over at my apartment at eleven o'clock."

He reached for the telephone on the table. "What's that address again? Twenty-five Central Park West?"

"No," I said. "Penthouse B, Waldorf Towers."

I almost laughed at the look of surprise on his face. "I didn't know you'd moved," he said.

"That's just one of the things I did this afternoon. I like to be within walking distance of the office."

FOUR

THIS TIME WHEN I CAME into the lobby, they knew me. The two girls at the desk looked up and smiled. "Good morning, Mr. Gaunt," they said, almost in chorus.

"Good morning," I replied.

The guard who took me upstairs yesterday came out from behind the desk. "Good morning, Mr. Gaunt," he said. "I have the key to your elevator. I'll show you how it works."

"Thank you, Mr. Johnson," I said.

He smiled, pleased that I remembered his name. I followed him to the back of the corridor. There was another elevator next to the one we had used. He took the key from his pocket and placed it in a lock where the call button usually was. He turned it. The doors opened. I followed him inside.

"All you have to do is press the Up button," he said. "There are no stops between the lobby and your floor. You do the same in reverse when you come down."

I nodded, then I smiled. "No bells on this one?"

"No, sir," he said straight-faced. "That's only in Mr. Sinclair's elevator. He had it installed last year after a crank came in with a gun."

I waited for a moment, but he didn't continue. I wondered what it was that Sinclair did that almost led to his getting shot. He handed me the key.

"Your visitors will be directed to the executive reception area on the forty-seventh floor," he said. "From there, they take another elevator that runs only between the five floors to fifty-one. That elevator is always attended, all the others in the building are self-operated. There are only three keys to this elevator, one for yourself, one for Miss Fogarty, your executive secretary, and the last one is always at Main Lobby reception." He pressed a button and the doors opened again. "Is there anything else I can tell you?"

"One thing," I said. "On what floor is my office?"

A look of faint surprise came onto his face. "Fifty, of course, sir."

"Thank you, Mr. Johnson," I said and punched the Up button.

Miss Fogarty was waiting for me as the elevator doors opened. She was in her late twenties, tall, slim, brown-eyed with darkly burnished auburn hair tied neatly with a black ribbon behind her head, a simple Dior dress in basic black with one unobtrusive gold pin on her shoulder. "Good morning, Mr. Gaunt," she said. "I'm Sheila Fogarty, your number one."

I held out my hand. "Good morning, Miss Fogarty," I said.

Her hand was cool and slightly damp. I suddenly realized that she had to be as nervous as I was. I began to feel better. I smiled at her and she returned my smile. "Let me show you around," she said.

She turned and I noticed she had a good ass and that the seams of her stockings were straight on good legs and slim ankles. "The layout on this floor is exactly like Mr. Sinclair's on the floor above. Yours is the only suite of offices."

I followed her down the corridor. Everything was white, highlighted only by paintings. Someone with taste had evidently gone to a great deal of expense to select them. If I wasn't wrong there were some genuine Miros and Picassos.

She caught my gaze. "All the paintings are from Mr. Sinclair's private collection." She opened the first door. "This is the projection room."

I glanced inside. It was neat and luxurious, holding about twenty-two people in armchair comfort. I nodded and she closed the door and led me to the next room.

"This is the large conference room," she said. The table inside seated twenty people. "Between this and the small conference room, there is a private kitchen, and a permanent chef is on standby everyday for lunch if you should want to have it in."

The small conference room seated ten people and was a miniaturized version of the other. We walked back toward the elevator.

"Off the reception area," she said, "there are three private waiting rooms so that your visitors need never run into each other." She opened a door. "They're all very much alike."

They were also like the one I had been in on the floor above. A cool blonde was now sitting at the desk in the reception area. She got to her feet as we came near.

"This is Miss Swensen, your receptionist," Miss Fogarty said. "Miss Swensen, Mr. Gaunt."

The blonde smiled. "Pleased to meet you, Mr. Gaunt."

I returned her smile. She, too, was a carbon of the girl in Sinclair's office. "My pleasure, Miss Swensen."

We crossed the reception area. She opened another door. "This is my office."

There was another girl in the office. She looked up as we came in. She rose to her feet as we approached. "This is Ginny Daniels, my assistant, your number two. Miss Daniels, Mr. Gaunt."

"Happy to meet you, Mr. Gaunt," she smiled. She was in the mold, only with dark hair. For a moment I wondered whether Sinclair had them manufactured especially for their own use.

"Miss Daniels," I said. We shook hands. Her hands weren't as damp as Fogarty's had been. But then she had much less to lose. She was only number two.

"There are two entrances to your office," Miss Fogarty said. She indicated a door near her desk. "This one from our office and one directly from the reception area. Your visitors will be shown in from there unless you instruct otherwise."

I didn't say anything.

She opened the door to my office and let me walk in ahead of her. I stood there for a moment. It was almost a duplicate of Sinclair's office. The same ten windows on each side, the same view. There was only one thing that was different. The office looked new, untouched and unused.

"Who was in this office before?" I asked. Whoever it had been had disappeared without a trace.

"No one," she said. "For some reason, I don't know why, this office has been vacant ever since we moved in four years ago."

I glanced at her briefly, then walked over to my desk and sat down behind it. Sinclair had to be a strange man. No one sets up offices like these and then doesn't use them.

"Would you like a cup of coffee?" she asked.

"Thank you," I said. "Black with one sugar."

She left and returned in a moment, placing the coffee tray on my desk. I looked at it while she poured the coffee. At least he did things in style. The china was Wedgewood. She used silver tongs to drop one lump of sugar in my cup. "Like that?" she asked.

I raised the coffee to my lips. "It's fine," I said.

She smiled again. "In the center drawer of your desk," she said, "you will find two folders. One has the personnel records of Miss Swensen, Miss Daniels, and myself. You understand, of course, that we are provisionally assigned to your office. If you have other personnel or preferences we shall understand."

"No problem," I said. "I like what I see so far and I have no ties."

She smiled. "In the other folder is a list of the names and positions of certain key executives. Mr. Sinclair especially asked me to remind you to review that list as there will be a meeting at ten thirty in his conference room to introduce them to you."

"Thank you," I said. Fogarty would do all right. She had tact and style. She didn't say introduce me to them.

"Now, if I may, let me explain some things about the mechanics of the office." She came around the desk and stood beside me. I was aware of the faint, gentle perfume.

"The telephone is a conventional call director with ten lines. Outside lines are available by dialing eight or nine first. Of course we are available to get all numbers for you. There are also two direct lines that bypass the switchboard for your personal use, and direct intercoms to each of our desks.

"On the wall opposite you you will see three television screens. The first is tied into our own network and will always project the current network program. The other two are conventional sets and show all channels. All are controlled from this set of buttons next to your telephone.

"On the inside wall of the office there is a built-in bar which is revealed by this button." She pressed it and the bar opened.

It was stocked and ready for action. I nodded approvingly.

"To the right of the bar, you will notice a door. That is the entrance from the reception area. It is electrically controlled and locked from our desks or yours. To the left of the bar is a private bathroom. It is complete with a dressing room, shower, and sauna or wet steam; there is also a small bedroom should you desire to rest."

I got up and walked over to the bathroom and opened the door. I went inside. It was everything she said it was and more. With a setup like this there was never a reason to go home. I went back into the office.

The telephone buzzed. She picked it up. "Mr. Gaunt's office." She looked at me. "Mr. Sinclair for you."

I took the phone from her hand and walked around the desk. She left. "Mr. Sinclair."

"Just a moment, I'll put him on," his secretary's voice said. There was a click.

"Are you comfortable, Mr. Gaunt?"

"I am, thank you."

He chuckled. *"Just keep that in mind whenever you think of complaining because the neighbors upstairs are making too much noise. Remember you asked for that office."*

I laughed. "I'll remember, Mr. Sinclair."

"I'd appreciate it if you could come up to my office a few minutes before the ten thirty meeting," he said. "I would like you to meet Dan Ritchie before we go in."

"I'll be there at ten twenty."

—

DAN RITCHIE WAS A PRO. He took being kicked upstairs without rancor. His grip was firm. "Glad to meet you, Steve," he boomed. He studied me for a minute, a puzzled expression in his eyes. He turned to Sinclair. "I had the impression somehow that he was much younger."

Sinclair had the same puzzled expression on his face. I smiled at them. "You age quickly in this business."

Suddenly Sinclair caught on. A glint of amusement came into his eyes. Also a curious kind of respect. "You sure do," he said. "Sometimes it happens overnight."

He didn't know it. But it happened about eight o'clock that morning. I had had my shower and finished buttoning up my shirt as I walked back into the living room.

"Okay, fellas," I said brightly. "Any of you think of ordering breakfast?"

"Christ! Look at him," Jack groaned from where he was stretched out on the couch. "He stays up all night wearing us out with his questions, then showers and comes out looking bright as a new penny. How did you do it? With benny tabs?"

I grinned at him. "Just live right, I guess."

"It's youth," Joe Griffin, his chief research man said. "He almost doesn't look old enough to vote, much less be president of a major network."

I turned to look at him. He put his finger right on it. My big problem would come not from what I wanted to do but from the grayheads who would look at me and think I was nothing but a loudmouthed kid. I turned and picked up the telephone. The only way to lick them was to join them.

The barbershop had no one who could do what I wanted, but the beauty parlor did. The promise of fifty dollars sent the girl up real quick.

She was a cute little brunette in a pink smock. She carried a little black cosmetic case and chewed gum. She came into the room with a bewildered expression. "They got some kind of cuckoo word down there that a lady up here wants to put gray in her hair."

"They got it right," I said. "Except it isn't a lady. It's me."

She almost swallowed her gum. "Now I've heard everything," she said. "You nuts or somethin'? I'm leavin'. You're all cuckoo."

I pulled out the fifty and waved it in front of her face. "I mean it. Don't go."

She looked up at me. "What you wanna go an' do that for? You look like such a nice kid with your wavy brown hair."

"I'm up for a very big job," I said seriously. "And they think I look too young to get it. Now you wouldn't want me to lose my big chance, would you?"

"No," she said, hesitantly, her eyes going around the room. "I wouldn't want to do a thing like that."

"All you have to do is to shade some gray into it. Not too much, just enough to age me a little."

"Sure," she said. "I guess I can do that."

"Come on then," I said and led the way into the bathroom. When I came back into the living room forty minutes later, I was dressed and ready to leave for the office.

"I don't believe it!" Jack sat bolt upright on the couch.

They clustered around me. "What do you think?" I asked.

Jack shook his head. "It's got to be the greatest," he said. "It really doesn't make you look older, but it gives you a kind of solid authority. You know that I mean?"

I knew what he meant. The edging of gray she combed into my hair somehow worked out just right with my eyes. I still looked young but not that young anymore.

"Okay," I said, going to the door. "Time to go down to the mines."

"Wait a minute," Jack said. He picked up the loose-leaf book. "Don't you want to take this with you?"

I grinned. "Come on, teacher. Since when do they let you take the books into the examination room?"

—

I WAS WRONG ABOUT ONE thing. The offices weren't duplicates. Sinclair's conference room was bigger than mine. There were twenty-eight people at the table. I walked slowly around the table and shook hands with every one of them and tried to tie their names to what I had read last night. It worked pretty good. My memory was better than I thought.

They were all very pro about it. I could see them studying me but not one of them cracked. They weren't about to give me anything, they were going to sit it out until they could figure the drift.

After ten minutes, Sinclair left with a casual remark about leaving the team to get acquainted. Ritchie left with him.

There was a silence in the room now that you could really cut. I sat alone at the head of the table. And that's just what I was. Alone.

I glanced around the table. Strange how a little thing like gray hair helped even up the score. I kept my voice deliberately low so that they would have to strain to hear me.

"You're wondering about me and I'm wondering about you. None of us knows each other.

"But in the next few months we're going to find out. Some of you will like me, some of you will not. That's unimportant.

"What is important is that Sinclair Television is going to climb out of the cellar of broadcasting. What is important is the ratings. That's the standard by which I will measure you and by which you will measure me."

I paused. They were still watching me. "In Washington, when a new president takes office, he is allowed a cabinet of his own choosing. I like that. It's real democracy."

I could feel them tightening up. This was bottom-line talk. "I will expect each of you to submit his resignation effective thirty-one January and have it on my desk by tomorrow morning."

There was a collective explosive sigh. I waited a moment until they swallowed that. Then I threw out the lifeline.

I got to my feet. "My secretary is preparing a schedule of appointments. Sometime within the next few days, I will meet individually with each of you and review the problems of your departments. Thank you, gentlemen."

I went downstairs to my own office. Within ten minutes all hell broke loose. Sinclair stormed up and down my office, raging.

"You fired everybody! How the hell do you expect to run the network? All by yourself? Even you can't do that!"

I smiled up at him. "The gods descend from Olympus."

That stopped him. He looked down at me. "What do you mean?"

"They told me you never came down from your floor." He began to smile. I continued. "Let me set the record straight. I didn't fire them. I asked for their resignations effective in January. I didn't say I would accept those resignations."

He chuckled. "You really shook them up."

"That's the idea," I said.

"You play rough."

"This isn't touch tackle. I meant it when I said I was going to move this network."

"Okay," he said after a moment. "It's your ballgame." He glanced at his watch. "I've booked the private room at Twenty-One for lunch. I want you to meet the board of directors. And I've asked PR to set a press conference for you on Friday."

"Lunch is all right," I said. "But Friday is out. I won't be here" I gave him time to swallow that. "Time enough for a press conference when I have something to say. Right now I have nothing to tell them."

"Where will you be?" he asked.

"In Los Angeles."

"What the hell have you got to do out there that's more important than staying right here?"

I met his eyes straight on. "I'm going to try to steal Saturday nights back for us."

FIVE

"IS MY FATHER WITH YOU?" she asked as soon as I came into the room.

I shook my head.

"That was his car you came up in," she accused.

I looked at her; she was dressed and ready to leave, her small valise packed and standing in the middle of the room. She made no move toward it.

"He loaned me the limo," I said. "He thought it would be more comfortable than a taxi."

"He knows?"

"Yes," I said.

She seemed to deflate. She crossed the room and took a package of cigarettes from her purse. "How did he find out? Did you tell him?"

"You know better than that, Barbara," I said. "He already knew. He even knew that I was taking you to the doctor."

"Damn!" she said. "He never lets go." She looked up at me. "I'll fire that damn maid. Now I'm sure she told him. She was the only other one that knew. She's always listening at keyholes."

"He's your father," I said. "It's only natural that he should care—"

"What the hell do you know?" she snapped. Her voice turned savage. "He doesn't care about me or anybody. All he wants to do is to control everything. That's why my mother ran away from him. But even that didn't stop him. He hounded her until she killed herself. And that's just what he wants to do to me."

"Easy, girl," I said.

She laughed bitterly. "You don't know. But wait until he gets his hands into you. Then he'll own you. And you'll understand. I remember what he told my mother.

"'Nobody leaves Spencer Sinclair,' he said. 'Unless I want them to.'"

She ground her cigarette out. "I don't want to go back to my apartment."

"That's up to you. You're a big girl. I just came up to get you out of here."

She came toward me, her eyes wide. "Let me stay with you, Steve."

"Forget it."

"Please, Steve." She reached for my hand. "Only for a few days until I get my head unscrambled. I don't want to be alone in that apartment."

"You're out of your mind," I said. "My place is going to be like Grand Central Station the next few days."

"I'll be good. I won't be in your way."

"Why me?" I asked. "You have other friends."

She looked up at me, a hurt coming to her eyes. She let go of my hand and went back to her valise. "Okay, Steve," she said quietly. "I'm ready to go now."

I picked up the valise and we went down to the car. I don't think we spoke two words on the way to town. The chauffeur kept glancing curiously at us in the mirror. It was obvious that she knew him, but she ignored him too.

The car stopped in front of her apartment on Park Avenue and the doorman came rushing up to get her valise. I got out with her.

"You okay now?" I asked.

She nodded.

"Take care and get some rest. I'll give you a call later to see how you're doing."

"Sure," she said.

I kissed her cheek and she went into the building. It was almost five o'clock by the time I got back to my office and the memos and phone calls were stacked up to the ceiling. I got involved and before I knew it, it was eight o'clock and Jack Savitt was on the phone.

"Still at your desk?" he laughed. "You're setting a bad example."

I glanced over at the pile of papers still to be gone through. "Yeah."

"I've been on the horn," he said. "I think I can put your package together for you."

"Good."

"Shall I come over and talk about it?"

I glanced at my watch. "No. Meet me over at McCarthy's Steak House on Second Avenue in fifteen minutes."

"I'll be there."

I put down the telephone and hit the buzzer. Fogarty came into the office. "Pack up the rest of this stuff," I told her. "I'll go over it at home."

She nodded and I went into the bathroom and washed up. I looked at my face in the mirror. It was tired and there were lines on it that hadn't been there in the morning. I grinned. It all went with my gray hair. I wondered how long it would be before I wouldn't need the treatment.

I held a hot towel to my face and it felt good. When I put it down, some of the lines were gone. My eyes were still a little bloodshot. Maybe I needed glasses.

Fogarty had an attaché case ready for me. I looked at it. It was brand new and had my name discreetly engraved on its side. She snapped it shut, locked it and gave me the key. "Everything is in order," she said. "And I red-flagged the things that were urgent."

Joe Berger was standing at the door as I came in. "Congratulations, Steve," he said.

"Thank you, Joe." We shook hands. I followed him to a booth along the wall.

His pretty wife Claire smiled and called her congratulations from the cash register as we walked by. I smiled and waved to her. "What'll be your pleasure?" he asked.

"Jack Savitt is joining me."

"I know. He called, he'll be about five minutes late."

That was about normal for Jack. There should be at least two more calls like that before he showed up.

"I'll have about four martinis," I said. "Then a salad with blue cheese dressing, roast beef rare with the bone, baked potato with sour cream, and that's it."

"Take some advice from an expert, Steve?" he asked.

I nodded.

"Develop a taste for Scotch. It's easier on your stomach. Every ulcer case I know lives on martinis."

I laughed. "How about Coca-Cola?"

"That's even better. When my son was a baby the doctor told me to give him Coke syrup to settle his stomach."

"Okay, Joe," I laughed. "Now send over the martinis."

He went away shaking his head. Jack was right on schedule. Two phone calls and three martinis later, he came bustling in.

He dropped into the seat opposite me and looked at the table. "What number is that?"

"The third," I said, tapping the glass.

He looked up at the waiter. "Bring two doubles quick." He turned back to me. "It isn't that I need it. It's just that I don't want to take advantage of you."

I grinned. "That'll be nice for a change."

The waiter came back with the doubles. I began to speak but Jack held up his hand. Quickly, he drained one glass and was halfway into the other before he put it down. "Okay, now you can talk," he said.

"What about my package?"

"It wasn't easy," he said.

I was silent. That meant exactly nothing. It was agent talk for expensive.

"I got about thirty-six for you. About five from each of the majors, the rest from independents."

"How many good ones?"

"Average four out of six and the other two aren't too bad. At least they're not real dogs." He finished his drink. "I wanted one for one, but they wouldn't go for it."

I nodded. He had done well. Usually the picture companies hung you up for four lemons for each really good feature they gave you.

"Now, hold on to your seat," he said. "They'll cost you four hundred thousand dollars each and you've got exactly twenty-four hours to commit or there's no deal. And they want the money now because they want to take it into this year's figures."

I stared at him.

The price was exactly double the going rate for films up to now, but I knew that was the only reason they would let them go. They were in a bind too. They had to make this year's figures look good or there would be screams from the stockholders. And they were more afraid of their stockholders just now than they were of the theater owners who had forced them into an agreement to withhold the post-1948 pictures from television. Their stockholders could cost them their jobs, while the exhibitors still had to come to them for product.

"Okay," I said. "Buy them."

He stared at me. "You know what you're doing, right? That's over fourteen million dollars."

"I said buy them."

"Don't you even want to know what pictures they are, what stars are in them—"

My tone was abrupt. "You're the expert, Jack. I trust your judgment. You said you didn't want to take advantage of me."

"But it's your job. If the pictures are no good—"

I broke in again. This time my voice was cold. "That's where you're wrong, Jack. It's not my job. If the pictures are bombs, it's your agency that's on the line. My job allows for mistakes but if you stiff me, WAM never sells another show to Sinclair. And there goes your agency because all the business you get from the other networks isn't enough to pay the rent on one floor of your offices."

His face was pale, and faint beads of perspiration came out on his forehead. He finished his second drink, sipping it slowly without taking his eyes off me. After a moment he spoke. "They're good pictures."

I let up on him. "Then what are you worried about?" I smiled. "Relax and let's get our dinner. I'm starved."

But, oddly enough, he didn't seem to have much of an appetite.

—

IT WAS AFTER ELEVEN O'CLOCK when I let myself into the apartment. I wasn't at all tired. I opened the attaché case and spread the papers on the dining room table.

By the time I finished with them and fell into bed, it was after one o'clock. My eyes burned and they smarted when I closed them, but in less than a moment I spun out. I couldn't have been sleeping more than a half hour when the door chime began to ring.

At first it seemed an echo in my head and I tried to turn it off. At last I opened my eyes. It took me a moment to get used to the darkness. The chime sounded louder now that I was awake. I struggled out of bed and went through the apartment to the front door and opened it.

She wore a fur coat wrapped tightly around her. She clutched a small purse in her hand and her blue eyes looked up at me, wide, dark and afraid.

I stood there for a moment, then I stepped back and she threw herself into my arms. She was shivering and crying. I closed the door.

"You didn't tell me you moved," she sobbed.

I held her.

"I went to your old apartment first. The doorman told me where you had gone." She looked up into my face, her eyes wet with tears. "Are you very angry with me, Steve?"

I shook my head.

The words tumbled out of her. "I couldn't stand it there anymore. I was alone. So alone. I kept thinking about what you said. About other friends. For the first time I knew something. I don't have any other friends. Not really. Just fun and games friends. That's all.

"I drank half a bottle of whiskey. It just tasted lousy. I tried turning on. I smoked three sticks. Nothing happened. Then I decided to go to sleep. I took a Nembutal. By the time I got out of bed to take the fourth pill, I knew I wasn't going to sleep.

"I stared at myself in the bathroom mirror and all I could see was my mother. I was going to wind up just like her. They would come in in the morning and I would be lying there. Then I got frightened.

"I tried calling you, but they kept telling me that the number was disconnected. By that time I was in a panic. I had no place else to go, so I came looking for you."

She brushed at her eyes with her hand. Her coat opened and I saw she had nothing on but her nightgown. "Let me stay here just for tonight. I'll leave in the morning. Please."

"You're here," I said. "Let's go to bed."

I took her into the bedroom. "Go wash your face. Your eye makeup's all over it."

Obediently she went into the bathroom; I killed the lights and climbed into bed. I could hear the sound of the water splashing in the sink. A moment later the bathroom door opened and the light spilled into the room from the doorway behind her.

"Do I look all right now?" she asked.

I couldn't see her face, it was in the shadow, but I could see her silhouette through the gown. I laughed to myself. What I could see looked all right. "You're fine."

She hit the light and came into bed. I made room for her. "No, Steve," she said. "I want you to hold me."

I put out an arm and drew her head down to my shoulder. She was quiet for a minute, then she sat up suddenly. With a quick motion, she pulled the nightgown over her head, then she snuggled back against me.

"That's better," she murmured. "I want to feel your flesh against me." She turned again and drew my hand to her breasts.

I could feel the firm strength in them and hard nipples puckering gently in my fingers. The heat began to rise in me. Now it was I who could not sleep. I moved restlessly.

She took my penis in her hand and soothed it gently. "I'm sorry, Steve," she whispered. "We can't fuck for a week."

"I know," I said gruffly. "Let's try to sleep."

Her hand was still. I closed my eyes. After a few minutes she spoke again. "Kiss me good-night, Steve."

I kissed her gently, her lips pressed back lightly. She closed her eyes and her voice was barely a whisper. "Steve."

"Yes?"

"Promise me something."

"What?"

"First promise." She was like a child.

I lay back on the pillow. "Okay. I promise."

"In the morning you won't look at my cunt. They shaved it and it looks funny."

I laughed quietly. "For Christ's sake, go to sleep."

I could have saved my breath. She was already asleep. Her hand relaxed and fell away from me. I looked at her. She seemed so young and vulnerable in the dark. I closed my eyes.

But the warmth and smell of her was of a woman and there was no rest for me. Finally I got out of bed. She didn't even stir. I went into the living room.

When I did fall asleep it was in front of the late show on television.

SIX

I WAS SIXTEEN YEARS OLD and in my junior year at prep school when my parents died. It was one of those senseless accidents that happened during the war. Because of the blackout regulations along the eastern seaboard, all automobile headlights had the upper half painted black so their beams would not be seen from the sky. When the other automobile crested the hill and the headlights shone right into my father's eyes, he turned to the right just a little to avoid crashing into him. That was just enough.

The big Packard went off the road, down a sheer drop of three hundred feet, bounced twice on the rocks, turning over, and settled under twenty-eight feet of water.

"You've got to be brave," Mr. Blake, the attorney, said to me as I sat dry-eyed in his office after the funeral. "It was quick and merciful. They never even knew what happened."

I glanced over at my Aunt Prudence who sat in front of the desk on the opposite corner. She was nothing like her name. A long time ago she had moved from New Bedford to Cape Ann. My father rarely spoke about his younger sister, but I had heard all the stories.

About how she had fallen in love with an artist and had followed him to Paris only to be deserted by him when he went back to his wife. Then other affairs, each whispered about, until one day she returned to New Bedford.

My father didn't know she was in town until she came into his office at the bank. She had a little five-year-old boy with her. He clung to her skirts nervously.

"Hello, John," she said.

"Prudence," my father said stiffly.

She looked down at the little boy. *"Dit bon jour au monsieur,* Pierre," she said.

"Bon jour," the little boy said shyly.

"He speaks only French," Aunt Prudence said.

"Who is he?" my father asked, staring at him.

"He's my son," she said. "I adopted him."

"Do you expect me to believe that?" my father asked.

"I don't give a damn what you believe," she said. "I only came for my money."

My father knew what she was talking about. But there was still that New England streak in him. Women were not to be trusted, even with their own inheritance. "The money is supposed to remain with the bank until you are thirty years old, according to the terms of Father's will."

"I was thirty last month," she said.

He finally looked from the boy to her. "So you are."

He picked up the telephone and asked for the trust-account records. "Times have been difficult," he said. "But I have managed to keep your estate intact, even increase it a little despite the fact you kept taking out all the earnings as fast as they accrued."

"That was the one thing I was sure you would do, John."

He began to feel slightly more confident with her. "The wise thing to do would be to leave it here. The earnings come to about thirty-five hundred a year. You could live very nicely on that."

"I suppose I could," she said. "But I have no intention of doing that."

"What are you going to do with the money?"

"I've already done it," she said. "I've bought a small inn on Cape Ann. I've got it all figured out. The inn runs itself and I can continue painting. Pierre and I can have a very nice life there."

My father tried to talk her out of it. She shut him up.

"I want to make a home for Pierre," she said. "Do you think I can do that here?"

Aunt Prudence went to Cape Ann. A few years later we heard from a mutual friend who had seen her that the little boy had died.

"It's just as well," my father nodded. "He didn't look very strong to me. Anyway he spoke nothing but French."

"Was he my cousin?" I asked. I was about six years old at the time.

"No," my father said sharply.

"But if he was Auntie Prue's little boy—"

"He wasn't her little boy," my father snapped. "She just adopted him because he had no home and no parents. Your Aunt Prue felt sorry for him, that's all."

That conversation must have made more of an impression on me than I had realized. I remembered it as I sat looking at her at the other end of Mr. Blake's desk. Now it was my turn. I wondered if she was sorry for me.

"Stephen." I turned from her to Mr. Blake.

"Yes, sir."

"You're no longer a child, but you're not yet a man, legally that is," he said. "But I think you should have something to say about yourself. Your father was not a rich man; he left you well provided for. There's enough money left to see you through school and college, even get you started in a profession should you choose. But there is the problem of where you will live.

"Your parents appointed me the executor of their estate, but did not provide a legal guardian for you. Under the law, the court must appoint one until you are of age."

My aunt and I turned to look at each other at exactly that moment. I could feel myself being drawn into her. I didn't wonder any longer how she felt about me. I knew.

"Mr. Blake," I said, still looking at her. "Couldn't my Aunt Prue—I mean, isn't it all right for Aunt Prue to be—"

There was a moment's silence, then we both turned to look at him. He was smiling. "I was hoping you would say that, Stephen. There shouldn't be any problem at all. Your aunt is your closest living relative."

Aunt Prue got out of her chair and came over to me. She took my hand and I could see the tears in her eyes. "I, too, was hoping that was what you would say, Stephen."

Then, suddenly, I was in her arms and I was crying and her hand was stroking my hair gently. "There, Stephen, there. It will be all right now."

A month later when I came down from school for summer vacation, I went straight to Aunt Prue. It was late in the afternoon and the warmth of the day was still hovering over the station. A few other passengers got off, but they soon left the platform and I was standing alone. I picked up my valise and trudged toward the small wooden station, wondering if my aunt had received my telegram.

Just as I reached the station door a battered Plymouth coupe pulled up and a young girl got out. She looked up at me for a moment; puzzled, then she spoke. "Stephen Gaunt?"

I stared down at her. There were smudges of paint on her face and her long sunbleached brown hair hung down over the blue denim work shirt she tucked carelessly into a faded pair of men's levis. "Yes," I said.

She smiled in relief. "I'm Nancy Vickers," she said. "Your aunt sent me down to pick you up. She couldn't come because she's right in the middle of a class. Throw your bag in the backseat."

She got into the car and I followed her. Expertly she shifted gears. She looked at me and smiled again. "You surprised me," she said.

"How?"

"'Go down to the station and pick up my nephew,' your aunt said. I thought you would be a kid, I guess."

I laughed a little flattered.

"How was the trip down?" she asked.

"It was a train. Dull. Stopped every twenty minutes or so to let some express go through." I took out a package of cigarettes and held it out to her. She took one. I lit her cigarette first, then mine. "Do you work for my aunt?"

She shook her head, the smoke curling up around her eyes. "No. I'm one of her pupils. I also model."

"Oh," I said. I hadn't known that Aunt Prue taught art.

She took my word for something else. "It's not so bad," she said. "Modeling helps me pay for my own lessons."

"What are you studying?"

"Painting mostly. But I take sculpture twice a week. Your aunt says it helps with form."

I glanced at her and grinned. "You look like you need help."

She caught my glance and laughed. "How old did you say you were?"

"I didn't," I said. "Seventeen, if you want to know." I added a year.

"You look older," she said. "You're big for your age. I'm not that much older than you. I'm nineteen."

We were out just past the edge of the small town and turned left on a road that seemed to lead to the beach. We were almost there when she made a sharp right turn into a hidden driveway.

The house was on a small knoll overlooking the water. It was sheltered from the road by a row of northern pines. She stopped the car in front of the house. "This is it," she said.

I looked out. The building was a typical Cape Cod cottage, but of course much bigger. There were two small painted wooden signs on either side of the picket gate.

The one on the left read, *CAPE VIEW INN AND COTTAGES FOR SELECTED GUESTS.* Later I was to learn that it was local snobbery that led to the use of the word, selected, instead of selective.

The one on the right read, *PRUDENCE GAUNT. CLASSES IN PAINTING AND SCULPTURE FOR QUALIFIED STUDENTS.* But in the end I learned that "selected" and "qualified" meant exactly the same thing to my Aunt Prue. There was still enough of New England left in her to select her guests and qualify her pupils on their ability to pay.

Nancy leaned across me and pushed open the door on my side. I felt the firm press of her breast against my arm. She looked up into my face just at that moment and smiled. She made no move to straighten up. I could feel the flush crawl up my neck into my face.

"You're in the main building," she said, straightening up finally. "Your aunt said you're to take your bags right in."

I got out of the car and pulled my valise after me. "Thank you," I said.

"It was nothing," she said. She put the car into gear again, but held the clutch before she started off. "The students live in the cottages behind the main house. I'm in number five if there's anything you want." Then she released the clutch and drove off around the house.

I waited until the car disappeared and then went up the steps and into the house. The foyer was empty. I put the valise down and wondered where to go next. I heard the sound of voices coming from behind a closed door. I opened it and stepped in.

The voice stopped suddenly and so did I. Four or five girls, standing in smocks behind easels, turned to look at me. I don't remember even seeing them.

The only thing I did see was a nude model standing on a small platform at the front of the class. I stood there with my jaw hanging. It was the first time I had ever seen a naked girl. I didn't know whether to go or stay and if I did know I doubt that I would have been able to do either; I was frozen to the spot.

"Close the door and sit down, Stephen, you're creating a draft," my Aunt Prue's voice came sarcastically from the front of the room next to the model. "Class will be over in a few minutes."

SEVEN

THE NIGHT WAS WARM AND filled with good things. I rolled over on my back and looked up at Nancy. She was sitting against the headboard of the bed, her knees drawn up against her chest. In the dim light I could see the light and dark of her flesh where the bikini had covered her from the sun. The reefer glowed for a moment and I could see the somber introspection on her face.

"Don't be greedy," I said. "Share the wealth." I took the reefer from her fingers and dragged on it. The good things came even better.

She took it back from me. I held the smoke inside me as long as I could, then I let it out slowly and rolled over, burying my face in her soft fur. I breathed deeply of the woman smell of her.

"That does it for me," I said. "More than all the pot put together."

She twisted my hair in her hands and turned my face up to her. She looked at me for a long time. I don't know what she tried to see there, but when she let me go, the same somber look was still on her face.

"You're not there, Nancy," I said. "What's wrong?"

For a moment, she was still, then she got out of bed. I could see her tiny brown nipples puckering as the cool air from the open window hit her breasts. "I never told you I was married, did I?" she asked hesitantly.

"No," I answered, sitting up in bed.

"I should have."

"Why?"

"Then things would have been different," she said.

"How?"

"This might not have happened."

I thought that over for a moment. I didn't understand her. The good things were still there. "Then I'm glad you didn't tell me."

"He's coming back tomorrow," she said.

"Who?" I asked.

"My husband. His ship's putting in at New London and I'm going down there to meet him."

"Oh," I said. Then, "When are you coming back?"

"You don't understand," she said. "I'm not coming back. He's been transferred to shore duty. We're going to Pensacola."

I was silent.

She misunderstood my silence. "I didn't want to tell you like this," she said. "I didn't want to hurt you. I was going to leave without saying anything, but I couldn't do that either. I'm sorry, Steve."

I took the cigarette from her and puffed at it. It was down close to my lips and I could feel the heat from its glowing tip against my lips. She took it from my mouth and ground it out in an ashtray. She drew my head between her breasts. I put up my hands and squeezed them close to my cheeks. Slowly I moved my head from side to side, running my tongue from nipple to nipple.

"I'm sorry, Steve," she said again, holding me tightly.

"Don't be," I said. "Everything is good."

"It is good, isn't it?" she said, a strange note in her voice. She pushed me backward on the bed and I climbed up into her.

I could feel the moist heat of her pouring over me as she went wild. She bucked frantically, making sounds like an animal in the night. I had all I could do to stay inside her. She climaxed suddenly. She screamed, "Don!"

She froze.

"I don't care what you call me," I said, fiercely thrusting myself into her. "Just don't stop fucking!"

"You son of a bitch!" she said, sucking me into her. "That's all you want."

I rolled over on top of her and jammed her until this time her climax carried me with her, the marrow from my bones pouring into her like the roaring surf of the ocean outside. "Steve! Steve!" Her fingernails raked my back.

I caught her hands and held them down. We lay there gasping for breath. "You got the name right this time."

She stared at me balefully. A moment later we were both roaring with laughter.

—

THERE WAS A LIGHT COMING from Aunt Prue's office when I came into the main house. I glanced at my wristwatch. It was after midnight. I started quietly up the stairs.

"Stephen."

I turned on the stairway and looked down at her. "Yes, Aunt Prue?"

She looked up at me. "Are you all right?"

I nodded. "Yes, Aunt Prue."

She stood there hesitantly a moment, then she turned back into the room. "Good night, Steve."

"Good night, Aunt Prue," I said and went on up to my room.

A few minutes later there was a soft knock at my door. "Yes?" I asked.

"It's Aunt Prue. May I come in?"

"It's open," I said. "Come in."

"I don't know how to talk to you about—" Her voice trailed away as she looked at me.

I looked down at myself to see what she was staring at. There were long red scratches down my shoulders and chest. I grabbed my shirt from the chair and put it on.

"She did that?" Her voice was angry.

"Before I answer, Aunt Prue, tell me who you're mad at?"

She looked at me for a moment, then she smiled ruefully. "Myself, I guess. I kept thinking of you as a little boy. I didn't realize you were almost grown up." She sat down on the edge of my bed. "I hope I didn't make a mistake in bringing you here."

"I knew about girls before I came here, Aunt Pruc."

"There's all kinds of knowledge," she said. "Not all girls are like Nancy."

I didn't answer.

"I've been meaning to have a talk with you," she said awkwardly. "But I didn't know quite how to begin."

I sat down on the chair opposite her. "Yes, Aunt Prue."

"You know there are things you have to look out for," she said, her eyes not quite meeting mine. "Girls can have babies and there are diseases that—" She stopped when she saw the glint of laughter in my eyes. "What am I talking about?" she said confusedly. "You know all about those things."

"Yes, Aunt Prue," I said solemnly.

"Then why didn't you stop me?"

"I didn't know how," I confessed. I smiled. "Nobody ever spoke to me about things like that before."

She looked at me steadily. "I think you ought to get a summer job. It's not good for you to be hanging around here all the time with nothing to do."

"That's an idea," I said. It was dull lying around on the beach all day.

"I spoke to Mr. Lefferts. He said he can use you down at the radio station afternoons. It won't pay much, but it's something to do."

And that was how it all began. Before the summer was over I was running programming and sales for Lefferts. And by the time I went back to school I knew what I wanted to be.

EIGHT

THE TELEVISION SET CAME ON with a blast of sound and woke me up. I stared at it stupidly. Channel 7. I got up and turned it to Sinclair. I called downstairs for orange juice and coffee, then got under a hot shower until the aches in my bones went away. When I came out, the orange juice, coffee, and morning paper were on the breakfast table. Barbara was still sound asleep when I left for work. Those three sleeping pills had finally caught up with her.

I was in early, but Fogarty was there before me. I dumped the papers I had taken home on her desk. She gave me the appointment schedule for the day. I made only one change. I moved Winant of engineering up to nine o'clock and made him the first appointment of the morning.

He was a tall, pipe-smoking man whose eyes looked out at me from behind steel-rimmed glasses. "Good morning, Mr. Gaunt," he said, placing a paper on my desk.

I picked it up. It was his resignation just as I had asked the day before. I looked at him.

"I thought since I was coming up here," he said easily, "I would deliver it in person."

I grinned at him. "Thank you."

Fogarty came in with my coffee. There was a cup on the tray for him.

"Hold all calls," I said as she left. I sipped my coffee and looked at him. "Mr. Winant, how do we stand in relation to color?"

"We've made all the surveys," he said.

"And?"

"We're waiting."

"For what?" I asked.

"To see how it's accepted," he said, uncomfortably. "NBC—"

"I'm not interested in NBC," I snapped. "I'm interested in Sinclair, dammit. Why are we waiting?"

"I'm an engineer," he said finally. "I don't make policy."

I smiled at him. "Now we're beginning to understand each other."

He was bewildered.

I made it easy for him. "If I tell you the policy is color now, how fast can we get it on the air?"

He finally began to look interested. "I can have the whole network in color by next September."

"Can you give me New York, Chicago, and Los Angeles by New Year's?"

"That's not much time."

"I know that."

He thought for a moment, tapping his pipe with his finger. He looked up at me. "If I get the go-ahead now, I can do it."

"Do it," I said. "You got the go-ahead."

He rose to his feet, relieved. "You've got yourself color. Do you want to know what it will cost?"

"If I wanted to know I would have asked," I said. "You just send up the estimate. I'll okay it."

He started for the door. I called him back, holding up his resignation. "Just one thing, Mr. Winant."

"Yes, Mr. Gaunt?"

"You said I would have it by New Year's, right?"

"New York, Chicago, L.A., right?"

"Okay. You deliver. I tear this up."

He stood there a moment, then he smiled. "It's as good as torn up right now, Mr. Gaunt."

I watched the door close behind him. I had a feeling he would deliver. Slowly I tore it in half, then put the two pieces in an envelope and wrote his name across it. I called Fogarty into the office and had her send it down to him.

It was time I began to build my own team. And he was as good a man to start with as any.

It was almost one o'clock when Jack called. "I just put down the phone to my coast office. They got the deal wrapped up. When can you get out there to sign?"

"Tomorrow."

"Great." He laughed. "How's that for service? WAM!"

"Yeah, WAM," I said.

"World Artists Management," he said with satisfaction.

"Stop bragging," I said. "Now I'm looking for insurance."

"Come on, Steve. You got to be joking. With those pictures all you need is—"

I cut him off. "A lead-in show. Something that will hook them before they get trapped by the other nets." I thought for a moment. "Any big star around that's willing to do an hour a week?"

"You're out of your skull," he said. "Anybody good is already signed."

"WAM! Go find me one." I put down the telephone.

Almost immediately, the phone signaled again. "Miss Sinclair on the wire," Fogarty said.

I hit the button. "Barbara."

"I love you," she said.

"You're nuts," I laughed.

"No, I mean it. I love you," she said earnestly. *"You're there. Like you're solid. Always there."*

"How are you feeling?"

"Great!" she answered. *"I'm having a ball."*

"What are you doing?"

"Right now I'm having breakfast in your bed. I hope you don't mind crumbs. And I had them roll in the TV and I'm watching it."

I was curious. "What are you watching?"

"An old Jana Reynolds movie. God, she could really sing."

"Yeah," I said. Absently I hit the remote on my desk. Sinclair TV came on. A quiz show. I hit the other button. The next set came on. *The Lone Ranger.* Par for midday. "What channel?"

"Don't tell Daddy," she laughed. *"ABC."*

I hit the button twice and Jana Reynolds came on just in time to be cut by the commercial. I turned off the sound.

"I like it here. One of the waiters even called me Mrs. Gaunt. I may never go home."

"Sure," I said, watching the screen.

"What time are you coming home?"

"Why?"

"I ordered a special dinner for us," she said. *"Caviar, Chateaubriand, pommes soufflés, Dom Perignon, candlelight, the works."* She giggled. *"I even ordered a fantastic negligee from one of the shops in the hotel."*

"You sound very domestic," I said, my eyes still on the screen. The commercial went on, forever. "I hope it wasn't too much trouble."

"None at all. As a matter of fact, I think I boosted your prestige a hundred percent in this place."

"At room service prices, baby, I could live without it."

"Put it on your expense account," she said. *"Tell Daddy that you're entertaining someone very special to the network. A big stockholder. After all, mother left me fifteen percent of Sinclair Broadcasting."*

"You twisted my arm. Now get off the line, I've got to get back to work."

"I love you," she said, and the phone clicked off.

I put down the receiver as Jana Reynolds came back on. The movie was about fifteen years old and she was in her prime then, about twenty-five years old but still playing nineteen and making you believe it. Too bad she couldn't go on playing nineteen forever.

But time caught up with her. Time, and three bad marriages, and booze, and drugs, and near suicides. It's like at a certain point someone turned off the juice. You got too much talent, baby, now take some of the shit. And she got it all.

Films were out. They passed her by. There were other nineteen-year-olds now. But somehow in spite of everything, her voice held up. Occasionally, she did concerts and nightclubs. The public still loved her and would come out in droves to see her in person, but then something would happen and the whole thing would blow in a front-page blast of headlines. She was bombed and wouldn't show up or if she did, she was falling down and in no condition to perform. But the headlines were there. They were always there. She was still a star. Even her discharge in bankruptcy was front page.

I stared up at the screen. She was still a star. I was reaching for the phone even before the thought crystallized in my head. A star. Wasn't that just what I was asking Jack to find for me?

"Now I know you're crazy!" he yelled.

"Who's her agent?"

"She hasn't any," he answered. *"There isn't one that would touch her. She's involved in lawsuits with everyone she's ever had."*

"What's the packaging fee on a hundred-thousand-dollar show every week?"

"Ten grand per," he answered promptly.

"For ten thousand dollars a week you won't handle her?"

There was a pause. *"I'm your boy. For ten thousand a week I'd handle Adolf Hitler."*

Spoken like a true agent. If nothing else, he was dependable. I never got to that dinner Barbara had planned for us. Instead, that night, I was on a plane to the coast.

NINE

IT WAS THREE MONTHS LATER when I ducked into the alley behind the theater on Vine Street where the show would be broadcast. It was five minutes to five, Pacific Standard Time. In five minutes it would be eight o'clock in New York and we would be on the air.

Inside was a madhouse. Tension was crackling like the whip in a jockey's hand on the home stretch. I cut behind several men who were moving scenery and made my way to the wings. There were men and wires and cameras everywhere. The stage manager was whispering into his chest mike to the director up in the booth.

I peeked out into the theater. It was jammed. The curtain was still down, but they watched the stage with an air of expectancy.

The call came while I was still peering at the house. "Three minutes to airtime. Places everybody." I turned back.

The stagehands who had been adjusting the set came running off. The wing cameras rolled into place and set.

The director came out of the booth for a final check. He nodded, but I don't think he even saw me.

He came to a dead stop. "Where's Jana?"

The stage manager stared at him. He half turned, then turned back to him. "She was here a minute ago."

"You fool!" the director screamed in a shrill voice. "She's not here now. Get her!"

A stagehand stopped. "I just saw her go back into her dressing room."

"Get her! Get her!" The director was hysterical now.

"Two minutes to airtime," the overhead speakers blared.

The stage manager pulled off his headset, dropping it on the floor, ran toward her dressing room. Several of the grips followed him. I was right behind them.

The stage manager was knocking on the door. *"Two minutes to airtime, Miss Reynolds."*

There was no answer.

He knocked again. *"Two minutes—"*

I pushed my way through the crowd in front of the door. "Open it," I snapped.

He tried the door. He turned to me, a sick look on his face. "I—I can't. It's locked."

I pushed him out of the way. I put my foot against the door and kicked it off its lock. I followed the door into the room.

She stood there, staring at me, a bottle in one hand, a glassful of liquor in the other. "Get out!" she screamed. "I'm not going on!"

I knocked the glass from her hand as she raised it toward her lips and the bottle from the other as she tried to put it behind her. I caught her hand as it came wildly at me with an outstretched claw and pulled her to me.

"Let me go, you son of a bitch!" she screamed, twisting viciously, kicking at me. "I want a drink!"

I held on to her. "No booze. That was our deal. You're going on!"

"I will not, you cocksucker!" she spit into my face. "I'm not going out there. You tricked me! They didn't come to hear me sing, they came to eat me alive! They came to see a freak."

I let her have it. Open palm, right across the face. It made a crack like thunder in the small room and she spun across it and wound up half on and half off the couch against the wall.

The overhead speakers blared, *"One minute to air time!"*

I crossed the room and pulled her off the couch. She stared up at me, naked fear in her eyes. "You're going on, you cunt! I didn't pull you out of the gutter to go to black at airtime. You stand me up, you don't talk to lawyers, you talk to your undertaker!"

I slapped her again just to let her know I meant it. Then I turned and dragged her after me toward the stage. The crowd in the doorway parted silently to let us pass.

The crawl was already on the monitors when we reached the wings, the announcer's voice came from the speakers. *"STV proudly presents... JANA REYNOLDS... LIVE!"*

She twisted toward me. Her voice was shaking. "I can't... I can't... I'm frightened!"

"That makes two of us," I said, turning her toward the stage. I put my foot on her ass and shot her out over the wires and cables to the center stage.

It was a miracle she didn't fall. She just had time to straighten up and glance at me. I grinned and gestured a "thumbs up" at her. She turned toward the audience as the curtain arced open and up.

The orchestra went into her theme song and for almost a minute you couldn't hear her voice because of the thunderous applause. They all knew the song. "Sing from the Heart." It had been her very own since she was fifteen years old.

I stood there watching her. It was like not to be believed. Whatever else was wrong and crooked inside her it wasn't her voice. Maybe not as young as it once was, maybe not as strong. But there was a magic there. A beauty, a sadness, a pain and a kind of joy too. For fourteen minutes until the first commercial, she just stood there and sang.

When she came off, she was sopping wet and half fell into my arms. I could feel her shaking. The audience was roaring. "They liked me," she whispered almost as if she couldn't believe it.

"They loved you." I turned her back to the stage. "Go back out there and take a bow."

She looked up at me. "But it will throw the timing of the show off."

"To hell with it," I said, pushing her toward the stage. "The name of the show is 'Jana Reynolds... Live.'"

She went back out and took her bow. When she came back, she was glowing.

"Now get back to your dressing room for your change," I said.

She kissed me quickly on the cheek and hurried off. I looked after her. I never told her that her bow didn't get on the air. The only thing that television never interrupts is the commercial.

Then I went looking for the couple we had hired to keep an eye on her. I finally found them alone in a small viewing room at the rear of the stage. She was jumping up and down in his lap. They were too engrossed to hear me enter.

I crossed the room swiftly, put a hand under each arm, and lifted her.

"What the hell—" the man said.

The girl sprawled on the floor.

I looked at him as he tried to zip up his pants. "Where were you when the lights went out?" I asked.

"We got her to the theater," he said sullenly.

The girl was on her feet now. "You weren't supposed to leave her alone. Not for a minute," I said.

"She was all right when we put her in her dressing room," she said.

"That's just it. You weren't supposed to leave her," I said. "You're both fired."

Twenty minutes later I had a new pair of watchdogs. Carefully I laid it out for them. They nodded. They knew the score. This wasn't the first time they had a job like this. This was Hollywood.

"After the second show, you take her right back to the spa," I said. The first show was beamed to the eastern and central time zones, there was still a second show to do for the coast. "You bring her back here on Tuesday for rehearsals and you stay with her. She does nothing alone. Eat, sleep, or sex without one of you there, understand?"

I looked at my watch. It was a quarter to six. I'd have to get moving if I wanted to make the seven o'clock flight back to New York.

I stopped and looked up at one of the monitors as I was leaving. She was singing again and she looked absolutely beautiful.

Suddenly I was tired. I didn't know how many more of these miracles I could take. I could sleep for a week. But there wasn't time.

I wanted to be in New York tomorrow morning for the flash Nielsens.

TEN

I TOOK A PILL TO sleep on the plane, but it did no good. I couldn't turn off my head. There was still so much to do. One show, one night even if it did turn out a big winner didn't make a network. And in the back of my head a trouble was ticking.

It was nothing I could put my finger on. It was all too easy. Maybe that was it. The hostess came up. "Is there anything else I can do for you, Mr. Gaunt?"

I turned on a smile. "You can get me another double martini."

"But you already had one double, Mr. Gaunt," she said. "Regulations allow only two drinks per."

"I know that," I said. "But the way I look at it, we're not breaking any rules. I still had only one drink."

She hesitated a moment, then nodded. I watched her walk away and giving up the thought of sleep, I opened the attaché case. I placed the papers on the table in front of me.

The drink was cold and dry. I lit a cigarette and dragged on it. If only I could lose the feeling I had that something was wrong. I stared at the papers without really seeing them.

On the top, everything seemed okay. The fall schedule was shaping up. It would be the best that Sinclair had ever put on. Maybe not the best, but the most commercial. I had kept all the solid shows, the good ratings, but the problem had been there were not enough of them. About seventy percent of the fall programming would have to be new.

It had meant a complete change of direction for the network. It also meant a change of thinking for most of the executive personnel and more than half of them couldn't cut it. That meant in addition to everything else I would have to find replacements for them if I wanted to take advantage of the resignations locked in my desk.

To this point, Sinclair had been proud of the fact that their programming won the most kudos and critical acclaim. They boasted of more Peabody Awards than any other network. What they didn't brag about was the fact that they also had the lowest ratings and billings. The new fall schedule was designed to change all that. I never knew any Peabody Award that sold an extra cake of soap.

From now on, the critics could cry in their beer because there would no longer be such shows as "Great Adventures in American History." How many times could Washington cross the Delaware and who cared? Bach, Beethoven, and Brahms, all three of them together if they came down from heaven or wherever they were and conducted the weekly "Sinclair Philharmonic Hour" couldn't entice a single viewer from "Gunsmoke" or "77 Sunset Strip." "The Classic Repertory Theater" didn't stand a chance against Red Skelton or Sid Caesar and Imogene Coca.

The critics would have to be satisfied with such programs as Chic Renfrew in the "Park Avenue Squatters" (a story of a Kentucky moonshining family who inherited a fortune); "The Flyboys" (a new kind of private-eye story involving jet pilots who fly their plane to adventure); and "The Sandman," a story of a western bounty hunter.

There were other goodies in store for them too. An hour-long country and western music program, originating in Nashville beamed right at the heartlands; "White Fang," a dog story designed to yap at the heels of Lassie and Rin Tin Tin; and last but not least, "Sally Starr's Family," America's favorite daytime soap opera now moving to prime time, three nights a week in color.

It was commercial all right. That was the one thing I was sure of. As each program was carefully leaked to the advertising agencies on Madison Avenue, the interest mounted. Already we had more unofficial commitments for billings than we had ever had before in our history. All that remained to firm it up was to have the pilots ready in time for the buying season. And that began next month. February.

Sometime in those weeks, each network would publicly announce its schedule for the coming fall and begin the rat race after sales. From then through April, the pilots would be shown and the juggling would go on as each of the networks played chess with its programs, moving one to one day, then to the other, to counter the opposition moves. Usually Sinclair was the last to announce its schedules.

This time was going to be different. This time we would be first. I was going to announce our schedule at the end of January. By the time the others should be set, they would have to chase after us. We should be all sold out. I hoped.

If I proved out wrong, thirty million dollars would go down the drain. And so would I. The only job I could get after that would be back at Mr. Lefferts's radio station in Rockport and I doubted if even he would want me.

Even the second double martini couldn't loosen the tightness in my gut. It was gray morning by the time we landed in New York and I still hadn't slept.

Jack Savitt was at the gate when I came off the plane. "We got trouble," he said, even before we shook hands.

I looked at him. He didn't have to tell me. It couldn't be anything good that got him out of bed to be at the airport six o'clock of a Sunday morning. Inexplicably the tightness in my gut disappeared. Whatever it was would be in the open now.

It was two words. Dan Ritchie. I had made one bad mistake. I had left his team intact. I should have canned all of them that first day. Silently I vowed never to make that one again.

"When did it start?" I asked.

"Wednesday morning. After you left for the coast. Joe Doyle called and said to hold everything. All deals were to be finalized out of Dan Ritchie's office."

Joe Doyle was business affairs VP for the network. I had found him extremely capable and he was one of those I planned to keep. "Why didn't you call me?"

"At first I thought you knew about it," he answered. "I knew you were up to your ears and I thought you pulled Ritchie in to help you out. After all, he had the experience. It wasn't until Friday that I managed to get him on the phone and get the scam."

"What did he say?"

"He was using his holier-than-thou voice. He said the board of directors was very concerned over the financial commitments you were making and that they wanted everything held up until there was time to study them."

"That's a crock of shit!" I exploded. "The board does what Sinclair tells them."

"I know it and you know it," Jack said. "But what good does that do us when I have to firm up all the contracts for the shows or I blow them and my clients? He must have put a bug in Sinclair's ear."

I was silent. None of it made sense. Sinclair wouldn't have let me go this far if he had intended to pull the rug. He had to know it would cost him a fortune to buy out of some of those commitments.

It was eight o'clock when I walked into my apartment and the phone was ringing. It was Winant. His voice was shaking with anger.

"I thought I was doing a job for you," he said.

"You are," I said. New York, Chicago, and Los Angeles were on in color last night.

"So how come I got fired Friday night?" Winant asked.

I couldn't keep the surprise out of my voice. "What?"

"I got fired," he repeated. *"Dan Ritchie called and told me I was through. He said something about my having acted improperly. That I did not get approval for the color program. I told him that you had approved it. He said that wasn't enough. That I had been with the company long enough to know that board of directors' approval was necessary for every capital outlay."*

"Okay," I said.

"Now what do I do?" he asked.

"Nothing. You report to your office tomorrow morning and do your work as usual. I'll take care of it."

I looked over at Jack as I put down the telephone. "You heard?"

He nodded, the worry deepening on his face. "What are you going to do?"

For an answer I picked up the phone again and got Fogarty on the wire. "Can you get your girls together and meet me in the office in an hour?"

"Of course," she said in a matter-of-fact tone as if it were commonplace to come in on Sunday.

"Good."

"Mr. Gaunt." Her voice was excited.

"Yes?"

"I saw the Jana Reynolds show last night. She was wonderful. Congratulations. And the movie afterward with Clark Gable was fantastic."

"Thank you," I said. "I'll see you in an hour."

I took a hot shower and got into fresh clothes. When I came out, Jack was drinking coffee liberally laced with brandy.

"Try some," he said. "Best thing in the world to get you moving in the morning." He held out a cup.

I took a swallow and it went right down to my toes. I could feel the zing. He was right. "Come on," I said.

"What's the script?" he asked, following me out of the apartment into the elevator.

I grinned at him. "What is it they say is the only way to fight fire?"

ELEVEN

I TOOK A PILL AND slept late on Monday morning. Deliberately, I didn't get to the office until almost eleven o'clock. By that time all hell had broken loose.

Fogarty had an unexpected sense of humor. "The explosion had to reach eight on the Richter scale," she said as she brought in my coffee and the messages. "Mr. Sinclair wants you to call him."

I glanced out the windows. "It looks like snow," I said.

She knew what I meant. "If he calls again I'll tell him you couldn't find the dogsled."

"The Nielsens come in yet?" I asked.

"Any minute. I have the first ARI reports. They look good."

They were on top of the stack of papers. I looked at them. They were more than good. If they were anywhere near correct we had stolen forty-four percent of the audience with the Jana Reynolds show, forty-one percent for the first hour of the movie, and thirty-eight percent for the second hour. It had to be something of a record. Sinclair had never bettered seventeen percent of any Saturday night hour.

I began to breathe a little easier. It wasn't over yet, but it was improving. I was glad now I had made personal calls to the presidents of the four major advertising companies. It was soft sell but hard truths. It was late yesterday afternoon when I began the calls.

"I'm sending you an advance copy of our fall schedule," I said. "You're getting it twelve hours before the papers have it and twelve hours before the rest of the street. I'm making the same call to each of the other three biggest agencies and the same offer to each of them. I'm holding twelve and a half percent of primetime across the board per week at a ten percent discount from the rate list for each of you. This offer is good until four o'clock tomorrow afternoon, after that it's straight rates. You study the schedule and I think you'll agree with me that Sinclair is the money network for next fall."

Each came back with the same question. "What makes you so sure?"

To each I gave the same answer. "Check your Nielsens on Monday. If we don't sweep Saturday night you can forget my offer. If you don't buy Sinclair big for next year, you're going to find it tough to explain to your clients."

The first call came before I finished studying the ARI reports. It was John Bartlett, president of Standard-Cassell, one of the four men I had telephoned. *"Steve,"* he said jovially, *"I decided not to even wait for the Nielsens. I got faith."*

He sure had. And it probably came from the same reports that I had. "Thanks, John."

"One thing," he said. *"I want first pick on programs."*

"You got it," I said. "On any program you buy fifty percent or better."

"That's a holdup," he said. *"But I'll take it if you can fit me in now on Jana Reynolds and the movie."*

"I can place you on Reynolds and first-hour movie beginning next month. Second-hour movie I can do now."

"You have a deal," he said.

"Thanks, John. I'll have Gilligan call your man to firm it up." I put down the telephone. My hands were shaking. I never had sold thirty million dollars of television time in one deal before.

The phone buzzed again. *"Mr. Sinclair wants to see you,"* Fogarty said dryly.

"Tell him I'm in a meeting," I said. "And have Gilligan of sales up here right away."

The phone buzzed almost before I put it down. *"Mr. Sinclair hopes that you won't be too busy to attend a special board of directors meeting at two thirty this afternoon."*

"Tell him I'll be there," I said. I reached across the desk and poured myself some more coffee. It was flat and lifeless. I hit the signal and Fogarty came in.

"See if that bottle of Hennessy's X O is still behind the bar."

The brandy helped. I could feel myself lifting. It was snowing. I walked over to the window and looked out. The big soft flakes floated gently down. Gilligan came in. "You wanted me, Steve?"

"Yes," I said. "Come over here and look out."

He came over to the window and stood beside me.

"Somewhere down there, the snow is falling on people," I said. "And from up here we can't even see them."

He had a puzzled expression on his face.

"Did you ever think that someday, Bob, you'd be above the snow? Somewhere where you could see it falling below you and it couldn't touch you?"

I looked at him. He didn't know what I was talking about. But the man upstairs knew, Sinclair knew the snow could never fall on him. That's why we were all kept on the floors below. Nothing could touch him. We fought and scratched and scrambled and when it was all over, he walked away arm and arm with whomever was the winner.

Fogarty came into the office. She was smiling as she gave me the flash report. I looked at it. We owned Saturday night. We were eight points ahead of the next nearest network on the Nielsen. I gave the report silently to Gilligan and went back to my desk.

Almost before I sat down the phones got hot. We didn't get out to lunch. By the time I walked into the directors' meeting, all the advertising agencies had bought their quotas.

—

I WAS A FEW MINUTES late and Dan Ritchie was already seated in the chair next to Sinclair that I usually occupied. The only vacant seat was at the foot of the table. I walked over to it and sat down.

"Sorry to be late, gentlemen," I apologized. "But I've been jammed."

"So we gathered," Sinclair said, his face expressionless.

Dan Ritchie couldn't wait. "Are you familiar with the press release in front of you?"

I looked down at it, then back at him. "I should be," I answered. "I issued it."

"You realize, of course, you issued it without authorization, not having cleared it with the board of directors?" His voice was dry and cold.

I looked at Sinclair. "My understanding with Mr. Sinclair was that as president of Sinclair Television I had complete autonomy and authority to run the network as I thought best."

"But you did know that all your actions to date had been approved by the board?"

I nodded. "I knew that. And I had been given no indication that there had been any change in procedure. Since previous actions were approved *post facto,* I assumed the same would apply to anything I did."

Ritchie was silent for a moment while he picked up some papers and went through them. I tried to read something into Sinclair, but his face was an impenetrable as a block of granite.

"I have here a cost breakdown on the schedule you so precipitously announced," Ritchie said. "Do you realize it will involve an expenditure on our part of better than forty million dollars?"

I nodded.

"And added to that will be another eleven million dollars to convert the network to color?"

"That's correct," I said.

"You feel such an expenditure is economically sound for our company?"

"Yes," I said. "If I did not think so, I would not have committed the company."

"Do you also think it a proper action on your part to announce the resignation of certain officers of the company without prior consultation with them?"

"Yes. I have had their resignations in my desk ever since I came here."

"You did not have mine," he said. "But you announced it nevertheless."

"An oversight," I said.

"What do you mean, an oversight?" He was angry now.

I looked at him and kept my voice down. "I'm sure that before this meeting is adjourned, I will have your resignation."

His face began to flush, but I didn't give him a chance. I looked around at the table.

"I know you're busy, gentlemen, so I will be as brief as I can. The estimated billings for primetime in the current season is one hundred sixty million, of which thirty percent—or forty-eight millions—were advance sales. I have at this moment confirmed sales for fifty percent of next season's primetime amounting to one hundred twenty millions against projected total sales of two hundred forty millions. I could bore you with a percentage of increase over last year but I won't bother. The changes in programming initiated this last week by the movie and the Jana Reynolds show will increase the current year by a projected twenty-five million. So much for sales and programming.

"As for color, gentlemen, it is here and we may as well face it. If we waited five years when we would have to do it it would cost us better than fifty percent more than now. Meanwhile, we get an advantage of twenty percent increase in rates."

I looked around the table. "The increased costs will only result in greater billings and profits. Concerning personnel, I believe I have eliminated none but supernumeraries whose value to the company has long since disappeared."

They were all silent.

Sinclair spoke quietly. "The chair will entertain a motion for a vote of confidence in Mr. Gaunt and full ratification of his policies and schedule."

The motion was made and carried unanimously with two votes abstaining. Ritchie's and mine.

Sinclair's voice was dry and cold. "The chair will entertain a motion for adjournment."

In less than two minutes the meeting was over and there were only the two of us left in the boardroom. Ritchie and myself.

I gathered up my papers and looked down the long table. Ritchie sat there, hunched over as if he were in physical pain, his hands clasped tightly together on the table.

I stopped next to him on my way to the door. "I'm sorry, Dan," I said.

He looked up at me. His face was scrunched and gray. "The son of a bitch!" he said heavily. "He didn't even stop to say good-bye."

I didn't speak.

"He set me up for it," he said.

"He set us both up."

He nodded. His eyes blinked rapidly. "All he had to do was ask me to leave. It didn't have to be like this."

He walked over to the window and looked out at the snow. "Now I know why the windows in the new building can't be opened. They knew there would be days like this." He turned to look at me. "I saw him do things like this before. I even used to admire him for it. He could never do a thing like that to me, I thought."

A wry grin didn't make it to his eyes. "I thought," he repeated. He came back to me, his hand outstretched. "Good luck, Steve."

His handshake meant it. "Thank you, Dan."

"Protect yourself at all times, like they say. And never take your eyes off the referee."

TWELVE

I KEPT LACING MY COFFEE with brandy all afternoon. It kept me going. It also kept me from thinking too much. About myself, about Dan Ritchie, about Sinclair, about everything except the network. Finally it was nine o'clock and we were finished.

"That wraps it," I said, looking over at Fogarty.

"Yes, sir," she said in that quiet way she had. She began to gather up her papers.

"Fogarty, fix me a drink."

"Yes, sir." She went over to the bar. "What would you like?"

"Very dry martini. Double."

In a few minutes I had it. It was very good. "Was bartending one of the courses you took at Katherine Gibbs?"

She laughed. "No. That was on-the-job training."

I laughed. "Fix yourself a drink, Fogarty. You deserve one."

She shook her head. "No, thank you. I'll just get my things together and get going. The trains will be running late in this snow."

I had forgotten she lived in Darien. The way the New Haven was run she would be lucky to get home at all. "If there's any problem, Fogarty, you go to a hotel and charge it to the company."

"Thank you, Mr. Gaunt," she said. "Is there anything else I can do?"

"Yes. Make me another one of those delicious martinis before you go." I finished the rest of my drink.

I took the new drink from her hand. "Miss Fogarty," I said. "A martini like this is a good enough reason for a raise." I sipped the drink. "Tomorrow morning tell payroll that you get twenty-five dollars more a week."

"Thank you, Mr. Gaunt."

"You won't do it, Miss Fogarty, will you? You think I don't mean it. That I'm smashed, and it's the liquor talking."

"I think no such thing, Mr. Gaunt," she protested.

"That's a loyal secretary," I said. "Miss Fogarty, I've come to a decision."

"What's that, sir?"

"We've got to stop being so formal with each other. You call me Steve and I'll call you Sheila."

"Yes, Mr. Gaunt."

"Steve."

"Yes, Steve."

"That's better, Sheila. Now we can get down to the really important things. Am I or am I not the president of this network?"

"You are, Mr.—er—Steve."

"Then that makes everything very simple. Let's fuck." I took another sip of the martini.

A strange note came into her voice. "I think I'd better get you home."

I drew myself up proudly. "You're turning me down."

She didn't answer.

"You're fired," I said. "As president of this network, I'm firing you for refusing to perform your duties."

She watched me without speaking.

I sat down. The liquor left me suddenly. "You're not fired. I apologize, Fogarty."

"That's all right, Mr. Gaunt. I understand." She smiled. "Good night."

"Good night, Fogarty," I said.

—

THE FIRST FALL OF SNOW in New York is one of the most beautiful things I have ever seen. White and clean and crisp and clinging to shapes that nature never intended. I walked home through a white cubistic world that Braque would have given his left nut to paint, stopping only for an occasional traffic light. The snow formed a white peaked cap on each red and green traffic light, making them look like single-eyed cyclops going complacently about their business in the storm.

I was covered with snow by the time I reached home.

"It's rough," the doorman said, leaning on his shovel.

"Yeah." I didn't think it was bad at all. But then I didn't have to clear the walks.

The first thing I saw when I let myself into the apartment was the candles glowing on the table. I stopped. I had the strange thought that I had entered the wrong apartment. But then I saw the giant can of Malossol and the Dom Perignon in the ice bucket. It was all there.

"Barbara," I called out.

She came from the bedroom, carrying a single rose in a crystal vase. She looked at me for a moment, then placed the rose in the center of the table. "That does it, don't you think?"

I was still in the doorway. "What's the occasion?"

"It's snowing," she said.

"I know that," I replied.

"The first snow of the new year," she said. "I thought we should celebrate."

I looked at her. "Sure." I turned and put my hat and coat in the closet. When I turned back to the room, she was standing next to me.

"What's wrong?" she asked. "You sound strange."

"Nothing. I'm tired," I said. "I need a drink."

"I have an almost frozen bottle of vodka," she said.

"That should do it." I followed her to the bar. The bottle was encrusted with ice. She poured the drink. I waited for her.

She shook her head. "You go ahead."

It went down like beautiful liquid fire. I held the empty glass to her. She refilled it. This time I sipped.

She watched me. "It's been three months."

I nodded.

"Did you wonder what happened to me?"

I shook my head. "I figured you could find your way."

"But you knew I was lost."

"Aren't we all?" I said.

She poured herself a drink. She held her glass toward me. "Not you," she said. "You're never lost. You know exactly where you are. All the time." She swallowed her drink quickly and poured herself another. "Maybe this wasn't such a good idea, after all."

"It was a fine idea."

"I know how hard you've been working. That's why I kept out of your way. I thought this would be a surprise."

"I was surprised."

A wall of tears suddenly masked the blue of her eyes. "I think I'd better go."

"Don't go," I said. "I can't eat all this by myself."

She stood there. "Is that the only reason you want me to stay?"

"The snow outside is up to your ass. And there aren't any cabs."

She was silent for a moment, her eyes searching my face. "I love you," she said. "Aren't you even going to kiss me?"

I took her in my arms. Her mouth was soft and wet with the salt of her tears. I'm sorry, Steve," she whispered. "I'm sorry."

I pressed her head against my chest. "There's nothing to be sorry about."

She twisted in my arms. Her voice was strained. "I tried to warn you," she cried. "I tried to tell you what he was like. But you wouldn't listen, you wouldn't believe me."

I was bewildered. "What—who?"

"Daddy!" She spit the name out. "I was at his house for dinner last night and I heard him. He was on the phone to somebody.

"'We'll fix that cocky little bastard. He'll find out who's running Sinclair Television.'"

She clung tightly to me. "Don't feel too badly, Steve," she whispered against my chest. "You'll find another job and show him."

I turned her face up to me. "Is that why you came here tonight?"

She nodded. "I didn't want you to be alone."

"You're beautiful," I said. I smiled at her. "I didn't get fired. But I did find out who's running Sinclair TV. And so did your father. Me."

She threw her arms excitedly around me. "You did it, Steve? You really did it?"

I nodded, picking up the bottle of Dom Perignon. "Let's get this open. We've really got something to celebrate."

She kissed me quickly. "You open the wine."

I smiled as I watched her walking around the room turning off the lamps. Finally they were out and she came toward me in the golden light of the candles. I gave her a glass of champagne.

"There, isn't that better?" she asked.

"Much better," I said. We clinked our glasses. The bubbles tingled in my nostrils.

But it didn't help. I fell asleep at the table sometime between the Chateaubriand and dessert.

THIRTEEN

SOMEWHERE THE TELEPHONE WAS RINGING. I pushed my way up through the black, reaching for it. It stopped ringing before I could get to it. I heard a soft voice whispering into it.

I opened my eyes.

She turned back to me, putting down the telephone. "Go back to sleep."

"Who was it?" I asked.

"Your office," she said. "I told them you were still asleep."

"My office?" I snapped awake. "What the hell time is it?"

"Noon," she said.

I stared at her. "Why didn't you wake me?"

"You were tired." She smiled. "You know you sleep like a baby. Soft and gentle."

I got out of bed. "What kind of a dressing did you use on that salad? Seconal?"

She sat up. "You didn't need it. You knocked off a bottle of vodka and two bottles of champagne all by yourself."

"I don't remember."

"You passed out at the table. I had to call room service to help get you to bed."

"Is there any coffee?" I asked.

"There's some on the dining room table. I'll get it for you."

I went into the bathroom. When I came out she had a steaming cup on the tray. I took it from her hand and sipped it. "That's a help," I said. "But I'll need more than that to get started. You'll find a bottle of cognac on the bar."

She watched me lace the coffee. "You're drinking more than you used to."

I looked at her silently.

"Okay," she said. "I'm not the one to talk."

"That's right," I said. "Stay loose."

"Good advice. Why don't you take it yourself?" She came closer. "You're uptight."

"I got a lot of things on my head."

"You were wrong," she said. "You didn't get him. He got you."

"What do you mean?"

"You're drinking more and fucking less. That's the true sign of a big executive."

I didn't speak.

"I could have saved myself the bother," she said. "I wore the new nightgown. I saved it from the last time I was here. But it didn't work that time either."

I watched her walk into the bathroom and close the door. I looked down at the coffee cup in my hand. She was right. It had been three months now. Ever since I got the job. I put the cup down on the dresser. When she came out of the bathroom I was back in bed.

"What's the matter?" she asked, a quick concern in her voice. "Don't you feel well?"

"I never felt better."

Suddenly she was kneeling by the side of the bed, holding my face in her two hands, covering it with quick tiny kisses. "I love you, I love you, I love you," she said in between them.

"Don't get personal," I said, pulling her up on the bed beside me. "You'll blow your cool."

—

IT WAS TWO THIRTY IN the morning when I stopped the car in front of Aunt Prue's house. The bright, full, winter moon bouncing from the snow turned the night into day.

"The house is dark," Barbara said as we crunched our way through the snow to the front door. "You'll frighten the hell out of her, waking her up at this hour."

I reached up and took the key from its hiding place over the doorframe. "Chances are she won't even know we're here until we come down in the morning."

Light spilled into the foyer from her small office. "Chances are that you're wrong as usual," Aunt Prue said from the doorway.

She came into my arms and for a moment I had that surprise I always had when I realized she was never as tall as I thought she was. Somehow you always think of your elders as bigger than you. I kissed her.

"How did you get up here?"

"Drove from New York."

"In this storm?" she asked.

"The snow stopped a long time ago. The turnpike's all cleared."

She turned to Barbara and held out her hand. "I'm Prudence Gaunt," she said. "And my nephew hasn't changed a bit since he was a boy. He still forgets his manners."

Barbara took her hand. "Barbara Sinclair. And I'm very pleased to meet you. Steve's been talking about you all the way up."

"Lies probably." But I could see that she was pleased. "You must be frozen. Let me fix some tea for you."

"With rum, Aunt Prue," I said. "If you haven't forgotten your own recipe."

In the morning we went walking in the snow on the beach. The sun was bright and danced like diamonds on the snow. We got back to the house, our faces red and shining, in time for lunch.

Aunt Prue was at the door. "There've been five calls from New York for you."

I looked at her. "What did you tell them?"

"You weren't here," she said.

"Good. If they call again, tell them you haven't seen or heard from me."

"Is there anything wrong, Stephen?" she asked.

"Nothing's wrong," I said. "I wanted to get away for a while. I needed a vacation."

"What about your job?"

"It will keep."

After three days we had enough of the snow, so we went up to Boston and caught a plane for Bermuda. We spent a long weekend in the sun and the water. For the first time in three months I was able to fall asleep without wheels in my head. I went back to the office on a Monday morning.

Fogarty followed me into the office, almost staggering under the pile of papers. She put them down on my desk. "You've got great color, Mr. Gaunt."

"Thank you. I've been in the sun. How's everything going?"

She made a face. "Panicsville. Nobody knew where you were and everybody believed that I knew and wasn't talking."

"Sorry if it made it rough on you."

"That's my job. I told them I was your secretary, not your keeper."

"Good girl."

She gestured toward the papers. "Where do you want to begin?"

I looked at the small mountain, then I picked them up and dropped them into the wastebasket. I looked at her. "How's that for a beginning?"

"Fine," she said, unflustered. She glanced at her notebook. "Now, about the telephone calls. Mr. Savitt wants you to call him as soon as you arrive; Mr. Gilligan—"

"Never mind the phone calls." I got to my feet and went to the door.

In spite of myself, the question popped to her lips. "Where are you going?"

"Upstairs," I said.

There was a look of surprise on his face as I came into his office. I had walked right past his secretaries. "I was just about to call you," he said. He held a sheet of paper toward me. "Congratulations."

I didn't look at the paper in my hand.

"Saturday night held up," he continued. "We averaged a better than thirty-eight percent audience share the second week. I think you've made your point."

I put the paper back on his desk without looking at it. "No, Mr. Sinclair," I said. "You've made your point."

"I don't understand," he said.

"I didn't either at first, but now I do," I said. "And I don't like any of it. I quit."

FOURTEEN

HE STARED AT ME FOR a long silent moment. Then he nodded. "Just like that?"

"Just like that," I replied.

"Am I entitled to ask why?"

"You are," I said. "But I don't think you'll understand."

"Try me," he said.

"I don't like being used," I said. "I came here to do a job. Not to be dropped in a ring and aimed at someone's throat so that you could turn on."

He was silent.

"That business with Dan Ritchie need never have happened," I went on. "You could have let him out with his dignity. There was no reason to destroy him."

His voice was soft. "You believe that?"

I nodded.

"Dan Ritchie had to be destroyed," he said in the same tone. "I thought you, more than anyone else, could see that. You said he was too old when you came here."

"I didn't advocate euthanasia," I said.

He turned cold. "There's only one way to deal with a cancer. Cut it out. If you don't, you die. It's as simple as that. Dan Ritchie was a cancer. He had been with this company twenty-five years and he went sour. You knew that. I knew that. But the board of directors did not. They thought he was the same as he had always been. And more than one of them were quite willing to believe him when he said that you were wasting the company's money and assets.

"Sure, I could have let him go. But that wouldn't have convinced them that he was wrong. There was only one way to do it and only one person who could. You."

"And if I had lost?" I asked. "What would have happened then?"

"You couldn't lose. I stacked the deck when I let you spend the money."

He hit the buttons on his desk and all the television screens leaped into life on the wall behind me. "Look at that," he said.

I turned and he pressed the buttons again and the channels began flipping like a kaleidoscope. "There it is," he said. "The greatest medium of influence the world will ever know. And we're just beginning to learn about it.

"Five years from now it will determine who the next President of the United States will be, ten years from now it will put the world in our backyard, fifteen years from now it may take us to the moon." He jammed all the buttons angrily and the screens went to black.

"And that's what you want to walk away from," he said. "All because the game is too rough. And you're too sensitive, you don't want to hurt anybody's feelings.

"The rating game you play is a children's game. When you run a network, you're helping to shape and make the lives of people the world over. It can be for good, it can be for evil. But it has to be your choice. Only you can be the judge. You're alone at the top. And the more viewers you have, the more effective you can be. I thought you saw that, maybe I was wrong."

He was still for a moment. "I hadn't intended to make a speech," he said. "A long time ago in Phrygia there was something called the Gordian knot, and legend held that the man who untied it would be king. Alexander came and cut it with his sword. It was as simple as that.

"I made the fiftieth floor our Gordian knot. It remained empty four years. I intended it for the man who would succeed me. And all you did to get it was to ask. For only one reason. No one had ever thought of asking before. I thought you would be Alexander. He, too, was very young."

He went from his desk to the window. He didn't look at me. "I'll accept our resignation," he said over his shoulder. "But first I want you to read that memo I gave you when you came in."

Silently I picked up the sheet of paper from the desk. It was a rough draft of a press release.

SPENCER SINCLAIR III ANNOUNCED TODAY THAT HE IS ASSUMING THE POSITION OF CHAIRMAN OF THE BOARD OF DIRECTORS OF SINCLAIR BROADCASTING COMPANY. HE ALSO ANNOUNCED THE APPOINTMENT OF STEPHEN GAUNT AS PRESIDENT OF SINCLAIR BROADCASTING COMPANY AND ITS CHIEF EXECUTIVE OFFICER. MR. GAUNT WILL ALSO RETAIN THE PRESIDENCY OF SINCLAIR TELEVISION. MR. SINCLAIR STATED THAT…

I didn't bother reading the rest of it. "You could have told me."

He turned to look at me. His lips twisted in a wry smile. "You didn't give me much of a chance."

"Are you still willing to do this after the way I spoke?"

"I gave you the memo, didn't I?"

I looked down at it again. President of Sinclair Broadcasting Company. Like being on top of the world. I put the memo back on his desk. "No," I said. "Thank you, but no."

Surprise edged into his voice. "Why?"

"I'm too young to die," I said and went back downstairs to my office.

—

IT WAS EIGHT O'CLOCK AND we still hadn't gone out to dinner. We were in bed. I ran my finger down the curve of her spine and cupped my hand over her buttock. I squeezed it. Solid.

"Like that?" she asked.

"What's not to like? I'm an ass man. I thought you knew that."

"You're a lot of things," she said. She dragged on the stick.

I took it from her mouth and rolled over on my back. I dragged on the reefer and let the smoke stay deep in my lungs. "Is there any more champagne left in that bottle?"

"I'll see." She sat up and reached for the champagne in the bucket. She refilled my glass, gave it to me, then refilled her own. "Clear sailing," she said.

I could feel the tiny bubbles doing their thing all the way down to my toes. Everything was working fine. Champagne and pot. Dom Perignon and Acapulco Gold. Unbeatable.

I put the glass and the reefer on the end table and reached for her. She came into my arms as if she had been born there. I drained her mouth. "You're warm," I said. "Inside and out."

"I love you," she said.

I fed on her breasts. The telephone began to ring and I moved down to her belly.

"The telephone's ringing," she said.

"To hell with it," I said, moving down to her fur. But she had already picked it up. "Tell them I'm out to dinner."

A strange expression came over her face. "My father's downstairs. He wants to come up."

I took the telephone from her hand. "Yes."

"A Mr. Sinclair for you, sir," the doorman said. "Shall I send him up?"

I looked at her. "Yes." I put down the phone and got out of bed. I went into the bathroom and rinsed my mouth. I splashed some water on my face and brushed at my hair. I slipped into a robe and went back into the bedroom.

She had pulled a negligee around her shoulders and was sitting up in bed. I bent over and kissed her. "Don't go away," I said. "I'll get rid of him quick and be right back."

He had style and good instincts and both were working for him at the moment. "I hope I'm not interrupting."

"Not at all," I said. I led the way to the bar. "Would you like a drink?"

"Whiskey and water, no ice."

"Scotch whiskey?"

"Of course," he said.

I fixed his drink and poured myself a brandy. We drank. He came right to the point.

"What went wrong this morning? I thought I made everything very clear."

"You did," I said. "Nothing went wrong. I just realized that it was too much, too soon. Especially after listening to you. There's still a great deal I have to learn."

"You'll do all right," he said. "You learn fast."

"Sure. But no matter how fast I learn, it will be at least two years before I can take on the things you want to throw at me."

"Do you still want to leave?" he asked.

"No," I said. "Not now."

He smiled suddenly. "Thank you," he said. "The last thing in the world I wanted to do was to drive you out."

"I know that," I said.

"Then what do we do?" he asked. "Ritchie left a hole in the company structure."

"I'll fill that hole," I said. "With one condition."

"What's that?"

"You stay on as president and chief executive officer of Sinclair Broadcasting. I'll need you to keep me from going off the deep end. And if your offer is still good two years from now and you haven't changed your mind, I'll take you up on it."

He looked at me. "Okay. You're exec VP of the broadcasting company and president of the TV, is that it?"

I nodded. "That's it."

"Done." He held out his hand. "Tell me something, I'm curious."

"About what?"

"What would you have done if we hadn't worked out a deal?"

"I wasn't worried," I said casually. "I really don't have to work for a living." Behind him Barbara had come into the room. I couldn't resist it. "I forgot to mention I was married last week. To a very wealthy girl whose father wants to take me into the family business."

He looked at me as if I had suddenly gone mad.

"Hello, Father," Barbara said.

He didn't have just style, he had great style. The shock was gone in a fraction of a second and he held his arms open to her. She went into them and he turned to me with a big smile on his face. "Congratulations, son. You're a very lucky man."

"I know that, sir."

His smile broadened. "You don't have to be so formal now that you're in the family. Call me Dad."

FIFTEEN

"DAMN IT!" SHE EXPLODED. "NOW I can't even fasten this brassiere!" She flung it angrily across the room and turned back to the mirror. "Look at me. Christ!"

I came up behind her and putting my arms around her waist, I cupped a breast in each hand. "Let me be your brassiere."

She stared at my face in the mirror. "You like it," she accused. "You'd be proud if they asked me to do Elsie the cow commercials."

"There's nothing wrong with liking big tits. It's the most popular American fixation."

She twisted out of my arms and pulled a dresser drawer open violently. The drawer came out in her hands and spilled its contents over the floor. She sat down in the middle of the pile of underthings and began to cry.

I knelt beside her and pulled her head down to my chest. "I feel such a slug," she sobbed. "I can't do anything right."

"Relax," I said. "The worst is over. It's only another few months now."

"It's like forever," she said. "Why didn't you talk me out of it?"

I did. The first year we were married. But by the second year, her mind was made up and there was no stopping her. "Every woman is entitled to her child," she had said. "That's where it's at."

I knew better than to remind her of that just now. Instead I pulled her to her feet. I sat her down in a chair. "I'll fix you a drink."

I made it a good one. She took one taste of it, made a face and put it down. "It tastes awful," she said. "Give me a cigarette."

I lit one and handed it to her. "I'm down," she said. "I've never been so down in my life."

"Drink your drink. It'll make you feel better."

"You wouldn't have a reefer around, would you?"

"You know better than that. Bill said it might not be good for the baby. You wouldn't want the baby born stoned, would you?"

"Just because he's a doctor he thinks he knows everything," she snapped. "I suppose it's better if the baby's born bombed? Whiskey's okay?"

I didn't answer.

She picked up the drink. "You finish dressing and go ahead. I'm not going out."

"But they're expecting both of us."

"Make excuses then, for Christ's sake. Tell them I'm nauseous or something. God knows you're good enough at making excuses for not coming home to dinner. Think one up for them." She swallowed some of her drink. "Besides I can't stand that fat little Jew anyway. He reminds me of a pig."

I stared at her. "Your stinger is showing."

"I wouldn't like him if he stood in the pulpit of St. Thomas's Episcopal every Sunday," she said. "He only wants to use you."

"Doesn't everybody?" I turned back to the mirror and finished knotting my tie. "But that's my job. To be used by people."

"Christ, aren't you noble?" she sneered. "You're beginning to believe that crap my father hands out that the president of a network is a servant of the people."

"It could be worse," I said, slipping into my jacket. "Are you getting dressed or are you going to sit there all night with your tits hanging out?"

There were eight of us at the round table at Twenty-One. Sam Benjamin and his wife, Denise; Jack Savitt and an actress client he was showing off, Jennifer Brace; Sam's brother-in-law, Roger Cohen and his wife, whose name I didn't catch until three weeks later; and Barbara and myself.

I looked across the table. Sam was enjoying himself. He was doing one of his tricks. Making a hundred dollar bill disappear, then finding it, first in the actress's décolletage, then in Barbara's cigarette case. Barbara seemed to be enjoying herself.

At least she laughed more than anyone else at the table. But then, maybe she hadn't seen his tricks before.

I smiled to myself. Sam loved table magic. Sometimes I wondered whether he was a frustrated performer, actor, or publicity man, or maybe a combination of all three. In a kind of way, that was how I came to meet him.

—

JACK AND I HAD JUST finished lunch at the Norse Room in the Waldorf and were walking back to the Park Avenue entrance when we saw the crowd in front of the Empire Room. Then I saw the four Brinks men with drawn revolvers. Behind them were two more guards, carrying a big aluminum trunk that was fastened with two giant gold padlocks. Four more guards brought up the rear.

"What's happening?" I asked.

"I'll find out," Jack said quickly. He charged up the steps to the Empire Room and stopped to talk to a man at the door. A moment later he was back.

"It's a publicity stunt," he said. "Some new producer invited the press and every important exhibitor in the country to show how a picture should be sold."

I looked at the crowd and recognized some of them. They were among the toughest and most cynical men in the business. "It's got to be a pretty good stunt to get them out."

"It is," Jack said. "My friend told me there's a million dollars in cash in that trunk."

"This I gotta see." No one at the door stopped us. Everyone had his eyes on the trunk, now standing on a table.

I looked around the room. It was plastered with signs and buntings. They all said the same thing.

SAMUEL BENJAMIN PRESENTS

Icarus

THE EXHIBITOR'S MILLION-DOLLAR MOVIE

I grinned to myself. At least here was a motion picture distributor who wasn't lying down for television. He was fighting back with their own language. He was also fighting with more than that. There were giant blowups in color—a magnificent half-nude male, whose muscles shimmered under his skin, holding an almost naked girl in one arm while with the other he fought off armies. Other blowups had the same figure soaring over the massed warriors in a curious harness of feathered wings but never without the naked girl.

"Ladies and gentlemen," the PA system boomed.

All eyes turned to the stage. This was the first time I saw him. He was small and seemed almost as broad as he was tall. He wore a black suit and a white shirt. He had black hair and a ruddy face that seemed to be sweating.

"Most of you don't know me," he said. *"My name is Sam Benjamin. And most of you don't know my picture. Its name is Icarus. But I promise you just one thing."* He paused to wipe his face with a white handkerchief that was already sopping wet. *"After today, you won't forget either of us."*

He gestured and the guards picked up the trunk and turned it toward him. He took an immense gold key from his pocket and opened the locks, then stepped back.

The guards knew what they were supposed to do. They picked up the trunk and turned it over. Bundles and stacks of bills tumbled out onto the table, overflowing the edges and spilling to the floor. It seemed as if it would never stop. A deep collective sigh rose from the crowd.

I looked at them. There was an expression of rapt absorption on their faces. They could not take their eyes from the pile of money.

I looked back at the little man on the platform. Suddenly he was not that small anymore. He had been right. They would never forget him.

"Let's go," I whispered.

Jack turned to me when we reached the lobby. "The guy's nuts. To take a chance with a million bucks like that. What if—"

I cut him off. "Get me a rundown on him."

"You're serious?"

I nodded. "I've never been more serious in my life." There was only one kind of person who would pull a stunt like that. He had to be either a man who had everything, or a man who had nothing and was gambling everything. And it didn't matter how it turned up. The man had guts.

What I learned made me ever more curious, and the next morning I went over to his office to see what he was really like. It was a small four-room office in one of the Rockefeller Center buildings. There were people running around, desks everywhere, even in the corridors, papers on the floor.

I stood there in the middle of what passed for the reception room and watched the confusion. After a moment, a man came up to me. He wore a worried expression. I didn't know it then but he was Roger Cohen, Sam's brother-in-law and principal source of finance.

"Are you an exhibitor or a salesman?" he asked.

"In a kind of way, I'm both."

"What I want to know," he said hoarsely, "is—are you buying, selling, or collecting?"

"Buying," I said.

A smile came over his face. "In that case, come right in. Mr. Benjamin will see you right away."

Sam was on the telephone when we came in. He looked up and waved me to a seat. There were papers on it. Roger hurriedly took them off.

"You got it," Sam said into the phone. "Fifty percent rentals on the film, I pay all the co-op ads up to one grand per week."

He put down the telephone and reached his hand over the desk. "Sam Benjamin's the name."

I took his hand. It was a fooler. There was nothing soft and fat about his grip. "Stephen Gaunt."

He looked at me. "*That* Stephen Gaunt?"

I nodded.

"Why?" he asked.

"You need money," I said. "We have it."

"I don't know where you got your information," he said quickly. "But it's all wrong. We're doing fine."

I got to my feet. "Then I'm wasting your time."

"Wait a minute," he said. "Not so fast. What have you got on your mind?"

"Two hundred thousand for your picture for TV."

"Can't do it. If the word gets out, the exhibitors will boycott me."

"Money now," I said. "We'll announce the deal in two years. Your picture will have played off by then."

"Did you bring the check?" he grinned. "I gotta pay the rent today or they'll throw me out of here."

SIXTEEN

WE TURNED DOWN THE OFFERS of a lift and walked home through the warm summer night. We crossed Fifth Avenue and looked in the windows of Saks. They were bright and filled with color and featured sport and cruise clothes. I looked at her. "It wasn't so bad, was it?" I asked.

"No," she answered shortly. She seemed lost in her own thoughts and we walked on. She didn't speak again until we turned the corner on Forty-ninth Street. "What makes him so important to you?"

"Film," I said. "He may be a way for us to get feature movies."

"What's so difficult about that?" she asked. "There's plenty to be had."

"Sure," I answered. "But how long do you think the supply will hold up? Television uses more feature film in one week than Hollywood's average annual production over the last twenty years."

"Why don't you just make them yourselves?"

"We will, in time. But the economics aren't right just yet. Until then, we're in an open market and I would like to protect myself against higher prices."

"What makes you think you'll get bargains from him? He's not the type."

I looked at her with respect. She wasn't her father's daughter for nothing. "Right," I said. "But he needs us. He's ambitious. He wants his own picture company. And we can help him get it. It works both ways."

By this time we were at the Towers. We went into the building and got on the elevator. She began to say something, but then glanced at the elevator operator and held it until we had entered the apartment.

She sank exhausted into a chair. "Thank God for air conditioning. You can't imagine how that heat beats me with all the weight I'm carrying."

"You were going to say something in the elevator but you didn't."

"Oh." She lit a cigarette. "I still wouldn't trust him if I were you."

"What makes you say that?"

"Little things. The way he acts." She ground the cigarette out. "Nothing tastes right."

"You started something, finish it."

"He has no sense of loyalty, for one thing," she said, almost defiantly. "Take the way he acted toward his brother-in-law, Roger, tonight.

"The first time we went out with him, he treated Roger as if he were his partner. It was Roger this, Roger that, Roger what do you think. I didn't understand that until you told me that it was Roger who financed him all these years."

"So?" I asked.

"You saw the way he acted tonight," she said. "As if Roger were his lackey and didn't exist at all. One tiny little bit of success and he treated Roger with contempt. Every time Roger opened his mouth, Sam shut him up, until Roger just sat there like a poor stupid idiot."

"Sam was just feeling good," I said. "He's entitled to crow a little. It's not every picture that grabs a three-million-dollar gross in twelve weeks."

"Sure," she said. "But not at the expense of the man who's been carrying him for half his life."

"I'm positive he means nothing by it," I said. "Did you see the new Lincoln convertible he bought Roger?"

"I saw it. But I wonder if he's paid Roger back the money he owed him?" She got heavily to her feet. "I feel all sticky and sweaty. I'm going to shower and go to bed."

I thought that was the end of it, but she was still awake watching television when I got into bed beside her two hours later.

"I still don't like him," she said.

By that time he had long gone from my mind. I had spent the evening in the living room jumping channels. Tuesday night was still a problem for us. "Who?" I asked.

"Sam," she said. She turned on her side away from me still watching the TV screen. "Rub my back."

I moved my hand in a circular motion over the middle of her back. "How's that?"

"Just a little bit lower." I did what she wanted. "That's better." She was silent for a moment. "Did you see the way he took that hundred-dollar bill from that actress? He stuck his hand so far down her dress I thought he was going to pull her tits out along with the money. Not that she didn't have them right up there for everybody to look at."

I laughed. "If it's tits he was interested in, he went after the wrong girl."

"You were looking at them, too. I saw the expression on your face. On *all* your faces. You all wanted to fuck her. I could tell."

"You're jealous," I said.

"You're damn right I am! If you think I like looking like this while cunts like her push their titties at you, practically begging you to fuck them, you're crazy."

"I wasn't interested," I said. "Anyway, it wasn't me she was after, it was Sam."

"Yes." She giggled suddenly. "It was really funny. He's so crass and vulgar. At one point when he thought no one could see him, he took her hand and put it under the tablecloth on his cock. From the expression on his face I thought he was going to come."

I laughed, continuing to rub her back. "Good for him."

She was quiet for a moment. I started to remove my hand. "Don't stop. You're making me deliciously horny."

"How do you think I feel?" I asked.

She reached behind her and found me. "Hey!" she exclaimed. She began to turn toward me.

"Don't move," I said, putting my hands under her hips and moving her back toward me. She was wide open for me and I drove all the way in.

I heard her gasp. "I can't breathe!" she cried. "I feel you up in my throat!"

I laughed and moved my hands up to hold each breast. I leaned over her shoulder and ran my tongue down the side of her cheek to her throat. Her buttocks were hard and grinding against my groin. A blare of sound came from the television set. Involuntarily I glanced at it.

She turned her face back toward me just at that moment. "Damn! I knew it had to happen sometimes," she said. But her voice was warm and pleased and she didn't stop trying to take more of me into her. "I knew you would find a way to fuck and work at the same time."

—

I GOT OUT OF BED and turned off the television set. She put her head against my shoulder when I came back.

"It was good, wasn't it?" she asked.

"Yes."

"It didn't make any difference that I'm bigger now, did it?"

"No."

She raised her head and looked at me. "My cunt is still the same? I mean—it isn't stretched or—"

"It's better," I said. "It's tighter, and wetter, and hotter."

"I'm glad," she said. She put her head back on my shoulders. "I'm sorry I was such a drag. But the last few weeks everything seemed to get to me. Your working late, my not being able to move around, the heat of the city and the noise. I'm even tired of the air conditioning. If only once I could get some fresh air to breathe—"

"That's easy," I interrupted.

"In this city?" she asked. "Where can you go? Central Park?"

"How about the Cape?" I asked. "Aunt Prue would be glad to have you. And you wouldn't be bored. There is always something going on up there."

"But what about you?"

"I can come up on weekends." Suddenly I wanted her to go. It would make things easier all around. "During the week I have to work and I'm not much use to you. At least, this way, we'll both get some time in the sun."

But I was wrong. The first weekend she was away, I was in California, the second weekend I spent in the office going over the annual report to the stockholders, which had to be at the printers by Monday.

And the third weekend was too late.

SEVENTEEN

I HAD JUST BEGUN A meeting with the sales managers when Fogarty came into the office. "I know you said hold all calls, Mr. Gaunt," she apologized. "But your aunt is calling from Rockport. She says it's very important."

I picked up the telephone. Aunt Prue spoke before I had a chance to utter a word. "Barbara is ill, Stephen. I think you had better come up here right away."

My stomach began to tighten. "What happened?"

"We don't know yet," she answered. "I brought her breakfast as usual and found her on the floor in a pool of blood."

"Is she all right?"

"She's on her way to the hospital in an ambulance," she answered. Her voice began to crack. "You come up here as quick as you can."

The phone went dead in my hand. I looked over at Fogarty. I didn't have to say a word, she could read the news on my face. She picked up the telephone. I was there in less than two hours by chartered plane.

Aunt Prue was in the waiting room of the hospital when I got there. "How is she?" I asked.

"She lost the baby," said Aunt Prue in a dull voice.

"I don't give a damn about the baby!" I almost shouted. "How is she?"

"I don't know. She's been in the operating room since she got here."

I went down the corridor to the nurses' post. "I'm Mr. Gaunt," I said. "I'd like to get some information about my wife. She was just brought in here a few hours ago."

"Just a moment, Mr. Gaunt, I'll find out." She picked up a phone and dialed a number. "Info on a new admission. Mrs. Gaunt." She listened for a moment, then nodded. She depressed the bar and dialed again. She looked over at me. "I'm calling operation status."

After a moment, someone answered. "Check on Mrs. Gaunt," she said into the phone. "Her husband is here." She listened for a minute, then put down the telephone and came over to me.

"She's on her way down to her room," she said in a professionally soothing voice that did nothing for me at all. "If you'll go back to the waiting room, Mr. Gaunt, Dr. Ryan will be with you in a moment."

"Thank you," I said and went back to Aunt Prue.

It was fifteen minutes before he came into the waiting room. He knew Aunt Prue. He was a young man, but his face was gray and tired and his eyes were bloodshot with strain. He didn't waste words. "If you'll come with me, Mr. Gaunt, I'll fill you in while we're on our way."

We went out into the hall and into an elevator. He pressed a button and it began to climb slowly, as only a hospital elevator can.

"Your wife is very low," he said in his quiet voice. "By the time she was discovered she had lost a great deal of blood. Apparently she began to bleed in the night while asleep, but did not wake up until she actually began to abort. Then she tried to get out of bed for help, but she was already too weak and collapsed. My guess is that it was almost three hours before she was discovered. It's a miracle that she was alive when she was found."

The elevator door opened and we followed him down the hall to her room. We paused outside the door. "What's her chances?" I asked, my words strangely impersonal in my own ears.

"We're doing the best we can. We had to replace almost all her blood." He looked right into my eyes. "I took the liberty of calling a priest in case she was Catholic."

"She's not," I said. "She's Episcopalian." And I went into the room.

A nurse looked over her shoulder and saw us and moved away from the side of the bed. I looked down at her. There was a tube running into her arm, another into her nostril. She was white, whiter than I had ever seen anyone. I moved over to the bed and took her hand.

After a moment she seemed to become aware of me. Her eyelids fluttered and opened. Her lips moved, but I couldn't hear her.

I put my face very close to her. "Don't try to speak, Barbara," I said. "Everything will be all right."

Her eyes looked into mine. Again I felt the wonder of their blueness. "Steve," her voice was the barest whisper. "I'm sorry about the baby."

"It doesn't matter," I said. "We'll have others."

Her eyes searched mine. "You mean that?"

"You'll know I do," I said. "As soon as you get out of here."

A faint smile came to her eyes. "I love you," she said.

"I love you," I said. She seemed to give a small sigh of happiness and her lips parted. "I've always loved you. You know that," I said.

But she didn't and she never would. I didn't even know she was dead until the doctor came over and gently took my hand away from her.

—

AFTER THE FUNERAL I WENT back to the apartment and locked the door and turned off. I didn't want to see or speak to anyone.

For the first few days people tried telephoning, but I wouldn't answer and anyone who came was turned away downstairs. By the third day no one called, not even the office. They had all gotten the message.

I wandered through the apartment like a disembodied ghost. She was still there. Everywhere. The perfume of her was in the bed, her clothes were in the closet, her makeup was still spread over the bathroom.

The television set was on, but I didn't even look at it. It was just on and after the third day of never being off, the tube burned out and I never bothered having it replaced. Now it was really quiet. Deadly quiet. Like the grave. Like where Barbara was.

Sometime during the fourth day the doorbell rang. I just sat on the couch. Whoever it was would go away. The bell rang again. Insistently.

I got up. "Who is it?" I asked through the closed door.

"Sam Benjamin," he said.

"Go away," I said. "I don't want to see you."

"I want to see you," he shouted. "Do you open this door or do I have to break it in?"

I opened the door. "You saw me," I said and started to close it.

But his foot was in the door now and his weight was against it, all two hundred pounds of him. I went back with the door.

He straightened up, puffing. "That's better," he said, closing the door behind him.

"What do you want?" I asked.

He looked at me. "It's time you got out of here."

I walked away from him and back to the couch. He followed me. "Why don't you leave me alone?"

"I should," he said. "You're really no concern of mine."

"That's right," I said.

"But I still need you," he said.

"That's what Barbara said about you."

"She did?" He looked at me shrewdly. "She was smarter than I thought." He walked over to the dining room table and looked at the remnants of food on the plates. "When did you eat last?"

I shrugged my shoulders. "I don't remember. When I get hungry I call downstairs."

"Do you have any booze here?"

"Behind the bar," I said. "Help yourself."

He went to the bar and took down a bottle of Scotch and poured two glasses full to the brim. He came back to me. "Here, take one. You need a drink."

"I don't want any."

He put the glass down and, sipping his own drink thoughtfully, wandered off into the apartment. After a few minutes I heard him in the bedroom, then it was quiet. I stared at the glass of whiskey and ignored him. Or tried to. But after about fifteen minutes and he still hadn't come out, I went after him.

There was a pile of clothing lying on the floor. He came out of her closet with another armful and threw it on top of the rest. He saw me and stopped.

"What the hell are you doing?" I yelled. "Those are Barbara's clothes!"

"I know it," he said, puffing a little. "But what good are they doing to do you? Unless you intend to wear them?"

I began to put them back. He knocked them out of my arms and with surprising strength pushed me back. I swung at him, but he grabbed my wrists and held them.

"She's *dead!*" he said sharply. "She's dead and you might as well accept it. She's dead and you'll never bring her back. So stop trying to climb into the grave with her!"

"I killed her!" I said wildly. "If I hadn't sent her away, she would still be alive. She wouldn't have been alone when it happened."

"It would have happened, anyway. Everybody dies in their own time."

"You know," I said bitterly. "You Jews know everything. Even about death."

"Yes. Even about death," he said gently and let go of my wrists. "We Jews have six thousand years of experience with death. We have learned to live with it. We had to."

"How do you live with it?"

"We cry," he said.

"I forgot how. The last time I cried I was a little boy. I'm grown up now."

"Try it," he said. "It will help."

"You'll have to teach me," I said nastily.

"I will," he said. He looked around the room and took a hat from my closet and put it on his head. He turned to face me.

I stared at him. The too-small hat on his head, his ruddy shining face, the gleaming black-rimmed glasses. It was all too ridiculous. I almost began to laugh but something stopped me.

"At every funeral and once a year on Yom Kippur, the Day of Atonement, we say a certain prayer for the dead. It's called Kaddish."

"And that makes you cry?" I asked.

"It never fails," he said. "Because it's not only for your dead but it's for all the dead since time began." He took my hand, "Now say this after me—*Yisgadal, v'yiskadash—*"

He waited and I repeated the words after him. *"Yisgadal, v'yiskadahs—"*

I saw the tears come into his eyes behind his shining glasses. He opened his mouth to speak, but his voice began to fail him. *"Sh'may rabbo—"*

I felt the tears burning their way to my eyes. I put my hands up and covered my face. "Barbara!" I cried.

I cried.

I cried.

I cried.

BOOK TWO:
SAM BENJAMIN

NEW YORK, 1955-1960

ONE

HE WOKE FROM HIS SLEEP feeling drugged and heavy. He was quiet for a moment, then pushed himself up in the bed. The door opened and Denise stood there looking at him.

"So you finally made it," she said.

He stared at her. "I feel lousy. I got a mouthful of stones."

"You ought to have," she said without sympathy. "Must you try to drink all the whiskey in town in one sitting?"

"Don't hok me," he said, without resentment. "I got a headache."

She was silent for a moment. "I'll get you some aspirin."

She went into the bathroom and he struggled to his feet and stepped on the scale next to the bed. He looked down and cursed. Two hundred and twenty pounds.

Denise heard him as she came back into the room. "It's the drinking," she said, handing him the aspirin and a glass of water.

He swallowed the aspirin, making a face. "I eat pretty good, too."

"You eat too much, you drink too much," she said. "You got to start somewhere. Dr. Farber says stop drinking. The weight's too much for your heart. You're not getting any younger."

"Don't tell me," he said wearily. "I know. Just tell Mamie to get me some breakfast." He started for the bathroom.

"Coffee and toast?"

He stopped and looked back at her. "You know better than that. The usual. Four eggs, bacon, rolls, the works. I need the energy."

"It's your funeral," she said.

"Then you'll be a rich widow."

She smiled at him. "Promises, promises. Ever since we met that's all I got from you."

He went to her and kissed her cheek. "Mama, get breakfast. You talk too much."

She touched his face and left the room. He stood there for a moment after she left, listening to her voice as she called instructions to the cook, then he went into the bathroom.

As usual, the telephone rang while he was sitting on the john. Denise's voice came through the closed door. "It's for you. Roger."

"Damn it," he said. "Tell him I'll be right out." He pushed the flush and shouted over the roar of the water. "And call the phone company. I want an extension in here."

He went back into the bedroom and picked up the telephone. "Yes, Roger."

"We're confirmed for the Rome flight. Alitalia, nine o'clock tonight." Roger's voice was hesitant. *"You sure you want to go?"*

"Of course I'm sure," he snapped.

"We're four hundred thousand to the good now," Roger said. *"You make that deal and it's gone."*

"We don't make that deal and it will go away," he said. "In dribs and drabs and we won't know what happened to it. We got to keep movin' or we lose it all."

"What makes you so hot to keep pushing?" Roger said.

"I been waiting all my life for this chance," he said. "And I'm not goin' to pass it up."

"But half that money is mine," Roger said.

"I'll guarantee your half," he said, knowing full well that they were only words. If it went, he would have no money to guarantee Roger anything.

Roger knew it, too. *"That Gaunt has got your head turned, I swear. What if he doesn't come through?"*

"He'll come through," Sam said confidently. "He's the one person around that can see beyond the edge of his nose. Besides, he's lucky for me."

Roger knew when to stop. *"What time will you be down at the office?"*

"In about an hour," he said. "I'll pack a bag and we'll leave from there."

When he put down the phone, Denise had returned. "You're going through with it?"

He nodded.

"You don't have to," she said. "We have enough. The kids don't need it."

"I need it. I've been around a long time and if I don't make it now I'll never make it. Just once I would like everybody to know I'm as good as they are."

She touched his hand. "You're better."

He smiled. "You're prejudiced," he said and went back into the bathroom.

—

HE HEARD THE FAINT "PING" and was instantly alert. The cabin was dark and overhead the seat-belt sign had just gone off. He glanced over at Roger.

Roger was asleep, in the awkward position most perfectly adapted for aircraft sleeping, his mouth slightly agape. He always bragged that he could sleep anywhere. As a boy he had slept on subways and after that everything was easy. Apparently he was right.

It wasn't like that with Sam. Something about hanging thirty-five thousand feet in the air in a heavy metal container did something to his gut. No matter how much he drank or how many pills he took, his eyes remained steadfastly open.

Carefully he stepped out into the aisle over Roger's outstretched feet and made his way forward through the dark cabin. Everyone seemed to be sleeping.

He went through the curtains into the lounge, blinking at the light. The lone stewardess sitting there jumped to her feet.

"Can I get you something, *Signor* Benjamin?"

"You know my name?" he asked.

"Si, signore," she smiled. "Doesn't everyone know the name of the famous *prodottore?"*

It was real Italian con. Especially with his name on the passenger list. "Whiskey and water."

He sat down as she turned to the galley. He took off his glasses and polished them with his handkerchief. She placed the drink in front of him. He put his glasses back on and almost finished the drink in one draft. He looked up at her. "Where's the rest of the crew?"

"Sleeping," she said. "It's still four and a half hours to Rome and there's not much to do."

He nodded, finishing his drink. "Bring the bottle over here and sit down."

"It's against regulations, *signore.*"

"It's also against regulations for members of the crew to sleep while on duty. But we know about such things, don't we?"

She glanced at him, then nodded. *"Si, signore."* She took the bottle of whiskey from the galley behind her and put it on the table between them. She sat down opposite him.

He poured some whiskey into his glass. He sipped at it slowly this time. He was beginning to feel better.

"You are going to begin production of another film, *signore?*"

He nodded.

"With Marilu Barzini?"

It hadn't been a con. She did know after all. "Yes."

"She is very beautiful," the stewardess said. "And very talented."

"You speak as if you know her?" he guessed.

"She and I used to make the rounds together," she replied. "But she had much more determination than I. And much more beauty."

He studied her. There had been a faint hint of wistfulness in her voice. "Why did you stop? You are quite lovely yourself."

"Thank you, *signore,*" she said. "But I could not do what she did. I could not live on promises. This job gave me security."

"I will be at the Excelsior for a few days. Come and see me. Perhaps it is not too late."

"You are very kind, *Signor* Benjamin. Perhaps I will come and visit you. But for the career it is too late. I am quite content now."

"Are you?" He made a gesture with his hands and a hundred-dollar bill appeared between his fingers.

She looked at it, then at him. "What is that for?"

"Contentment," he said, pushing it in front of her. He took her hand and guided it to his lap under the table. "I told you I thought you were lovely."

She made a motion as if to withdraw her hand, but he held it firmly while he opened the zipper and let himself free. She stared into his eyes behind the polished shining glasses, then her fingers tightened around the heat of his erection.

"Better get a towel first," he said quietly. "I'm a quick comer."

Ten minutes later he was back in his seat and sound asleep. He didn't open his eyes until the big plane touched down at the Rome airport.

TWO

SAM CLOSED THE SCRIPT AND put it down. "I need a drink." Charley Luongo, his Italian representative, had the drink ready almost before the words were out of his mouth. "What d'yuh think, boss?" he asked, the Brooklyn accent still in his voice although he had not been in America since he was sixteen.

"It's strong stuff," Sam said. "I don't know."

"It's not her usual style, that's for sure," Roger said.

"Yeah." Sam pulled at his drink.

Marilu Barzini made her name running around naked in Italian epics like *Icarus* and *Vesuvius.* Then she went into several American films as a sex symbol. Now she wanted something more. To be an actress. And she was willing to make sacrifices. She was cutting her price from one hundred and fifty thousand dollars a film to fifteen thousand for this one just to get someone to do it. And despite that, until Sam came along, she had no takers.

Now he knew why.

It was downbeat. It was grim. Perhaps it would be great. But there was no way of telling whether it would become a commercial success or just another *Open City* or *Bicycle Thief* to play the art houses and gather a few critical posies.

He looked over at Charley. "If there was some way we could brighten it up," he said. "Get some humor into it."

"No chance," Charley said. "She's got her mind set on it. 'Just like that, no changes,' she says. Pierangeli, the director, agrees with her."

"He should," Sam said. "He hasn't made a money picture in his life."

"But he's won every film award in Italy and Europe," Charley said.

"Great," Sam said unenthusiastically. "Let him try hocking that to the banks."

"What are you going to do?" Roger asked.

"I'm going with it," he said. "I haven't any choice. Win or lose, it's going to be an important picture. How they did it I don't know, but they got the best actors in Europe for it. It's up to us to promote the ass off it so we don't lose."

"You have a plan?" Roger asked.

"I have an idea," he said. "But it depends on the cooperation I get from her."

The telephone rang and Charley picked it up. "Pronto," he said. He covered the mouthpiece. "They're downstairs now."

"Tell them to come up," Sam said. He went into the bedroom and closed the door, then into the bathroom and washed his face. He dried himself and then looked in the mirror. The lines of fatigue were in the corners of his eyes. Maybe after this was over he could get a little sleep.

As usual, her sheer beauty stopped him as he came through the door. He held his breath for a moment. It was almost too much. No woman could be like that. But she was.

"Sam, darling" she said in a warm voice. She held out her hand and leaned forward for his kiss.

He kissed her cheek. "I don't believe it," he said truthfully. "You are too beautiful."

She smiled. She had learned to live with compliments and accept them as normal. "Thank you, Sam."

"Hello, Nickie," he said. Niccoli was her husband everywhere except in Italy. They shook hands. He turned to the third man. "*Signor* Pierangeli," he said. "It's an honor to meet you."

The director nodded shyly. He spoke very little English. "*Signor* Benjamin."

Marilu couldn't wait. "The script, Sam, you read it? What do you think?"

Sam looked at her. "I like it. But I don't think it will go. I have some ideas that I want to present to you and if we agree, we will go forward."

"No changes, Sam," she said imperiously.

He looked at her for a moment, then shrugged his shoulders. "If we can't even discuss my thoughts, Marilu, then there isn't the faintest chance of our ever making a deal." He walked to the bedroom door and opened it. "And that means you'll never make the picture because I'm the only one who believes you're enough of an actress to do it. And enough of an actress to become the first foreign actress to win an Academy Award."

He shut the door behind him. He could feel the sweat standing out on his forehead. He went into the bathroom and washed his face. He wished he had a drink.

There was a soft knock at the bedroom door. "Yes?" he called out.

It was Nickie's voice. "May I come in, Sam?"

Quickly he took off his jacket and threw it into a chair. He pulled open his collar and tie and leaned back on the bed. "Come in."

Nickie came into the room. He was a slim, good-looking man and, oddly enough, a good producer. He did not have to depend on Marilu for his projects. It was the other way around. He had first seen the potential in her and brought her along from just another buxom Italian girl to the star she had become.

"You have to understand Marilu," he said in a soft voice. "She's very emotional."

"I appreciate that," Sam said. "But you must remember that I'm tired and exhausted. That I just flew four thousand miles and stayed awake all night to meet with her and if we can't discuss anything, it's useless."

Years of dealing with temperament gave Nickie the patience of Job. "I think she would like to talk with you now. She already regrets her sharp remark."

"I think it would be better if we met after I had a little sleep," Sam said. "Then I might be more patient myself."

"If I might make a suggestion, Sam," Nickie said smoothly. "Meet her without Pierangeli. She'll be less defensive and more willing to listen to reason without him around."

"You arrange it, Nickie. I'll be ready anytime this evening from cocktails on."

"Cocktails and dinner," Nickie said. "She will be here."

"And you?"

Nickie met his gaze. "You meet her alone. Believe me, it is better. This is your picture, not mine."

"But I thought you were to be the producer?"

"I will," Nickie said. "But I will be your employee. And it is just as well that Marilu understands this immediately. That way she will realize there is only one final authority."

"Thank you, Nickie," Sam said. "I appreciate that."

Nickie smiled at him for the first time. "Don't worry, Sam, it will be a commercial picture. Together we will see to it.

They shook hands and Nickie left. Sam stretched out and was asleep in a moment.

—

IT HADN'T ALWAYS BEEN LIKE that. As he fell asleep, he remembered the first time he had come to Rome. Almost four years ago.

The flight had been miserable. He found himself squeezed into an economy section seat between two Italian ladies who chattered incessantly and kept passing pieces of fruit back and forth in front of him. He cursed the stinginess of Roger, who had made the reservations for him. Roger could never see the necessity of first-class air travel. After all, the flights never lasted that long.

He landed in the blazing heat of an August morning and the chauffeur and car that were to meet him at the airport never showed. He climbed hot and sweating into a taxi, which took him to the Excelsior Hotel.

A reception clerk showed him to the room. He stared at it in dismay. It was narrow and dark, facing a rear courtyard. "There is a mistake," he said. "I ordered a suite."

"No, *signore,*" the clerk said politely, showing him the reservation. "This is what has been ordered."

Sam looked at it. Roger had done it again. He was willing to bet now that he hadn't even ordered a car to meet him. He gave the confirmation back to the clerk. "I would like a suite."

Sam followed him downstairs to the reception desk. The assistant manager was definite. "There are no suites available, *signore.*"

Sam gestured with his hand. The corner of the hundred-dollar bill peeked from it. The assistant manager saw it. "Perhaps something could be found, *eccellenza,*" he said, turning to study the chart.

Sam watched him as he shuffled cards in the frame. "I want the best you have. I will be holding some very important meetings."

"The Ambassador suite is available," the assistant manager said. "But it is very expensive, *signore.*"

"I'll take it."

"Very well, *signore.*" He turned back to Sam. "For how long will you need it?"

"A week, maybe ten days."

"It will be payable in advance, signore."

Sam took out his Diner's Club card.

The manager shook his head. "I am sorry, signore. We do not accept credit cards."

Sam took out his checkbook from an inner pocket.

"No personal checks, signore. Unless credit has been arranged in advance."

"You do accept traveler's checks?" Sam asked sarcastically.

The irony was lost on the assistant manager. *"Si, signore."*

Sam put the attaché case on the counter between them. He opened it and let the man catch a glimpse of the neat rows of traveler's checks it contained. He pulled out one package and snapped the case shut. He countersigned a check quickly and passed it across to the man.

"But it's for a thousand dollars, *eccellenza,*" the assistant manager said. "The suite is only—"

"That's okay," Sam interrupted. "It's the smallest I have. You just apply it and let me know when that's used up."

"Si, eccellenza," the assistant manager said, almost breaking himself in half bowing. He personally escorted Sam up to the suite and pocketed the hundred-dollar bill with effusive bows.

Sam ordered a bar set up in the living room and when he went into the bedroom, the valet was already unpacking his bags. He looked around him with satisfaction. This was more like it. Roger would blow a cork when he found out what it cost, but it didn't matter. He would have to learn.

He began to get rid of his clothes. They were sticky and uncomfortable from the flight. He went into the shower and by the time he came out, the telephone began to ring.

And it was never to stop ringing as long as he was there. The thousand-dollar traveler's check had done its job well. And so had the assistant manager. It was better than being announced on the six o'clock news.

The first call he took was from Charley Luongo.

THREE

HE CAME OUT OF THE shower and wrapped himself in the immense robe that served double duty as a bath towel. The bar was already set up and he poured himself a heavy Scotch and took it over to the window and looked out.

His view faced the American embassy and the Via Veneto as it curved toward the old city. The sight of the American flag somehow cheered him and he raised his glass and silently toasted it.

The ringing of the telephone called him back into the room. He picked up the phone. "Yes?"

"Mr. Benjamin? This is Charley Luongo." The accent was unmistakably Brooklyn.

"Charley Luongo? Do I know you?"

"No, Mr. Benjamin. But I know of you. You are an American producer who is coming to Italy to look at some films."

"You are well informed," Sam said. "What can I do for you?"

"You can give me a job," Charley said.

"Doing what?" Sam asked.

"Anything. You name it." Charley's voice was serious. "I translate, chauffeur, guide, negotiate, secretary, pimp, I have experience. Two years assistant production manager on *Ben Hur*, one year sales department and advertising, Columbia Pictures, two years independent production, *Cinematrografica Italiana*. Good references. Besides, I'm honest.

I'm not like these local guineas who will steal you blind if you don't keep your hands in your pockets all the time."

"You're not Italian?"

"I'm Italian, but I was brought up in the States. I came here before the war with my parents. I was just sixteen. I was drafted into the American Army when they invaded."

"Okay," Sam said. "I'd like to see you."

Almost before Sam put down the telephone, the doorbell rang and he was there. He was tall and slim, with brown eyes and fair hair, slightly balding.

They shook hands and studied each other. "How did you find out about me?"

"The assistant manager is the brother-in-law of the girl I'm living with. He called me as soon as you were checked in."

"If you're as good as you say you are, how come you're not working?"

"The Italians get first crack at the jobs," Charley said.

"But you said you were Italian," Sam said.

"I am," Charley answered. "But I hold an American passport. My father was a naturalized citizen."

"I don't know," Sam said doubtfully.

"Why don't you try me for a week?" Charley said. "Then, if you're not satisfied, we'll call it quits. I don't get so much. I'll work for forty thousand lire a week."

Sam thought. That wasn't very much. About eighty dollars. "Okay."

"Thank you, Mr. Benjamin," Charley smiled.

The telephone rang. Without hesitation, Charley picked it up. A rapid exchange in Italian followed. He covered the mouthpiece with his hand and turned to Sam. "A producer wants to show you a picture."

"What picture?"

"It's called *Crazy Baby.*"

"Is it worth looking at?"

"No," Charley said. "He's been trying to unload it for two years now. Every major company passed it up."

"Tell him I'm not interested," Sam said.

Charley spoke a few more words into the telephone and put it down. "Maybe I could be of help if I knew what you were looking for?"

"A big exploitation picture in color. I want a lot of production values, costumes, and naked broads. Something I can buy cheap and promote the hell out of in the States. You know what I mean."

"Okay," Charley said. "Now I know. Maybe I can help you. I know a guy that's got four hundred grand in a costume picture called *Icarus*. It's the legend about the Greek boy who wanted to fly like a bird and the feathers melted in the sun. It's got everything you want. And the producer is busted. He'll take anything you will give him."

"I like it already," Sam said. "Get him on the phone and arrange a screening for me."

Charley took a small book out of his pocket, opened it and put it down next to the phone. He called the operator and gave him the number.

"Would you like a drink?" Sam asked.

"No, thank you," Charley said. He tapped his stomach. "I have an ulcer."

Sam grinned at him. "I guess you're American, all right."

That was where they began. Sam was fortunate because Charley was as good as his word. They were able to buy *Icarus* at the right price and later make an almost equally good deal for a sequel, *Wings of Icarus*. It was then that Sam gave him a bonus of a thousand dollars and raised his salary to two hundred a week. He made him managing director of the Italian company with one small office off the Via Veneto and Charley was his for life.

—

THE ROOM WAS DARK AND he felt the hand pressing on his shoulder. He rolled over and sat up.

"It's almost eight o'clock," Charley said. "Marilu will be here any minute."

"Jesus, I better shower," Sam said. He got out of bed. "Make a reservation for me at Capriccio's for dinner."

"I ordered dinner served up here," Charley said.

Sam looked at him. "Do you think that's wise? She's not just another cunt."

"She's an Italian actress," Charley said flatly.

"But what about Nickie?"

"It was his idea, wasn't it?"

Sam didn't answer, he started for the bathroom. "If she comes, you keep her busy until I'm dressed."

"Okay," Charley said. "I'm taking Roger out to dinner. We'll be at Gigi Fazzi around the corner if you should want us."

As it was, Marilu was an hour late and Sam was half bombed by the time she arrived. He had been as nervous as an adolescent. He drank Scotch after Scotch and now the whole world had a rosy glow.

When the knock came at the door, he rose to his feet, weaving slightly. Charley opened the door and she came in.

The breath caught in Sam's throat and in a moment he was terribly sober. She had that effect on him. It was unbelievable. Again the sheer beauty and femaleness of her brought a physical pain to his gut.

She came right to him. He kissed her cheek, his nostrils filling with the warm scent of her. "I'm so glad you're not angry with me, Sam."

He smiled. "Who can be angry with so beautiful a woman?"

She returned his smile. "You're becoming very Italian, Sam."

She walked over to the tables. "Champagne and caviar!" she exclaimed. Like a child, she took a small spoon, scooped the caviar to her mouth. "Delicious!"

She didn't seem to notice that Charley and Roger had disappeared. Still at the table, she poured two glasses of champagne and turned, holding one toward him. "A toast, Sam."

He took the glass although he hated champagne, or for that matter, wine of any kind. "What shall we drink to?"

"To our film together," she said.

They drank. She lowered the glass and looked at him. "I am very happy."

"I am too," he answered.

The telephone rang and he answered it. He had placed the call to Stephen Gaunt in New York early that afternoon and it had finally come through. "I'll take it in the bedroom," he said. "If you will excuse me?"

She nodded and he went into the other room and picked up the telephone. "Steve?"

The secretary's voice said, *"Just a moment, Mr. Benjamin, I'll put him on for you."* There was a click and it was Steve. *"How's the pasta over there, Sam?"*

"Haven't had time to try it yet," he said. "I called to find out what you thought of the script."

"The Sisters?"

"Yeah."

"It's strong meat. But I like it. The only thing I wonder about is Marilu Barzini. I know she's great running around naked, but can she act?"

Sam glanced up. He noticed the door moving slightly. "Hold on a minute," he said, putting the phone on the bed.

He walked back to the door and opened it suddenly. Marilu almost fell into the room. She looked at him, a startled expression on her face.

He smiled, and taking her hand, led her back into the room with him. He sat down on the bed and picked up the telephone. "I'm sorry, Steve," he said. "You were saying?"

"Is there someone there?" Steve asked.

"Yes," he said.

"Can you talk?"

"Yes," he answered. "What about Marilu?"

He held the phone out so that she could hear what Steven had to say. *"Like I said, if she can act, it's got a chance, but it needs lightening up. And some real ballsy sex, not so much of that goddamn imagery."*

"If I can deliver what you want, will you come in with me?"

"I can't now, Sam. You know my board of directors. Once you have the picture, though, it's another story."

"Will you give me a commitment for four hundred thousand subject to delivery?"

"Two fifty is the best I can do. Providing the script meets with our approval. Of course it's all subject to the final viewing of the film."

"What if I told you I think she'll come up with an Academy Award for her performance in this picture?"

"If she delivers, I can believe it. You going to go through with it?"

"Yes," Sam said. "After all, isn't it what you told me to do? Get out of the *shlock* business into something respectable?"

Steve laughed. *"Okay, Jewish Father. One way or the other, count me in."*

"For three hundred," Sam said.

"Three hundred," Steve laughed. *"Good luck. And give that broad I hear breathing into the phone one for me, will you?"*

The phone went dead in his hand and he put it down. He looked up at Marilu. "Well?"

"Who was that?" she asked.

"The president of one of the big American companies."

"Why is it that no one will believe that I can act?" she said angrily. "All they think I am is a body."

"There's nothing wrong in that."

"But sooner or later they must come to something else. Look at Lollobrigida, Loren—they are appreciated as fine actresses also."

"And you will be, too," he said soothingly. "*After* we make this film."

Her anger was suddenly gone. "Do you really think so, Sam?"

He nodded.

"And that I will win the Academy Award?"

It was then he knew he had her. "If you do what I say."

Dramatically she sank to her knees before him. "I will do anything you say, Sam. You are my mentor, my guide." She buried her face in his lap.

His reaction to her was so swift as to take even him by surprise. She turned her face up to him, a secret smile in her eyes. He found himself blushing. "I am also a man," he said.

"Of course," she said calmly, her fingers finding his zipper and opening it. "First you are always men."

FOUR

HE ALWAYS HAD BIG DREAMS. And the first was about his height. In his dreams he was always six feet two inches, lean, hard, and broad-shouldered, the kind of man the girls looked after and sighed. It didn't take him long to realize that no matter how many stretching exercises he did he would never be more than the five feet six inches heredity had bestowed on him. It was then that he made up his mind, if he couldn't be six feet two, he could *act* six feet two.

Fortunately for him, heredity had also bestowed on him a square, powerful frame and the strength of a young bull. If it were not for that he would have been killed before he was sixteen. The neighborhood in the East Bronx made no allowances for his size when measured against the loudness of his mouth. By the time he graduated from high school, he figured out that he couldn't beat everyone in the world and began to control his quick tongue. From that time on, he began to do well.

He graduated from the City College of New York, then Fordham Law. He passed the bar examination of the State of New York and after two years clerking in a cousin's law office quit the law profession forever. There was not enough in it for him. He was not interested in the small matters that would come his way and the big ones would always go to the already established attorneys.

It was 1933 and the depression blanketed the country. He considered himself lucky to find a job as an assistant manager of a local movie theater on Broadway near One hundred and thirty-seventh Street. The only reason he got the job was because he had promised the owner of the small chain of theaters, three in all, that he would throw in for free and, on his own time, such legal services as the boss would require. All for the magnificent salary of $22.50 per week.

In 1934 came the projectionists' strike, then the whole industry erupted. The theater manager left rather than cross the picket line and Sam found himself promoted. Now he was a big man. Thirty dollars a week. And oddly enough, he loved the business.

He loved motion pictures. Every one of them. Good or bad. He saw them all when they finally played in his theater. Some of them two or three times. And once again he began to find himself dreaming.

It had been like that the morning he came out of the subway on the corner across the street from the theater. It was warm, and the shimmering heat already lay on the city streets.

He stood on the corner and looked across at the theater. The biggest sign of all was a banner strung underneath the marquee: *20° COOLER INSIDE!*

Above that in neat, white, block letters, the feature was advertised.

JAMES CAGNEY · LORETTA YOUNG

TAXI

Early Bird Matinee 25¢

Selected Short Subjects

He crossed the street and stopped at the box office. "Good morning, Marge."

"Good morning, Sam," the cashier replied.

"How are we doing?" he asked.

She looked down at her sheet. "Not bad. Seventy admissions." She looked at him. "The pickets didn't show this morning."

He looked up and down the street. "Maybe it's too hot for them."

"It seems strange without them," she said. "They always brought me coffee from the store on the corner."

He looked down the street again. She was right. The pickets had become a fact of life, and the theater entrance seemed naked without their red and white painted signs. "I'll check on them when I call downtown with the morning figures," he said.

"Don't take too long. I've been in this booth since nine thirty and I need some relief."

"I'll be back in a minute," he promised.

Old Eddie, the ticket taker at the door, smiled at him. "Good morning, Mr. Benjamin. Seventy tickets this morning." His voice was as pleased as if he owned the theater.

"Morning, Eddie." He went on in. The soothing dark flowed over him and he heard the voices coming from the screen.

The feature was on. He took one look and stopped, entranced. This was his favorite scene.

The little Jewish man with the long, flowing beard and wide, black, flopping hat walked up to the taxicab parked at the curb and in Yiddish asked directions to the synagogue.

James Cagney turned his map-of-Ireland face to the man and, in equally perfect Yiddish, gave him directions. An appreciative murmur of laughter came from the audience. Sam laughed with them.

Sam went up the steps toward the balcony. The manager's office was on a small landing about halfway up. He opened the door and went inside.

The pimply faced young man, the boss's second cousin, now the assistant manager, looked up at him. "Good morning, Sam."

"Good morning, Eli. Anything in the mail?"

"The usual," Eli said in a bored voice. "Just the press books for next week's pictures. A couple of bills. The ice company won't deliver tomorrow unless we pay up. I told them you would call them."

"How many did they bring in this morning?"

"Four cakes."

"We'll need more before the day is out if this heat keeps up," Sam said. "You go down and relieve Marge. I'd better call them now."

He picked up the telephone and got the manager of the ice company. They agreed to send over two more cakes of ice at four o'clock in the afternoon after he promised to pay them something on account.

He put down the telephone and looked at the press book for next week's feature. It was an MGM picture and the book was elaborate. They always did the best job. They had the best of everything. Stars, stories, directors. He began to turn the pages wondering how many accessories and lobby cards the front office would send him. There were always stingy with supplies even if they only rented them from National Screen instead of buying them as the downtown theaters did. He heard the door open behind him and turned around.

It was Marge. She looked at him reproachfully. "You didn't even call last night."

"It was late," he said. "I didn't get out of here until after one o'clock in the morning. I thought you'd be asleep."

"I told you I would wait up."

He began to feel annoyed. That was the trouble with being nice to them. Bang them twice and they began to feel that they owned you. "I was tired."

She closed the door carefully behind her. "Are you still tired?"

He smiled suddenly. "Not that tired."

She turned the key in the lock and came toward him. She was a big girl, almost a head taller than he. He liked big girls and she was big everywhere. Big tits. Big ass.

He got to his feet and she came into his arms. She leaned back against the desk so that she would not tower over him as they kissed. His fingers fumbled at the buttons of her blouse.

She laughed lightly, sure of herself now. Quickly she undid her blouse and the big breasts heavy in their brassiere, pushed forward. He fumbled with the catch and uncovered them. With an almost animal cry he buried his face against them.

She held his head tightly against her with one hand and with the other she pulled open the buttons of his trousers. He sprang swollen into her hand, moistening her with his lubricious fluid.

"Do you have something to put on?" she whispered.

He stared at her. "Here? I didn't expect—"

She pulled her hand back as if she had touched a hot poker. "We better stop then," she said. "I can't take any chances. It's too close to my period and that's the most dangerous time."

"Oh Christ!" He was angry. "Really? You're not going to stop now. I'll pull out before I come."

"You promise?"

"I promise."

"I don't want to have a baby," she said, dropping her skirt and stepping out of it. She stood there a moment, looking around. "Where are we going to do it?"

She was right. There wasn't even enough room in the small office to stretch out on the floor. "Turn around," he said, roughly placing her hands on the desk, so that she was half bent over.

He let his trousers fall around his ankles and entered her from behind, his arms reaching around her, cupping and holding her breasts.

"Oh God! You're going right through me!" she cried.

He held her tightly, thrusting himself against her. He went soaring off into a world all his own. Filled with tremendous breasts and buttocks and lubricious cunts. He closed his eyes.

At first the roar seemed to be in the distance, almost a part of their coupling, then the explosion hit and the force threw them back against the wall of the office and to the floor.

The desk upended and the chair splintered in the corner. He lay there for a moment, gasping for breath, her weight full on him. Then he moved.

"Are you all right?" he asked.

"I think so," she said hesitantly. "What happened?"

He knew the answer instinctively, almost before he heard the cries from the theater. He pushed her away and got to his feet, pulling up his trousers. Now he knew why the pickets didn't show up this morning. "Better get dressed," he said. "I think the theater's been bombed."

He was out of the office and down the staircase before she could answer. The glass at the back of the lobby was shattered. Old Eddie was standing next to a twisted door, blood streaming from a cut on his forehead.

"I saw them, Mr. Benjamin," he cried. "They threw it from a car. A black car that stopped in front of the theater."

Sam looked out. The lobby was destroyed and almost impassable with broken glass. A wave of people came from inside the theater. They pushed against him. "Eddie, open the side doors," he said. "Okay, folks," he shouted. "Nothing to worry about. You'll all get refunds."

The side doors swung open, spilling the white daylight into the theater. Fortunately there was no panic.

The customers filed out slowly. He went over to Eddie. "Where's Eli?"

"I haven't seen him," the old man replied.

Suddenly a sick feeling came over Sam. He turned and ran through the broken glass in the lobby. The young man was still in the box office. That is, what was left of him. Apparently the box office had taken the full brunt of the bomb.

In the distance he heard the sirens of the fire engines. It was just luck that it wasn't he who was in the booth. Pure blind fucking luck.

FIVE

HE SAT THERE UNCOMFORTABLY IN the back of his father's tailor shop off Southern Boulevard as the old man went about the business of closing up for the evening. Every now and then his father would glance at him and shake his head, murmuring, "What will I tell your mother?"

He was thirty-five years old then and his parents still had the ability to make him feel a child. That he was an assistant manager of the Roxy Theater downtown didn't matter. Nor did it matter that his salary was ninety dollars a week, more than anyone else in the neighborhood. All that mattered was his latest mishegoss.

His father turned the final key and they stood outside in the street. "Button up," his father said. "The wind will give you your death."

Sam looked at the bent old man, then buttoned his coat. They began walking along the street toward the apartment.

His father stopped him suddenly and looked up into his face. "I didn't say anything, did I, when you said you didn't want to be a lawyer after all the money we spent putting you through college, did I?"

Sam shook his head.

"When your mother hollered, didn't I say, let him? He's a man, he must find his own way? Even when you went to work in that crazy business, the movies, did I say no? I said good luck to him. If it makes him happy, good luck."

Sam didn't answer.

"When you didn't want to get married to that Greengrass girl, did I fight with you, even if her rich father said he would give you twenty thousand dollars to open your own law office? No. I said an American boy has a right to decide for himself who he wants to marry. As long as he don't come home with a shiksa, it's okay. This is not the old country."

Sam held his tongue.

"But this is too much," his father said. "This I can't give my okay to. This I can't say to your mother: let him. This is stupid."

They were at the apartment house now and went inside. The hallway was filled with the many odors of his youth. It was Friday night. Chicken soup. They began to climb the stairs to the apartment.

"It isn't as if you were a kid. You don't have to go. Before the draft gets to you, you'll be overage."

"That's just it, Pa," Sam said. "If I don't get in now, it'll be too late. They'll never take me."

"Oho, and that will be such a tragedy?" his father said, stopping on a landing and poking him in the chest to emphasize his words. "And what will you be missing? A chance to get your head shot off or maybe worse? Just because we named you Samuel? Leave the fighting to the goyim. They're good at it. You stay home where you belong and mind your business."

"That's just it, Pa," he said. "I am a Jew and this is my business. If we're not the first to want to stop Hitler, who else is there to do it for us?"

"But your job at the Roxy? How do you know they'll keep it for you after the war?"

"It doesn't matter, Pa," he said. "I was about ready to quit anyway."

They reached the apartment door. His father took out his key. Before opening the door, he turned to Sam. "Does this mean you'll have to give back the Roxy pass?"

Sam smiled. It all came down to that. The one thing his mother had to lord it over the neighbors was the right to get into the Roxy for nothing anytime she wanted. "I don't think so, Pa," he said. "I'll make arrangements to take care of it."

—

HE WANTED WAR, HE GOT it. He didn't have to wait until they reached the battlefields of Europe. For him it began his third day of basic training at Fort Bragg.

It was six o'clock in the morning and they had been formed up in the freezing wet rain of the early spring morning for almost an hour. Finally they were dismissed for breakfast. They broke ranks and began to hurry through the rain to the mess hall. About to go in he was pushed aside.

"Move, Jew boy," the cracker voice said in his ear. "It's enough we're goin' to fight your war for you. Let us in for breakfast."

He stopped, blocking the doorway, and turned to look at the man who had spoken. There were three GI's behind him. He recognized the look on their faces. He hadn't spent his life in the East Bronx for nothing. "Which one of you said that?" he asked in a tight voice.

They glanced at each other and the tallest pushed forward. His voice was an icy challenge. "I did, Jew boy." He never finished speaking.

Sam never gave him a chance. He jerked his knee into the soldier's balls. The GI gasped and bent forward, clutching at himself. Sam clasped his two hands together in a clenched, joined mallet and brought them viciously down on the soldier's neck just behind his ear. The man pitched forward and again Sam brought up his knee, catching him in the chest. The soldier looped backward into the mud and lay there face up, out cold.

It happened so quickly the others were still standing there watching. Sam turned to them. "Anybody else want to do my fighting for me?"

"What's holding up this damned line?" an authoritative voice shouted.

They snapped to attention as a lieutenant came toward them. He stopped and looked down at the fallen soldier.

"What the hell's goin' on here?"

They were silent, still at attention.

"At ease," he snapped. "What happened?"

No one spoke up. He turned to Sam. "You. What happened?"

Sam met his gaze. "He slipped on the step, sir. I think he hit his head against it."

By now the GI on the ground was beginning to move. His friends went to help him. The lieutenant looked at them. "Get him down to the dispensary," he said. He turned back to Sam. "What's your name, soldier?"

"Benjamin, sir. Samuel Benjamin."

"You report to me in thirty minutes," he said, swiveling on his heel and leaving before they had a chance to salute again.

A half hour later Sam was standing in front of his desk. "At ease, soldier," the lieutenant said.

Sam relaxed.

"Where did you learn to fight like that?"

Sam looked down at him. "Sir, I was brought up in a tough neighborhood."

The officer looked at the papers on his desk. "What are you doing out there with those rednecks? Why didn't you put in for OCS? According to your Form 20 you've got all the qualifications."

"Sir, I thought this was the quickest way to fight Germans."

The lieutenant nodded. He looked down at the papers again, then back up at Sam. "You're a fucking idiot," he said. He made a few notes on the sheet of paper in front of him, then stamped it and pushed it over to Sam. "Sign that."

Sam looked at him. "What is it?"

"I'm approving your request for Officer's Training," the lieutenant said. "You don't think I'd send you back out there after what just happened? Those rednecks'll kill you long before you ever get to fight Germans."

In less than two hours Sam was on a bus leaving camp. He felt a sense of relief. Three days in the Army had convinced him. Being a private was not the thing to be.

A little more than three months later he came home on a pass. The second lieutenant's gold bars gleamed on his tailored uniform.

His mother took one look at him and burst into tears. "What have they done to you?" she cried. "You're so thin."

He was hard and chunky and solid muscle. He weighed one hundred and seventy pounds, the least he had weighed since he was twenty years old. And the least he would ever weigh in his lifetime.

He spent three years overseas and never saw a German, never carried a gun, never fired a shot. Somewhere along the line they had found out he knew how to run a projector. And he spent the entire war showing films to battle-weary troops in rest and recreation areas.

SIX

"SO YOU'RE A HERO," HIS father said, pulling down the lever on the big pressing machine and letting a cloud of steam escape over the trousers blocked on it. "So what good is it? You ain't got a job."

Sam sat there uncomfortably, looking at his father. The old man's face was red with heat. "I'm not a hero," he said.

"With all those ribbons on your jacket, you're a hero." There was finality in his voice that ended the argument.

Sam gave it up. He had explained too many times they were only service ribbons that denoted various theaters of the war. North Africa, England, Sicily, Italy, France. Their colors shone brightly on his chest.

"First we got to get you looking good again," his father said. "You look terrible."

"I'll be all right once I catch up on my sleep," Sam said.

"You'll never catch up." The old man took the pants from the press and put them on a hanger. "Not until you stop running around every night with those shiksas. You think I don't know why you don't want to come home to live when we have your room all nice and fixed up for you? No, you'd rather live in that little room of your own downtown where the only thing you got to look out on is traffic and noise."

"It's not a little room, Pa, it's an apartment."

"You call it an apartment. I call it a closet." He took a jacket from the hanger and put it on the press and gave it a burst of steam as he looked up at the clock. "That damn schwartzer," he swore. "Eleven o'clock already and still he's not here. And then they wonder why they can't keep a job. Treat them good and they shit all over you."

He left the press open and walked to the front door and looked out. He came back to Sam. "He's not even on the street yet." He slammed down the press angrily. "So what are you going to do?" he asked. "You won't get a job, your old job at the Roxy you don't want, you won't come home to live, you're breaking your mother's heart. You're almost forty years old, you're not a baby anymore, what do you want?"

"I'm tired of working for someone else," Sam replied. "I'm looking to buy my own theater."

"Oho, a *fluchenshiesser!*" His father stopped the press and looked at him. "A big shot I got for a son. Tell me, big shot, what are you going to use for money?"

"I've got some money saved up," Sam said.

"You got some money?" the old asked in a doubtful voice. "How much?"

"About ten thousand dollars," Sam said grudgingly.

"Ten thousand dollars?" The press hung open, spouting steam as the old man forgot to close the value. Sam could see his father was impressed. "Where did you get that much money? You didn't do anything they'll put you in jail for?"

"No," Sam smiled. "I just saved my pay, that's all."

"Maybe so stupid you're not after all," his father said. He cut off the steam value. "Is that enough to buy a movie house?"

"The kind of theater I have my eye on, it's enough," Sam said. "If I need a little more I can always borrow it."

The old man was silent for a moment as he pressed down on the jacket, then he turned to Sam. "Promise me one thing."

"What?"

"If you should have to borrow money, you won't go to strangers. Your mother and father ain't exactly so poor that they can't help out their only son if he should need it."

—

HE CAME OUT OF THE theater on Forty-second Street and stood under the marquee looking east across Eighth Avenue toward Broadway. The bright lights of the many marquees sparkled like so many flashing colored gems. He turned and looked back into the theater he had just left. Somehow it seemed small and dingy compared with the others up the block.

The agent came out rubbing his hands against his coat to get the dust from them after locking the door. "All it needs is a coat of paint, Mr. Benjamin, and you're ready for business."

"I don't know," Sam said doubtfully.

"Everything else is perfect, you can believe me," the agent said. "The projectors and the sound system is like new. The old owner just had them reconditioned before he dropped dead, poor man."

"What's the clearance?" Sam asked.

"Fifth run," the agent said quickly. "Same as the theaters up the street."

Sam looked up the block again. Clearance was the system they used in order to determine which houses could play the pictures first. But a lot of good it would do him way down here near Eighth Avenue. The traffic began at Broadway. By the time they reached this theater, the cream would have been skimmed. "No," he said.

"You're making a mistake, Mr. Benjamin," the agent said earnestly. "It's a hell of a buy. If it weren't for the unfortunate—"

"It's not what I'm looking for," Sam said with finality.

"For the kind of money you want to spend, I suppose you're looking for something like the Bijou," the agent said sarcastically.

The Bijou was the only grind house on Broadway. Just off the corner of Forty-second Street, it always had done a great business at the box office. But its operating costs were too high for its size. It had also bankrupted quite a few theater operators. Right now, it was dark again.

"That's more like it," Sam said. "What can you do for me on that?"

"Nothing for the kind of money you're talking about," the agent said.

"How much would it take?" Sam asked.

"Serious?"

"Serious."

"The rent alone is five thousand a month. That's ten thousand deposit for the first and last month, add five thousand for the second month, seven thousand for union bonds and deposits, three thousand for the electricity come to twenty-five thousand already. The furnishings and equipment is mortgaged at forty thousand and there's about fifteen thousand left in the chattel. I figure it will take about fifty thousand to move in."

Sam studied the agent and at the same time mentally checked his balances. With everything, he could put together about fifteen thousand dollars.

"Don't forget, the weekly payroll will run you about fourteen hundred, and because you're on Broadway all the distributors want top dollar and percentages," the agent added.

Sam nodded. "Let's go over and look at it."

"Do you think you can swing it?" the agent asked.

Sam looked at him. "You never know until you try."

The figure was closer to thirty-five thousand. That still left Sam short twenty thousand dollars.

He sat in the chair behind the counter in his father's store and together they watched the big Negro presser work the machine.

"You told me not to go to strangers," he said. "So I came to you first."

"How much do you need?" his father asked.

"Twenty thousand dollars," he said.

"You think it's a good investment?"

"I'm putting every penny I have into it," he said. "That's fifteen thousand dollars."

His father was silent for a moment. Then he went behind the counter and opened a drawer. He took a checkbook from it and opened it up. He turned and looked back at Sam. "How do you want I should make out the check?"

—

HE ALMOST LOST IT ALL before he opened. The guarantees asked by the major distributors for their films guaranteed only one thing. If he grossed maximum box office he would be bankrupt in twenty weeks, anything less speeded up the process.

He sat despondent in the little office just behind the lobby studying the sheets of figures in front of him. He would have to make up his mind. It was only ten days to the first of the month and if he was not open by then he blew it all.

There was a knock at the open door and he looked up.

A tall, good-looking blond man stood there. "Mr. Benjamin?"

He nodded. "Yes."

The man entered the office, taking his card from his pocket and placing it on the desk. "Here is my card." There was a faint accent.

Sam looked down at it.

Erling Solveg, Svenska Filmindustri.

"Yes, Mr. Solveg, what can I do for you?"

"I represent the Swedish film industry," he said. "We are looking for a Broadway showcase for our pictures. We have several films that are worthy of your consideration."

Sam looked down at the card, then back at the man. By this time he was near the desperation point, almost ready to try anything. "Are they dubbed?" he asked.

"No," the man answered. "Some are subtitled."

"Won't do," Sam said shortly. "No one will sit for it in this house."

"But Burstyn and Mayer are doing all right across the street in the Rialto with Italian pictures," Mr. Solveg said.

"*Open City* got great reviews," Sam said.

"We believe our films are just as important."

"I'm sorry," Sam said. "But if they're not dubbed we haven't a chance."

Solveg thought. "There is one. It has two American soldiers in it. They speak English all the way through the picture. The rest of the cast speaks Swedish and German though."

"The Americans have big parts?"

"They're the leads. You see, they play two soldiers escaping from the Nazis. They find sanctuary in a nudist camp. It's really very funny. And the color is quite good, too."

"Nudist camp?" Sam was interested.

"Yes," Solveg said quickly. "But in very good taste. Nothing lewd in it. I would like it if you could find time to screen the picture."

"Has it got a state censor board seal?"

"We screened it for them," the man replied. "They approved it with a few small cuts that we have already made. It doesn't affect the picture at all. We're prepared to make you quite a good deal on it, if you like it."

"What kind of a deal?"

"We'll contribute five thousand dollars a week to the advertising for ten weeks on a guaranteed run. Film rental will be twenty percent of the gross after house breakeven, nothing below that.

"Who's the distributor?" Sam asked.

"No one," Solveg said. "We haven't set that yet."

"You have now," Sam said, without hesitation. "You give me American distribution rights and you got a deal for your picture.

"Wouldn't you like to see the film first?" Solveg was puzzled.

"Not unless we have a deal," Sam said. "There just isn't that much time to waste if we're going to open in ten days.

Opening night, Sam sat with his mother and father in the back of the theater. By the time the two soldiers got to the nudist camp the audience was roaring with laughter. His mother hid her eyes behind her hands and peeked out at the screen between parted fingers. "But they're all *nacketaheit,* Sam," she said.

"Look, Mama, don't talk so much," his father said testily. "Maybe you'll learn something."

"What's to learn?" his mother asked. "They're *alle goyim.*"

Sam slipped out of his seat and walked back to the lobby. The crowds were already lined up into the street and they were jammed around the box office.

Sam looked at the sign over the window.

ADMISSION FOR THIS PERFORMANCE: $1.25.

He went back into his little office and picked up the telephone that connected him with the cashier. "For the nine o'clock show put the price up to one seventy-five," he said into it. Then he put his face in his hands and began to cry.

He had his first hit.

SEVEN

THE CALL CAME FROM THE ticket taker in the front lobby. *"There's a Mrs. Marxman here to see you, Mr. Benjamin."*

"Mrs. *Who?*"

"Mrs. Marxman," the ticker taker repeated. *"She says she has a ten o'clock appointment."*

"Oh, yes." Suddenly he remembered. "Send her up." He put down the telephone and began straightening the papers on his desk. This was the girl his father wanted him to see when he had mentioned at dinner last Friday night he had been searching for a good secretary.

His father had wiped his face with a napkin and looked at him. "What kind of secretary do you want?"

"You know," Sam said. "A girl who could do things without you having to tell her twice. One with a little *tsechel* for a change."

"I got just the girl for you," his father said.

"You have?" Sam as suspicious.

"Yes," his father said. "You remember Cohen, the chicken flicker?"

"No." Sam shook his head.

"During the war he became the biggest chicken black marketer in the Bronx."

"She's a very nice girl," his mother said, coming back to the table. "A fine person. Educated, too."

"Wait a minute," Sam said. "All I'm looking for is a secretary. I'm not looking to get married."

"Neither is she," his father said quickly. "She has a little child, a girl."

"Then she is married?"

"Not exactly," his father answered. "She's a widow. Her husband was killed in the war. I heard she's thinking of going back to work."

"How did you hear?"

"From her brother, Roger. He comes every month to collect the rent for the store. Cohen owned the building and when he dropped dead, they found so much property he owned that his son, Roger, went into the real estate business. He's doing very well."

"Then why doesn't he give her a job?" Sam asked.

"You know how it is. Family. Besides she doesn't really need the money. Cohen left both his children well fixed."

"Then why does she want to go to work?"

"She's getting bored hanging around the house," his father said. "You're looking for a secretary? So, see her. Maybe you'll like her, maybe you won't. Besides I promised her mother I would arrange an appointment."

"She's a lively girl," his mother said. "Tall, too. Here, have some more soup."

Sam watched her refill his plate. It was a trap and he knew it. But there was no way within reason he could escape it. He would have to see the girl. But that was all. If they thought he was going to hire her they were crazy. He didn't manage to get this far by being stupid.

"Okay, I'll see her. Have her come to the theater ten o'clock Monday morning."

His parents were right about one thing, he thought. She was attractive, about an inch taller than he, dark brown hair and blue eyes. "Please sit down," he said, indicating the chair in front of his desk.

"Thank you," she said. But she remained standing.

Suddenly he realized the chair was piled with papers that he had been planning to go through. "Excuse me," he said. He went around the desk and took the papers from the chair. He stood there looking around the office for a place to put them.

She smiled. "At least my brother wasn't lying. He said you really did need a secretary."

"I really do," he said. He still held the papers. "What made you think your brother was lying?"

"You know Jewish families," she said. "They think I should run right out and get married again."

He stared at her. "I know what you mean." He finally gave up searching for a place to put the papers and dumped them on a corner of his desk. He went back and sat down behind it. "I get the same thing from my parents."

"To tell the truth," she said, "I thought it was just another trick on Roger's part. I didn't want to come down and see you."

He laughed. "I thought my folks were pulling the same gag on me. I already figured out how to tell you you weren't right for the job.

She laughed with him. He liked her laugh. It was warm without being self-conscious. She sat down in the chair. Now her voice was businesslike. "Just what duties would be involved in the job, Mr. Benjamin?"

He looked around helplessly. "You know. The usual. Typing, filing, keeping track of things generally. I need a girl with brains, more than just a secretary. Sort of run things while I'm out of the office."

"It sounds very interesting," she said.

"It is. I got big plans. I'm not going to stop here. It's more than just one theater. I'm going into the distribution business. I'm going to sell films all over the world."

"I see," she said.

They fell silent and he looked at her. He liked the suit she was wearing. She was smart without being loud. Absently he reached for the cigar in the ashtray on his desk. He put it in his mouth and chewed on it. Then he put it back in the tray, took out a fresh cigar and lit it. "Do you mind if I smoke?"

"No," she said.

"Would you like a cigarette?" he asked.

"Thank you," she said.

He began to search the top of his desk for a package he knew to be there somewhere.

"That's all right," she said. "I have some." She took a pack from her purse and put the cigarette between her lips. He struck a match and leaned across the desk to light it.

The cigarette lit, he leaned back in his chair. They were silent for a moment, then both started to speak at the same time.

"I'm sorry," she said.

"That's all right," he said. "What were you going to say?"

She hesitated. "It sounds like the kind of work I could be interested in. Is there anything you want to know about me that might help you make up your mind?"

"I suppose so." He looked down at the desk. "You worked in an office before?"

"Yes," she said. "After I graduated Hunter College, I worked for a real estate company until I got married. My shorthand and typing are a little rusty, but I'm sure they'll come back quickly with a little practice."

"How long were you married?"

"Two years," she said. She hesitated. "That is, two years until my husband was killed. We were actually married less than a month when he went overseas."

"I'm sorry," he said.

There was a long pause. "You know I have a daughter?"

He nodded.

"She's three years old now. She's no problem if I go to work. I have a good nurse for her."

"The job doesn't pay that much," he said. "I'm only just starting the business."

"The salary isn't important. Is there anything else you would like to know?"

"Yes," he said, looking at her.

"What's that?"

"Your name."

She looked into his eyes. "Denise," she said.

—

WITHIN TWO WEEKS AFTER SHE came to work for him, Sam knew it would be all right. She had everything under control, the books, the mail, the accounts.

The Naked Fugitives, as Sam titled the picture for the United States, continued to do capacity business. It looked like a solid run for a year if he wanted to keep it there. And he was in no hurry to pull it. There was nothing else that seemed likely to take its place.

He began to turn his attention to distribution. Several majors approached him to handle the picture, but their terms were always too high to allow him to make more than the small guarantee they offered. They kept telling him that the Broadway run was a fluke, that it was a New York picture and that outside New York it would fall flat. He began to hold meetings with various states rights distributors.

These were small companies, one- or two-man operations in most cases, but they were able to market films that would otherwise be sloughed by the majors. But again, in most cases, there wasn't much money to be made. He studied various formulas and in the end came back to the one that had been successful for him.

What he needed was distributors or partners to finance the advertising and publicity campaigns. To attract attention to the picture that would not ordinarily accrue because of the lack of well-known stars and box-office names. He spent two weeks traveling around the country visiting key cities. These were the cities that offered the greatest grossing potential, generally contributing almost eighty percent of a film's take. When he returned to New York, he had a plan all worked out. What he did not have was the financing to implement it.

Once again, he began to feel tight and frustrated. This was the same thing he had felt before, the feeling that drove him from job to job. The feeling that he kept running into stonewalls.

He approached the banks, but they were not willing to lend him the money. According to them, there was not sufficient security in the distribution rights to a film, no matter how good it looked. They had been burned before on similar propositions.

The factors and high-interest people were willing to take a limited flyer. Enough to get him by but not enough to really accomplish what he wanted. For a brief moment, he was tempted to take their offers, but the combined effect of the high interest he had to pay, and the fifty percent of his profit they wanted after that stopped him.

In reality, his plan was a simple one. He had ten theaters lined up around the country. Each theater was willing to make a four-wall deal with him. In effect, they were leasing the theater to him to show the picture. He would guarantee them a minimum profit and they would share fifty-fifty with him on the overages. The guarantees plus the advertising that he would have to pay came to three thousand dollars a week per theater. Thirty thousand a week for the five-week period, which was the minimum he could contract for, one hundred and fifty thousand in all.

He could come up with thirty thousand himself, another twenty thousand he felt sure his parents would givc him, especially after the quick repayment he had made on the original loan. Solveg promised to contribute fifty thousand dollars again on the part of the Swedish film industry. That still left him short by fifty thousand dollars.

He pushed back the papers on his desk and looked at his watch. It was almost eight o'clock. He rubbed his face thoughtfully. He had better shave and get ready. He had arranged to meet Denise at the Brass Rail for dinner. They had a nice dining room upstairs and she had gone home to change. The telephone rang and he picked it up.

It was Denise. "Sam?"

"Yes," he said.

"Are you all right?" she asked.

"I'm fine," he answered. "Just a little tired, I guess."

"Look, I have an idea," she said. "It's miserable out and raining. Why go out to dinner? Come on up here and relax. I have a couple of huge steaks I can throw on the fire."

"Sounds great to me," he said. "When do you want me up there?"

"Come now," she said. "I have everything ready."

—

HE SAT IN THE LIVING room of her West End Avenue apartment, a drink in one hand and an illustrated children's book of *Snow White* in the other.

"Is that Snoopy, Uncle Sam?" Myriam asked, pointing to an illustration.

"No, that's Grumpy," he said.

"I don't like him," the child said.

He laughed, putting down his drink and rumpled the child's head. "Nobody likes him. He's got bad manners."

"I have good manners," Myriam said. "Everybody likes me."

"I'm sure they do," Sam said.

The child crawled off his lap. "Don't go away. I'm going to get another book."

"I'll be here," Sam promised. He picked up his drink again and looked around the apartment. His parents were right about one thing. Apparently she didn't need the job. The rent on this apartment was more than he paid her each week.

The doorbell rang.

"Will you get it, Sam?" Denise called from the kitchen.

He opened the door. Her brother, Roger, stood there. He came in and they shook hands. "I can only stay a few minutes," Roger said. "Denise told me you were coming up for dinner and I thought I'd drop by and say hello."

Denise came in from the kitchen. "Why don't you stay for dinner?"

"I don't want to intrude," Roger said, looking at Sam.

"You won't be intruding," Sam said.

"Fix yourself a drink," Denise said. "Dinner will be ready in a minute. I'll set another place."

"How's it going?" Roger asked, over the drink.

"Good," Sam replied. "We're still playing to capacity."

"It's a good picture," Roger said. "I especially like that scene where the Germans can't find the American soldiers because naked everybody looks alike and they want everybody to put clothes on."

Sam smiled. "It's a good scene."

"How's your distribution plans coming along?"

"Slowly," Sam answered. "It takes time."

"What's the problem?"

"The usual. Money," Sam replied.

"How much do you need?"

Suddenly it all made sense to Sam. He wasn't here just for dinner. Denise had arranged it all.

Later when Roger had left and they were having a second cup of coffee in the living room, he turned to her. "You didn't have to do it."

"I wanted to," she said. "I believe in you."

It happened quite naturally. They leaned toward each other, then she was in his arms. They kissed. Suddenly his size didn't matter anymore. He felt tall.

"Why me?" he asked. "I'm fifteen years older than you, short and fat." He gestured toward a photograph of her late husband. "Not a bit like him."

Her eyes were steadier than her voice. "You're a man. Compared to you all the others, everyone else, is a boy."

A small sound came from the open doorway. They turned. The child was standing in the doorway, rubbing her eyes. "I had a bad dream."

Sam picked her up and brought her back to the couch between them. "It will go away," he said soothingly.

She looked up, first at her mother, then at him. "Are you going to be my daddy?"

"Why don't you ask your mother? She seems to have it all worked out."

EIGHT

"I'D LIKE YOU TO GET some new clothes," she said one evening as they sat down to dinner.

"What for?" he asked. "I got all new clothes just before we got married. They're perfectly good."

"Sure," she agreed. "For a racetrack tout. Not for a successful businessman."

"I'm in the picture business," he said. "They don't dress like everybody else."

"Okay," she said. "If that's what you want. If you like looking short and fat."

"I am short and fat," he said. And that was the end of it. He thought. Until he went to his closet the next morning.

He turned back into the room. "Where the hell are all my suits?" he yelled.

"You're shouting," she said. "It's not healthy."

"It's healthy to walk around naked?" he yelled. "What did you do with my suits?"

"I gave them to the Salvation Army," she said.

He was speechless.

"I made an appointment for you at the tailor," she said. "Ten o'clock this morning. I'm going with you."

"Okay, okay," he said. "But what do I wear in the meantime?"

"The suit you wore yesterday," she said.

They bought a half dozen suits. All the same cut, three in black, three in dark blue.

Even he had to admit afterward that he looked better. The new shoes with the built-up heel didn't hurt either.

A few days later she turned from her desk in the small office they shared and waited until he finished screaming over the telephone at the theater manager in Oklahoma City.

"You don't have to shout," she said quietly. "The way you're carrying on you can save yourself the cost of the phone call."

"What do you expect me to do?" he yelled. "When the son of a bitch is trying to screw me out of two grand?"

"You're shouting now," she said. "And I'm only three feet away from you."

"Of course I'm shouting. I'm angry."

"You can be just as angry in a quiet voice," she said. "And people will have more respect for you." She got to her feet. "You don't have to yell anymore to make people listen to you. You're successful. You're a big man. They'll listen if you whisper."

She walked out of the office and his eyes followed her to the door. He turned back to his desk. That was always the trouble with women. They were never happy until they changed you. All the same, maybe she had something. Just like with the suits. It wouldn't hurt to try it. He could always go back to shouting if it didn't work.

That night when they were in bed, he turned toward her. "You know you were right," he said.

"About what?" she asked.

"About shouting," he said. "I don't really have to. It was just a habit, I guess. Maybe it was just my way of showing I was boss." He pulled her toward him.

She held him away. "There was something else I wanted to talk to you about."

"Can't it keep until later?" he asked like a little boy. "I want to get laid."

"That's what I want to talk to you about," she said. "Later you'll be asleep."

He reached over and turned on the lamp, sitting up in bed. "What is it?" he asked, looking at her.

Her face began to turn pink. "I can't talk about it with the light on and you staring at me like that."

"You want I should go in the next room and pick up the telephone?"

"Don't make jokes," she said. "This is serious."

"I'm not joking," he said. "Tell me already."

Her face was completely red now. Her eyes fell. "That's just it. You're so impatient, you're always in a hurry."

"What the hell are you talking about?"

She looked up at him. "We're married almost six weeks," she said in a low voice. "And I've only had maybe two orgasms."

A note of concern came into his voice. "Why didn't you say something before? Maybe you ought to see a doctor, there might be something wrong."

"There's nothing wrong," she said. "It's just that—you see—you're always in such a hurry. Bing, bang, boom. You're on, you're off, you're out, you're asleep. Then I lie there awake half the night trying to figure out what happened."

"There's nothing to figure out," he said. "All you have to do is get it off sooner."

"I can't," she said in an unhappy voice. "You'll just have to give me more time."

"How can I do that? You know me. Once I get started, there's no stopping."

"Maybe it would help if you thought of other things when you find yourself getting too excited."

"If I think of other things I'd lose my hard," he said.

"I read somewhere that if you counted to yourself, it helps," she said.

"I don't know," he said doubtfully. "Did you have the same trouble with him?"

She knew who he meant. "I never had an orgasm with him at all," she said honestly. "Before I had a chance to think about it, he went overseas."

Sam was silent.

"I don't mean to upset you, honey," she said, reaching for his hand. "I love you. You know that."

"I love you," he said, looking at her. "I want it to be right for you. I'll try.

He turned off the lamp and bent over her and kissed her. She moved his face down to her breasts and held him tightly there while he nuzzled like a child. A few moments later, he was inside her.

"Is it all right?" he whispered.

"Beautiful," she answered, all warm and flowing.

He grew stronger inside her and she began to respond to her fierce thrusting. "I'm getting there," he whispered hoarsely. "Should I begin counting now?"

"Yes. Yes," she replied, unable to control her own responses.

"One… two… three… four… How long do I have to keep this up?" he gasped.

"As... long as you can," she cried.

"Five... six... Oh, Jesus... seven... eight." He was almost shouting now. "I'll never make it... Nine... Here it comes... oooh... ten. There go the rockets!"

She clung tightly to him, rising and falling with him until the tide within them was completely spent. After, they were silent and a kind of languor came over her. She felt his breath on her cheek and opened her eyes.

He was looking at her. "Was that better?"

She nodded.

"You never felt like that with him?" His voice was almost fierce.

"No, never," she answered.

He stared at her for a moment, then his face relaxed into a smile. "Is it all right if I sing the next time?" he asked. "I always was lousy at arithmetic."

—

BY THE TIME SAMUEL JUNIOR was born, late the following year, they had settled into a comfortable kind of life. Between the theater and the distribution company, Sam netted in the neighborhood of fifty thousand dollars a year and had developed a reputation in the trade for merchandising and handling a specialized kind of film. Exploitation pictures they were sometimes called. The subject matter was almost always something unusual, something that at the first glance did not seem to have promotional qualities, but Sam found the key to them and for the most part they worked. There was only one trouble with the business. None of the pictures was sufficiently broad in its basic audience appeal to break through into the general market.

That was where he had to go for the really big money. Seventeen thousand theaters against the few hundred that he sometimes could play. He kept his own counsel, not even sharing his ambitions with Denise, who in those years was fully occupied with the two children. Quietly he watched and studied the market and then one day in 1955 decided to take his big step.

He sold his lease on the theater and moved the distribution company into small offices in Rockefeller Center. Television had thrown the film industry into a panic. Grosses were off and theaters were threatened with closure all over the country.

His reasoning was simple. What had worked for him on a smaller scale would now work in the larger market. Promotion, publicity, and exploitation even more than the picture itself would attract people to the local box office. But, again, it had to be the right kind of picture. One that would appeal to all kinds of audiences, young and old, if it were to work. And it had to be the kind of picture that would lend itself to the old-fashioned circus publicity he intended to give it. He also knew where he would have to go to find it.

Italy. Italian film-makers had climbed aboard the *Ben Hur* chariot after MGM finished its famous remake. They had taken advantage of the many sets and props gathered for that film and he had heard of a number that were in production that might fit his plan. All he needed was money.

Denise invited Roger and his new wife to dinner.

NINE

SAM LOOKED UP AS ROGER came into his office. Roger put a sheet of paper in front of him. "Here are Charley's latest figures from Rome on the Barzini picture.

"What do you think?" Roger asked.

Sam shrugged. "That's the auditor's report. I knew those figures two weeks ago."

"Why didn't you say something to me?" Roger asked. He was annoyed with himself. He should have remembered that the auditors were two weeks behind.

"What was there to say? We're in this far, there's nothing else to do but keep on going."

"You still could have told me." Roger was angry. "I *am* your partner."

"I didn't want to worry you," Sam said. "I figured with Anne just about to have the baby you had enough on your mind."

"Enough on my mind?" Roger's voice rose sharply. "You think I'm a child? That I didn't know we're looking bankruptcy in the face? I said we should never have got into this damn film!"

Sam stared up at him without speaking.

"But you're supposed to be the expert?" Roger continued sarcastically. "This picture is going to win all the awards, you said. The only award it's going to win will be Chapter Eleven in bankruptcy court."

"Hold it a minute!" Sam snapped. "It's a hell of a picture. I showed Steve Gaunt the first two reels and he flipped over it."

"So he flipped over it," Roger said. "I still didn't see him come up with any money toward it."

"You know he can't do that," Sam said. "Not until it's finished."

"You're being conned, Sam. Why can't you see it?" Roger was nasty now. "That boy is as cold as ice. I know his reputation by now. He uses everybody. You think I don't know the type, the friendly goy, always with a smile on his face, while behind your back he's looking how to murder you?"

Sam's voice was mild. "Okay, Roger. You're upset so I'll make allowances. Now go back to your office and calm down. We'll talk again when you're able to make sense."

"I can make sense right now," Roger said. "Perfectly good sense. Just give me my money back, that's all. I'm not greedy. You can have it all if you think it's that good."

"You don't mean that." Sam said.

"You don't think so?" Roger stared down at him. "Try me."

Sam shuffled the papers on his desk and picked up a letter with a check attached to it. He handed it to Roger. "There's a check from Supercolor Laboratories for two hundred grand they're lending me on account of the agreement I made to give them all our film processing and printing. I was going to send it to Italy for the production account. Now it's up to you.

"If you still feel that way, keep it. But if you think everybody in this business is crazy the way you think I am and that they don't know what they're doing, someday you'll regret it. But make up your own mind. You can put it in the production account or keep it. But either way, after this, I don't want to hear no complaints from you."

Roger looked down at him. "If I keep it, what do you do?"

Sam met his gaze. "I managed this far, I'll manage the rest of the way."

They both knew that all it would take for Roger to put the check back on the desk was for Sam to ask. But it had gone too far. Sam's back was up. He would never ask. That would be too much like begging. And he had his own kind of pride.

He knew from the expression on Denise's face when he got home that evening that she already knew. He didn't say anything, went straight to the bedroom and began to change his clothes. He got into a shirt and slacks, kicked his feet into a pair of slippers, and went into the living room. The ice and the Scotch were already on the coffee table. He fixed himself a drink, turned on the television for the seven o'clock news, and sat down on the couch. He took a long sip of his drink.

The children came into the room as was their custom after they had finished their dinner. They climbed upon the edge of the couch and kissed him. "Hi, Daddy."

He smiled at them. "Hi. Have a good dinner?"

Myriam nodded, Junior didn't even bother to answer. He was watching the television set.

"What are you watching, Daddy?" Myriam asked.

"The news," he said.

"'Sea Hunt' is on," Junior said. "Channel Two."

"You can watch it after the news," Sam said.

"It'll be half-over by then," Junior said.

Sam grinned and rumpled the boy's hair. "Okay. You can go and watch on your set if you want."

"Thanks, Daddy." Junior was gone before the words were out of his mouth.

Sam looked at his daughter. "How about you? Don't you want to watch it, too?"

"I'd rather stay here with you," she said.

Sam looked at her. This was not usual. Ordinarily she and her brother took off as soon as he gave the word. She climbed down from the edge of the chair into his lap. They sat silently for a few minutes; when a commercial came on, she pulled at his arm.

"Daddy, are we rich?"

Sam grinned. "I don't think so."

"Poor?"

"We're not poor."

"Then if we're not poor, we're rich," she said, finality in her voice.

"I never thought of it like that," he said. "That's one way of putting it."

"Are we as rich as Uncle Roger?"

"What makes you ask that?"

"Aunt Anne just left before you came home. She and Mummy were talking. She said Uncle Roger had more money than we do."

"That's right. But there's nothing wrong in that."

"She also said Uncle Roger was tired of supporting us." There was a puzzled look on her face. "I thought you supported us."

"I do," he said. "That's why I go to work every day."

"Then why was Mummy crying?"

"She was?"

The child's attention was caught by the television screen. Sam turned her face back to him. "When was Mummy crying?"

"Aunt Anne said that if you didn't act nice to Uncle Roger, he would not give you any more money. And then we would be poor because you would lose everything."

"She said that?" Sam's voice was soft.

"Yes," Myriam answered. "Then she left and Mummy began to cry."

Sam sat there silently for a moment. He took another sip of his drink and watched the screen. But it didn't register. Anne wasn't that far wrong. If he couldn't get the money to finish the picture, they could very well be poor. Perhaps not poor in the sense that he remembered his parents had been when he was a child, but poor compared with what they had now.

Myriam stirred on his lap. "I think I'll go and watch 'Sea Hunt.'"

"Go ahead," he said.

"We won't be poor?" she asked. "Like those little children in India that we take up collections in school for? All starving and with no clothes to wear?"

"Don't worry. That'll never happen."

"I'm glad." She smiled suddenly. "I don't think I would like that very much."

—

"YOU DIDN'T EAT," HE SAID as they left the dinner table.

"I wasn't hungry." Denise followed him into the living room.

He turned on the TV and lifted the cover from the ice bucket. "It's all melted," he said, annoyed.

"I'll get some more." She took the bucket from the coffee table and left the room.

He flipped channels until he found something he was interested in watching, then sat back on the couch. He put some Scotch in a glass and held it in his hand until she came back with the ice. He put several cubes in the glass and stirred it with his fingers.

"That's a sloppy habit," she said.

"Adds a bit of flavor."

She turned and looked at the screen. "Another Western? Don't you ever watch anything else?"

"I like Westerns," he said defensively.

"I'm going to bed." She left the room before he had a chance to answer.

He sat there a second, watching the screen, then got to his feet and followed her to the bedroom, the glass still in his hand.

"Okay," he said, closing the door behind him. "Get it off your chest."

She turned to him from the closet where she had just hung her dress. "I don't like the way you've been acting. You don't talk to anybody anymore. You do things without thinking of anyone else. You act as if you're the only person who knows anything."

He took a sip of his drink.

"You've changed," she said. "I don't know what got into you. You never used to be like that."

"Is that what your brother told you?" he asked.

"I haven't spoken to Roger," she snapped.

"No. You spoke to Anne. He told her what to tell you."

"Anne can see things without anyone having to tell her what to say. So can I."

"What do you want me to do?"

"You can call Roger and explain things to him. He's hurt. Maybe then he'll give the check back to you."

"No," he said. "There's nothing to explain. Roger took that check because he wanted to. I didn't force him. Roger was right. It's me who was wrong. But not only then. All the time. I should never have a partner. I'm not the type. I have to be my own boss. That was why I went into business myself in the first place."

"But he was your partner. He had all that money tied up."

"I paid him back," he said. "You know that. Every penny he ever put in. That two hundred thousand was his share of the business before we went into this picture."

"Roger says Stephen Gaunt has turned your head with his promises," she said.

"Roger is full of shit!" he snapped, angry for the first time. "Stephen's promised me nothing. He's only said that he likes the picture so far, that's all." He drained the last drop of liquor in his glass. "Roger should have stayed in the real estate business. That's all he knows."

"But what about the money?" she asked. "You need it to finish the picture."

"I'll find it somewhere else."

"Where?"

"I don't know," he said, looking at her. "But I'll find it. And on my own terms. From now on, the only partner I'll ever have is you."

He put the drink down and walked over to her. She came into his arms and he drew her head down to his chest.

"I'm worried, Sam," she said.

"So am I," he confessed. "But talk to Myriam tomorrow morning. She overheard you and Anne talking and thinks we're going to be poor. There's no point in having her worry, too."

"She heard us?"

Sam nodded. "She told me you were crying. She thought she might have to go without clothes and be hungry."

Tears suddenly came to Denise's eyes. "The poor child."

She went over to the dresser and picked up a tissue. "I'm all right now," she said. She blew her nose. "I think I could use a drink."

They went back into the living room and he fixed drinks for the two of them. They sat down just as a new program came on.

"My God, another Western," she said, getting up to change channels.

"Don't change it," he said. "Steve told me about this one. It's a new kind of Western. Psychological. He thinks it'll be very big."

She watched it for a few minutes, then turned to him. "It looks like every other Western to me. They're still shooting at each other. Steve doesn't know what he's talking about."

But Sam didn't even hear her. He was caught up in the events on the small screen in front of him. She was wrong. This show was different. He knew that Steve was right. It would be a big winner.

Toward the end of the program, she turned to him. "What are you going to do?"

He looked at her. "First, I'm going to Italy to take a look at the picture for myself and find out what's really happening and exactly how much more we'll need to finish. Maybe I can find a way to cut some of the expense. We'll see."

"And then?"

"Then we'll see what happens next," he said. He turned back to the set to watch the climax of the show. The little screen had a hypnosis all its own. It took your mind off your problems into another world.

And in a way it was just as well. For in the end, it was Stephen Gaunt who found the solution for him.

TEN

THE LITTLE PLANE GAVE A sickening lurch as they dipped down over the mountains toward the small airfield at Palermo. The pilot swore in Italian as he adjusted the stabilizer, then turned to Charley and explained something rapidly.

Charley nodded and turned back to Sam who was sitting directly behind him. "The pilot wishes to apologize for the bump. He says it's been several years since he's flown one of these and he's a little out of practice. He flies Constellations usually. But he says not to worry, by the time we go back to Rome tomorrow, he will have practiced a little more."

Sam still felt the dip in his stomach and the faint taste of bile that had come up as the plane dropped. "Helluva time for him to tell us," he said. "I don't care how much he practices as long as he does it on his own time. Not with me in the plane."

The radio chattered and the pilot replied. He took the plane in a wide sweeping curve out over the sea.

"What now?" Sam asked nervously.

"Nothing," Charley replied. "We just cleared for landing."

"What's he gonna do?" Sam asked. "Land us on a fishing boat?"

Charley laughed and looked down. It was a bright sunny day and the sea was a calm, clear blue. Here and there, the sails of a few small boats skipped by beneath them. Up ahead of them was Palermo, baking in the summer heat. Neatly the plane went between two mountains and dropped onto the field.

Sam let his breath out in a sigh as the wheels touched the ground. They rolled toward the small building.

Charley looked back at him. "The car will be waiting to take us to the hotel. You'll have a chance to grab a quick shower before we drive to the location."

"Why don't we go right up?" Sam asked.

"It wouldn't do any good," Charley said. "It's lunch time, nobody'll be working."

The location was a small village in the mountains about an hour and a half ride up a winding narrow road from Palermo. They drove through the village square with its inevitable church and in a few minutes were at the scene.

Sam blinked his eyes. A moment ago he would have been willing to swear he was back in the sixteenth century—everything, the people as well as the houses, seemed so old. And here, there were trailers, bigger than the village huts, big brute lamps, generators, reflectors. There in the field in front of him, aiming at a small hut, was the big Mitchell camera, protected from the sun by a black cover.

The driver pulled his little Fiat to a stop just behind one of the trailers. He leaned forward and patted the dashboard of his car as if to congratulate it on getting them there. *"Va bene,"* he said.

Sam got out of the car and looked around. Across the road from him, in a field, some men were playing bocce, others were just lying around in the shade, some had their hats pulled down over their faces and were sleeping. Those who were awake returned his gaze with idle curiosity. More would have been an effort in the heat.

"That's Nickie's trailer in front of us," Charley said, leading the way.

Sam followed him and they went up the small steps. Inside it was dark and cool; the first room was fixed up as an office with two small desks and a typewriter. It was empty.

Charley went over and knocked on the door to the second room. "Hey, Nickie," he called. "Are you awake?"

There was a scuffling sound from the other room. A moment later, a girl came from it. *"Signor* Luongo," she nodded. She went over to the desk, sat down behind the typewriter, and began to comb her hair.

A moment later, Nickie came out. He was wearing slacks and a sport shirt, but his feet were bare and his eyes were sleepy. He smiled when he saw Sam. "Ah, Sam, it's an unexpected pleasure," he said, holding out his hand.

Sam took it. "I thought I'd take a run over and find out how we were doing."

Nickie looked at him. "It's good well. A little bit slowly perhaps, but we are getting very good film."

"The film is good," Sam said. He didn't say anything about being behind schedule. Time for that later. "I'd like to take a look around."

"My pleasure," Nickie said. He turned to the girl and shot a few rapid words at her. She nodded and turned back to her typewriter as they went out.

"This is the small house that *The Sisters* live in," Nickie said as they walked toward the camera. "We took off the roof so that we could shoot inside. It's a real house."

Sam looked around. The bocce game was still going on across the road. "Why aren't they working?" he asked.

"They're waiting for the director to call them for the next shot," Nickie said.

"What's holding him up?" Sam asked.

"I'll find out." Nickie exchanged a few words with one of the men slouching in the shade near the camera. He turned back to Sam. "They're waiting for the sun to be right. In about another half-hour."

"What the hell are all those brutes doing out here if you wind up waiting for the sun?" Sam asked.

"We use them for fillers and night shots," Nickie answered. "But Pierangeli insists on the real thing wherever possible."

"How much film did you get in the can today?"

"A few scenes," Nickie said.

"How many minutes?"

"Maybe two."

"And this scene? How long will it run?"

"Maybe a minute, maybe less."

"And for that you wait for the sun?" Sam asked angrily. "I thought you were going to protect me? The picture is already double the budget. Where is my protection?"

"We had bad breaks, Sam," Nickie said uncomfortably. "The weather, we had a lot of rain when we wanted sun, sun when we wanted rain—"

"Why the hell didn't you shoot with the weather instead of waiting for it?"

"That's the way Pierangeli works," Nickie said. "I can't change him. Nobody can."

"I'd like to see him," Sam said angrily.

"He's over in Marilu's trailer," Nickie said. "They're rehearsing."

Pierangeli had already left Marilu by the time they reached her trailer. Her maid greeted them. Marilu was resting, she exclaimed. *"E vero, il Maestro* and the *Signor* Ulrich, the German actor, have been rehearsing with her over an hour and now they have gone to give her a chance to compose herself before the shooting begins again."

"What the hell were they rehearsing that got her so tired she has to rest?"

Charlie shot him a look, but no one answered, and they started back toward the set. Charley fell behind and whispered as they were walking. "Pierangeli is a realist."

"So?"

"This is the scene after she and the German were screwing in the field back of the house and she comes in all fucked and glowing and her sister accuses her of going with her guy."

"I still don't get it," Sam asked.

Charley looked at him. "You mean—he really had them do it?"

Charley nodded. "Pierangeli believes the camera will see it on her face."

"But what about Nickie? Surely, he—"

"It's for the film, for art. There's nothing personal in it."

"I'll have to tell that to Denise sometime," Sam said. "But she'll never believe it."

Men were already at work by the time they reached the set. The cameraman and his helpers had the cover off the camera and were busy with the lenses. The soundmen were wheeling their portable recorder into position. Other men were straightening up the ground in front of the house, sweeping the small steps, oiling the door hinges so that they would not squeak at the wrong moment.

Sam looked around. He did not see Pierangeli. "Where's the director?"

Nickie pointed.

Sam followed his hand. Pierangeli was sitting on the ground, his back against the small stone-wall fence in front of the house. His knees were drawn up and his head rested on his arms crossed on the knees. His wide-brimmed black hat was pulled down over his face, shielding him from the sun.

Sam started toward him. Nickie stopped him. "Not now," he said. *"Il Maestro* is getting in the mood. We never interrupt him before he shoots a scene."

Sam stood there watching. After about five minutes Pierangeli raised his head. He looked around at all the workmen as if he were surprised to find them there. Then slowly he got to his feet.

He walked behind the camera and peered through the viewfinder. He said something to the cameraman and, leaving him, walked over to the doorway in the front of the house. He kicked some dirt back that the men had swept away. Then he glanced up at the sun, squinting, and turned back to look at his shadow against the house. Apparently everything was all right, for he made an invisible signal as he walked back behind the camera. There was a piercing blast on a whistle.

"Silenzio!" an assistant's voice roared.

A second later all that could be heard was the faint hum of a motor, then that, too, died away. Without looking around, Pierangeli held up his hand. *"Avanti,"* he said in a quiet voice, bringing his hand down sharply.

The door opened and the girl who was playing the younger sister came out, a pail in her hand. She threw the water out across the steps. She started back when she heard the sound. She looked up.

Sam turned and followed her gaze. Marilu was coming through the gate in the stone fence. There was something about the way she looked, something about the way she moved, her hips and legs and breasts swinging. No one had to be told. Everybody knew it just by looking at her.

Sam turned again and looked at the little man standing next to the camera. Under the wide-brimmed hat all he could see was the man's eyes. They were watching. Everything. As a camera sees everything.

Sam turned and gestured to Charley. They walked back across the road out of earshot. "Come on," Sam said. "We're going back to Rome."

"But I thought we were going to spend the night here." Charley said.

"No point in it," Sam said. "They have their own way of working. Maybe it's slow, maybe I don't understand it. Maybe it will cost twenty cents more. But they know what they're doing and it will be worth it."

ELEVEN

ONE MOMENT HE WAS SITTING there, alone in the last row of the projection room, and reflected light from the screen flickering across his impassive face. The next moment, when they looked back, he was gone.

Wearily, Jack Savitt held up his hand. "Okay, fellers, that's it."

The film stopped as the lights in the room came on. Jack got to his feet. Jimmy Jordan, head of television production for Trans-World Pictures, looked at him. "What happened?"

"How the hell do I know?" Jack answered.

"It's a perfectly good show," Jordan said. "What turned him off?"

"Whatever it is, you can be sure he will tell you. Himself."

"We put a lot of money into that pilot," Jordan said.

"So did Steve," Jack said. "A hundred grand ain't peanuts." He started for the door. "I'm going back to my office. I'll call you from there."

Steve was seated in the car when he came out of the building. Silently he got in beside him and turned on the motor. "Back to your office?"

Steve shook his head. "I've had enough for the day. Take me back to the hotel. I'm going to try for a little sleep."

"Good idea," Jack said. "You've been hitting it pretty hard the last two days. You don't get over that time lag without some rest."

He put the car into gear and they drove off the lot, past the guards at the studio gate who waved to them and onto the freeway back to Los Angeles. He pulled a cigarette from his pocket and lit it. He passed it over to Steve and took another for himself.

"They cheat," Steve said suddenly.

Jack was startled. "What did you say?"

"They cheat." Steve's voice was flat and angry. "They promise one thing, then deliver another. They lie, they cheat, they steal. What makes them think just because they have a big film factory that they can slough off the things they do for us? If it wasn't for our money, they would all be out of business."

Jack turned off Highland Avenue and swung right on Sunset Boulevard heading for Beverly Hills. "They have problems," he said. "The picture division is always holding the budget on the TV division."

"That's a lot of shit," Steve said. "We gave them a hundred grand for that pilot. It cost a hundred and fifty according to their figures. That includes their twenty-five percent overhead charge, which means all they laid out was another twelve thousand five hundred. Then they try to tell us they got a lot of money in it. No wonder all we get from them is crap."

"It's not Jimmy's fault," Jack said. "He's a good man. He's doing the best he can."

"I know that," Steve said. "I'm not blaming him."

"They'll want an answer on the show."

"They can keep it. I don't want it."

"You're blowing a hundred grand."

Steve put the cigarette out in the ashtray. "It won't be the first time."

They were silent until they were passing Sunset Plaza Drive. "Turn up here," Steve said suddenly.

Jack made a sharp right, followed by some curses from the driver of the car behind him. "Where do you want to go?"

"Just drive," Steve said.

They followed the winding road for a few minutes, then came to another small street. "In here."

The street came to a dead end after three hundred yards, just beyond a small apartment house. "You can pull in here," Steve said, indicating a small parking area opposite the apartment house.

Jack cut the engine. "What now?"

"Come with me," Steve said, getting out of the car.

Jack followed him across the parking area to an iron gate blocking a hidden driveway. Steven took a key from his pocket and opened the gate. He led the way up the driveway; it curved suddenly and there was the house, almost hanging over the road they had just left. The entrance was at the back of the house. Steven took out another key and opened the door.

They entered at the top and walked down a flight of stairs. On the first landing Steve gestured to a big picture window cut into the inside wall. "The bedroom."

He pressed a button and the bedroom lit up. Through the window it looked like a stage setting. The giant round bed almost in the center of the room. He opened the door and they went inside.

Jack looked at him. "No outside windows?"

Steve pointed at the ceiling as he pressed a button at the side of the bed. There was a low humming sound as the ceiling rolled back and light flooded into the room. He pressed another button and the glass that separated them from outside moved back into the wall. Overhead the sky was a bright blue and already the evening stars were beginning to shine in it.

"The bed rotates also," Steve said, pressing still another panel. The bed began to turn toward them; at the same time a television screen came down from a recess in the corner. "There are three sets," Steve explained. "No matter which way you turn the bed."

"Jesus!" Jack said.

Steve hit a master switch and everything began to roll back. "Come on."

He led the way down to the main floor to an enormous living room. Jack stared at it. The house was a giant A-frame chalet with windows that went thirty feet up. Everything was there. The kitchen, cleverly recessed behind the bar, the dining area, the enclosed terrace. Outside on the small terrace was an oval-shaped pool about twenty feet by twelve, which seemed suspended over the city. Below them the traffic crawled along the Strip.

"You bought it?"

"I built it."

Jack shook his head. "You're full of surprises."

Steve looked at him.

"I never figured you for a Hollywood Hills type," Jack said. "More like Beverly or Holmsby Hills, even Bel Air."

"That's family style," Steve said. "I'm a loner type."

Jack laughed. "You giving up girls?"

"Does this look like it?"

Jack shook his head. "I guess not," he laughed. "But you're young yet, you'll marry again."

"Maybe." Steve's voice was even.

"I suppose you've got the stereo to go with the setting?"

"Of course." Steve pressed a panel. Music suddenly filled the house. It seemed to come from everywhere.

Jack held up his hands. "Okay. You got me. Let's go to bed."

Steve laughed and turned off the music.

"You got to have a housewarming," Jack said. "When are you moving in?"

"Not for a while yet."

"It looked ready to me," Jack said. "What else do you have to do?"

"Nothing else," Steve replied. He turned and started back up the steps. "Let's go."

When they were back in the car and on their way down the hill, Jack glanced at him. "When do you think you will be ready?"

"In time." Steve shrugged his shoulders. "Who knows? One year, five, ten. The job won't last forever. No job does. Then I'll come out here to live."

"And what will you do?"

"I'll figure that one out when I get to it," Steve said. He was silent for a moment. "Do you like the house?"

"I'm crazy about it," Jack answered. "There's only one thing wrong with it."

"What's that?"

"By the time you get to it, you'll be too old to enjoy it."

Jack turned the car into the driveway of the Beverly Hills Hotel. A bellboy stopped him as he walked into the lobby. "A telegram just came for you, Mr. Savitt."

Jack tipped him and walked over to the desk. He took it from the room clerk and opened it. He read it quickly and made a face. "Damn!" he said.

"Anything wrong?" Steve asked.

"Your friend Sam Benjamin's really done it this time. He's got checks bouncing all over town."

"I didn't know he was in trouble," Steve said.

"The Barzini picture went way over budget and he ran out of money. I just got word that Supercolor Labs are closing in on him for their two-hundred-grand loan."

"You don't seem sorry about it," Steve said.

"I couldn't care less," Jack answered. "He's a loud-mouthed little bastard. He's been overdue for this one." He became aware of Steve's sudden silence. "I forgot. You like him."

Steve's voice was flat. "Yes."

"I don't get it. He's not your kind of guy."

"You also thought I wasn't the Hollywood Hills type."

"Okay, okay," Jack said. "But just between us. Why?"

Steve was silent for a moment. "Maybe it's because he's the only man around who isn't always trying to suck my ass. Or maybe it's because he knocks down doors."

TWELVE

IT WAS AFTER TEN O'CLOCK when Denise closed the door behind them. She turned the safety lock and slumped against the door, drained and exhausted. After a moment, she went into the living room.

There was still some ice in the bucket. Maybe a drink would pick her up. She put the ice in a glass and poured some Scotch over it. She added a little water and, sipping at the drink, turned on the television set. She went back to the couch and sank into it. The set blared into life, but she didn't see it. It wasn't the same without Sam. Nothing was the same without him.

All through dinner, they had been careful not to talk about him. Not until the very end. Then it had been Roger who had brought him up.

"When's Sam coming back?" he had asked.

"I don't know. He's trying to rush the picture through editing and music."

"Is it going well?" he asked.

"Sam says it is," she had answered.

"I hope so," Roger said phlegmatically. "For the children's sake, if no other reason."

It was Anne, always a little stupid and tactless, who brought up the subject they had all been carefully avoiding. "Where's your engagement ring?" she asked pointedly.

Unconsciously, Denise had looked down at her empty finger, then up at them. She had been very proud of the ten-carat diamond that Sam had bought her after the success of *Icarus*. She rarely took it off, sometimes even slept with it. "At Provident Loan," she said. Then a little defiantly she added, "Along with the diamond wristwatch and wedding band. We needed the money."

Roger looked at her, then at his wife. After a moment, he turned back to her. "The money couldn't have lasted very long," he said.

"It didn't."

"What are you doing for money now?" he had asked.

She hesitated a moment. "We're managing." They were managing all right. That is if you could call being two months behind on the rent and owing the butcher and grocer, managing. "Sam's parents sent some money up from Miami." His mother and father had moved down there a few years ago when he sold the tailor shop and retired.

Awkwardly Roger put his hand inside his jacket. He took out a check and pushed it across the table to her. She looked at it. It was made out in her name for one hundred thousand dollars.

Her voice was not quite steady. "What's that for?"

"You're my sister," he said in a gruff voice. "I don't like to see you struggling."

She fought back the tears that were threatening to come to her eyes and pushed the check back to him. "No."

He stared at her. "Why not? It will cover the checks that Sam has out and put an end to your problems. Then maybe he can come home and not have to hide out over there in Italy."

"If you want to give Sam the money," she said, "you'll have to give it to him. He would never forgive me if I took it from you."

"I can't talk to Sam, you know that," he said. "You don't have to tell him that I gave it to you. Tell him it was the last payment due you from Papa's estate."

She shook her head. "I can't do it. I never lied to him before and I'm not going to start now."

"You're a fool—" Anne began to say.

"Shut up!" Roger said quickly. He picked up the check and put it back in his pocket. He looked at his watch. "We'll have to be going now. It's almost time for the baby's feeding."

They got to their feet and she walked to the door with them. She waited while Anne got into her mink coat.

"The dinner was delicious," Anne said, kissing her cheek.

"Give the baby a kiss for me," Denise replied. She turned to her brother. "Thank you," she said. "You know I mean it."

He nodded heavily. "Yes. By the way," he said as if it were an afterthought. "I've paid up the rent and the back bills so you don't have to worry about them."

"How did you know?"

"You forget, the accountant who works for Sam also works for me."

—

THE PROGRAM ENDED AND THE late news came on just as the telephone began to ring. She jumped from the couch and ran to the telephone. She hadn't heard from Sam in almost a week.

"Hello?"

The long-distance operator's voice sang through the wires. *"Mr. Sam Benjamin, please. Long distance calling."*

"Mr. Benjamin isn't here just now. This is Mrs. Benjamin, can I help you?

"Do you have another number at which he can be reached?" the operator asked.

Another voice cut in. It was a man's voice and had a familiar sound. *"I'll speak with Mrs. Benjamin,"* it said. *"Hello, Denise, this is Steve. Stephen Gaunt."*

"Steve," she said.

"How are you? And the kids?"

"We're all fine," she said. "Sam isn't here. He's in Italy."

"Do you have a number at which I can reach him?" Steve asked. *"It's very important."*

"He's at the Excelsior Hotel in Rome," she answered. "If you can't reach him there, try Cinecittá Studios. They're editing the picture out there."

"How's it coming?" Steve asked.

"Sam says it will be a great movie."

"I'm sure it will," he said. *"I liked the project from the very beginning. Matter of fact, that's why I'm calling. I think I have a deal for him."*

"I hope so," she said. Then the dam broke and she began to cry and the whole story spilled out of her. The fight with Roger, the shortage of money, the struggle to finish the movie before the creditors closed down.

He listened quietly, letting her talk herself out. *"Why didn't Sam call me when he got into trouble?"*

"I don't know," she said. "You know Sam. It was his pride that led to the fight with Roger. Maybe it was that. Maybe he didn't want you to know that he got into trouble. Maybe he didn't want to bother you because you have your own problems."

"That's stupid," Steve said. *"What are friends for, anyway, if you can't call on them when you need them?"*

She was silent.

"Anyway, stop worrying about it now," he said calmly. *"Everything will be all right."*

There was a quality in his voice that reassured her, that gave her confidence. "I feel better now, Steve," she said. "I'm sorry I broke down."

"Forget it," he said. *"Do you still make that wild brust flanken with white horseradish?"*

"Yes." She had to laugh at the way he pronounced the Yiddish words.

"Good," he said. *"I'll call you when I get back to New York and you'll invite me up for dinner."*

The telephone clicked off and she put it down. She turned off the television set and went into the bedroom. Steve had said it would be all right. And it would be. She knew it. She felt it. For the first time in weeks she slept without taking a pill.

THIRTEEN

THE LOS ANGELES OFFICES OF Sinclair Broadcasting were on the top floor of a new twenty-story office building on Wilshire Boulevard in Beverly Hills. Steve's office was on the southeast corner of the building, facing toward Hollywood and downtown Los Angeles. When Jack came into his office the next morning, Steve was standing, a cup of coffee in his hand, looking out the windows.

"On a clear morning you can see Mount Baldy from here," Steve said. "That's almost forty miles away."

"Yeah," Jack said. "But how many clear mornings do you get out here?"

"More than you think," Steve said. "The smog gets better Nielsens than it deserves."

A secretary's voice came from the intercom on Steve's desk. *"I have Mr. Brachman of Supercolor on the line from New York for you, Mr. Gaunt."*

"I'll pick it up," Steve said. He went back to his desk, pressed a button, and picked up the telephone. "Ernie, good morning."

"It's morning for you, baby," Brachman said. *"But it's almost lunch time for us slaves here in New York. We got half a day's work under our belts already."*

"Tough titty." Steve laughed. "I read your annual report. You guys are the only people in the business making any money. All you do is print the film and rake it in."

Brachman laughed. *"It's not bad,"* he admitted. *"But what's on your mind? The service all right?"*

"The service is fine," Steve said. "I just wanted a favor from you."

There was a note of relief in Brachman's voice. *"Anything. Just ask for it."*

"I hear that you're closing down on Sam Benjamin. I want you to lay off."

There was a moment's silence. *"I don't know whether I can do that, Steve. It's out of my hands now. It's in legal."*

"You're the president of Supercolor, aren't you?" Steve's voice was expressionless. "Nothing's out of your hands."

"Wait a minute, Steve. I'm like you. I got stockholders to answer to. We loaned Benjamin two hundred grand for his picture and he used the money to pay off his brother-in-law. If we hold off we can lose the picture to other creditors and where would that leave us?"

"Don't shit me, Ernie," Steve said. "You loaned Benjamin that money to make sure that you got the printing on it. No other reason. You couldn't care less what he did with it."

"Right. But that was only if everything was all right and there were no problems. But we also take a chattel on the picture to protect ourselves."

Steve's voice was still flat, but there was an edge of steel in it now. "Who's your biggest customer, Ernie?"

"You are." The answer came without hesitation. It was true and they both knew it. Supercolor did all the printing for Sinclair's filmed shows.

"And we never ask a penny's loan or advance, do we?"

"That's right. But—"

Steve interrupted, his voice deceptively soft. "Next year's contract will come up soon. As usual, Technicolor, Deluxe, and Pathe will bid on it. As usual, you will come with about the same pricing. I have to present those bids to my board with my recommendations."

Brachman went down in flames. But gallantly. *"Okay, Steve. You want a favor, you got it. I told you all you have to do is ask. I only hope we don't get hurt by it."*

"You won't get hurt. It's a great picture," Steve said. "Thank you, Ernie. I appreciate that."

He put down the telephone and turned to Jack. The agent stared at him. "Have you gone out of your mind, Steve? You just put your neck in a noose. That Ernie Brachman's a bad guy and if he blows the dough on that deal, I wouldn't put it past him to go to Sinclair and say that you used your position to push him."

Steve looked at him. "Then it's up to us to see that the deal doesn't blow, isn't it?"

Jack ran out of words. After a moment, he got to his feet. "You got anything stronger than coffee around here this morning? I need a drink."

Steve gestured to the bar. While Jack poured himself a shot of whiskey, Steve refilled his coffee cup. Jack tossed the drink down and came back to the desk.

"Bad policy to be on the sauce this early in the morning," Steve said mildly.

"Okay, okay," Jack said. "I have a hunch that you aren't finished with this little caper just yet. Let's have the rest of it."

Steve smiled and sat down. "Your hunches have a way of being absolutely right. You just got yourself a new client."

"I have?" Jack asked. "Who?"

"Sam Benjamin," Steve said. "And you're going to make a distribution deal for his picture."

"How the hell am I goin' to do that when he has his own distribution company?"

"Not domestic. You're going to sell the foreign distribution rights."

Jack stared at him. "You mean he hasn't got a foreign distribution deal on this?"

Steve shook his head. "I know he hasn't. I have the TV deal for it and he has to clear all distribution deals through us."

"Christ! A picture like that could be worth more money abroad than here. They love that kind of a movie."

"You're getting the message," Steve nodded. "But I want big numbers."

"How big?"

"A half million or more."

"That makes it tough. There are only the majors that can go for that kind of dough. And they never paid that much money for foreign distribution rights."

"Trans-World Pictures will," Steve said.

—

IT WAS ONE O'CLOCK IN the morning and Sam sat in the chair, staring owlishly out of the window at the lighted facade of the American embassy across the street. He picked up the glass of champagne from the table next to him. He made a face and turned back to the room. "Drink up," he said. "There's still four more bottles left."

The girls sitting on the couch giggled. He looked over at Charley. "The least you could do is come up with some cunts who speak English," he grumbled. "Tell 'em what I said."

Charley began to translate, but he interrupted him. "No, wait a minute, I got a better idea."

He got up and walked unsteadily over to the couch. He looked down at the girls. "Tell 'em the first girl to give me a hard-on wins a bottle of champagne."

The girls giggled again. He turned to Charley. "You sure they don't speak English?"

Charley nodded. He spoke rapidly to the girls. They chattered back at him. He looked at Sam. "They say they're not whores. They're actresses and they want to be treated with respect."

Sam stared at the girls. After a moment he spoke. "Throw 'em out." He went back to the chair and sat down, his back to him. He picked up his glass of champagne. Again he made a face. "Jesus! Haven't we got any real whiskey left in the place?"

"No, and I can't get any. They cut off our credit this afternoon."

"That ain't all they'll be cutting off," Sam said dourly. "Tomorrow they'll be cutting off my balls." He took another sip of champagne. "Pure shit! A man can't even get a respectable drunk on this *pishachs*. If I ever get the money, I make a resolution never to drink anything but Scotch whiskey for the rest of my life. No ice, no water, nothin'. Just pure whiskey, that's all. At least that way when I want to get shikker I can depend on it."

He got out of the chair and went back to the girls. "I heard about you kids using Seven-Up and Coca-Cola for a douche, but did you ever try Dom Perignon '55? It's got to be the best."

The girls laughed. One of them spoke rapidly to Charley. Charley laughed.

"What did the cunts say?" Sam asked. "Tell me."

"They said we're wasting time out here, why don't we all go to bed?"

"It's okay with me," Sam said. "But if they think they're wasting time out here, wait until we get into the bedroom. Then they'll find out how to really waste time. I couldn't get it up if you pumped it full of starch."

Charley said something to the girls and they got up and went into the bedroom.

"You can get started," Sam called after them. "Don't wait for me."

The door closed behind them and he turned to Charley. "I never promised you a steady job, did I?"

Charley shook his head. "Take it easy, boss," he said soothingly. "Something will turn up."

"Sure," Sam said sarcastically. "And I know exactly what. My toes." He looked around the room. "Tell me, how do you go about sneaking out of a suite like this without paying up?"

Charley didn't answer.

"Come on." Sam picked up a bottle of champagne and started for the bedroom. At the door, he turned to look back at Charley. "Well?"

Slowly Charley walked over. Sam opened the door and stood there. "Well, I'll be damned!" he said. "I thought you said they didn't understand English. They did get started without me."

Charley looked into the room over Sam's shoulder. The two girls were naked in the bed and wrapped around each other in a wild tangle of arms and legs.

Sam turned to look at him. "I think they're in love," he said solemnly.

Charley nodded. "Looks like it."

"I don't think we should disturb them," Sam said, gently closing the door. The telephone began to ring as they walked back into the room. "Now who the hell is that?"

Charley picked up the telephone. "Pronto." A voice rattled in the receiver. He looked at Sam. "A Jack Savitt calling from Los Angeles for you."

"To hell with him," Sam said. "Tell him I'm out. He's probably found out the paychecks I gave a couple of his clients bounced."

Charley started to speak again, but a voice cut him off. He was silent, listening, then turned to Sam again. "He says it's not about the rubber. He says he's got a deal for you on the picture."

"Give me the phone. What are you waiting for?" Sam practically tore it from his hands. "Hello, Jack," he said into it. "What's on your mind?"

He listened and the sweat began to break out on his forehead. He pulled out a handkerchief and wiped at it. After a moment, he spoke. "Yes, yes… Good-bye."

He put down the telephone and turned to Charley. Suddenly he grabbed him around the waist and hugged him, lifting him off his feet. "You were right, you guinea bastard, you were right!"

"Put me down," Charley yelled. "Are you crazy or somethin'? Do you want to get a rupture?"

The yelling brought the naked girls to the door of the bedroom. They stood there staring at them. Sam picked up two bottles of champagne and gave one to each girl. "Back in the box for you lovers," he said, pushing them into the bedroom and closing the door behind them.

He turned to Charley. "Come on, let's get out of here to find a bar with real whiskey and celebrate!"

"Celebrate?" Charley asked. "What are we celebratin'?"

"We've been saved by the bell," Sam said. A look of wonder suddenly came over his face. "Really. Jack Savitt's coming over here the day after tomorrow with the president and the international sales manager of Trans-World Pictures. They want to make a deal for the foreign rights to our movie!"

FOURTEEN

***"BRUST FLANKEN!"* SAM LOOKED AT** the table in disgust. He looked up at Denise. "The least you could do when I bring somebody home to dinner is to lay on a steak. This is for relatives."

Denise smiled. "Steve asked for it."

Sam turned to him. "You got to be out of your mind. It's instant heartburn!"

Steve grinned. "I like it. I can get a steak anywhere in the United States, but brust flanken like this, I can only get here."

"You can't even pronounce it properly and you like it? Broost flahnkin, not bruhst flanking."

"You say tomatoes, I say tomahtoes. Let's eat," Steve smiled, holding out his plate.

Despite his complaint, Sam put away twice as much food as anyone at the table. When dinner was finished, he got to his feet. "Not bad," he said to Denise.

Steve grinned at her.

She smiled back at him. "Why don't you both go into the living room and talk," she suggested. "I'll help Mamie straighten up."

Sam made two drinks and gave one to Steve. "Did you see those reviews?"

Steve nodded. "They were great. Crowther said it was the best film in the last ten years."

"When that boy flips, it's really got to be somethin'," Sam chortled. "The lines are around the block from the time the theater opens until it closes. And L.A. is the same. Raves and SRO."

"When are you going into general release?" Steve asked.

"I'm in no hurry. I want to wait for the Academy nominations. Meanwhile I'll let the picture build. Nobody can say that I don't know how to get the most out of a film. If we pick up the New York Critics Award and then the Academy, I'll need a steam shovel to handle the money."

Steve held up his drink. "Good luck."

"You too," Sam said. He drank. "Not bad for my first picture. And they said I didn't know what I was doing."

"What are you planning next?" Steve asked.

"Right now I'm concentrating on this one. I got an advertising campaign aimed right at the Academy. But I got Marilu and Pierangeli signed for a follow-up picture."

"Anything else?"

"Isn't that enough?"

Steve looked at him. "Not if you want to build a real company like you say. You can't do it on foreign pictures alone. No matter how good they are."

"How do I get domestic pictures? The majors get all the cream. All I can pick up is the *shlock.*"

"You can start by acquiring a few properties and making them," Steve said.

"I'm not crazy altogether," Sam said. "I know I'm no producer."

"You got this one made," Steve said. "You're a producer."

"This was different. Marilu was a star. She came to me with it. Everything was blocked out for me. All I had to do was come up with the loot."

"Isn't that what most of the majors are doing right now?" Steve asked.

"But they have the money. I can't compete with them."

"You don't have to right now," Steve said. "Trans-World will go partners with you on anything you like after this picture. They need product."

"You really think so?"

"I'm sure of it," Steve said confidently. "Why don't you try them?"

Sam thought for a moment. "No. It won't work. I haven't got any properties. And I wouldn't know one if I fell over it. Show me a picture and I can tell you in a second whether it's got anything. But a property? That's something else."

"It's not that difficult if you keep your eyes open," Steve said. "For example, there are two that I can suggest right now."

Sam looked at him shrewdly. "Two?"

Steve nodded. "One's a play that's going into rehearsal next week. It's a comedy by a new playwright, about young marrieds in Greenwich Village. For seventy-five thousand dollars you can grab the screen rights and a piece of the play. It's called *Washington Arch.*"

"Lousy title," Sam said.

"Maybe, but the play'll be a big hit."

"You said there was another."

"This one's a book. I read the manuscript. The author's tongue is hanging out for money. Fifty thousand and you've got it. It's out in January and it can't miss being number one on the best-seller list. This one's got a great title. *The Steel Rooster.*"

"That *is* a good title," Sam said. "I like it. What makes you so sure it will be number one?"

"It's all about fucking," Steve said. "And I don't know anyone who doesn't like to read about that. But besides, it's a hell of a story."

"I'll think about it," Sam said.

"Do that," Steve said. "I'll send a copy of each over to you. The price might go up if you show an interest in the properties."

"They'll find out anyway if I want to buy them," Sam said.

"Not if you work through Jack Savitt," Steve said. "He can act for you without revealing your name until you're ready. His reputation is good enough for them to accept his statement that he has a legitimate interest in the property."

"Okay," Sam said. "I'll look at them as soon as I get them."

Denise came into the room. "Everything all right?"

"Just fine," Steve said. He got to his feet. "I'll have to go. I'm catching a morning plane to the coast."

Sam looked at him. "You ride that plane like an ordinary guy rides the subway."

Steve laughed. "That's a good way to put it. Subway in the Sky." He turned to Denise. "Thank you for the *brust flanken*. It was delicious."

Denise smiled. He kissed her cheek.

"You still can't say it," Sam said, walking to the door with him. He stopped there. "Look. If we get any nominations for the Academy, I'll take a big table. Will you join us?"

"I usually don't make dates five months in advance," Steve said. "But in this case, I'll make an exception. You get the nominations. I'll be there."

—

THE WALLS OF THE GRAND ballroom in the Beverly Hilton Hotel were stretched with people. Holding on to the hand of his date, he fought his way through to Sam's table. The first person he saw was Denise. She was sitting between her children, a proud smile on her face.

He stopped next to her and bent to kiss her cheek. "Congratulations, Denise," he said. "I'm sorry I'm late."

She could hardly hear him over the noise. "Isn't it wonderful?"

"Yes," he said. He turned to Myriam. "My God, you're all grown up. You're not too old to kiss."

"On the cheek," she said, turning her face just like her mother.

He kissed her and turned to Junior. "Big night, Samuel?" He held out his hand.

The boy took it shyly. "Yes, Uncle Steve."

He turned back to Denise. "I'd like you to meet—" He stared at the girl, suddenly realizing he had forgotten her name. The time lag must be worse than he thought. "Green-eyed Girl," he said. "Mrs. Benjamin."

"Irene Murdoch," the girl said. "Pleased to meet you, Mrs. Benjamin. Congratulations."

"Where's Sam?" he asked.

"He's off with the Barzinis. They're taking pictures," Denise said. "Sit down and have a drink."

He held a chair for the girl and sat down beside her. "I can use one," he said. "I just got off the plane an hour ago and had to change and pick up—" He looked at the girl in bewilderment. Damn, he had forgotten her name again. "—Green-eyed Girl here and come over."

He put some ice into two glasses and added Scotch. He handed one glass to the girl.

"At least you remember what I drink."

He grinned. "I'm not that bad, Green-eyed Girl." But it had been an accident. He only gave her Scotch because that was what he was drinking.

A crowd of people surged toward the table. He looked up. Sam was in the center of them, his tie askew, in his arms a number of Oscars.

He saw Steve and let out a yell. "You made it!" He dropped the Oscars on the table and hugged him. He kissed him on both cheeks.

Steve grinned at him. "Congratulations."

"Five of them. How about that?" Sam yelled. "We walked away with everything. Best picture, best actress, best director, best screenplay, best everything!"

"You did it," Steve said.

Sam sat down abruptly. "I need a drink." He picked up the bottle of Scotch and held it to his mouth. The liquor ran down over his shirt.

"Sam!" Denise put out her hand. "People are looking!"

"Let 'em," Sam yelled happily. "That's what they came here for."

Jack Savitt came up with his girl and they sat down. Jack leaned across the table to Steve. "It's a wild night."

Steve nodded.

Ernie Brachman, tall and distinguished in his dinner jacket, stopped by the table. "Congratulations, Sam."

"Congratulate yourself, Ernie, you son of a bitch!" Sam shouted at him. "The smartest thing you ever did was to lay off me."

Ernie smiled again, but this time only with his lips. He bowed and walked away.

"Sam," Denise reproached him. "You shouldn't have spoken to him like that."

"Fuck him!" Sam said. "That prick pisses ice water. The only reason he strung along with me was because it was good business."

He turned back to the table and began to stand the Oscars upright like toy soldiers in front of him. "Look at that," he sang. "Five of them."

His eyes were more than just slightly glazed. "You know what that means? You know what it means? Each and every little one of them is worth a million dollars at the box office. Five million dollars." He looked around the table. "Now maybe they won't think I'm so stupid. Or that they can push me around anymore. I'm just as big as any of them. I got the number-one play on Broadway. The number-one book on the best-seller lists. And now I got the number-one picture in the world.

"I'm not Sam Benjamin the fat little *shmuck* exhibitor anymore. I'm Sam Benjamin, number one in the picture business. Nobody pushes me around.

"And you know what I'm goin' to do tomorrow?"

The table was silent as he looked around at them. "You know what I'm goin' to do?

"Tomorrow I'm goin' to open up the TV bidding for the picture. They'll pay me a million dollars for the right to show it five years from now."

He stared belligerently at Steve.

Steve didn't answer him.

It was Jack who finally spoke. "I thought you had a deal with Steve."

"Friendship is one thing, business is another," Sam said, still looking at Steve. "The picture is worth a million dollars. Isn't that right, Steve?"

Everyone turned to Steve.

His gray eyes were calm as he watched Sam; slowly he nodded. "I guess you're right, Sam."

"Are you goin' to pay me a million dollars for it?"

"No." Steve's voice was even. "I'm going to pay you exactly what we agreed on. No more. No less."

Sam stared at him for a long moment. Then he suddenly smiled. "That's right." He took a deep breath. "I'd hate to sit in a poker game with you." He got to his feet. "Take me home, Mama," he said to Denise. "I'm drunk."

Jack watched him go, then leaned over to Steve. "I was right about the little bastard. Like someone once said, 'Impossible when he's broke, insufferable when he's solvent.'"

THAT DAY LAST SPRING

AFTERNOON

SHE WENT OUT OF BED like a cat. One moment she was there beside me, warm and purring, the next, like an animal scenting danger, she was at the window. She peered out between the drapes. There was something about the way she stood there, tense and watching, the sun turning her all gold and shining.

I rolled over on my stomach. "Come back to bed, Blonde Girl."

She didn't move. "You've got a visitor."

"So have you," I said.

It was like she didn't even hear me. "He's walking around back to the carport. A little guy."

"Maybe if you'll stop looking, he'll go away."

"He might be somebody important," she said. "He's got a silver Rolls."

I looked at her. The long blonde hair, the blue eyes, the full breasts with tiny nipples, the moist golden fur. And I gave up. "Why don't you invite him over?"

"That's an idea." She pulled back the drapes and stepped outside on the terrace. "Yoo hoo!" she hollered, waving. "Over here!"

This I had to see. I got out of bed and walked over. The moment I saw the car I knew who it was. And that it only meant one thing. Sam Benjamin had not given up. He had sent a persuader. Perhaps the best persuader in the world.

Dave Diamond, a/k/a *"The Shtarker,"* your friendly neighborhood banker. That is, if you were in a million-dollar neighborhood. Otherwise known as president of the California Consolidated Banks.

She called again and he turned. For a moment he seemed frozen to the spot, his mouth agape. Then he dashed back to his car and jumped in. The next moment he was halfway down the driveway.

I leaned over the terrace railing and yelled as he came past us. "What's the matter, Dave? Didn't you ever see a naked girl before?"

The Rolls screeched to a stop. He stuck his head out of the window. "What the hell are you doing up there?"

"Sunbathing," I said.

"You gotta be crazy," he shouted. "In broad daylight. The cops'll grab you."

"It's the one thing you can't do at night," I said. "Come on up and join us."

"Not unless you get some clothes on," he said. "My depositors wouldn't like it if I was dragged downtown for showing myself off in public."

I looked at her. "What do you say, Blonde Girl?"

"He's cute."

I leaned over the railing. "You heard her. Come on up."

He was pulling the car against the curb as we went inside. I pulled on my Levis as she went into her closet. The bikini she wore when she came out looked like she had even less on than when she was naked. She went to the door and opened it.

He came into the apartment, his eyes darting suspiciously from side to side. "I thought you *had* a girl," he said.

"He's got a new one now," she said brightly.

"Blonde Girl," I said. "I'd like you to meet the guardian of my money. Dave, this is Blonde Girl."

"He guards my money, too," she said.

He looked at her with new interest. This was his favorite language. "I haven't seen you in the bank, have I?"

"No, Mr. Diamond," she demurred. "I don't bank in the main office. I have one of those small accounts at the Sunset Plaza Branch. You know, twenty-five-thousand-dollar minimum balance. But I did get the sweetest letter from you when I opened my account."

He preened visibly. "Well, if there's anything you need, just call on me. Do you work around here?"

"No," she answered. "I work in Chicago."

"Chicago?" he asked. "And you live here? When do you work?"

"Every other Monday," she said sweetly. "Can I get you something to drink?"

He stared at her for a moment while he digested that. "Scotch. If you have it."

"I have it." She left the room.

He looked after her appreciatively, then turned to me. "I don't know how you do it," he said. "You always come up with the greatest. How did you find her?"

"She found me," I said. "Just like you did. Tell Sam the answer is still no."

"Now wait a minute," he said. "You didn't even hear what I was going to say."

She came back with a bottle of Chivas Regal, ice, and glasses. She put them down on the small table. "You men just help yourselves," she said, unfastening her brassiere. "I'll take a shower while you talk."

Dave couldn't keep his eyes from her breasts as they sprang free. He watched her until the bathroom door closed behind her, then turned to me. "You put her up to that," he accused me. "You know I can't talk when I have a hard-on."

I laughed, filling a glass and giving it to him. I took my own glass. *"L'chaim,"* I said.

"Up yours," he said.

We drank.

"Why not?" he asked.

"I won't be used anymore," I said. "This time Sam can do it by himself."

"He still owes me twelve million," Dave said. "But I'm not worried anymore. He's got it made."

"Good for you," I said. "I wish you both luck. Now you go back and tell him I'm not interested."

"You sit out here three years lookin' for action an' when it finally comes your way, you don't want it."

"It's not the kind of action I want," I said.

"What is it you want?" He was becoming annoyed. "You want to be head of a studio? Everybody wants to be head of a studio. But there are only so many—"

"Okay, Dave—enough. You know better than that. You know what I want. I want my own company. Where I'm the boss. Like Sinclair. Like Sam."

"Sam says you'll be boss if you come in."

"Sam's full of shit. How can I be boss if somebody else owns the company?" I refilled my glass. "And what the hell does a plate-glass company know about the picture business, even if they are the biggest plate-glass manufacturers in the world?"

"You gotta stay up to date, Steve." Dave eyeballed me. "This is no longer a game for the little guys. Look around. Trans America, Gulf and Western, the Avco Corporation. With companies like that you need more than peanuts to play in their league."

"Exactly what are you saying?"

"No hard feelings, Steve," he said. "But if you're still looking to buy a company, forget it. Nobody wants your money anymore. They want paper. Backed with the name of a big company, all fancy with gold lettering that they can take down to the Street and play games with. You ain't got enough money to beat that game. Nobody has."

I was silent for a moment. "Then you think this is the best I can do?"

He nodded.

I turned and looked out the window. It was as simple as that. Three years shot to hell. Three years of waiting for the right thing to happen. Now it was over. It would never happen.

"What if I could match the offer?" I asked.

Dave was ironic. "Thirty-two million dollars?"

"But it's mostly paper."

"So?"

I took a deep breath. "Then what's in it for me?"

"More than you ever thought," Dave said. "If I can tell 'em you're interested I can arrange a meeting."

"I already met with Sam."

"Not with him," Dave said quickly. "With Johnston of Palomar Plate. He's the emmiss. He's the one who really wants you and insists that you're part of the deal."

"Why me? We've never met."

"He makes it a big point. Says he has known about you all his business life. He thinks you're the only one in this industry that makes any sense at all."

I lit a cigarette and looked at Dave thoughtfully. "You know him?"

"We've met," Dave said noncommittally. That meant he didn't know him at all. In Dave's position, not being on a first-name basis was a cardinal sin. "You've heard of him?"

"Yes." Everyone had. Last month his picture was on the front cover of *Time.* Along with an article inside on conglomerates. And how he had taken his company from the quiet conservatism of eighty million a year to where it is now, almost eight hundred million a year. All in a short time, merely by exchanging pieces of paper.

I remembered the portrait. It was a typical *Time* cover. Filled with the kind of symbolism of dollar signs and gold stock certificates and the products of the companies he now controlled.

"Don't say no until you talk to him. He promises you complete autonomy."

"He told you that?"

"Personally," Dave assured me.

"What else did he promise you?"

Dave looked uncomfortable.

"Come on, you can tell me," I urged. "We're friends."

"Five millions of deposits," he said reluctantly.

I whistled. "All for talking me into it?"

Dave shook his head. "You have nothing to do with it. He likes the way we operate. We're not an old-fashioned bank. We swing. Besides, we get our twelve million back from Sam."

"Is that why you came to see me?"

There was an expression in his eyes that told me he meant what he was saying. "Not only that, but because I think you'll be good for each other. He respects you and won't try to run your business for you the way some of the others do."

I knew what he meant. It was amazing how quickly otherwise normal, competent businessmen get hooked on the film business. Then all the rules they have lived by go out the window. "Not even a girlfriend he wants to make into a star?"

"I can answer that." Blonde Girl had just come out of the bathroom, a long towel tied sarong-like around her.

I looked up in surprise. Dave peered over the edge of his glasses. "You?"

She nodded, casually filling a glass with ice and then pouring some whiskey over it. "Yes."

I just watched her. She turned to me. "I know Ed Johnston very well. He's a straight-up guy. Never once did he say anything about getting me into the movies."

It was beginning to make sense now. I remembered when she first moved into the apartment about three months ago. Then how she always seemed to be there at the window, never going out. Her casual line about working every other Monday in Chicago. Chicago was Palomar Plate's home base. I still didn't speak.

"You angry with me?" she asked.

I shook my head. "You should have come over sooner. We've been missing a great thing."

"You were all wrapped up with that other girl," she said.

"There's always room for one more."

"I'm old-fashioned. Besides I could wait. The money was good. It was no strain."

"And what did you find out?" I asked.

"Nothing that he didn't already know. You're an okay guy and I told him. He's prepared to like you and I think you'd like him." She finished her drink and put the empty glass back on the table.

I turned to Dave. "Okay, I'll talk to him. But no commitment."

Dave smiled for the first time. "Good. He's in Vegas. He's got his company jet out at Burbank in case we want to join him for lunch."

I looked at my watch. It was a quarter past twelve. "Okay, sounds good. I was getting hungry, anyway."

"We'll go out to the airport in my car," Dave said quickly. "I'll save the flying until we get to the plane."

"You'll go in your car," I said. "Blonde Girl will come with me."

—

I LEARNED A LITTLE BIT more about Ed Johnston on the way down to Vegas. Blonde Girl told me a few personal items. Like he was married, two children, and on the square side of the sheets. Warm but square. No tricks, no kinks, everything simple and straight. Sometimes dull but with a great deal of strength and staying power.

Dave filled me in on the business side. He was the youngest captain ever to command an aircraft carrier. He left the Navy after the Korean War despite the attempts made to keep him in, which included a promotion to rear admiral in the Reserve. He joined Palomar Plate as executive VP and within one year became president and chief officer. Within five years he began his period of diversification and acquisition. First in related lines, then going further and further afield until now Palomar Plate controlled one of the big meat-packing companies and a large hotel chain whose newest hotel was the Flaming Desert in Las Vegas where we were going to meet. He was also reaching for one of the major transcontinental airlines and had just acquired a large tract of land in Los Angeles where he planned to erect another Century City on the style of the Alcoa project.

I could understand all of them. The one thing I did not understand was why he wanted a film company. That made no sense at all in the scheme of things.

It was a quarter to two when we were ushered into his suite in the tower of the hotel. The luncheon table was already set, but he was on the telephone.

He waved us to a seat and kept on talking. I tuned in carefully. "The red herring is already out," he was saying in a calm voice. "Let's wait for the reaction before we start fiddling with the points. If it goes well we're in good shape. Time enough to change if it looks like it's dragging ass." He put down the telephone with finality and got to his feet. He held out a hand. "I'm Ed Johnston. I've been looking forward to meeting you."

"Thank you," I said.

He shook hands with Dave and kissed Blonde Girl on the cheek. "You just earned your bonus," he said. He turned back to me with a smile that took the edge off his words. "How do you like the bodyguard we found for you?"

I laughed. He was direct enough. "I couldn't have done better for myself."

"Let's eat," he said, sitting down at the table. "I ordered delicatessen. They tell me this hotel has the best in the world. Anything to drink?"

A waiter appeared quickly and began taking our orders. I got myself a Scotch and water and felt better with a glass in my hand. He had a diet Coke.

We ate quickly and efficiently and in twenty minutes the table was cleared. He looked at me. I glanced at him, then at Dave. Apparently it was up to me to begin.

"I have just one question," I said.

"Shoot," he said.

"Why?"

A puzzled look came over his face. "Why what?"

"The film business," I said. "It seems to me you have enough on your plate now. Everything solid and real. Why go for something as risky and ephemeral as that?"

He just sat there studying me.

"I could understand if you were after a major studio with land available for development. That would fit into your scheme. But the only assets here are films." I put my drink down. "You can't turn that into a construction project."

"There are other attractions," he said. "CATV is already here, next there will be Pay TV, soon there will be TV tape cassettes, someone will have to work day and night just to fill the demand. And our tape division is one of the largest in the country."

It was my turn to sit on my hands.

"The idea isn't new. Other conglomerates have the same idea and are already in the field. I think the time is right for us. For our kind of operation, especially if we stay loose. My idea is to have a production and distribution company that can supply all media as the demand arises."

"Sounds good. I'm sure you have a very practical plan." I got to my feet. "But I've taken enough of your time already, Mr. Johnston. May I wish you the very best of success?"

He stared, a disbelieving look on his face. "You're not interested?"

I shook my head. "Thank you. But it's not for me."

"If it's the money. I'm sure that can be—"

"That's not it."

"What is it then?" All the power and frustration were deep in his eyes.

"You spoke about everything but the most important ingredient—"

It was his turn to interrupt me. "Talent? I was just coming to that."

"No, Mr. Johnston, that's not it, either. Talent you can buy." Blonde Girl was right. He was square. "The most important ingredient in our business is Fun. If you haven't got that, you've got nothing. All you're offering is just a job."

I started for the door. "Don't worry about me, Mr. Johnston," I said, "I can get a cab to the airport."

Blonde Girl caught me as I was going through the casino on my way to the front lobby. "Hey there, wait up for me!"

I grinned at her. "Your boss send you?"

"He just fired me," she said.

"You shouldn't have blown your job because of me," I said.

"If you think I was going to let a lousy little thing like a job come between us, you're crazy," she said. "They just don't make rigs like yours no more."

AFTERNOON

THE TELEPHONE CALL CAME AS we started up the steps from the casino. A bellboy in the uniform of a major general looked at Blonde Girl and stopped me. "Mr. Gaunt?"

"Yes."

"There's a telephone call for you." He led the way to the telephones around behind a bank of slot machines. He picked one up. "I have Mr. Gaunt on the line," he said, giving me the telephone.

I hit him with a dollar and took the phone.

"Mr. Gaunt, you're a hard man to find." Diana's very proper English answering-service voice held a sneaky edge of triumph.

"Okay," I said. "How'd you do it this time?"

"Easy," she said smugly. *"The police found your car for me at the Burbank parking lot. Air-traffic control gave me your flight and destination."*

"That's another hundred I owe you." We had a thing. Each time she tracked me down without my leaving word where I would be, she got a hundred dollars. Each time she missed I would get a month's free service. I had yet to collect.

"It seemed serious or I wouldn't bother you," she said. *"A Samuel Benjamin, Junior, called collect from San Francisco. He asked for Uncle Steve and said it was important."*

"Give me his number. I'll call him back."

"He was in a pay booth and said he couldn't stay there but that he would call again in half an hour. That is exactly twenty minutes from now."

"All right, when he calls, relay it through your switchboard."

"Any special room number?"

"No," I said. "Just have them page me at the crap table."

I put down the telephone and left the booth. Blonde Girl had fallen in love with a slot. "It's about ready to come," she said, her fingers caressing the level. "I can tell."

It came up a grapefruit, orange, and lemon. "Try sucking it," I said. I walked around the slots and there they were. Green table magic, with people stacked like sardines. With a money machine like this going for him, Johnston had to have rocks in his head to want the picture business.

I pushed my way up to the table just as a shooter sevened out. The stickman pulled in the dice and pushed them back with two more sets added for choice.

I looked around the table but nobody seemed to be reaching. They all had the look of players who didn't trust their luck. I picked up a set and rolled them between the palms of my hands to get the feel. They felt good. I nodded and laid a hundred on the pass line and covered with a hundred on any craps.

"New lucky shooter," the stickman called in a hoarse voice, pulling back the other dice. "Get your bets down. New shooter coming out."

I crapped out twice in a row, letting my cover bet ride. Third time I picked up the dice, I switched the bets. At six to one on any craps, I had forty-two hundred. I left two hundred on the any craps and went for two grand on the pass line. The other two thousand was in the box in front of me.

I naturaled twice, doubling, then came up with the ten point. I bought all the numbers and went on a wild ride. I needed ten pairs of hands to pick them up and lay them down and lost all track of time. I looked up in surprise when the major general came back with the page. "Your call's come through."

I nodded and picked up the dice. I rubbed them once and threw them. They snapped against the backboard and rolled over to a stop. I didn't have to look to know I sevened out. That's the way it is with dice. They were worse than girls. Take your attention away from them for even a moment and they went cold on you.

I picked up the chips from the box in front of me. When I turned around Blonde Girl was standing there. I gave her the chips. "Cash them in for me."

I followed the major general to the telephone. "Sorry, Mr. Gaunt," he apologized as he gave me the phone.

This time I laid a hundred on him. "No harm done," I said. "You probably saved me a fortune."

He went away smiling and I turned into the phone. "Okay, Diana," I said.

"I have Mr. Benjamin on the line for you."

"Good. Put him on. But stay on the line with me," I said. "I might need you for follow-through."

"Righto, Mr. Gaunt."

There was a click, followed by a faint hum. Over the hum came Junior's voice. *"Uncle Steve?"*

"Yes, Junior," I said.

"I'm in San Francisco."

"I know."

"I got big trouble," he said.

"What happened?"

"I'm up here with a couple of friends." His voice began to tremble. *"I went out for a few minutes this morning, when I came back there was fuzz all over the place. They were pushing everybody into the wagon. Afterward two of the fuzz in plainclothes hung around. I got a hunch they were waiting for me, so I ducked around the corner."*

"What was the bust for?" I asked.

"The usual thing," he said. *"Every now and then, the fuzz gets a bug up their ass. But there was no reason for them to grab us. We were nice and quiet and never made no trouble."*

"Was there anything in the apartment?"

"Not much," he said. *"We were all pretty low on dough. Some pot, a little speed, but no acid."*

"No hard stuff?"

"No shit, no coke, Uncle Steve," he said. *"We're all straight kids."*

"In whose name was the apartment?"

"I don't know," he answered. *"It was empty, so we just moved in. Every day a guy came around and we slipped him a few bucks and he went away."*

"You don't sound in any trouble to me, Junior," I said. "All you gotta do is shake that town for a while. They can't be after you. There's no records."

"I can't go like this," he said.

"If you need money, I'll shoot some up to you."

"It's not that." He hesitated. *"There's a girl. I'm worried about her."*

I knew about the girl. His father had told me that morning. But I wanted him to tell me. "Yes?"

"You see, she's pregnant. And she's a kid herself," he said.

"Your baby?"

"No. But she was such a sweet kid that we all kind of adopted her. We wouldn't even let her smoke or go on a trip."

"Then what are you worried about?" I asked. "They'll take good care of her. Better than you have."

"Maybe," he said. *"But will they love her?"*

I was silent.

"She's a very sensitive kid," he said. *"She needs to be loved, to know that someone cares. That's how she wound up like she did."*

I was still silent.

"I can't leave until I know she's all right," he said. *"You know, kind of let her know that I didn't run out on her like everyone else."* He took a deep breath. *"If I went up to Juvenile to see her alone, the way I am, they'd put the arm on me right away. I thought, maybe—if you had the time—"*

"Okay," I said. "I'll come up. Where are you now?"

"In a telephone booth on North Beach," he said.

"Got any money on you?"

"About six bits.

"Go over to the KSFS-TV offices on Van Ness across the street from the Jack Tar Hotel and ask for Jane Kardin in the legal department. By the time you get there she will be expecting you. Tell her what you told me and have her check out where they took your friend and arrange a visit. Wait there in her office for me. I'll be up on the next plane from Vegas.

His voice was suddenly very young. *"Thanks, Uncle Steve. I knew you wouldn't let me down."* He hesitated a moment. *"You think your friend would spring for a sandwich? I haven't had anything to eat all day."*

He was still a kid. "Sure. Go across the street to Tommy's Place. I'll look in there for you before I go up to the offices. Good-bye."

"Good-bye, Uncle Steve." He clicked off and I heard Diana come on.

"There's a Western Airlines flight leaving for San Francisco from McCarran in twenty minutes," she said. *"I made a reservation for you while you were talking."*

"Good girl. Now call Jane Kardin at Sinclair Broadcasting KSFS and tell her I'm coming up and to look after the kid until I get there."

"Will do, Mr. Gaunt," she said. *"'Bye, now."*

Blonde Girl was waiting when I came out of the booth, the money in her hand. "What's up?" she asked.

"What was Johnston paying you?"

"Five hundred a week and expenses," she said.

"How much you got there?" I asked, indicating the money in her hand.

"Twenty thousand three hundred," she said, handing it to me.

I took the money and counted off ten thousand and gave it back to her. I stuck the rest in my pocket. "That's for you."

She looked at me with big eyes. "What's it for?"

"Severance pay," I said, leaving her there in the casino. I went out and got into a cab. She came to the door just as the cab pulled away. She waved and blew me a kiss.

I blew a kiss back to her and by the time the cab pulled out onto the Strip, she had already gone back inside.

The way the good-bye rate for girls was climbing for me since this morning, if I wound up with one tonight I would have to keep her.

—

LOS ANGELES HAD BEEN HOT and muggy, Las Vegas, sun-bright and dry. San Francisco was wet and clammy. I shivered going into the airport from the plane. Blue jeans and a pullover weren't enough.

Jane Kardin was waiting at the ramp with a raincoat. I slipped into it gratefully. "Makes me wish I were still your boss, Lawyer Girl. So I could give you a raise for this."

"Since you're not my boss anymore, you can kiss me hello."

Her lips were warm and sweet. I looked at her. "Hmm. I had almost forgotten how good it was."

She smiled. "I've got my car outside."

I looked around as we began to walk. "What did you do with the kid?"

"I left him out at Tommy's Place eating his way out from under a mountain of knockwurst."

It turned into real rain by the time we got into the car. The windshield wipers began to click as we moved out.

"What did you find out about the girl?" I asked.

"She's gone."

"Gone?" I echoed.

She nodded without taking her eyes off the road. "By the time I tracked her down at Juvenile, her parents had already come and picked her up."

"What about Junior?" I asked. "He must have been upset."

"I thought he looked relieved," she said flatly. "After all, he is a man."

She was entitled to that one. I hadn't exactly been the gentlest of people with her. We were swinging pretty good. But that was almost four years ago. Before I left Sinclair and she wasn't a lawyer then. She was a model.

She came out of the Ford Agency in New York. I remember the way she had walked into El Morocco the first time I saw her. She had calm eyes and stood there looking around.

It was a premiere party and I went right up to her. "Can I help you, Miss—?"

The expression in her eyes didn't change. "I'm looking for John Stafford, the director."

I hadn't seen him and I wouldn't know him if I did. "He just left," I said promptly, taking her arm. "Let me get you a drink."

She looked around without moving, then back at me. "No, thank you," she said coolly. "I don't see anyone I recognize. And I don't like staying at parties where I don't know anyone."

"I'm Stephen Gaunt," I said. "And now you have no excuse."

She laughed. "They told me about New York men."

By this time we were moving. I made a signal and the maître d' fielded it. "Your table is just over here, Mr. Gaunt."

"You're from out of town?" I asked as we sat down.

"San Francisco," she said. She looked up at the maître d'. "Bourbon and ginger."

She liked sweet drinks, sweet talk, and sweet men. After about a week she decided I wanted too much, I wasn't sweet enough.

"You're looking to get married," I said.

"That's right. Anything wrong in it?"

I shook my head. "No."

"But it's not for you?"

"That's right."

"You're honest at least."

"Anything else I can do for you?" I asked.

"Yes," she said.

I looked at her, thinking *here it came.* They were all alike. She surprised me.

"I want a job."

"I'll send you over to the head of casting," I replied.

"Not that kind of a job."

"What kind of a job?"

"I just received word from home that I was admitted to the bar," she said.

I looked at her. "You're a lawyer?"

She nodded. "Modeling just helped pay the way. Now I want to work at it."

"You make more money as a model."

"So?"

"Okay," I said. "I'll send you in to see the head of Legal."

"I don't want to work in New York," she said. "I don't like it here. I want to work in San Francisco."

"There's more opportunity here."

"But I have family there. And friends. And I'd be much happier. Here everything is a turn-on."

Our station in San Francisco needed an attorney. She turned out to be good at it too. The proof was that she kept her job, even got a promotion after I had left.

She found a parking place next to the restaurant. Samuel was sitting behind a huge schooner of beer. "Hey, Uncle Steve, you know they got ninety-one kinds of beer here?"

"Wipe the foam off your whiskers and kiss me," I said. "It's been a long wet trip."

"I'm sorry, man," he said, shaking his head. "I didn't know she was goin' to hang us up like that. I wouldn't have bugged you."

"It's okay," I said, sliding into the seat opposite him. "I had nothing better to do.

Anyway I've been lookin' for an excuse to come up here and see Lawyer Girl for the longest time."

"Too much," said Lawyer Girl. "I'd better be going now."

"No you don't," I said, pulling her down onto the seat beside me. "We don't know whether we're out of trouble yet."

Samuel looked at her, then at me. He shook his head. "I should have known it."

"Know what?" I asked.

"You had to come up with the best lookin' legal brain in the world."

We all laughed as the waitress came to the table. "Beer all around," I said.

"No," Lawyer Girl interrupted. "Bourbon and ginger for me."

"I gotta go," he said, sliding out of his seat. "Be right back."

The waitress came with the drinks. I hoisted my glass. *"Ciao."*

"You finally made it."

I looked at her.

"You know I used to have little-girl dreams about you. That you would come up here someday and you'd be different somehow...." Her voice trailed off.

"I *am* different," I said. "I'm not your boss anymore."

She shook her head. "You're still the same. You belong. Wherever you are is where it's at. What made you think of me? I thought that by now you had forgotten."

I didn't answer.

"Or is it that you have a file cabinet somewhere in the back of your head and in every drawer there is a listing of girls in different towns that you can call on for various services? Is that it, Steve? Am I filed under Legal?"

"Okay, Jane," I said. "Did you get your money's worth?"

She flushed. "I apologize."

Samuel came back with a peculiar look in his eyes. He sat down easily and picked up his glass of beer.

"If you're goin' to turn on in public toilets," I said, "shave. The smell of pot sticks to your beard."

"I just used half a joint," he said defensively. "I was getting a little uptight."

"What for?" I asked. "You're out clean."

"You," he said. "Suddenly I got scared. I brought you up here on a jerkoff. You must think I'm pretty stupid."

"I know better than that. You didn't get me up here just because of the girl."

He looked at Lawyer Girl. She started to get up.

"Maybe I'd better go. You might have something personal to talk about."

I put my arm out to stop here. "You're in this. You didn't ask for it. You stay." I looked at him. "That right, Samuel?"

He nodded. She sank back into her chair.

"Okay, Samuel," I said. "Get it off."

He took a deep breath. "My father was up here the other day."

"So?"

"You know him, Uncle Steve. He did one of his tricks. He tried to lay a hundred on us. I told him we didn't want it. Later he sent his chauffeur back up with two fives." He took a sip of his beer. "He also wanted me to come home."

"Nothing wrong in that," I said. "After all, he is your father. And your mother isn't on cloud nine over what you've been doing either."

"Aw, come on, Uncle Steve, you're not going to get on my back, too?"

"Not me, Junior," I said. "The one thing I believe in is the right of every human being to go to hell in his own peculiar fashion. I don't give a shit what you do."

"I don't quite believe that. You care about me."

"True enough," I said. "I cared about your sister, too. But I couldn't live her life for her. And I can't live yours for you. All I can do is be there if you want me."

He drained his glass. "Can I have another beer?"

I signaled the waitress. She came with the beer.

"I do want you to help me," he said.

"How?"

"Doesn't it seem strange to you that the day after my father comes up to see me we get busted?"

"Is that what you think?"

He looked down at his glass. "He said he could blow the whistle if I didn't do as he wanted." He looked up at me. "I got to find out the truth, Uncle Steve. It's very important to me."

"How do you expect me to help you with that?"

"You ask him, Uncle Steve. He wouldn't lie to you."

"No. I have a better idea."

"What's that?" he asked hopefully.

"You ask him. After all, he's your father, not mine."

AFTERNOON

SHE WAS RIGHT THERE IN the parking lot where I left her before I went to Vegas. Gleaming black, her chrome shining in the slanting rays of the sinking sun.

Junior let out a low whistle as we came up to her. He ran ahead of me and touched the car reverently. "Too much," he said in a hushed voice.

I took the key out of my pocket and opened the door. He was in the car before I could move. He sat there, brushing his fingers lovingly over the fascia of the dashboard and the toggles, then leaned his head back and closed his eyes. "Smells like pussy."

I tapped him on the shoulder. "In the back."

He scrambled over the back of the seat like an overgrown monkey and rested his chin on the headrest, staring over at the dashboard as I got into the car. "Does it really do two-forty?" he asked, pointing at the speedometer.

"I don't know. I never had it all the way up."

Lawyer Girl got into the car. "I still don't know what the hell I'm doing here."

I grinned at her. "You were bored."

"I have a date tonight," she said defensively.

I gestured to the phone. "Call up and cancel it."

"Man, you got everything in this car," Junior said. "Where's the john?"

"Driving," I said. The phone began to buzz. I picked it up. "Okay, Diana. You're getting rich."

"The calls are piling up, Mr. Gaunt," she said. *"Messrs. Johnston and Diamond called from Vegas. They're on their way to see you. Mr. Benjamin called from the Beverly Hills Hotel, he wants you to call him. Mr. Sinclair called and asked me to tell you that he was at the Bel Air Hotel and would you please drive directly there from the airport."*

"Anything else?"

"That's all for the moment, Mr. Gaunt," she said sweetly.

She disconnected and I put the phone down and started the motor. The beginning roar faded into a steady hum. I put the car into gear and moved out of the parking lot. I got on the freeway smack in the middle of the rush-hour jam.

"Listen to that motor," Junior said from the back. "I can feel it in my balls."

"I'll never understand what men see in cars," Lawyer Girl said.

I caught Junior's eye in the rearview mirror. He shook his head. She was right. It was a private world. I snaked through the traffic and cut off the freeway at the next exit. I would make better time on the back roads.

Lawyer Girl picked up the telephone. "How do I work this thing?"

"Press that button down," I said. "When the operator comes on, give her the number you see printed on the receiver and the number you want."

She clicked the switch. A half minute later she was talking to her date in San Francisco. Honey dripped from her voice sickeningly. "Truly I am sorry, David. But this matter came up at the last minute and I couldn't call before now." There was a moment's silence, then when she began to speak again, her voice turned frosty. "You forget one thing, David. I am an attorney. And an attorney's first responsibility is to his client." She slammed the phone down.

I grinned at her. "So that's all I am to you. A client."

"Oh, shut up," she snapped. "Give me a cigarette."

"In the glove compartment," I said.

She opened it and took a cigarette from the tray I kept in there. She lit it, took a deep drag, and a peculiar look came over her face. "This tastes funny."

I sniffed the air. "That's pot. Regulars are on the right, menthols in the middle."

She started to throw it out the window. Junior's hand stopped her. "Fire zone," he said, taking the cigarette from her fingers. "Do you want to get a ticket?"

"What are you talking about?" she asked in an annoyed voice.

"Look," he said, jerking a thumb at the rear window behind him.

I looked into the mirror. The police car was on my tail. Junior put the cigarette in his mouth. "This is good hash."

I looked at Lawyer Girl. Her face was suddenly pale. I reached over and patted her hand. "Easy, Jane," I said. "Try a real cigarette."

She looked at me. "You're both crazy." Her hand was trembling under mine.

I took a cigarette from the glove compartment and lit it. I gave it to her.

She sucked the smoke deeply into her lungs. The color began to come back into her face. "I could be disbarred if they caught me with that."

I stopped for a traffic light and the police car pulled up next to us. "Beautiful car," the young patrolman called.

"Thank you," I said. "Want to drag?"

He grinned back at me. "Can't. I'm on duty."

The light changed and I let them pull out ahead of me. They went to the next corner and turned off. "Okay, Junior," I said. "Kill the reefer."

He started a protest, but then he caught a glimpse of my eyes in the mirror. Silently he pinched it out and put the roach in his pocket.

I turned onto Coldwater and began to climb up the mountain. The traffic had begun to ease off and I opened her up a little. She took the corners like a ballerina.

"Man, this is better than flyin'," Junior said.

I glanced in the mirror. He was doing fine. The reefer had hit him.

"Where we goin'?" he asked.

"I'm dropping you at my place," I said. "Then Lawyer Girl and I are going to a meeting with her boss."

—

THE BEST WAY TO DESCRIBE the Bel Air Hotel is Hollywood genteel. The conservative crowd went there. Spencer was waiting for me in his suite. No bungalows for him. He wanted every comfort close by, no long wait for service while the boys trotted a half mile with his breakfast.

He rose to his feet when we came in. The years were kind to him. He wore well. I took his hand. The grip was as strong and firm as ever. "This is a surprise," I said.

He smiled. "I'm glad to see you." And he meant it.

I introduced Lawyer Girl. "She works for you," I said. "House counsel at KSFS in San Francisco."

He turned on the charm. "No wonder they say the West is more progressive. Back East the lawyers don't look like you."

"Thank you, Mr. Sinclair."

"I wouldn't have called you like this. But some important matters came up that we must talk about." He looked at Lawyer Girl.

She picked up. "If you gentlemen have business to discuss, why don't I wait in the cocktail lounge?"

"Would you mind, my dear?" he asked. "I'd be very grateful."

We watched the door close behind her. He turned to me. "She seems a fine girl. Is she a good lawyer?"

"I imagine so," I answered. "They seem to like her up there."

"How about a drink?" he asked.

I nodded and followed him to the small bar set up in the suite. I mixed two Scotch and waters.

"Make mine light," he said.

I added more water and gave him the drink. "Okay?"

"Fine."

I followed him back to the couch and we sat down. He was silent for a few moments while we sipped our drinks. "I suppose you're wondering why?"

I nodded.

"I'm sixty-five," he said. "The board wants me to stay on for another five years. They're willing to change or waive the mandatory retirement rule."

"They're smart," I said.

"I don't want to," he said.

I sipped at the drink.

"It's three years since you left," he said. "It doesn't get easier and I can't keep up with it." He put down his drink and looked at me. "After the foundation and me, you're the biggest stockholder in the company."

I knew what he meant. The fifteen percent of the stock that came to Barbara from her own trust fund and her mother's estate. "I won't give you any problems," I said. "I gave you the voting privileges on it and I'll pass it on to anyone you tell me to."

After a few moments, he spoke. "That's not what I want."

"What is it then?"

"I want you to come back," he said.

I looked at him. Then I got up and went to the bar and made myself another drink. I drank some and went back and sat down.

"I have thirty percent, the foundation, twenty-five. With your stock, that's seventy percent," he said. "And there's no one around that I would trust with it."

"You've got some good men there," I said.

"They are good men," he said. "But they're not you. They are men who are working at their jobs. If another network wanted them tomorrow and the price was right, they would be gone. They're not Sinclair."

"You're the only Sinclair," I said.

"No, I'm not," he answered. "You're a Sinclair. And it's not just the name. It's an attitude, a being. You know what I mean.

I knew. What he was talking about was a way of life. A Sinclair didn't build a business for business's sake, or even the money. What they did was build monuments. Bridges to the future that would last after they were gone. He didn't understand that this was his monument. Not mine. I was silent for so long that he began to speak again.

"I never wanted you to leave. You know that."

I nodded. "It was the best thing to do. For all of us."

"I didn't agree with you then. I don't agree with you now," he said. "Others have made bigger mistakes and ignored them."

"They weren't me," I said.

"You and your sense of perfection. Don't you realize yet that no one—nothing—is perfect?"

"It wasn't that."

"What was it then?" he asked. "You did what you set out to do. You saved your stupid friend's business for him. He didn't care what happened to you. All he thought it would take to pay you off was money. What did you have to feel guilty about…? to punish yourself for? In the long run, no one was hurt. Not your friend. Not us. Only you."

"Not that, either," I said.

"Tell me, then. You owe me that much."

I said simply, "I wore out."

"I don't understand."

I sipped the drink. "It's not that difficult. I fought all the wars. Over and over again. And they were always the same wars. The ratings war. The talent war. The business war. How many wars do you have to win to prove yourself?

"Maybe I'd won too many. Maybe it was time I lost one just to taste the newness of defeat. At least it was something different."

"That's not all of it," he said.

He was smart. "True."

"What else was it?" he asked.

"I had a dream," I said. "I was part of the biggest opportunity man ever had to talk to man. And we were blowing it. Because of the wars. There was so much we could do. And we didn't."

"It's not too late," he said. "If you come back, you can shape it in your image. I'll support you."

"It is too late," I said. "It's gone past that now. Too much has happened. The whole thing has become too complex."

He looked at me. "I'm sorry."

I didn't say anything at all.

"Do you still mean what you said about voting your stock with me?" he asked.

"Yes."

"Would you have any objection if we sold the company?"

"None at all," I answered. "If you think that's best for it."

"I've been approached by several conglomerates," he said. "I haven't talked to them. Maybe now."

Something was beginning to happen. For the first time in what seemed like a hundred years, I began to turn on. "Do you mean that?"

He nodded. "Yes. Why?"

"I have an idea," I said. "Supposing I could show you how you could get all the financial benefits that would come by selling the company without really selling?"

"I've had merger offers before."

"Not the same thing," I said.

"What's different about it?"

It took me three minutes to explain it to him. I could see he was intrigued.

"Do you think you could do it?" he asked when I was finished.

"I don't know," I said. "Give me six hours and I'll let you know."

"You can have more than that," he said. "I'm in no hurry."

"I'll know in six hours. Where will you be this evening if I have to get in touch with you?"

"Right here," he said, an expression of surprise on his face. "Where did you think I would be? I'm too old for your kinds of games."

I turned left on Sunset from the Bel Air gate. It was dark and the headlights of the oncoming cars flicked on and off in our eyes.

"He's not at all what I thought he was," she said. "He's really quite charming."

"He can be when he wants to," I said.

"He's supposed to be as cold as ice," she said. "But he's not like that with you."

I looked at her. "In a kind of way we're still family."

"I don't understand," she said.

"I was married to his daughter once."

"Oh," she said. "I see." She took her own cigarette. I held the lighter for her. "Maybe you'd better take me to the airport now."

"Why?" I asked.

She drew on the cigarette. "You seem to be kind of involved tonight. I'd only be in the way."

"Don't be a fool," I said. "If I didn't want you down here, I wouldn't have asked you to come."

She was silent. "Do you want to go to bed with me, is that it?"

"Yes. Partly."

"What's the partly?"

"You're an attorney," I said. "Stick around. I may need one before the night is over."

I don't know whether she liked that. She didn't speak until we turned into the driveway at my house. I pulled into the carport and killed the lights.

She made no move to get out of the car. Like she was waiting to be kissed. I took her into my arms. Her lips were soft and warm and hungry. We clung together for a hard minute, then she broke away.

"Don't start," she said. "I can't go through that again."

"You seemed to survive all right."

"How do you know?" she asked. "I wasn't playing. Why do you think I ran back to San Francisco?"

"You had a job waiting."

"That's what I kept telling myself. That I was just another girl to you. That at times you didn't even remember my name. But it wasn't the way I felt."

I didn't answer.

"It's been more than three years," she said.

"Give me your hand."

She put her hand in mine. I could feel it trembling slightly. "I'm not a monster."

"Did you ever think about me? Once in the four years? Just once?"

"I thought about you this afternoon," I said. "Isn't that enough of an answer?"

"No." She withdrew her hand and looked at it. "Would you believe I haven't been with another man since you?"

"That explains it," I said. "No wonder you're so uptight. We'd better get inside."

She threw me an angry look and got out of the car, slamming the door. I caught her as she came around my side and held her.

"Is that all you think it is?" she snapped.

"It can still be pretty good," I said. "Don't knock it until you try it."

She pulled free of me and went up the walk to the house. I followed her.

I could hear the shouting voices as soon as I opened the door. We went down the steps past the bedroom.

Sam and Junior were standing in the center of the living room shouting at each other. For background they had the newscast of the latest riot at Berkeley on the television set.

"Hello," I said and walked around them and turned off the television.

"You're still not so big I can't knock you on your ass!" Sam shouted, moving toward Junior.

I slipped between them.

Junior grabbed my arm. "He told the pigs! He blew the whistle! Ask him, he doesn't even deny it!"

"Cool it!" I said sharply.

Junior stared angrily at me for a moment, then turned and stormed outside to the terrace. He lit a cigarette and stood there looking down at the city.

I turned back to Sam. He glared at me, his face still mottled with anger. "Isn't it enough that you cost me my daughter?" he said bitterly. "Do you have to take my son, too?"

BOOK THREE:
SAM BENJAMIN

HOLLYWOOD, 1960-1965

ONE

THE STUDIO POLICEMAN AT THE Trans-World gate waved to him as the limousine entered the lot. "Good morning, Mr. Benjamin."

"Good morning, John," Sam said, from the backseat. "It looks like it's goin' to be a nice day."

"Sure does, Mr. Benjamin," the policeman answered. "No smog."

The limousine rolled in and turned right on the road next to the gate. It moved past the first row of administration buildings and stopped before a two-story office located on a corner of its own. The car pulled into a parking place with a small sign: *RESERVED FOR MR. SAMUEL BENJAMIN.*

A maintenance man was polishing the brass plate next to the entrance, *SAMARKAND PRODUCTIONS.* He nodded as Sam went in. "Good morning, Mr. Benjamin."

"Good morning." Sam continued on down the corridor to his office. It took up the whole far corner of the building. He entered through his own door. At the same time his secretary entered from her office.

"Good morning, Mr. Benjamin."

"Morning, Miss Jackson," he said, going behind his desk.

She placed some papers before him. "Mrs. Benjamin just called. She said you forgot to take your gout pills before you left the house." She walked over to the bar and came back with a glass of water, which she gave him with two pills.

"Okay," he said, grumbling. He swallowed the pills. "I bet I'm the only man in the world ever to get gout eating kosher hot dogs."

She placed another pill before him. "What's that?" he asked suspiciously.

"Your diet pill," she said. "You're allowed fifteen hundred calories today. Mrs. B. said you had three hundred for breakfast and that you were going to have eight hundred at dinner. That means cottage cheese for lunch."

"Shit," he said. He swallowed the other pill. "Now can we go to work?"

"Yes, sir," she nodded. She picked up the papers from the desk and looked at them. "Rushes for *Washington Arch* will be at screening room three at eleven o'clock."

"Okay."

"Here are comparative box-office figures for *The Steel Rooster.* First seventeen engagements. It's running seventy to one hundred and twenty percent ahead of *The Sisters.*"

"Good," he said. "I'll look at them."

She consulted her notes. "Mr. Cohen called, from New York. He would like to speak to you, five o'clock his time."

He nodded.

"Mr. Luongo called from Rome. The new Barzini picture is now seven days behind schedule."

"That's par for the course," he said. "We've only been shooting for three weeks. Better call him back. I want to talk to him."

"Mr. Schindler and Mr. Ferrer of the production department would like a meeting with you at your convenience. They have the production estimates and budgets ready on *The Prizewinner* and would like to go over them with you."

"I'll see them before lunch," he said.

"Yes, sir. Mr. Craddock called. He would like to have lunch with you in his private dining room at twelve fifteen."

He looked at her. "I wonder what he wants?" Craddock was head of production and executive vice-president of Trans-World.

"Did you read the trades this morning?" she asked in an almost hushed voice.

"No," he answered.

She placed the *Hollywood Reporter* and *Variety* in front of him. "Look at the lead story in both papers."

They had almost the same headlines.

BENJAMIN NEW PRESIDENT TRANS-WORLD?

The stories were almost the same, too. Both made a big point of the fact that practically all the pictures Trans-World had in production or planning were his. They reviewed the success of the current release, *The Steel Rooster,* and gave highlights of his past successes, *The Sisters* and *The Naked Fugitives.*

He looked up at her. "First time I heard anything like this. Nobody spoke to me."

"It's been the big rumor around the lot the last few weeks," she said.

"I still don't know nothin' about it." But inside him he was flattered. "I have enough of my own headaches," he added. "Who needs any of theirs?"

"What shall I tell Mr. Craddock?" she asked.

He looked at her. "Twelve fifteen will be okay."

She left the office and a moment later had Charley on the telephone for him. He yelled into the transatlantic phone. "What do you mean seven days behind? What the hell's goin' on over there?"

—

RORY CRADDOCK WAS NOTHING LIKE his name, which suggested a big bluff Irishman. Instead when you walked into his office, you find a slim, intense man who ate Gelusils all day long to calm his constantly nervous stomach. For the past eight years he had been head of production for Trans-World. His secret for success was a simple one. He never approved a project until all his superiors urged him to do so. Once he had that, if anything went wrong it could not be said that he was to blame.

He sat at his desk staring at the trade papers. Nervously he popped another Gelusil into his mouth and studied the story. When he had first read it that morning, he had almost called New York to find out who had planted it and if there was any truth in it. But then he had thought twice about the call and didn't make it.

He had been around long enough to recognize the tactic. The story had been a feeler, an exploratory gesture on the part of the management to see how it would be accepted. He checked with the stockbroker. Apparently it had gone down well on the market. There was a great deal more activity than usual in Trans-World stock and the common had gone up almost two points.

He wondered what effect it would have on him. The Gelusil was almost completely dissolved by now, leaving a clayey taste in his mouth. He took a sip of water from the glass always on his desk.

That Benjamin might become president of the company was not important to him. But the fact that he might take charge of production was another story. Up to now there had been no threat to his area of responsibility. Impulsively he had called and asked Benjamin to lunch. Now he wondered whether that had been a wise move. One of his strong points was never to show concern. The next thing he had to do was legitimize the lunch.

He reached for another Gelusil, then stopped. The implication that it was his fault production at TW had come to a standstill had not been entirely true. There were several projects he had been ready to okay, but he had not been able to muster the support that he required. Two of them in particular he thought had a great chance.

One was the *Fatty Arbuckle Story.* He had a great screenplay based on a novelization of the scandal that had caused the industry to form its own censorship board. He had spoken to Jackie Gleason about playing in it.

The other was a remake on a grand scale of the old Zane Grey novel *Riders of the Purple Sage,* which had been one of Tom Mix's greatest successes. Gary Cooper had said he would do it if the script was right.

The Gelusil was still in his hand. He put it in his mouth and sucked on it. Suddenly he had the idea. It was so good and so simple he was surprised that he had not thought of it before. It would serve all his purposes. Answer the critics about his lack of production and show Benjamin that he was in his camp just in case there was any truth in the rumor.

TWO

"GO RIGHT IN, MR. BENJAMIN," the secretary said, opening the door to the inner office. "Mr. Craddock is expecting you."

"Thank you." Sam went into Craddock's office. The door closed softly behind him. He stood there a moment.

Craddock rose from behind his desk, hand outstretched. "Good morning, Sam," he said. "So glad you could come over."

Sam took his hand. The way Craddock had spoken, you would think Sam had come a thousand miles to see him instead of just across the studio street. "Morning, Rory."

Craddock came out from behind the desk. He took off his glasses and put them on top of a pile of scripts, making sure that Sam noticed them. Sam picked up the cue. "You read all those?"

Craddock gestured modestly. "Part of the job. You can't imagine how much crap I have to go through each week just to find something worthwhile. Sometimes I think I need another pair of eyes."

Sam was properly impressed. "I never could do it. Haven't the patience."

"That's my job," Craddock said. He pressed down the button on the intercom.

"Yes, Mr. Craddock?"

"We're going upstairs now," Craddock said. "Hold all calls."

"Yes, Mr. Craddock. Enjoy your lunch."

Craddock released the key on the intercom and turned to Sam. "Hungry?" He led the way to the staircase to the private dining room.

"I'm always hungry," Sam said. "But I'm on a diet." He climbed the steps ahead of Craddock. They came out on the small terrace that had been enclosed in glass to make the dining room. It commanded a view of the entire studio.

"Everybody's on a diet," Craddock smiled. "That's why we have two menus. The diet lunch or the regular."

"What's the difference?" Sam asked.

"The regular is a thick New York steak, French fries, and salad with Roquefort dressing. The diet is a hamburger patty very lean with cottage cheese and sliced tomatoes."

"Aah, fuck it," Sam said. "I'll have the regular."

The colored butler bowed. "Mr. Craddock, Mr. Benjamin, sirs. May I have your requirements for a libation?"

"My usual. Dry sherry," Craddock said.

Sam looked at the butler. "Scotch on the rocks." He turned back to Craddock. "There goes the diet. The hell with it."

Craddock smiled.

"You wouldn't believe it," Sam continued. "But I figured out that I lost over fifteen hundred pounds dieting the last ten years. So why am I still two hundred ten?"

The butler came back with the drinks on the tray. Sam took his. "Cheers," he said.

"Cheers," Craddock said.

They drank.

"Might I be so bold as to ask the way you would like your steak done, Mr. Benjamin, sir?" the butler bowed.

"Rare," Sam said.

"Thank you most exceedingly, sir." The butler bowed again and disappeared into the pantry.

Sam turned to Craddock. "Where did he learn to talk like that?"

Craddock laughed. "Remember the Arthur Treacher pictures? I think Joe saw them all." He led the way to the table. "I hear the *Washington Arch* rushes look just great."

Sam nodded. "They're coming along."

"You're getting everything you want at the studio? Services, cooperation?"

"Couldn't be better," Sam said.

The butler placed the salad in front of them. Sam began to eat voraciously, Craddock toyed with his. He never ate salad, anyway. It was too much for his delicate stomach.

"I suppose you're wondering why I called this morning?" Craddock asked.

Sam nodded, without speaking. His mouth was full.

"We're very happy to have you here at Trans-World," Craddock said. "And we've been cudgeling our brains trying to find a way to implement our association."

Sam looked at him. He still did not speak.

"You know you are one of the three producers in the business now whose name the public recognizes?"

Sam shook his head. "No."

"There are only two others I can name," Craddock said. "Hal Wallis and Joe Levine. All the others are just known to the trade."

"I never thought of that," Sam said.

"It's true," Craddock said. "And you did it with only a few pictures in a few years. They spent all their lives at it."

Sam didn't speak.

"We're very interested in any other properties you might have in mind," Craddock said.

"I'm looking at some things," Sam said. "But beyond *The Prizewinner* I have nothing definite yet."

"Too bad." He seemed to be sincere. "We would like to do more."

The butler laid their steaks down. Sam looked at his. Hot, charcoal-blackened, with a patty of parsley butter melting right on the middle of it. The juices flooded into his mouth. He cut into it. Everything was right. Blood-rare and tender.

"Did you ever think of producing some pictures for someone else?" Craddock asked. "Other than your own company?"

Sam shook his head.

"It would be a way to fill in your time," Craddock said. "While you were preparing your own properties."

"I'm not really a producer," Sam said.

Craddock laughed. "If you're not a producer, I wish we had ten more like you."

Sam was silent. He still didn't know what was up Craddock's sleeve. But the steak was good and what the hell, it beat eating a diet lunch. "What have you got in mind?"

"I may be talking out of turn," Craddock said. "But I think I can get the boys back East to go along with me. I think we ought to make a ten-picture deal."

"Ten pictures?" Sam was surprised.

Craddock nodded. "You do five pictures for us, we finance five pictures for you. On our pictures we pay you double the producer's fee you charge your own pictures and give you fifty percent of the profits. Your pictures we do the same way as we do now, only we reduce our share of the profits to twenty-five percent of the foreign instead of the present fifty percent."

Sam finished his steak. "It's an interesting idea."

"I think it's a practical one," Craddock said. "And good for both of us."

Sam nodded. There was something in what Craddock said. Two hundred and fifty thousand dollars producer's fee was a lot of money per picture. And there was no sweat in it. He didn't have to chase the property, the script. All he would have to do was to ride herd on it. It all depended on the properties, however. He couldn't allow them to saddle him with their dogs. "Would I have approvals?"

"Absolutely," Craddock said. "We wouldn't dream of asking you to do something you wouldn't want to. You would have all approvals. Script, director, cast. That goes without saying."

"Do you have anything in mind?" Sam asked.

Craddock nodded. "I have two great ones ready right now. The only thing I need is the right kind of producer. One is a Western that could be for Gary Cooper, the other for an actor like Jackie Gleason. In the right hands they're both big winners."

Sam looked at him. With actors like those, the pictures could be shlock. The actors themselves were too good and too expensive.

"Look," Craddock said. "Let me send the two scripts over to you. You read them and then we'll talk some more."

"Good idea," Sam said.

The butler appeared beside the table. He bowed. "And now, gentlemen, sirs, for dessert we have hot Washington State delicious apple pie with vanilla and chocolate ice cream *á la mode.*"

Sam was completely destroyed. "I'll take it all," he said.

It wasn't until after lunch, as he walked back across the studio street, that he realized not once had Craddock mentioned the story in that morning's trade papers.

THREE

"STEVE."

He rolled over on his back in the warm sand. He put up an arm to shield his eyes from the sun, already beginning its plunge into the Pacific. "What is it, Golden Girl?"

She crawled across the sand to him and placed an arm on either side of his chest and looked down at him, blocking the sun.

He dropped his arm to her thigh. Her flesh was as warm as the sand under him. He waited quietly.

"You were far away," she said.

"Not really," he answered.

"What were you thinking?"

Strange how alike they were. All of them. After a while they wanted to crawl inside your head. "Nothing," he said. "Maybe just that I wish there were a thousand days like this. No telephones, no people, no problems."

"You wouldn't be happy," she said.

He thought for a moment. "I guess not."

"Are you up to a party tonight?" she asked.

He didn't answer.

"I know it's not what I promised. But it's Sunday night and tomorrow you're going back East, anyway, and I have to start looking for work sometime." He still didn't speak.

"Ardis called me this morning while you were sleeping. The Gavins are giving a party at their new house in the Colony. It's for Sam Benjamin, the producer. Bobby Gavin just got the second lead in the Western he's doing with Gary Cooper and says there's a great part in it for a girl and that I'm just right for it."

"You go," he said. "I won't mind."

"No." She shook her head. "I promised to stay with you. If you won't go, I won't."

He knew better. Whether he took her or not, she would not go to the party alone. Even if she had to call her fag hairdresser.

"Bobby says I've got a good chance for it, too. This is one job Benjamin can't give his girlfriend."

"Girlfriend?"

"Yes," she answered. "Marilu Barzini. She's got the wrong accent. Ardis also told me he's bringing her to the party with him."

"Okay."

"Okay, what?"

"Okay, we'll go," he said.

The house was not that large, but it had a great terrace extending over the sandy beach toward the ocean and the crowd spilled out into the warm night. Someday Bobby Gavin would be a star. That is, if his wife Ardis had anything to do with it.

She was at the door as they entered. "Selena!" she exclaimed. She turned to Steve. "And you came, too. I'm so glad."

"I wouldn't miss one of your parties, Ardis," he said, kissing her cheek.

"Go on inside and grab yourself a drink," she said. "There are loads of fun people around."

They left her as she turned to other arrivals and pushed their way into the crowd toward the bar. It was not easy. Selena was a very popular girl and having Steve with her did not hurt. By this time it was well known in Hollywood that the president of Sinclair Broadcasting did not attend many parties.

They finally made it to the bar. Steve turned back to the room, a Scotch in his hand. Selena was off with some friends. The noise pressed down on him after the quiet of the day on the beach and he moved outside to the terrace. He stood there at the railing looking at the ocean.

On the horizon were the lights of a coastal steamer. The breakers spent themselves on the beach. It had been almost a year since he had seen Sam. Almost a year since Sam made his new deal with Trans-World.

Somehow he could never see Sam in the Hollywood environment. There was something completely alien about the little man. But he had come out and he had the big house in Beverly Hills and the children went to the Beverly Hills School and Denise.... He wondered about Denise. He felt an odd disturbance over the news that Marilu was Sam's girlfriend. That was not in character for Sam, either.

He pushed it from his mind. It was none of his affair, anyway. They were all adults and had their own lives to live. Chances were that none of them approved much of his own way of life.

Sam and Marilu arrived late. Late by Hollywood standards. Ten thirty. At that hour, the guests were beginning to leave. Monday was a workday and those who were working had to be at the studios early and those who were not working would not let it show.

There was a sound of greeting at the entrance. "I was beginning to worry you couldn't make it," he heard Ardis say.

Steve turned to watch. The whole party seemed to gravitate toward Sam and Marilu. Sam was smiling, his face slightly flushed and perspiring. He'd already had a few drinks before he got there.

Marilu was standing beside him. Steve looked at her. There was no doubt about it. Whenever she came into a room all the other women paled by comparison. She stood next to Sam, with the inner air of assurance that only a woman truly secure in her beauty can achieve.

Someone put a drink in Sam's hand and he gulped it thirstily. "We were held up by a call from Rome," he was explaining, when he saw Steve watching him from outside. He stopped speaking suddenly, a kind of embarrassment crossing his face. Then he finished his drink and made his way out to the terrace.

"Steve!" he exclaimed. He embraced him and kissed him on both cheeks, European fashion. "Why didn't you let me know you were in town? We could have arranged something."

"It was a quick trip," Steve said. "Just the weekend. I'm back to New York tomorrow."

"You should have called me, anyway. It's been too long."

"You've been busy."

"Not too busy for you. Never too busy for old friends." Marilu came up to them. "By the way," he added, "do you know Marilu Barzini?"

Steve bowed. "We met at the Academy Awards. But it was brief, almost two years ago, and there were many people around."

"Steve Gaunt," Sam said to Marilu.

Marilu nodded. "I remember. You're the young man who runs the television. Sam spoke of you from Rome when we were talking about making *The Sisters.*"

Steve stared. The telephone conversation came back to him. So it had begun even then. She had been the girl in the room with Sam. "You have a fantastic memory."

"I never forget anything." The way she said it made Steve believe it. She would never forget anything that was important to her or her career.

Someone came and pulled Sam away, leaving Marilu with him. "Can I get you a drink?" he asked politely.

"Champagne."

He signaled one of the waiters. The champagne was in her hand in a moment. Steve lit a cigarette. "Are you enjoying your stay here?"

She smiled. "I like America."

"Do you plan to stay long?"

She shrugged her shoulders. "Sam has a picture he wants me to do, then they want to sign me for two others afterward."

"How nice. What picture?"

She made a face. "A Western. Can you imagine that? Me, in a Western. But Sam says it is a very good script. And it is with Gary Cooper."

Steve looked across the room. Selena was watching them. Suddenly he was tired. He hoped she would not find out tonight that there was no chance for her to get the job.

"I owe you my thanks," Marilu said.

He was startled. His mind had been away. "Thanks? For what?"

"That time in Rome," she said. "If you had not encouraged him the picture might never have been made."

"The picture would have been made."

Sam came back to them. He took Marilu's arm possessively. "We have to be going. There's another party I promised to drop in on."

"Too bad," Steve said dryly.

"Yes," Sam said. "I wish you were staying over a few days. There's so much I'd like to talk to you about."

"I have a board meeting in New York that I can't miss."

"You call me the next time you get in town," Sam said.

Steve nodded. His eyes caught a glimpse of Golden Girl. Obeying an impulse, he gestured to her. "Just one moment, Sam. There's an actress I'd like you to meet."

Golden Girl came up to them. Sam turned toward her. "Golden Girl, I'd like you to meet Sam Benjamin," Steve said. "Sam, this is Selena Fisher. She might be just the girl for that Western you're doing."

Sam looked at him. "That's cast already. The announcement's going out tomorrow. Marilu's going to do it." He turned back to Selena. "But you come in to see me, my dear. I'm sure there are other things that I am doing for which you would be right."

Over Sam's head, Steve met Marilu's eyes. They were cool and green. Green like a savage animal in the night. He smiled at her. She did not smile back. It was like a declaration of war.

He knew.

She knew.

Sam did not.

FOUR

THEY GOT INTO THE BACKSEAT of the limousine. "Dave Diamond's place in Bel Air," Sam told the chauffeur.

"No," Marilu said. "Take me back to the hotel."

"It will be just a few minutes, honey," he said. "I promised Dave I'd stop in for a nightcap on the way home."

"No," she repeated stubbornly. "I have had enough of those stupid parties."

"But it's important. Dave's coming up with the financing for your next two pictures."

"If it is that important, then drop me at the hotel and you go." She drew back into the corner of the seat, turning her face away from him, looking out the window at the traffic on the Coast Highway.

"Okay." He said to the driver, "Change that to the hotel."

They were silent until the car turned onto Sunset Boulevard and began to climb into the hills toward Los Angeles. "What's bugging you?"

"Nothing."

"It's got to be something," he said. "You were fine when the evening started."

She didn't answer.

He reached for her hand, but she shook him off. "Okay. Have it your way."

They didn't speak until the car reached the outskirts of Brentwood. The lights of a small shopping center faded behind them as she turned to him.

"Are you going to stay the night?"

He shook his head. "No."

"Why not?" she asked.

"Jesus, honey. I've already stayed out one night this week," he said. "I only got so many excuses I can pull on Denise. She'd kill me."

She made her voice deliberately contemptuous. "If she does not know by now she must be stupid."

He didn't answer.

"You American men are cowards," she went on. "I can understand not divorcing. There are many reasons. Property. The tax. But Nickie did not hesitate for one minute. He left his wife and moved in with me."

"This isn't Europe," he said defensively. "It's different here. They don't accept things like that."

"So I must live alone in a hotel like some *putana* you visit when you have the need?"

He reached for her hand and held it this time. "That's not true, honey," he said earnestly. "And you know it. You know how I feel about you."

"How do you feel about me, Mr. Benjamin the great producer?"

"Don't get sarcastic," he said. "I love you."

"If you love me then you would stay with me tonight. Tonight I need you. You know how I hate to sleep alone."

"I can't," he said desperately.

She burrowed her hand into his lap. "You know how I like to sleep. With my hand holding you. All night."

"Don't make it worse for me," he said. "Maybe I can work something out tomorrow night. I promised I would be home tonight."

"You promised!" She pulled her hand back violently. She began to cry.

"Marilu!" Clumsily he tried to stroke her hair.

Viciously she struck his hand away. "Don't touch me!" she sobbed.

He felt the blood come up on the back of his hand where her fingernails had raked him. He put his hand to his mouth and sucked on it.

"I don't know why I listened to you," she sobbed. "Nickie told me you were not like him. That you did not care for me as he did. That you only wanted to use me."

"Use you?" He was angry, the entire scene was too much for him. "Use you, you cheap guinea cunt? I got you up to a half a million dollars a picture and a piece of the gross and you say *I* used *you?* You came for one reason only. You go where the money is."

She stopped sobbing abruptly. This was the first time he had ever raised his voice to her. The expression on her face changed. "You do love me" she said in a suddenly sure voice.

"Of course I love you, you bitch," he snapped at her. "Why the hell else do you think I am with you? Risking my marriage, the laughter of my friends who think I'm an old man grabbing for his last hard-on?"

She took his hand and pressed it to her lips, tasting the blood on it. "I hurt you," she half crooned. "I'm sorry, your baby is sorry."

He let out a deep breath. "It's all right. Forget it."

The limousine turned into the driveway of the Beverly Hills Hotel. She moved closer to him on the seat. "Will you come in for just a little while?"

He didn't answer.

"I promise not to keep you too long," she said, turning the palm of his hand to her mouth and letting the tip of her tongue reach into it. "Just long enough to show you I am really sorry."

Her ideas of a little time and his were completely different. He felt the weariness seeping through him. "Tomorrow night. I must be up very early in the morning."

"You promise?"

He nodded.

"You are no longer angry with me?"

"No."

The limousine stopped and the chauffeur got out and walked around to the door. He opened it and stood there waiting.

"It was your friend," she said abruptly.

Sam was surprised. "My friend?"

"Yes," she said. "The television man. It was the way he looked at me. He did not like me."

"You're mistaken," he said. "Steve is a big fan of yours."

"No. He does not like me. I could tell. Else why did he call that girl over for the part in the picture?"

"He didn't know you were going to play it."

"Yes, he did," she said. "I told him just before you came back. Still he called her over, anyway."

Sam said nothing.

"It is maybe because he is a good friend of your wife's that he looks at me like that."

"Like what?"

"Like I am a tramp." She got out of the car. "I do not want to see him again."

He got out beside her. "I'm sure you're mistaken. Steve isn't like that at all."

"He is your friend. I will not say any more," she said. "It is not right for a woman to come between two friends."

"The next time he comes out, I'll arrange a luncheon," Sam said. "Just the three of us. You'll see you were mistaken."

"Maybe." She turned her cheek for his good-night kiss. "Good night, Sam."

He stood there until she disappeared into the hotel and then wearily got back into the car. All he could think of was climbing into bed and going to sleep. He hoped Denise was not waiting for him. He wasn't up to telling a lot of lies about tonight.

—

DENISE WAS IN BED WHEN she heard the car enter the driveway. She put down the book she had been reading and listened. She heard the creak of the front door, then his footsteps mounting the stairs. Quickly she turned off the light, pulling up the covers.

The bedroom door opened softly and some of the light from the hall spilled into the room. She closed her eyes tightly and tried to make her breathing soft and even. He came silently into the room and she could sense him looking down at her. She did not move and after what seemed a long time, he turned and went away.

She listened in the dark to the soft, quiet sounds of him undressing. The dull thud of the shoes, the rustle of his shirt and trousers. She heard him go into the bathroom, then into the adjoining guest room to sleep.

She turned her face into the pillow and began to cry. They were soft, stifled sobs. Hollywood. She hated it.

FIVE

"I'M A ONE-MAN STUDIO," Sam bragged uninhibitedly. "When *Look, Mama, the Fat Clown's Crying* starts shooting tomorrow, it will make the seventh picture I have in production this year. Not bad for a guy his second year in Hollywood, is it?"

Steve watched him across the table. Sam's enthusiasm was contagious. "Not too bad," he agreed.

Sam looked around the crowded studio commissary and leaned toward Steve, lowering his voice. "You know when I came out here you could shoot clay pigeons in this restaurant. Now it's packed with people. Most of them working on my pictures." His voice lowered still further. "You know they say Rory Craddock would have been out of here if he hadn't made the deal with me. I'm supporting the whole fucking place."

Steve laughed. "But what do you have to do to get a drink around here?"

Sam's face fell. "Damn, that's one thing I should have thought of before we left my office. All you can get here is wine or beer. But I didn't want to be late. Marilu is joining us on her lunch break."

"Can I get a beer?"

Sam signaled the waitress. "Beer for Mr. Gaunt." He turned back to Steve. "I'm glad you called me. I wanted you to get to know Marilu. She's a wonderful girl besides being a great actress."

The waitress put the beer in front of Steve. "How's her picture going?"

"Fantastic," Sam said. "The rushes are unbelievable. When Coop couldn't do the picture because of a conflict, I thought we were heading for the crapper. But then I came up with Jack Claw and he's great. But it's Marilu who makes the big difference. She puts the class into it, so that it's not just another Western."

"I'm glad." Steve looked across the table at Sam. "How are Denise and the kids?"

"Denise is just fine," Sam said. "And they're right about this place. It's the greatest in the world to bring up children. You should see them. They love it out here."

"I'd like to see them," Steve said.

"Sure thing," Sam said, "I'll fix it up one night. You'll come over the house for dinner. I'll get Denise to send over to the kosher butcher on Fairfax for some of that favorite *brust flanken* of yours."

"Just let me know," Steve said. "My mouth's watering already."

A hum of noise came from the entrance. Steve did not have to look to know that Marilu had arrived. She paused there, signing autographs for the visitors, and then came down the aisle toward their table. They rose.

Sam stepped out into the aisle to make room for her between them on the banquette. He kissed her cheek. "You look marvelous, dear."

"This makeup is terrible," she said. "But you're kind." She turned to Steve. "So nice to see you again, Mr. Gaunt."

He took her outstretched hand. "My pleasure, Miss Barzini."

"We're so formal it's not American," she said. "Please call me Marilu."

"If you call me Steve."

She looked at his glass. "Is that beer?"

He nodded.

"I'm so thirsty, do you mind?" She picked it up and drank from it. She put it down with a sigh. "We were on the back lot all morning and the sun was so hot."

Sam called the waitress. "Two more beers. Aah—the hell with it. Make it three beers. I've had enough of this diet-drink crap."

The waitress nodded. She stood there. "The usual for lunch, Mr. Benjamin?"

"Yes," he said. He looked at Steve. "The food isn't bad. You can order almost anything without being poisoned."

Marilu didn't eat, she pushed the food around while Sam picked the French fries off her plate. Steve finished his steak and sat back with his coffee.

"Do you spend much time out here, Steve?" Marilu asked.

"Quite a bit," he said. "Almost half my time. I'm wondering if it isn't a good idea to move my offices out here."

"Sooner or later, you'll have to," Sam said. "This is where the action is."

The waitress came to the table. "Your office is on the phone, Mr. Benjamin. Shall I bring the phone to the table?"

Sam shook his head. "Don't bother. I'll be quicker if I take it at the desk."

They watched him go down the aisle and pick up the telephone. He began to talk rapidly into it.

"He works too hard," Marilu said. "He never stops."

Steve looked at her without answering.

She returned his gaze evenly. "Do you work like that also?"

He shrugged his shoulders. "Yes and no."

"That's a very European answer," she said.

"I try not to. But I get caught sometimes."

"You are like all Americans," she said. "Business comes first. Then if there is any time left over and you are not too tired, there are other things."

He smiled, but there was no amusement in his eyes. "I'm not biting."

She returned his smile but also without amusement. "You do not like me." It was more a statement than a question.

"I didn't say that."

"My English is not that good. Perhaps I say it better like this. You do not approve of me."

"I don't think it matters. It is none of my affair."

"You are very American. So correct," she said. "But you are his friend and you think I am not good for him."

"Are you?"

"I think so. In many ways. For his career, for his—what do you say—ego?"

He didn't answer.

"Sometime in every man's life there should be a woman like me," she said. "I am better for him than some cheap little starlet who will try to take him for everything. I give him as much as he gives me. With me he is a man."

"He always was a man," Steve said.

Sam came back to the table, his face flushed and angry. "Goddamn idiots!" he said, sitting down. He looked at Marilu. "I'm sorry, but I have to break our dinner date. The director and the writers are in a hassle over the script and I have to meet with them tonight to settle it. We begin shooting in the morning."

"Oh," said Marilu. "And I've made plans. I was cooking pasta myself tonight."

Sam looked at her, then at Steve. "I have an idea. Why don't you have dinner with her? And if I get through early enough I'll join you afterward."

"Perhaps Steve has another engagement?" Her eyes rose to meet Steve's gaze. There was a hint of challenge in her voice.

"I don't."

"Good," Sam smiled. "You've never really tasted pasta until you've eaten it the way she makes it."

"I'm looking forward to it already. What time and where?"

"Eight o'clock. Bungalow three, Beverly Hills Hotel," she said.

"That makes it easy. I'm staying there, too."

She got to her feet. "I'm due back on the set."

They watched her leave and Sam turned back to Steve. "I'm so glad you didn't turn her down," he said. "Do you know, the poor kid thought you didn't like her?"

—

HE CAME FROM THE COOL dark of the air-conditioned Polo Lounge and stepped out the side doors into the heat of the fading day. He blinked for a moment and then walked along the flower-scented path. Bungalow three was just past the accounting offices. He climbed the steps and pressed the bell.

After a moment, the door opened. A dark-haired middle-aged woman in a maid's black dress answered the door. She curtsied. *"Signore."*

It was only slightly cooler inside. He glanced toward the windows. They were wide open.

Marilu came into the room as he turned back from the windows. "You can't eat pasta in an air-conditioned room," she said. "It does something to it."

"Yes," he said. "It makes it cold."

She looked at him not knowing whether he was being sarcastic. "Yes."

"I'm sorry," he said quickly. "It was just a wisecrack."

She smiled. "I do not understand American humor quite good yet."

"You will," he said. "It just takes time."

"Let me take your jacket."

He suddenly noticed she was wearing an ordinary cotton housedress that couldn't have cost more than three dollars at the Broadway stores, and no makeup. He took a deep breath. It made no difference what she wore. She was a for-real woman.

She took his jacket and placed it in a closet. "There are drinks on the bar," she said. "Help yourself. You can also take off your tie. I have to go back into the kitchen."

He watched her leave the room. It was all there under the housedress. Nothing but her. He was sure of that from the way it clung damply to her body. He pulled his tie loose and went over to the bar.

He was in the midst of pouring himself a large Scotch when her voice came from the kitchen. "Don't take too large a drink. I don't want you to lose your taste."

"Don't worry, Italian Girl," he said. "I'm just beginning to acquire one."

SIX

THE MEAL WAS SIMPLICITY ITSELF. First the antipasto, with the celery and the lettuce crisp, the radishes and scallions firm and crunchy, garnished with a chilled can of tuna, thin slices of Genoa salami, black and green olives, and tiny red and green peppers. Then the pasta. *Lasagna al forno.* Al dente with a delicious sauce and folded with layers of meat and pieces of Italian sausage. The Chianti classico was chilled just enough, and for dessert there was *zabaglione* which she beat at the table herself. Black, strong *espresso* from a little machine placed in the center of the table and that was the end of it.

He leaned back in his chair. "I don't believe it. I ate so much."

"Not as much as I."

"I don't know where you put it." It was true.

She had eaten like it was going out of style. She laughed. "I have more experience than you."

The maid came and began clearing the table. Marilu got to her feet. "Let's go back into the living room."

The telephone rang. She went to the small desk and picked it up. "Hello."

It was Sam.

She listened to him speak for a moment. "I'm sorry," she said. "Yes, tomorrow then." She looked over at Steve. "Sam would like to talk with you."

Steve took the telephone from her hand. Sam's voice was in his ear. *"I'm hung up here, I can't get over. Was I right about the pasta?"*

"You were right."

"How long you going to be in town? I want to get together with you. I have some ideas."

"A few days."

"Tomorrow will be rough," Sam said. *"But the day after?"*

"Good for me," Steve said. "Just have your girl call my office with the time."

"Okay," Sam said. *"Thanks."*

Steve was surprised. "For what?"

"For being nice to my girl. I appreciate that."

He rang off and Steve put down the telephone. Marilu was standing at the bar. She turned to him with two glasses of Fior d'Alpi in her hands. He felt the trembling in her fingers when he took his glass from her. "Are you all right?"

She nodded. "I'm fine."

"You must be exhausted," he said. "Working all day in that heat, then coming back here and cooking. I'd better go and let you get some rest."

"No," she said tightly. "Don't go."

"You'll feel better if you get into bed."

"I'm fine," she said. "I didn't cook that meal. I had it catered. Billy Karin's Casa d'Oro on Santa Monica Boulevard. He's the only one that cooks it like we do at home."

"You're kidding."

"You look shocked," she said. "Why should you be? This is Hollywood. Nothing is what it seems, nothing is real."

He didn't speak.

"I can't cook," she said. "I never learned. When I was fourteen years old in Marsala, a film director who came to our town with his company saw me. I was big even then. Two weeks later I went to Rome with him. My father was glad. He had seven other mouths to feed."

She turned away suddenly. "You see, Sicilians aren't quite as tight about their honor as they would have you think. It's amazing how far ten thousand lire went then."

Ten thousand lire was less than twenty dollars. "I'm sorry."

"Why should you be?" she said with her back to him. "I learned something from my father. That everything has its price. Even honor. And I've done well with that lesson.

"After the director, there were others. There was always someone. And now it's Sam." She turned around. "So you were right about me."

He saw the tears standing in her eyes. "Not entirely. Are you in love with him?"

She met his gaze. "No. Not in the sense you mean it. But I do love him in my own way. I respect him."

"Then why?" he asked. "You don't have to do it anymore. You're a star now."

"I say that to myself. But I don't believe it," she answered. "I'm afraid. I'm afraid if I don't have someone, I will fail."

"It's not true," he said. "Whatever you are, no one did it for you. You did it yourself. You were there in front of the camera. You, alone. Not someone, but you. Up there on the screen in front of the whole world. You."

She raised her glass to him. "You're a very kind man, Stephen Gaunt. Thank you."

"You're a very beautiful woman, Italian Girl, and whether you cooked it or not, it's still the best pasta I ever tasted."

"And what about you?" she asked. "You don't talk much about yourself."

"There's not much to talk about."

"None of them have anything to talk about. But they manage. They never stop. But I have seen you twice now and each time you just listen. They are all busy telling how great they are. But not you. Are you great?"

"I'm the best there is."

She looked at him seriously. "I believe that. Are you married?"

"No," he said. "I was."

"Divorce?"

"She died."

"Oh." A look of sympathy came to her face. "Did you love her?"

"Yes." He hesitated. "I never knew how much, though, until it was too late."

"That is the way it is. We never really have appreciation for the things we have."

He glanced at his watch. "It's eleven o'clock. I'd better go if you want to look good tomorrow morning in front of that camera."

"I am not working tomorrow."

He was curious. "What do you do on your days off?"

"Tomorrow I have some fittings in the morning. Then I come back here and wait for Sam to call. If he can, we will have dinner together."

"And if he can't?"

"Then I will have dinner alone. Watch some television and go to bed. The day after will be better though. I am working then. It is always better when I am working."

"Don't you go out? To the movies? Anyplace?"

She shook her head. "No. How would it look? Marilu Barzini, the star, going out alone? But it's all right. I am used to it."

"It's not good," he said. "To lock yourself up like that."

"It will not be for long," she said. "I have made up my mind. I am not signing the contracts for those other two pictures. I am going back to Italy. There I can be free. I am at home."

"Does Sam know that?"

"No. How could he? I just made up my mind tonight."

"Will you come through New York on your way back?"

"If you ask me to," she said.

"I'm asking you."

"Then I will come."

He moved toward her and she came into his arms. She rested her head against his chest and they stood together for a long time. Then he turned her face up to him and kissed her gently. "Good night, Italian Girl."

"Good night, Stephen Gaunt."

He picked up his tie from the couch. She gave him his jacket. Silently, without another word, he left. She stood there looking at the closed door for a long time. Then she went into the bedroom, feeling better than she had in a long long time.

—

"DID YOU SEE THIS, SAM?"

He looked up from his bacon and eggs. "See what?" he asked, his mouth half full. Denise gave him the Reporter. She pointed to the small story on the front page.

BARZINI TO RETURN TO ROME AFTER RIDERS.

He glanced at it and nodded. He resumed eating.

"I thought you had her signed to two more pictures," Denise said.

"We agreed to skip them. She's not happy here. She prefers working in Rome."

Denise tried to keep the sudden lightening of her heart from showing in her voice. "Will it affect your plans in any way?"

"Sure," he said, swallowing a mouthful of food. "Maybe I'll be able to get home early some nights now that I don't have to follow her around holding a can every time she wants to take a pee."

"Like tonight?"

He put down his knife and fork and took her hand. "Yes, Mama. Like tonight."

SEVEN

STEVE CAME INTO THE APARTMENT just after midnight and the telephone was ringing. He picked it up. "Hello."

The faint accent echoed in his ear. *"Stephen Gaunt?"*

"Yes."

"You told me to call you when I am coming to New York."

"Italian Girl, when are you coming in?"

"I am in New York," she said. *"At the airport. My plane just landed."*

"The picture finished?"

"Yesterday. I had a few scenes to dub this morning or I would have been in earlier."

"Does Sam know you've left?"

"No." She hesitated. *"I thought it would be better if I just went off quietly. I tried to call you, but you were never there."*

"Do you have a car meeting you?"

"No. I decided to leave this morning. I left my maid there to finish packing and follow me."

"I'll have a car there in thirty minutes."

"It's all right. I can get a taxi."

"Don't forget you're a star, Italian Girl," he said. "Taxis are for the common people."

She laughed. "I'll wait then. I'll be in the lounge at United Airlines."

He put down the telephone and picked up the house phone. "Front door, please

Tell my chauffeur I want to speak to him." He hesitated. "No. Tell him to wait for me. I'll be right down."

—

THE PRESS AND THE PHOTOGRAPHERS beat him to her. Despite the late hour they seemed to come from out of nowhere. She was sitting on a railing that gave them a chance to photograph her legs, the short skirt seeming even shorter.

He stopped behind them and waited patiently.

She saw him and waved. "Stephen Gaunt!"

They turned to look and made a path for him to walk through. She came off the railing into his arms. They kissed and the flashbulbs went off like Chinese firecrackers.

"Once again," a photographer called. "My camera jammed."

She looked at him questioningly.

He grinned. "Why not?"

They repeated the kiss for the photographer. He turned to them. "I could keep this up all night," he said. "But Miss Barzini just came off a long flight and she is tired."

They began to walk out. Some of the reporters followed them. "Is it a romance?" one asked.

"We're old friends," he said.

"How long did you know each other?" another called.

"How about a month?"

They laughed. The luggage was already in the car. His chauffeur opened the door for them.

Marilu got in and he followed her. "Will you be in town long?" a reporter asked her.

She smiled at him. "I haven't decided yet."

Steve signaled his chauffeur and the car moved out into the road, leaving the reporters behind. He pressed the button that raised the glass divider. When it was closed, he turned to her.

"Welcome to New York, Italian Girl."

She sat there looking at him for a moment. Then she spoke. "You really mean that, don't you?"

"Yes."

"I believe you," she said. "It's strange."

"What's strange?"

"I am so used to not believing what people say. Yet when you say it, I believe you." She looked into his eyes. "Do you know—since that night we had dinner—I could not wait until the picture was finished. All I thought about was coming here to be with you."

He was silent.

"Do you believe me?" she asked.

He nodded.

"Why is it you do not speak?"

"I don't know," he said hesitantly.

She picked up his hand and brought it to her lips. "I, too," she whispered against the back of his palm.

—

SHE CLUNG TO HIM, THE heat of her engulfing him like the interior of a furnace, melting in its fierceness. "Stephen Gaunt," she cried. "I am lost! There is a whole world I never knew and I am afraid."

He held himself against her fire. "Don't be afraid," he whispered. "You're with me. Give yourself up to it."

"No!" Suddenly, frantically, she tried to get away from him, her hands striking at his chest and shoulders.

He trapped her against the headboard, his weight against her, his forearm across her throat cutting off her breath. She fought, rolling and squirming. Inexorably he increased the pressure. As suddenly as she had begun to struggle, she stopped.

She looked up at him, her mouth open, gasping for breath.

"You would have killed me," she said softly. A curious respect came into her voice. "You are not like the others."

Her body motionless, the sheath that was her being gripped him, tightened around him, pulsed rhythmically as she sought to empty him. He began to rise and fall, responding involuntarily to her demand.

"You like that?" she whispered.

"Yes."

She nodded, sure of herself once again.

He held himself still. "You know all the tricks, don't you, Italian Girl?"

She smiled. Suddenly, he rolled away from her and was out of the bed, looking down at her.

She followed him swiftly, her hand taking him to her mouth. "My strong, beautiful cock," she whispered. "Let me make love to it."

He stood there for a moment, feeling the tiny sharpness of her teeth on him, then tilted her face up toward him. "No. I want you to make love to me, not it." He picked up his robe from a chair. "And I want to make love to you. If I wanted to just fuck you I would have done it that night in California."

—

IT WAS ROGER COHEN'S VOICE on the transcontinental wire. *"Sam?"*

"Yeah," he said irritably. He was beginning to wish he had never taken him back.

"Do you know where your girl is this morning?" he asked sarcastically.

"Sure I do," Sam said, annoyed. "Marilu's at the Beverly Hills Hotel. We just finished shooting yesterday."

"Sure you're sure!" Roger then delivered his daily quota of aggravation. *"Then how come her picture is in this morning's newspapers draped all over Stephen Gaunt at Idlewild Airport?"*

"She's not?" Sam's voice was disbelieving.

"You want me to send you the clips?"

"Okay, okay, I believe you." Sam stopped for a moment. "The dirty cunt."

"What about our pictures with her?" Roger asked.

"We canceled them. She said she was unhappy here."

Roger's voice grew even more savage. *"That's great. Now you've made your five pictures for Trans-World and we're no closer to one for our own company than we were a year ago. Not even one with her. That one you gave to them also."*

"That million and a quarter producer's fee I got didn't hurt our company."

"How far do you think that will take us without pictures to distribute? Our expenses run more than fifteen thousand a week now. If we don't get some product real quick, we might as well close up shop."

"I'm working on some ideas," Sam said. "I'm just waiting on approvals from Craddock's office."

"How long will that take?"

"I should hear today," Sam said. "It's just a formality."

"I hope they're good ones," Roger said. *"We can use them."*

For a brief moment, Sam was angry when he put down the telephone. He should have known it. She had begun to change ever since that night she made dinner for Steve. She could have told him.

Then he felt the sense of relief. It was just as well. For a while she had him on a roller coaster and he didn't know how to get off. He was all right for quickies and one-shots, but an affair was too much for him.

He was perfectly happy to be too old for it.

EIGHT

"WE'VE GOT A TIGER BY the tail," Steve said. "We have to go into production ourselves. If we don't, we're at the mercy of every picture company in the business."

"We're not in the motion picture business," Spencer Sinclair said. "We're in broadcasting."

"We are the picture business," Steve declared. "And the newspaper business, and the publishing business, and baseball, football, and even in the politics business. We had as much to do with electing Kennedy as anyone."

Sinclair looked at him without speaking.

"What I'm saying, Spencer, is that we're in communications. And that covers everything. Everything. Our little twenty-one-inch screen feeds on the world with the appetite of a thousand tigers and if we don't provide for its food, there will soon be none left for us."

The older man moved the papers on his desk and looked at them. After a few moments, he glanced up at Steve. "What is it you think we should do?"

"We start now by going into the picture business," Steve said. "There are two ways we can approach it. By setting up our own production company or buying one."

"I suppose you have one in mind."

Steve nodded. "Trans-World."

"I thought your friend was taking that one over."

"More the other way around. Sam's a producer and a salesman, he's not really a businessman."

"What makes you think they'll be ready to sell?"

"I've studied their annual reports for the last five years. It's been four years since they've shown a profit and their losses amount to over twenty million dollars. Its principal asset is its film library which they estimate is worth one hundred and fifty million dollars."

"How many shares of stock do they have out?"

"Three million odd shares at about twenty-two. If we make a tender of thirty dollars a share I think we would have control in a week. Management went to sleep. They own next to nothing."

"That could be ninety million dollars," Sinclair said.

"It doesn't have to be cash," Steve said. "We can offer stock."

"No. I've no intention of diluting my equity. If I consider it at all, it will be for cash."

"That's up to you," Steve said. "You're the boss."

The older man smiled. "So why do I feel like I'm being pushed all over the place?"

Steve returned his smile with warmth. "Maybe it's because you don't get into the office enough, Spencer. And when you do, you're always faced with a major decision."

Sinclair laughed. "You never stop, do you?"

Steve was silent.

"Have the legal department look into this," Sinclair said. "There might be complications. Antitrust, FCC."

"They're already working on it."

"How about Trans-World operating losses? Will that affect our profit picture?"

"It would if we kept it," Steve said. "But all I really want is the library and the studio. I'll spin the distribution company off."

"Got an idea as to who might want it?"

Steve nodded.

"Who?"

"Sam Benjamin," he said. "He dreams of making Samarkand a major distributor and the one thing he hasn't got is a ready-made organization."

"What makes you think he'll go for it?" Sinclair said. "The way it looks we'll be skimming the cream."

"Not really," Steve said. "We'll still need a distributor for the pictures we make. The right kind of an arrangement and neither of us can go wrong. He's the best salesman in the business."

"Except one," Sinclair said.

Steve looked at him. "Who's that?"

"You." Sinclair laughed and got to his feet. "Sometimes I wonder why I even bother to come in at all."

"You know you wouldn't be happy if you didn't," Steve said.

"I guess so." Sinclair was thoughtful. "Well, in time I can let go. Then it will really be up to you."

Steve knew what he meant. There was a mandatory retirement age in the corporation. "Meanwhile, stick around," he said. "We need you."

"Thank you," Sinclair returned to his chair. "That was a pretty girl with you in that picture in the paper this morning. The Italian actress." He paused. "Anything serious?"

Steve shook his head. "Just a friend."

"I thought I heard somewhere she was a friend of Sam Benjamin's."

The old man didn't miss very much. "She might have been."

"I hope it's nothing that will affect your relationship with Benjamin," the older man said. "Especially if you have plans to work with him. I've always found it much more dangerous to fool with a man's mistress than his wife."

Spencer wasn't that far wrong. There was a call from Sam waiting for him when he got back to his office.

Sam's voice boomed through the wires. *"You prick!"* he laughed. *"You're fuckin' my girl!"*

Sam sounded anything but angry.

Steve said, "You have to admit I was a gentleman about it. I waited until you were through with her."

Sam's voice went serious. *"She's a nice girl, Steve. You'll be good for her. She needs someone like you."*

"That's enough crap, Sam," Steve said. "Marilu isn't the reason you called me."

"A little problem came up on my deal with Trans-World. I've completed the first five for them, now I'm ready to start on my own half, but they come up with a case of the shorts. They had a bad first six months and they have to get the new pictures into release."

"Don't tell me," Steve said. "Craddock just pulled a long face and explained how embarrassed he was, but the boys back East...."

"You know the son of a bitch then?"

"I know," Steve said.

"Why didn't you warn me?"

"Why didn't you ask me?"

Sam was silent for a moment, his breath heavy in the telephone. "They'll come up with seventy-five percent of the negative. They want me to come up with the other twenty-five percent."

"How much is that?" Steve asked.

"My end, about six and a quarter million for the five pictures. Dave Diamond will give me four. I want the rest from you."

"When do I get the pictures?" Steve asked.

"Three years after domestic release."

"You got a deal," Steve said. "On one condition."

"What is it?"

"You read the small print the next time. Craddock's pulled that deal before. It's his favorite escape clause. He never figured you could come up with the money."

"I'll fire my lawyer," Sam said.

—

THE FIRST THING HE NOTICED when he entered the apartment was her valises standing in the foyer. He made himself a drink, turned on the television set to the news program.

He didn't turn when the bedroom door behind him opened.

"I didn't think you'd be home this early," she said. "Sam called. Did you speak to him?"

"Yes," he answered.

"He wasn't surprised that I was here."

"Why should he be?" he asked. "Your arrival wasn't exactly a secret."

"I didn't mean to cause trouble between you."

"You didn't. He called me on business."

"I'd better leave now. I'm booked to Rome on a nine o'clock flight." She made a helpless gesture. "I'm sorry."

"For what?"

"For being a disappointment to you." Her voice trailed off.

"I wasn't disappointed," he said. "I was surprised."

"I don't understand," she said.

"With all you do know, you know nothing of love. What you're afraid of is to allow yourself to feel."

"Maybe." She held out her hand, European style. "Good-bye, Stephen Gaunt."

He made no move to take her hand. "Don't run away."

"I'm not running away," she said. "I'm going home."

"The same thing. You go now and you'll never find what you're looking for. You'll always be afraid."

She was silent for a moment, watching his face. "You mean you want me to stay, even after last night?"

"Yes."

"Why?"

He looked up. "Because I think we can love each other. And that's too rare a thing to lose even before it begins."

She sank to her knees in front of him and rested her head against his legs. "Stephen Gaunt," she said. "I think I am already in love with you."

NINE

LAZILY MARILU SWAM TO THE far end of the heated pool and climbed out. She stood there for a moment, savoring the warm lawn-scented Connecticut air. She reached for a towel and began to dry herself.

Behind her she could hear the faint murmur of their voices. She turned to look back at them. They were occupied with the sheets of paper in front of them on the table and did not look up. She turned back to look out at the blue waters of the Sound.

The pool was on the crest of a small rolling hill that rose from the waters of Long Island Sound beneath them. There was a boat dock there that extended almost eighty feet from the shore. Moored alongside was a large motor yacht, shining whitely in the sun, over one hundred and forty feet at the waterline. On the other side of the dock were two speedboats and a sailboat.

She thought how nice it would have been if they had been out on the sea today in the sailboat. Just the two of them, no one else. They could have dropped the sails and drifted and made love in the open cockpit under the sun. But that was not the way it was.

She turned and started back toward them. All afternoon Steve had spent with the old man explaining the figures on the little white sheets of paper. Steve's voice began to come clearly to her as she approached.

"The funds and the brokerage houses assure me they'll go for a deal. And that means control. They are very unhappy with present management. But they don't want cash."

"What will they take?"

She stopped at her chair and picked up a package of cigarettes. She lit one while Steve answered.

"Debentures equal to thirty dollars per share and a bonus of class B non-voting common stock equal to five dollars a share. They feel it serves their tax picture that way."

"It sure does," Sinclair said. "They don't pay any. At least not until the debentures and stock are sold or retired. But it still adds up to fifteen million dollars more than you thought."

"There are compensating factors," Steve said. "Firstly, we can expense the interest and cost of debentures; second, we don't have to lay out the cash; third, by the time we have to pay them off we will have had the use of one hundred and fifty million dollars worth of their film library. In effect we'll be paying them with their own monies."

"Do they understand that you're spinning off the distribution end of the company?"

"Yes," Steve answered. "They couldn't care less. They feel it's the losing end of the business. But I do have a problem there."

"Yes?" Sinclair asked.

"They're not interested in financing Samarkand."

"You mean Sam Benjamin?"

"Same thing," Steve said.

"Did they have a reason?" the old man asked.

"They had lots of reasons. But none of them the truth. What it comes down to is they won't do business with what they call a 'Jew promoter.'"

"If we have to take the distribution company, the deal's no good for us," Sinclair said definitely. "I'm not going to have that five-million-dollar annual operating deficit eat into our profits."

"I have a way around it," Steve said. "I think."

"You don't sound sure."

"You never know until you try," Steve said. "The way I see it, we can supply fifty percent of his production capital. What I had to do is to find the rest of the financing for him."

"Have you spoken to him yet?"

"No. I wouldn't do that until I had clearance from you."

"You've got it," Sinclair said. "But I hope your friend doesn't disappoint you. If he opens his mouth about this deal before we're ready, he can blow the whole thing."

"I know that," Steve answered. "I'm going to have everything set before I go out there to see him. We make the tender the minute he agrees."

"Do you really think it will work?"

"Why shouldn't it? We'll start with seventy-one percent of the stock in our pockets. It only takes nine percent more and we can consolidate the companies. And we should pick that up the first day."

"Okay. Just don't lead with your right," the old man said, getting to his feet. "I wouldn't like to see you catch one on the chin."

Suddenly Steve grinned. "I feel better now."

"Why?" Sinclair was puzzled.

"I was afraid you were getting soft," Steve said. "But your message comes through loud and clear."

Sinclair laughed and walked over to where Marilu was lying, "*Signorina* Barzini, I apologize for being so poor a host," he said in flawless Italian.

She answered him in the same language. "In my profession I have grown accustomed to it. Men are always talking business."

"It is your friend's fault," he gestured at Steve. "I think he is crazy to be talking business when he could be with you."

Still in Italian, she replied. "He is many things. To many people. But crazy he is not."

"That is very deep. And very Italian. Would you care to explain to an old man who does not quite understand?"

She hesitated.

"I do not mean to pry," he said quickly. "You do not have to answer."

"It is not that," she said. "I was just thinking how to answer."

He was silent.

"To me, he is the lover I thought I would never know. To Sam Benjamin, he is the friend that he never thought he would deserve. To you—"

She stopped.

"Go on," he said. "To me—?"

"To you—I think—he is the son you never had."

"And what is he to himself?" the old man asked. "What do you think?"

A dark sadness seemed to appear in her large green eyes. "To himself—he is not good enough. He is pursuing a dream that will never be real."

—

"WHO WILL HEAD UP PRODUCTION for you?" Sam asked. "He's the guy I have to live with."

"Jack Savitt," Steve answered. "He's selling his agency to Artists and Writers, Inc."

"Good," Sam said. "I like him."

"Let me get it clear in my mind," Roger said. "Trans-World—Sinclair takes over the studio and the foreign distribution companies. Samarkand—Trans-World, the domestic and Canadian companies. We finance production fifty-fifty. We share profits fifty-fifty. We each make pictures outside the financing deal but you can make them only for TV."

"You've got it," Steve said. "We're interested only in making features for television."

"Will they be distributed theatrically abroad?"

"Yes," Steve answered.

"Isn't that competitive with us?"

"I don't think so," Steve said. "The quality is not the same. Without the domestic market we're automatically limited."

"I'm satisfied with that." Sam turned to Dave Diamond. "What do you think?"

"I'm satisfied," the banker said. "I have everything set for the revolving loan. You begin with a credit of fifteen million dollars."

"What if I buy foreign pictures for domestic distribution as I have in the past?" Sam asked. "How do you fit into that?"

"The same as before," Steve said. "You have no restrictions. I would like first crack at them, but if it's your own money, you can do as you see fit."

"That's fair enough," Sam said. "There's only one thing I insist on."

"What's that?" Steve asked.

"I'm the one who tells Craddock."

Steve laughed. "Be my guest."

"I've been waiting to get that son of a bitch," Sam said. "When do you think we'll be ready?"

"As long as it takes your lawyers to read the papers," Steve answered.

"This is Friday," Sam said. "We'll sign on Sunday."

"The tender will go out Monday," Steve said.

Sam grinned. "I wish I could see Craddock's face when he hears about it." He turned to Roger, a note of triumph in his voice. "Samarkand—Trans-World. How about that? We're a major."

TEN

"IT'S DONE," STEVE SAID, COMING into the apartment. "We've got ninety-two percent of the stock the first day."

"Congratulations," she said.

"This calls for champagne." He took a bottle from the small refrigerator and filled two glasses. "Start packing," he said. "We're leaving for California in the morning."

"I'm already packed." She looked down at her glass of champagne, then back at him. "But I'm not going with you. I'm going back to Rome."

He was surprised. "What for? I thought you didn't like any of the pictures they offered you."

"Nickie came up with a proposition I do like," she said. "Marriage."

He didn't speak.

She took the cable from the small desk and gave it to him.

ANNULMENT APPROVED VATICAN YESTERDAY NO MORE EXCUSES COME HOME AND GET MARRIED LOVE.

NICKIE

His voice was soft. "So that's it."

"That's it," she said. She made her voice light. "Unless—"

He looked at her as her voice trailed off. "Unless what?"

She shook her head, her voice suddenly tight in her throat. "Nothing. It would not work, anyway. I am an actress and I have my work. We would not fit together."

"You could give up your work."

It was her turn to be surprised. "Are you asking me to marry you?"

"I guess so," he said. "That's what it sounds like, doesn't it?"

The tears came to her eyes. "But you never said you loved me. Even when—"

"I love you," he said.

She came into his arms. "What took you so long?"

"I'm stupid. I didn't know until I suddenly realized I was going to lose you."

She kissed him quickly and stepped away from him. She held up her glass to him. "Thank you, Stephen Gaunt. But, no."

He almost dropped his glass.

"Don't be so surprised," she said. "But we both know it would not work. I would not give up my career."

"You would rather be an actress than a woman?" he asked.

"I'm greedy. I've always been greedy," she answered. "I want both. With you I must make a choice."

"And with Nickie?"

"I have both. I know him. We have been together a long time. He knows me and he does not object." She sipped her champagne and smiled. "You can relax. You're safe."

He began to smile. A moment later they were both laughing. He held out his arms to her and she came into them again. "Italian Girl, tonight we're going on the town for the biggest night you ever had."

"No," she said. "Tonight we're staying in."

He kissed her. "I do love you. You believe that, don't you?"

She nodded. "I believe you. Because I remember what you said. That we can love each other. And we do. But I also know something else that you do not."

He looked his question.

"There are two kinds of love. One is the marrying kind. And ours is the other."

—

SAM COULD FEEL THE DIFFERENCE the moment he drove on the lot the next morning. The suddenly hushed greeting of the guard at the gate instead of the usual hearty bellow. The small clusters of employees who suddenly stopped talking to look after his car as it passed them. The pile of telephone messages on his desk.

"The trades are all calling," his secretary said.

"Tell them a statement will be issued later today," he said, knowing that Steve was meeting with the management of Trans-World that moment in New York.

"Mr. Craddock called and would like to see you if you have a few moments to spare."

The son of a bitch didn't waste any time, Sam thought. Let him come. We'll see how he likes getting his balls cut off. Aloud, he said, "Tell him I'm clear now."

He watched his secretary put down the telephone. "Mr. Craddock's on his way."

Craddock came in with a smile. He held out his hand. "Congratulations, Sam," he said in a sincere voice. "I think it's the best thing ever to happen to Trans-World."

Sam looked at him doubtfully. "You do?"

"You bet I do," Craddock said. "Something had to be done and the management back East was twenty years behind the times." He lit a cigarette. "Now maybe some pictures will be made. They forgot that's what this studio is for."

"You fucking idiot!" Sam almost shouted. "You're fired! Don't you know that?"

Craddock smiled. "Of course I know that."

"And you don't care?" Sam asked incredulously.

"Of course I care," Craddock said, drawing on his cigarette with obvious pleasure. "But, man, look at me. I'm smoking. Even inhaling. And that's the first time in ten years a cigarette isn't burning its way into my ulcer. By the way, who do they have in mind to replace me?"

"Jack Savitt," Sam answered without thinking, still in a state of shock.

"Jack Savitt." Craddock's voice was approving. "A good choice. Very qualified. He's already got an ulcer, so the job won't throw him."

Sam stared at him. If nothing else the man had the balls of a brass monkey. They couldn't be cut off. They had to be ground off. There wasn't another production head in town that had kept his job that long. That and the fact that he fought for every dollar he could get for Trans-World as if it were his own. If Sam had had someone like that operating in production for him, maybe he would never have been in the trouble he stepped into.

"I spoke to my attorneys this morning," Craddock said. "I told them to get ready to settle my contract. Do you have any idea how long it will be before they'll contact me?"

Sam shook his head. "That's Sinclair's department. It's their studio. I'm just leasing space here, that's all."

"That's okay," Craddock said. "I can wait. My contract still has three years to run."

Sam made up his mind. In a kind of way it was obviously the most logical thing he could do. "Look, Rory, with my taking over the distribution company I'm going to spend most of my time out of the studio. I need someone to take over production from me. And you're the guy. You know the plans, the product, and the studio. Are you interested?"

"You mean you want me to make pictures?"

Sam nodded. "I want you to do for me exactly what you did for Trans-World."

"I'm interested," Craddock said.

"Well then, damn it, if you're interested, get off your ass and find me some pictures to put into production. We have a distribution company that needs product."

"I'll get right on it," Craddock smiled and dragged on his cigarette. Suddenly the smile vanished and a look of pain crossed his face. He looked at the cigarette as if it had suddenly betrayed him, then ground it out in the ashtray.

"What happened?" Sam asked.

Craddock stared at him. "The damn cigarette began to burn hell out of my ulcer," he said angrily. "I should have known the feeling was too good to last."

ELEVEN

"WHAT DO YOU MEAN YOU don't want a *bar mitzvah?"* Sam yelled. "Your grandfather and grandmother are coming from Florida especially for it."

Junior had a stubborn look on his face. "Aw, c'mon, Dad. It's a ritual hangover, that's all it is. Like circumcision, it means nothing in modern society."

"Nothing?" Sam roared. "I'll give you nothing across your ass. You're going to make your *bar mitzvah* if I have to drag you down to the *shul* myself."

"Sam," Denise said quietly. "Don't get excited. Your blood pressure."

"My blood pressure's all right. What ain't all right is this little jerk's head. He needs somebody to screw it back on straight."

"Let's talk about it quietly," Denise said.

"Okay," Sam answered. "So we'll talk." He turned back to Junior and his voice dropped to an almost calm tone. "You'll make your *bar mitzvah* or I'll break every bone in your body."

Denise looked at her son. "You can go now. Let me talk to your father."

The boy left without a word. They waited until the door closed behind him. Sam looked at her.

"A fine mess you make of things," he complained bitterly. "I turn my back for a minute and look what happens. You can't even handle a simple assignment like getting your own son to make his *bar mitzvah."*

Denise was angry. "A simple assignment? The big executive comes home once in six months from the road and talks to his wife like she's an employee or something. What are you going to do next, Mr. Big Man, fire me?"

"If you were working for me, I would have—" He stopped suddenly and looked at her. A puzzled tone came into his voice. "Mama, why are we talking like this?"

She shook her head. "I don't know. I didn't start it. But for the last year you've been in another world. We never see you anymore."

"There was so much to do," he said. "The whole company had to be reorganized or else we'd wind up losing five million a year like they did. But it will be better now that I'm bringing Charley in from Rome to be my assistant."

"You'll find something else to take you away," she said. "We've been through that before. When Craddock took over production, when Roger took over administration, when you hired that man from Twentieth to be sales manager, but you're involved just the same."

"I'm the boss. If I didn't keep an eye on things, they'd get away from me."

"So then what do you need all those men for and pay them such fantastic salaries?"

"So that I can be free to concentrate on the big problems, that's why."

"I thought you just said everything was straightened out, Sam. What big problems are there?"

"I want to review our relationship with Sinclair. Do you know how much money I made for them with our pictures last year? Seven million dollars. That's more than we kept for ourselves."

She looked at him without speaking.

"The new Barzini picture alone will make them over four million," Sam added.

"I thought Steve got her to do that picture. She said she didn't want to come back to Hollywood, but she did."

"Why shouldn't she?" he asked. "Between her and her husband they're taking another three million home. All we'll get out of it is a lousy million and a half. I got word the other day that UA would like to take over foreign distribution of our product. And they're willing to take ten percent less for distribution and five percent less profit share."

She looked at him steadily. "I wouldn't be in such a hurry if I were you. After all, it was Steve who put you into this."

"He was only doing it for himself," he said. "If I didn't take over the domestic company he couldn't make the deal. Sinclair wouldn't go for the operating loss and antitrust would probably step in. He didn't do me any favors. I saved his ass. Besides giving him product for practically nothing."

"You'll talk to Steve, I'm sure he'll work something out."

"Sometimes he can get very stubborn," Sam said. "He's got the typical *goyishe* attitude that a deal's a deal."

—

"THE OLD MAN'S ON THE warpath," Junior said, throwing himself on the ground beside the pool in front of his sister.

Myriam looked down at him from the lounge. She put aside the script she was reading. "The *bar mitzvah* thing again?"

He nodded. "He's got a bug up his ass. Now it's because Grandma and Grandpa are coming up from Florida."

"I guess you'll have to go through with it, then. You know how he is about them."

"Yeah." He pulled off his shirt, revealing a thin wiry frame.

"Do you know if Mother's spoken to him about me yet?" she asked.

"I don't think so," he said. "Dad got started on me and I think she cooled it until he's in a better mood."

"Damn. I hope she doesn't wait too long. If I don't give them a definite answer with a week, I could lose my place. The Actors Studio has more applicants than they can handle."

He looked at her shrewdly. "You ain't never goin' to get there if you let your boyfriends keep using the glove compartment in your car for a storage place."

She stared at him. "You've been sneaking around!"

"I have not," he said quickly. "Mama wanted to use it and asked me to clean it out a little. You're just lucky I happened to look in there. If Mama had found the stuff that would have been your finish."

"What did you do with it?" she asked.

"I've got it in a safe place," he said. "I figure the next time I see Razz, I'll get him to ransom it."

"It's not Razz's."

"Then whose is it?" he asked.

"Mine," she said.

"Yours?" His voice was skeptical. "Okay. I dig the reefers. But the rubbers, too?"

She didn't answer. Her face was slightly flushed.

"You're okay, Sis," he said, a grudging admiration coming into his voice. "I hope I get lucky enough to find a girl like you when I start makin' out."

"You giving it back to me?" she asked.

"Yes," he said. "But I'm keeping five reefers. They're better than the crap they been pushing around school."

"You're not smoking?" her voice was shocked.

"Sure," he said. "All the kids are. But not much, though. Just a few drags at a time. It's groovy."

"You better take it easy," she said. "You're a little young yet."

"I can handle it," he said confidently.

She was silent for a moment. "And what about the rubbers?"

"You can have 'em back," he said. "They're a little too big for me."

—

DENISE LOOKED OUT THE WINDOW and saw them splashing in the pool. "Come, Sam, and take a look," she said.

He put down the paper and walked over to her. They stood there for a moment watching them.

"We're lucky," she said, marveling. "Did you ever think that time I came into your office we would be so lucky?"

"No," he said. He watched Junior streaking across the pool in a racing crawl, the water behind him churning into champagne-like bubbles. "That kid swims like a champion."

"They're good children, too," she said earnestly. "You should hear the stories I hear. The way kids act nowadays. It's unbelievable."

"Yeah," he said. "I know." He turned back from the window and picked up the paper again. "But he's still going to make his *bar mitzvah.*"

"He'll make it," she said. "Don't worry."

"He'd better," Sam said.

He seemed in a better mood now, she thought. Maybe this was the time to talk to him about Myriam. "You know, Sam," she said. "I've been talking to Myriam about her future. About what she wants to do."

He put down the paper and looked at her. "Yes?"

"She's a very pretty girl," Denise said quickly. "And she wants to go back East to school."

"What's the matter?" he asked. "USC isn't good enough for her?"

"No," she said. "She says she can't get the kind of training she wants here."

"What kind of training?" Sam asked.

"Dramatic training," she said.

"Dramatic training?" His voice began to rise. "You mean she wants to become an actress?"

"What's wrong with it?" she asked. "After all, you know how proud you were when she played the lead in those plays at school."

"That was different," he said. "That was school. You know how I feel about actresses. They're all whores. I won't have my daughter going around to casting offices like a tramp."

"Myriam's not like that," Denise said. "She's a serious girl. Last month when Lee Strasberg was out here, he gave her an interview and he thinks she has talent. He accepted her for the Actors Studio. And you know he just doesn't take everybody."

"Uh-uh," he said. "I'm not going to let her live in New York alone."

"She won't be alone," Denise said. "Roger said he would keep an eye on her."

In spite of himself, Sam began to feel a secret pride.

"You got to let her do it, Sam," Denise said. "You'll break her heart if you don't."

TWELVE

"YOUR FAT LITTLE FRIEND IS feeling his oats again," Jack said as Steve entered his office.

Steve sat down. Jack's secretary placed a cup of coffee in front of him. "What's happening now?"

"He elected to do the best three properties we found for him outside the agreement."

Steve picked up his coffee. "So?"

"Come off it, Steve. That's not fair and you know it," Jack protested. "How am I going to keep running the studio without a loss if he uses his minimum overhead charge for other company's benefits?"

"Has he announced a distributor yet?"

"UA," Jack said. "What are you going to do about it?"

"Nothing," Steve answered shortly. "He's within our agreement. He can elect to make his pictures with his own money if he wants to."

"You're not going to say anything to him?" Jack was angry.

"Not a word."

"Okay, then, I quit," Jack said. "I'll be damned if I'm going to find properties for him to screw us out of."

"Stop looking, then," Steve said mildly. "You have enough to do on our program. Let him find his own properties."

"Do you mean that?"

"Absolutely. There's nothing in our agreement that says we have to turn over to him any property we buy. The only reason for that is because we're partners."

"That's better," Jack said. He went behind his desk and sat down. "What if I see something great?"

"Buy it. We'll worry about finding a producer later. There's nothing in the agreement to keep us from doing that."

He put down his coffee cup, walked over to the window and looked out. The studio street was crowded. "They look busy enough out there."

"We're movin'," Jack said in a pleased voice. "Production begins on the first of our two-hour features next month and we're scheduled for one a month after that."

"Good," Steve said. "I'll start thinking of time slots then."

"We'll be ready earlier if you like."

"I'm in no hurry," Steve said. "The schedule's holding up. The new medical series, 'GP,' is getting good Nielsens. I notice, though, when we're in the hospital instead of outside, the ratings are slightly better. You might look into that and plan a few more inside stories."

"I'll check it." Jack made a note on his memo pad.

"Have you spoken to Sam recently?"

"He's not around much. I do all my business with Craddock."

"See if you can find out if he's on the lot. Maybe I can drop in and have a talk with him." He went back to the chair and sank into it wearily while Jack picked up the telephone. He leaned back and closed his eyes.

"Sam's on a swing around the exchanges," Jack said.

Steve opened his eyes. "I'll catch up to him the next time I'm out."

"Are you all right?" he asked.

"I'm fine. Just tired, that's all. I've been on a merry-go-round for a month."

"You need a vacation."

"No time," Steve answered. "Tomorrow morning I'm due in Montreal to try to lock up the Intercontinental Football League for the next few years. The day after that, Washington for the congressional hearings on broadcasting. Then Chicago for the NAB conventions. After that, London to check on the series we're doing in association with British TV."

Jack shook his head. "I wish I could be of more help to you."

"I know that," Steve smiled, taking a small pillbox from his pocket. "But one of the penalties that goes with my job is that everybody wants to see the president of the company. Could I trouble you for a little water?"

"No trouble." Jack filled a glass from the carafe next to his desk. "What's that you're taking? Vitamins?"

"No." Steve swallowed the pill. "But I take those, too. This is a benny. It'll hold me up for the rest of the day."

"That's rough stuff. You can get hooked on them."

"I only use it once in awhile. When I'm very tired," Steve said. "I didn't get much sleep last night. The plane came in late."

"You better try to get a real vacation," Jack said. "I wouldn't like anything to happen to you. Life wouldn't be worth living around here."

"I'll be all right." Steve got to his feet. "Now, how about looking at those pilots you say are so great?"

—

"HAVE THERE BEEN ANY KICKBACKS since you told them we're going with UA for the three pictures?" Sam asked.

"None at all," Rory answered. "I expected Jack to squawk—but nothing. It's been a month now. I guess they've been too occupied with their own problems."

"How are their pictures coming along?"

"Okay, I guess. They began production on one last week."

"Is it any good?"

Rory shrugged his shoulders. "Who knows? At any rate it's not much. What can you get for six hundred thousand dollars these days? A good property costs that much."

"Yeah." Sam felt curiously disappointed. He had been sure he would hear from Steve about their switch in distribution. It would have been a good jumping-off point for renegotiation. "And what about those properties we were after?"

"No dice," Rory answered. "They're gone."

"Gone? You mean someone else bought them?"

Rory nodded.

"How come?" Sam's voice began to grow tight. "I thought I said get them."

"I know what you said, Sam," Rory said smoothly. "But when I checked into it I found they were already sold."

"Who bought them?"

"I don't know," Rory answered. "The only thing I've been able to find out is that the same party got both of them."

"The same party?" Sam said thoughtfully. "Levine?"

"I don't think so. If it were Joe, you would have read it in the trades. I think it's a new syndicate and they're not making any announcements until they set a deal."

"Find out who they are," Sam said. "If they're looking for a deal maybe we can work something out with them."

"I'll do that," Rory said. He smiled. "There's one I'm pretty sure of. I put in a bid of a half million for *Blue Jeans* and next week it will be the number-one book in the country according to *The New York Times.*"

"Good," Sam said. "When do you think you'll hear about it?"

"Any minute now," Rory answered. "I've got a call into the Matson Agency right now. They were opening the bids this morning." The telephone rang. "That could be them."

He picked up the telephone and spoke into it. Gradually his smile faded. A moment later he put down the telephone. He spoke in a disbelieving voice. "That's gone, too. Seven hundred and fifty thousand dollars."

Sam stared at him. "Who bought it?"

Rory shook his head. "They wouldn't say. I gathered that it was the same group that bought the others."

Sam got to his feet. "I don't get it. Did you hear of any other properties that they might have acquired?"

Rory shook his head. "No. Only those three."

"I smell something rotten." Sam asked, "Don't you?"

"In what way?"

"It's almost as if somebody's trying to shaft us." He walked around the desk and looked down at Rory. "Who else knows we were interested in the properties besides you and me?"

Rory thought for a moment. "No one except our secretaries."

"And how did we hear about them?"

"The usual channels. The studio story department sent them up to us with the galleys and a report."

Sam took a deep breath, face flushing with suppressed anger. "The usual channels?"

Rory nodded.

"And you still think you haven't had any kickbacks from Sinclair?"

Rory's ulcer twinged. He reached for his Gelusil.

"Then you're not as smart as you think you are," Sam said. "Or maybe it's that I know Steve Gaunt better than you do. This is his way of letting us know he doesn't like what we're doing." Sam sat down heavily. "He's going to use those properties as a club to get us back into the fold."

"What are you going to do?" Rory sucked on the tablet.

"Two can play that game. Steve'll find out that I'm not just another *shmuck* like he's used to dealing with. I'll bust him."

"How are you going to do that?"

"Simple." Sam smiled conspiratorially. "You just let them know everything we bid on. And you bid on everything even if we don't want it. They'll top our bids and the next think you know they'll be so loaded with crap, they'll come yelling to us for mercy. Then we'll really shove it to them."

THIRTEEN

STEVE GOT TO THE RECEPTION just as Sam stood up to make his speech. He slipped into an empty seat at a table toward the back of the room and looked around.

Behind the main table, a giant banner was strung across the wall.

HAPPY BIRTHDAY SAMUEL BENJAMIN, JR.
OUR BAR MITZVAH BOY!

Sam banged a spoon against a plate to gain attention. Slowly the room began to quiet down. Sam stood there, weaving slightly, smiling. After a moment, he held up his hands.

"Friends, *Goyim* and *Landsleit,* welcome to my son's *bar mitzvah.*" He paused while everyone applauded. "In case you didn't notice when you came in, there are fifty white Rolls Royces waiting outside. When we leave here, they're taking us to the airport where there will be fifty white DC Eights which will fly us direct nonstop to Kenya, Africa. At the airport there will be waiting fifty white hunters with fifty white elephants. We will board those fifty white elephants and go on a safari into the jungle. Each of you will be given a white rifle to shoot your own rarest of creatures, a white tiger. As we approach the jungle, single file on the narrow path, the chief white hunter will hold up his hand and we will stop. And we will wait.

"And do you know what we'll be waiting for?"

The shouts of laughter came up from the room. "No, Sam. Tell us."

He looked around smiling. "For Joe Levine's *bar mitzvah* safari to clear out of the jungle ahead of us."

The roar of laughter grew even louder and applause broke out through the room. Sam smiled and held up his hands again for quiet.

"Thank you," he said. He looked around the room. "I've opened some of my pictures with smaller crowds than this. In case you're not doing anything next Tuesday—"

Again they began to laugh. This time Sam waited until they subsided by themselves.

"But, seriously, friends, some of you might be asking yourselves, why is Sam Benjamin doing this? Why is he going to all this trouble? After all, it's nothing but a *bar mitzvah* and boys make them every day.

"But it's more than that to me. How else can a poor boy from the Bronx who got lucky say to his son"—he turned to Junior and spoke directly to him—"I love you. And I'm proud of you."

In the silence, Sam bent down and kissed his son. Then he straightened up and looked into the room. "Thank you," he said simply and sat down.

Steve made his way up to the front table as the party began to break up. Sam was busy talking to some people and Denise was the first to see him.

"Steve," she said in a pleased voice.

He kissed her cheek. "Congratulations. It's a lovely party."

"I'm glad you came. It seems like it's the only time we see each other. I still owe you a *brust flanken* dinner."

"Someday when things are a little more quiet."

"Even if you keep the meat in a freezer, four years is a long time to wait," she said.

"Has it been that long?"

"Yes," she said. "the last time you saw the children was at the Academy Awards."

"It won't be that long this time, I promise." He turned to Junior with a smile. "Remember me?"

"Yes, Uncle Steve."

Steve grinned, taking an envelope out of his pocket. "My friends tell me this is the custom. Congratulations."

Junior took the envelope and peeked into it. A wide grin broke over his face. "A five-hundred-dollar bill," he said in an awed voice. "And I thought I was through collecting the loot!"

"Junior!" Denise's voice was shocked.

Junior grinned again, shoving his hand out to Steve. "Gee, thanks Uncle Steve," he said enthusiastically, pumping his hand up and down.

"You're quite welcome," Steve smiled. He turned back to Denise. "Where's Myriam? Since I'm here I'd like to say hello."

"She was here a moment ago," Denise answered, looking around.

"She's gone home," Junior said. "She said she still has some packing to do."

"That's right," Denise said. "She's going to school back East and she's leaving tomorrow morning."

"I'm sorry I missed her," Steve said. "Give her my best."

"I will," Denise smiled proudly. "You wouldn't recognize her, she's so pretty."

"Especially since she got her nose job," Junior piped up.

"Junior!" Denise's voice was sharp.

Steve laughed. "It's all right, Denise. I'll keep it in the family. I won't tell anyone."

"There's nothing wrong in it," Denise said defensively. "Many girls do it nowadays."

"Of course," Steve said in a soothing voice. "You'd be surprised at the number of beautiful actresses who have had it done."

"Yes," Denise agreed. "And especially since she's—"

Sam's bellow interrupted her. "Hey, Steve!"

They shook hands. "Congratulations."

"What do you think of my boy?" Sam looked at his son admiringly. "I think he's going to be a six-footer."

"He's too much."

"Come, let's get a drink," Sam said, taking his arm and moving him to the bar. "Two Scotches."

"Yes, Mr. Benjamin." The bartender put the drinks down in front of them.

"Cheers," Sam said.

They drank.

"How's it going?" Sam asked.

"The usual," Steve said. "Win a few, lose a few."

"I've been picking up a lot of properties the last few months."

"So I've noticed." Steve's voice was noncommittal.

Sam glanced at Steve's face, looking for hidden meanings. But he could read nothing there except polite interest. "I think we ought to have a meeting."

"I'll be in the studio tomorrow," Steve said.

"I'll call you in the morning." Sam turned and looked out at the room, a smile breaking over his face. "It's a hell of a party, isn't it? I bet there never was a *bar mitzvah* like this."

—

MYRIAM SNAPPED THE LOCK ON the last valise and stared down at it. She heard the car in the driveway and crossing the room quickly, turned off the light. She had had enough family for the day.

Slowly she began to undress in the dark. The tightness was still inside her. Nothing had gone right. At least as far as she was concerned. If it hadn't been for the *bar mitzvah s*he would have been out of here last week. Sometimes relatives could be too much. Especially her kid brother. Of all people... it was uncanny how aware he was of what she was thinking.

"Who are you looking at?" he had whispered at the table as their father got up to make his speech.

She didn't answer.

He followed her gaze. "That's Uncle Steve."

She still didn't answer.

"You've got the hots for him?"

"Oh, shut up!" she whispered angrily, feeling the heat creep into her face. She forced herself to look away and Daddy had begun his speech, distracting her brother.

But he had been right. It had always been like that for her. Even at the Academy Awards years ago when he came in with that actress. She could have gladly killed her. And after that, she even felt a twinge every time she read his name in the columns. He was always going with one girl or another. An actress or a model. Maybe that was what gave her the idea for herself.

When the speech was over and Steve started toward the table she felt a sudden impulse to flee. She turned to her brother. "Tell Mother I'm going home to finish packing." She left before he had a chance to answer, walking right past Steve on her way out. Strange, the way she felt about him and he didn't even recognize her.

She began to grow angry with herself. She was acting like a child, not a girl who knew the score. She walked over to the dresser and opened her purse. One stick left.

She lit it and dragged the smoke deep into her lungs. She felt calmer almost immediately. Slowly now, she unfastened her brassiere and dropped it to the floor. Naked, she went to the window and opened it.

She stood there, letting the cool night air flow over her while she blew the smoke out the window. She closed her eyes and leaned against the sill.

She wondered where he was now. He had come alone but that meant nothing. He probably had a late date and was balling some girl right this moment. She wondered what it would be like making love with him. She began to feel warm and put her hand down and touched herself. She was wet and flowing.

She dragged on the cigarette and went back to the valise and opened it. From a side pocket she took out the pink battery-powered vibrator. She sat down on the edge of the bed, dragged again on the cigarette and, putting it into an ashtray, lay back.

She turned the base handle and its small hum filled the room. It was suddenly loud in her ears. She wrapped her legs around a pillow and, covering the vibe, held it against her clitoris. She tripped off to the moon and the suddenness of her orgasm brought his name in a half scream to her lips.

"Steve!"

His name hung there in the darkness.

The tears came to her eyes.

Then sleep.

—

"HE FUCKED ME!" SAM RAGED, coming into the house. "He sat there smiling like a snake. 'I'm your friend,' he said. Then he shoved the umbrella up my ass and opened it!"

Denise stared at him in bewilderment. "Who are you talking about?"

"Steve, that's whom I'm talking about," he said angrily. "Your *goyishe* friend. Who just yesterday came to my son's *bar mitzvah* and ate our food."

"I can't believe it. Not Steve."

"Yeah, Steve," he replied. "All I wanted was a nice quiet talk. To straighten out the inequities in our deal. That's all."

"What happened?"

"He sat there righteous as a judge behind his desk. 'You should have come to me before you made the UA deal,' he said.

"I explained to him I had to do it for my own self-protection. The way things were working out, Sinclair was making two dollars for every one of mine.

"'You read the agreement,' he said. 'Nobody forced you to sign it.'

"'But I was doing you a favor,' I explained. 'You wanted to make the deal and I helped you out.'

"'You also made yourself seven and a half million dollars,' he said. 'But I'm your friend. If you're unhappy I'll let you out of the deal even though it's still got five more years to run.'"

"What did you say?" Denise asked.

He looked at her as if he just saw her for the first time. "I need a drink."

She followed him to the bar and waited while he poured himself a drink and swallowed it in one gulp. He filled his glass again and turned to her.

"'What about those four and a half million dollars worth of story and play properties that I bought?' I asked him.

"'You bought them. We didn't,' he says as calm as if he's talking about the weather. 'You didn't notify us as required by the contract.'"

He swallowed half the second drink. "I stared at him, trying to read his face. But there was nothing there. He needed me more than I needed him. I felt it. He had to be bluffing. I called him."

He finished the drink and put the glass down on the bar. He stared at it morosely.

"What happened then?"

"Nothing. The lawyers are meeting tomorrow." He looked at her, the hurt showing in his eyes. "I guessed wrong."

BOOK FOUR:
STEPHEN GAUNT

HOLLYWOOD, 1960-1965

ONE

FROM SOMEWHERE IN THE DARK the telephone jangled in my ears. I struggled up through the sleepy abyss and reached for it. "Hello."

"Steve?" The voice grated in my ear.

"Yes," I said, still too far off to recognize it.

"Angel, here."

It all came together and I was awake. Angel Perez was VP Daytime Programming. One time he had been an actor, then he switched to production. He was better behind the camera than in front of it. For the last year I had been using him as my unofficial assistant. I needed a man in New York to listen since I was spending most of my time on the coast now.

"Yes, Angel. What is it?"

"The house is on fire. I think you better get back here."

I swung my feet over the side of the bed. "What's happening?"

"The old man called a special meeting of the board yesterday."

"I know," I said. "I got the notice."

"You should have come in for it. I got word they blew your ass over the special programs."

I knew what he meant. They were good television but bad programming. They didn't get the ratings. I had already heard from the sponsors.

They weren't happy either.

"I told them to expect that," I said. "But we should do them, anyway. You have to put something in once in a while."

"Southern Products canceled. They didn't like your equality angle on the labor special. They said that you made a target out of them."

"I'm not responsible for their own guilt feelings," I said.

"So you'll be a dead hero."

"There's got to be more to it than just that."

"There's also your old friend," he said.

"I've got lots of old friends."

"Not like this one," he said. *"Dan Ritchie. He came in with another old buddy of yours, Sam Benjamin. They have a whole new idea to revitalize the network. They claim you drifted away from your policy of film and entertainment and that you're now embarked on a crusade to reform the world. They say that your involvement with the Kennedys blew your mind as well as your judgment."*

"You're remarkably well informed for being down on the thirty-first floor," I said.

"I'm reading the memos."

"Where'd you get them?"

"The old man. He called me upstairs and made me a committee of one to study the situation and report back to him." He paused. *"He knows how close we are. Maybe this is his way of warning you."*

"He say anything else?"

"No. You know the way he is. Freezeville."

It was typical Sinclair. "What time is it?" I asked.

"Ten o'clock here. Seven, your time."

"I'll be in this evening. Meet me at my apartment at eight o'clock."

"Good." There was obvious relief in his voice. *"I got a girl I want you to meet. Out of sight. An actress. Marianne Darling. She's got the whole town turned on. And she wants to meet you."*

"Me?"

"Yeah," he said. *"When she found out I knew you, she zeroed in on me like a rocket. Made me promise the next time you were in town, I'd set it up. Seems like she's followed your career in the papers or something. She knows more about you than you do."*

I was interested. "Okay. Bring her with you."

"I'll bring Faith, too," he said. *"Maybe we'll swing a little bit."*

Faith was his girl. "Fine. See you tonight."

I pressed down the bar on the phone, then released it. The operator came on. *"Yes, Mr. Gaunt?"*

"Get me on the ten a.m. to New York." I put down the phone and started out of bed. I had another idea. I called Jack Savitt at home and woke him up.

"I'm going into New York this morning," I said.

"Anything wrong?" he asked quickly.

"Nothing I can't handle."

"Want me to drive you out to the airport?"

"No. There's something else I want you to do for me."

"Name it."

"Sam Benjamin. Bring me up to date on him. What and how he's doing."

"I haven't heard much since he moved back to New York last year," he said. *"Only that he's in constant trouble and is slow paying his bills. He's had bad luck with his last batch of pictures. Dropped about eleven million."*

"I know that," I said. "What I want to know is what he's involved in now."

"I'll get right on it."

"You call me at my apartment in New York tonight."

"Have a good flight," he said.

I went into the shower. I turned it on hot, then ice cold, then hot again, and when I got out at least I wasn't asleep. But I was still logy and tired, so I took a benny before I shaved and by the time the shave was over I was alive.

There was a foul-up and the limo never got there so it was nearly six o'clock and dark by the time I caught the cab at Kennedy International. I was surprised to see the snow piled against the sides of the roads. Then I remembered. It was Christmas week in New York.

In L.A. it wasn't real. Not the snow—it was white plastic. Even Santa Claus wore a summer-weight costume. I pulled the topcoat around me.

"Where you in from?" the hackie asked.

"California," I said.

"Shmulck," he said. "You needed this weather?"

"I like it," I said. "It's a change."

"I'd move out there," he said. "Only my old woman won't leave the children.

The grandchildren, I mean. She couldn't wait to get our own kids out of the house and now the grandchildren run around screaming all day and she's in seventh heaven. I can't figure it out. I'll never understand women."

"That makes two of us," I said.

He grunted and settled into the driving. For the rest of the trip he was silent until I gave him a tip. He looked at the fiver and grinned. "Happy *Chanukah.*"

"Buy the grandchildren a Christmas present," I said.

I let myself into the apartment and turned on the lights. Everything was just the way I left it three months ago. Even to the fresh ice in the bucket on the bar.

I fixed myself a drink and picked up the phone just as it began to ring. Sheila's voice echoed in my ear. *"Welcome home, boss. I'm downstairs in the lobby with your messages."*

"Come on up." I fixed another drink. By the time I finished, the door chime rang.

She stood there, the snow still clinging to her black coat.

She smiled. "Hello, Stephen."

I kissed her cheek. "One of the nice things about coming home is you." I took her coat. "There's a Scotch on the bar for you."

We went to the bar and she picked up her drink. "Oh, boy," she said.

I didn't speak.

She finished her drink and put down the glass. "I'm glad you're back. Everything's gone peculiar."

"Tell me."

"There's an undercurrent. I can't put my finger on it. Earnings are off. Everybody's uptight. You're not there to cool it off and Sinclair sits in his tower and fires memos down the floors like paper airplanes, scaring the shit out of everybody." She stopped for breath. "I think I could use another drink."

I fixed it for her. "It was you who got Angel to call me?"

She nodded. "How did you know?"

"I guessed," I said. "Angel's no angel. And he's ambitious. Somebody had to convince him it was better to go with me than against me."

"Your being away at the coast all the time is no help," she said. "The staff keeps churning."

"Someday I'm going to move the executive offices out there. The only thing we need in New York is a sales office. The rest is crap and tradition."

"You call it what you like, Stephen. The fact remains it's still here." She didn't say the rest of it, but I knew what she was thinking.

This was where I belonged. I was president of the company. I had to be here, not so much to do anything but to defend my job. That is, if I still wanted it.

And that was at the heart of it all.

I didn't know anymore whether I wanted it or not.

TWO

THE YEARS TURN YOU ON. The years turn you off. I had them all. I had been running up the hill for so long it became a habit. If I slowed down a little, it looked to everybody like I was beginning to slide. So off I would go again.

I didn't blame Spencer. He had his own job to do. To watch the machine with a critical eye, to goose it if he felt it dragging. And I was the only one there for him to goose. I was the man in charge.

"Who knows I came in?"

"Pretty much the whole office by now," she said. "There were lots of lights still burning when I left. They want to be ready for you tomorrow."

"I won't be in tomorrow," I said. "I'll work the phones from here. Set up the auxiliary board."

She knew what I meant. I had a special multiple-line hookup direct from my office. Everything came through just as if I was in the office. The caller never knew that I wasn't there.

"Anything special?" she asked.

"Yes. Just keep Sinclair away from me. I don't want to talk to him."

"What if he insists?"

"Tell him exactly what I said. I'm too old to play any more games. And he should be, too."

She gave me the rest of the messages and closed her notebook. I walked back to the door with her and helped her into her coat. She looked up at me, a strange expression on her face. "Are you all right, Stephen?"

"Sure," I said. "Why?"

"I don't know. You seem a little strange. As if you don't really care that much."

"I'm a little bored with it. I've made this trip too many times before."

"It's more than that."

"Maybe I'm tired. I'll be all right in the morning."

She let it go at that. "Good night, Stephen."

I closed the door behind her and went back to the bar. I made myself another drink and sat there. Fogarty was no fool. She knew me. Maybe better than I knew myself. Could be she saw something in me that I didn't. I swallowed some of the drink and began to go through the pile of memorandums she left for me.

I lost track of the time. It could have been about a half hour before the doorbell rang. I finished the last memo before I got up to answer it.

I was half a mile away when I opened the door. The girl there brought me home in a hurry. She had long, dark blond hair halfway down her back, an oval face, and blue-violet eyes with four pairs of false eyelashes. She wore a short, fluffy lynx coat on which the snowflakes looked like a decoration. Her nose was pert and tilted just a little and her smile showed small, white, even teeth and a sensual lower lip.

"Hello," I said.

"I'm Marianne Darling," she said. "I'll make it easy for you. You can call me Darling Girl."

I grinned. "Come in, Darling Girl."

"I closed the door and took her coat. She wore a purple knit mesh micro and long matching purple boots that climbed up over her knees halfway across her thighs. There was at least six inches of white meat between the top of the boots and the bottom of her dress and from the way it clung to her, she wore nothing beneath it.

She walked ahead of me into the apartment. Her eyes went everywhere at once. I stood there watching her. "What do you think?"

She turned to me. "I like it. It's all male and leathery."

"What do you drink?" I asked, leading the way to the bar.

"What are you drinking?"

"Scotch."

"I'll take the same," she said. "It makes life simpler."

I poured her drink and splashed some more into mine.

She held the glass toward me. "Bang, bang."

We drank. She saw Fogarty's glass on the bar with the faint touch of lipstick on the rim. "I'm early," she said. "I didn't mean to interrupt."

"No interruption. My secretary came over to give me my messages."

"Oh," she said.

I took the papers from the bar and put them on the desk near the window. She followed me across the room and looked out. The snow was falling.

"It's lovely from up here."

I looked out the window. "Yes." I had almost forgotten how lovely it could be. I turned back to her. "You make yourself comfortable," I said. "I want to grab a shower. I'm still sticky from the trip."

"Okay." She wandered back to the bar while I went into the bedroom.

I got out of my clothes and left them on the bed. I got into the shower stall and turned on the hot water. The heat eased the pressure, the roar of the water soothed the nerves. I don't know how long I stood there when I heard her calling. "Yes?" I shouted back over the water.

"The phone's ringing. Should I answer it?"

"Please," I yelled.

A moment later the bathroom door opened. "It's from the coast. Jack Savitt."

I cut the water and opened the shower door. "Give me the phone from the wall."

She came into the bathroom and stood, hesitating.

"Right there," I said, pointing.

She looked at me doubtfully. "Is it safe?" she asked. "I heard—"

I laughed. "It's safe."

She gave me the phone gingerly. I took it. "Jack," I said.

"Who's the girl?" he asked. *"She's got a great sound."*

"You don't know her," I said. "What did you find out?"

"Pretty much what we figured. He got into a big hole and the banks turned on the heat. They're getting ready to step in and take over. He put Dan Ritchie on last week to unload everything he could to television for the quick and ready."

"How does it tie in to the move on us?"

"Ritchie still has friends in the home office. You have twenty-six specials scheduled. That's twenty-six features that can be shown if he can knock you off."

"Okay," I said.

"Anything else?" he asked.

"Not right now. I'll get back to you tomorrow."

I reached around the shower door and gave the phone back to her. I heard the click as she put it back on the wall. I closed the door and turned the water on again.

Through the opaque glass I could see her standing there, the purple of her dress making an odd design. She didn't move.

"Anything wrong?" I called.

"No," she said. "I'm just looking."

"Looking?"

"At you," she said. "It's a wild sight through that glass. It's like you're all over the place. Crazy effect."

I turned off the water. "Better give me a towel. Before you do something rash."

"I already did," she said. "Twice. Once when I gave you the phone and just now while I was watching."

"Give me the towel anyway," I said. "And stop wasting it. We've got a long night ahead of us."

I stepped out into the towel and wrapped it around me. I pulled another towel from the rack and began to dry myself.

"I'll get your back," she volunteered.

I threw her the towel. Her hands were quick and sure. "You're not Japanese?"

"Do I rook Japanese?" she laughed.

The bathroom door opened and Angel stood there. A grin split his face. "How cozy. I see you've already met."

"Fix yourself a drink," I said. "I'll be right with you."

"Okay," he said and disappeared.

I took the towel from her hand. "You, too."

She made a face. "And I thought I would help dress you."

I laughed and pushed her toward the door. "Go ahead, Darling Girl. I'm a big boy now. I can dress myself."

They were draped around the bar when I came out. I said hello to Angel's girl and fixed myself a drink. "Any of you kids had dinner?" I asked.

Angel shook his head. "No."

I looked at the girls. "Where would you like to eat?"

"Anything wrong with the room service here?" Darling Girl asked.

"No," I answered.

"Then why fight the snow? When we can be all comfy and cozy here," she said. "We can stay in, turn on, and ball."

Angel began to laugh. "What did I tell you, boss? Isn't she too much?"

I stared at her while I picked up the phone. "Maybe," I said. I saw the flush creeping into her face and the operator came on. "Give me room service," I said.

The steaks weren't too bad and once when Angel started to talk shop, I stopped him. "Tomorrow. Time enough."

The waiter took out the table and for a moment there was a silence. Then Angel got to his feet. "Come on, Faith, baby. Time for us to go."

I made no move to stop them. After they were gone, she still sat there. We stared at each other for a long time. "What are you thinking?" she finally asked.

"I don't get it," I said. "Why are you coming on so strong?"

She smiled. "Maybe I like you."

"Again. Why?"

"It's a long story." She got to her feet and walked toward the bedroom. "Someday I'll tell you."

THREE

I SAT THERE AT THE bar drinking Scotch. Everything seemed down for me. I just didn't want the effort. It could have been a half hour before she came back.

"Hey," she called from the doorway. "You goin' to sit up all night drinking?"

I turned to look at her. The only thing she had on was her boots. I stared at her. She had painted her nipples purple to match her costume.

She smiled. "Like it?"

"It's different."

"I have some smack," she said. "I rubbed it on my nipples. It makes them tingle." She came into the room and put a cigarette in her mouth. "Give me a light," she said, leaning toward me.

I held the match for her. The acrid odor of pot filled the room. "Want a drag?"

Silently, I took the joint from her. I pulled the smoke into my lungs. I felt nothing. Nothing was working.

She took the reefer back from me. "Man, you're way down."

I didn't answer.

"Do you want I should go?"

I took a long time making up my mind. "No."

She dragged on the reefer. Her eyes were beginning to darken. "You goin' to look at me all night?" She was beginning to slur her words.

"Maybe," I said.

She nodded. "Okay, if that's what you want." She crossed the room and put on the record player. "You won't object if I have some fun?"

I smiled. "Be happy."

She began to sway in time to the music. She dragged again and passed the reefer to me. I sat there on the bar stool watching her dance. She moved around the room, turning off the lamps until there was only a faint light coming from behind the bar. She cut into the bedroom and I put the reefer in my mouth and dragged on it.

She was back in a moment, holding something in her hand. I couldn't see it in the dim light. She moved toward me. "I'd like you to meet my true love."

I looked down at her outstretched hand. The slim pink vibrator shone faintly. She turned the base handle and it began to hum.

"Steve, meet Steve."

I looked at her. She was completely serious. "We really met when I was fourteen," she said. "And he's been with me ever since." She pressed it to her cheek, then down the side of her neck and around to her breasts. She reached for the roach with her free hand.

I gave it to her. She dragged once, then gave it back to me. Her eyes were swimming now. I put the roach out in a tray and refilled my glass. I watched her in the shaded mirror behind the bar.

She was moving with the music, her eyes half shut, passing the vibrator down across her stomach. She stopped suddenly and pressed it into the neatly trimmed, dark pubic patch.

Suddenly she opened her eyes wide and stared at me. Her legs began to tremble. "Steve!" she cried out and sank to her knees, the vibrator falling from her hands to the carpet where it lay humming obscenely.

After a moment, she picked it up and turned it off. She looked up at me, a faint smile coming to her lips. "That's crazy, isn't it?"

I shook my head.

"It's a wild orgasm," she said.

"I wouldn't know."

She got to her feet. "I've got to go to the bathroom."

I turned back to the bar. The room was a strange mixture of odors. Female, pot, whiskey. I picked up my drink.

"Fix me one," she said from the doorway. I turned to look at her. She was completely dressed. I threw some ice into a glass and poured the whiskey over it.

She took it from my hand. "Bang, bang." She swallowed the drink in one gulp and walked toward the door. She picked up her fur coat from the chair and wrapped it around her. She stood there looking back at me. "Good night."

"Good night."

The door closed behind her and a few minutes passed while I sat there with the drink in my hand. Then the house phone rang. I picked it up.

She was calling from downstairs. *"I forgot to tell you something."*

"What is it, Darling Girl?"

"I love you." She hung up.

—

THE DREAMS SOCKED IN THAT night. It happened every time I returned to the apartment. Barbara was there. Maybe Sam was right. I should have moved.

But I hadn't and there she was. We were that close and then—nothing. She was gone and would never come back.

I rolled over on the bed and pushed the dreams away. No more. I let myself open wide once and blew it.

I was not about to make the same mistake again.

It was better the way it was. No ties. No hangups. Everything cool. You came and went as you pleased. No guilt feelings because you had something else to do or something else on your mind.

But still I remembered the way it was when we began to make it. Beautiful. Like nothing I had ever known before or since. But, after that, the pain. Only the pain.

No more. I pushed at the dream and tried to sleep. Then the dream went all crazy and Darling Girl was dancing again. Only this time she wore Barbara's face and kept smiling at me with Barbara's smile.

The slow teasing smile she had when she was putting me on. I reached for her and Barbara vanished. I sat up in bed, looking into the dark.

The room was silent and empty. After a moment I got out of bed and took a sleeper. That did it. I went out like a light.

—

I WOKE UP TO THE music of the telephone. I was still logy when I answered it.

It was Angel calling from the lobby. *"I kept ringing your bell. I finally went downstairs and called."*

"Come on up," I said. I pressed down the bar and released it. The operator came on and I ordered breakfast. Then I staggered into the bathroom and threw some water on my face.

Angel was bugged with curiosity, but he didn't ask any questions. I didn't volunteer any information. I swallowed some coffee and we got on the trolley.

He moved fast. He had all the ratings, all the costs, and all the answers. He was bright, tough, and ambitious, and not about to let this one get away from him. Not while Sinclair was watching.

The pattern began to come clear as I listened to Angel. As smart as he thought he was, he lived on the surface. Underneath, Sinclair was already churning up the waters. All Angel could see was that the old man had called on him.

The arithmetic was simple. The specials blew two nights a month for us. At first there had been a great deal of enthusiasm on everyone's part, even the sponsors. At last something was being done that they could be proud to be a part of. Then the ratings came in.

Pride went before ratings. Down. They translated them immediately into sales response and were beginning to have second thoughts and were looking for a graceful way out. Up came the same old reasons. Blame it on the public. After all, it was they who switched channels.

Sinclair knew of my commitment to the project and this was his way of telling me that he was unhappy. He made the opening move.

Angel was just a piece on the chessboard.

But the old man was losing his touch. King's knight pawn to four was a bad opening for him. He was about to lose Angel.

"Good work," I said. "I like the way you're thinking and your approach is sound."

"Thanks, Steve," said Angel, creaming visibly.

I sat and thought for a moment. "Got a good backup man in Daytime?"

"Pete Reiser," he said. "I had him on game shows, but I think he's ready."

"Good," I said. "I'm moving you to Special Programming. That's one flight up and fifteen grand more a year. I'm going to let you handle the whole thing. I have every confidence that you'll straighten it out."

He stared. "You won't regret it, Steve. I'll work my ass off."

"I know you will. But you'll still have to keep an eye on Reiser until we're sure he can do the job."

"No sweat, Steve. I understand."

"I think you better get out to the coast and grab a firsthand look at the rest of the shows. I want to get your comments."

"I'll be on the plane tonight." He got to his feet. "By the way, I have the report ready for Sinclair. What shall I do with it?"

"Send it to him, of course."

"There'll be a copy for you as soon as my girl finishes typing it."

"Thank you."

I waited until he had left the apartment before I picked up the telephone. I didn't even have to check to find out the report had already gone to Sinclair. I would get it when he figured a safe enough time had elapsed. I woke Jack Savitt up at home.

"Angel Perez is coming out there," I said. "Bury him."

"He'll get the 'A' treatment," Jack said.

"When you complete those arrangements, you get on a plane and come in here."

"What for?"

"I want you to handle the Ritchie-Benjamin deal."

"Wait a minute," he said. *"That started top level. That means you're elected. Sinclair won't have anyone but the network president handle it."*

"You come in," I said. "I'll take care of Sinclair."

I put down the telephone and lit a cigarette. Sinclair wanted to play. He was entitled. After all, it was his bat and ball.

But he was going to be in for a few surprises. There was a whole new set of rules. And he would have to learn them, the first being that he shouldn't play games.

FOUR

ANGEL'S REPORT WAS ON MY desk when I went into the office the next day. I picked it up and skimmed through it. He was busy making points. The only person he didn't try to assassinate was Sinclair himself.

I grinned to myself. Angel was too eager. Sinclair could read right through this one. It was too obviously self-serving. But he did make one good point. With me at the coast most of the time, there was a lack of direction in New York.

It was nothing new. We had all seen it coming for a long time. I had brought it up to Spencer almost two years ago. But he had sloughed it off then. "Spread yourself," he had said.

I didn't even bother. I merely concentrated on what I thought were the major items on the agenda. The rest had to drag behind. But no more.

I threw the report into the trash basket. Reports didn't make television programs. I pressed down the intercom. "Let me know when Sinclair comes in," I said.

"He's right here," Spencer's voice came from the doorway.

I looked up and smiled. I got to my feet and held out my hand. "Mr. Sinclair," I said.

He made a wry face as he took my hand. "I recognize that tone of voice," he said. "So it's going to be a formal meeting?"

"It's time," I smiled.

"Before we begin, am I allowed to say that I'm glad to see you, Steve?"

I grinned. "I'm glad to see you, Spencer."

He nodded and sank into a chair in front of my desk. "Why did you send Perez to the coast?" he shot at me.

"To kill him," I said. "I don't like shits."

"I asked him to do a job."

"That was your mistake. He was working for me. It was me you should have asked."

"His report makes sense."

"So did mine two years ago. But you didn't want to do anything then. I predicted we would have problems. Now that we have them, you're ready to do something. You weren't then."

"He can't be too bad," he said. "After all, he did call you."

"After he gave you the report. He was just playing it safe."

"I'm chairman of the board and responsible for the financial affairs of the company. You can't say this year has been a roaring success."

"You forgot something," I said.

"What's that?"

"When you made me president of the whole company, I automatically became its chief operating officer. I don't like anyone usurping my authority. Not even you."

"Don't be so touchy, Steve, I was only trying to help."

"I know that. But you broke the rules. And you can't do that anymore. It's another kind of ball game now."

"You mean to say I can't take corrective measures when I see something wrong?" He was beginning to lose his temper.

"There is something you can do," I said. "Tell me."

"How the hell can I tell you anything when you're out of the office all the time?"

"Did you ever hear of the telephone?" I was deliberately nasty.

He cooled off. "What are you going to do now? The board is looking for answers. Our billings are off by eleven million dollars this year."

"Pressing the panic button won't get it back."

"You're spending too much time at the coast," he said. "Sales are suffering because of that."

"They won't hurt next September when our new programs begin."

"That's a long time off. It's less than a week to the new year. We still have this winter and summer figures to worry about. Let's face it, Steve. No one knows the agencies as well as you do. You have to come back here. You can't be in two places at once."

"Now you're making sense," I said. "I can't be in two places at once. But you're wrong about the other. There is someone who knows the agencies as well as I do."

He looked his question.

"Jack Savitt," I said. "You've forgotten that he's spent his life on Madison Avenue selling agencies as well as sponsors and networks his programs."

"But what about the studio?"

"He's done his job there," I said. "He got it started and running. He's also brought along some top backup men ready to take over. I think it's time we moved him up."

He was silent for a moment while he thought that one out. "What do you intend to give him?"

"I've asked him to come in and handle the Benjamin proposition."

"Wait a minute," he protested. "That's your job."

"It's the job of the president of Sinclair TV," I said.

"But you're still the president."

"That was my mistake," I said. "When I took over your job as president of Sinclair Broadcasting, I should have put another man in my old job. I think it's about time Sinclair TV had a new president."

"And what will you do?"

"The same thing you did when you had my job," I said. "Drive everybody crazy."

He began to laugh and got to his feet. He started for the door, then turned back to me. "Come up to Greenwich for dinner on Sunday?" he asked. "The snow is very pretty up there."

"I will, if I'm not back on the coast by then."

He nodded. "Just one more thing."

"Yes?"

"Have you figured out yet when I can retire?"

I answered promptly. "When you're sixty-five."

He laughed and went out the door. I looked after him and then began to smile to myself. He lost the skirmish and won the war. He was still smarter than I was. I suddenly realized that he had gotten everything he wanted.

—

IT WAS DARK BY THE time I left the office, and I didn't see her as I came out of the building. I crossed the curb to the car and was about to get in when she tapped me on the shoulder.

"You work late, Mr. Gaunt," she said.

I turned to her. She wore another kind of fur coat this time. Red fox, I think. With a hood that covered almost all her face and all I could see were her eyes, dark and shining.

"I've been waiting since five o'clock," she said.

"That's stupid. If you wanted to see me, why didn't you come upstairs?"

"Would you believe—I was afraid?"

"Of what?"

"That you wouldn't—didn't—want to see me."

"It still would have been better than standing out here all evening and freezing your ass off."

"It wasn't so bad," she said, taking an old-fashioned pocket flask out of her pocket. She held it upside down to show me it was empty. "After a while I didn't even know it was cold."

"You'd better get in the car," I said, taking her arm.

She didn't move. "No. I wasn't waiting for that. You don't have to take me with you. I just wanted to tell you I was sorry I made such an idiot of myself last night."

I didn't speak.

"I don't know what happened to me," she said. "It was like—all of a sudden—I came unglued."

There was something very young in her face. I took her arm again. "Get in the car."

Quietly she got into the big Continental limousine. I followed her and closed the door. The chauffeur turned and looked back at us. "Where to, Mr. Gaunt?"

"Where do you live?" I asked her.

"Riverside Drive and Seventy-eighth," she answered. She began to shiver and drew back into the corner of the seat, making herself very small.

The limo pulled out into the traffic. I turned the heater on full blast. The warm air poured over us. By the time we were in Central Park, it was like an oven.

"That better?" I asked.

"Y—yes," she said. "Do you have a cigarette?"

I lit one and passed it to her. She dragged on it. After a moment, she stopped shivering. She looked out the window at the snow in the park. "Where are we going?" she asked.

"You said Riverside and Seventy-eighth, didn't you?"

"I don't want to go there," she said.

"Okay. Where then?"

She looked at me, the smoke curling up from her face. "With you."

"I'm going home to sleep," I said, "I'm beat."

She was silent for a moment, looking at my face. "Okay, then it doesn't matter. You can let me off here."

We were in the middle of the park. The snow was piled high at the edge of the road. "You're crazy," I said. "It'll take you an hour to walk out."

"I like walking in the snow." She leaned forward and tapped the chauffeur on the shoulder. "Stop here."

He pulled the car over to the curb and she opened the door and got out. She stood there, the cold air pouring into the car. "Thanks for the lift."

She closed the door, climbed over a snowbank to the sidewalk and began walking. I watched her for a moment as the car began to move and passed her slowly. Her head was down and the hood was pulled over her face; all I could see was the tip of her nose. Then she was behind us and I sat back in the seat. A moment later there was a thud against the rear window behind me.

I turned and looked back. There was another thud as the second snowball hit the window. I saw her winding up with the third. "Hold it," I told the driver.

He stopped and I went out the door. The third snowball whistled past me. I scooped up some snow, packed it into a ball and threw it. It broke across her shoulder. "Got you!" I yelled.

I made the mistake of stopping to gloat and she caught me with the next snowball. It broke across the back of my neck and poured icily down my collar. I picked up some more snow and charged her.

She ran for a tree and, hiding behind it, bombarded me as I approached. I could hear her yelling with glee. Fortunately her aim didn't match her enthusiasm. By now I was close to the tree and she broke and ran again.

I caught her in the back with two in a row and then as she stopped short to scoop up some snow, crashed into her. We plowed into a snowbank and rolled over and over down the other side. We came to a stop and I rubbed her face with snow.

"This'll teach you not to be such a smartass," I laughed.

She was suddenly motionless, looking into my face. "You're laughing," she said. "You really can laugh."

"That's a stupid thing to say."

"No." She shook her head earnestly. "You're really laughing. And I never saw you laugh before."

Her arms went up around my neck. Her nose was cold, her lips were warm, and her tongue was like a fire searching my mouth. After a moment, we caught our breath.

Her eyes went into mine. "Yeah," she said. "Really. Yeah."

FIVE

JACK CAME IN ON THE red-eye from Los Angeles. That put him down at Kennedy at seven a.m. By eight fifteen my doorbell was ringing.

She came up like a shot. Her eyes were wide and frightened. She clutched the sheet to her. "Who's that?"

"Easy," I said. "My first appointment." I got out of bed and reached for my robe.

"Will it take long?" she asked.

"Couple hours."

"Oh."

"You come out whenever you want," I said. "You don't have to hide."

"I'm going back to sleep. If he leaves before noon, you come and join me."

"And if he doesn't?"

"I'll kill him and drag you back to bed." She pulled the sheet over her head and I went out to get the front door.

Jack was all hopped up. Even the nemmies he had taken on the plane hadn't worked. He kept jumping up and down all through breakfast.

"You mean the old man didn't even raise one objection, not one squawk?"

"Not one squawk," I smiled. "As a matter of fact, he seemed pleased about it."

"Does he know I'm Jewish?"

"I imagine so. There's very little he misses."

"My God," he said in an awed voice. "Imagine that? A Jewish boy, president of Sinclair TV. Ten years ago we couldn't even get a job here."

"Tomorrow the world," I said.

He stared at me, then abruptly sat down. "My legs are weak."

"You need some more coffee." I filled his cup.

"I'll be all right. It's just that it all happened so quick. When you called me the second time yesterday and told me, I couldn't believe it"

"You believe it now?"

He looked at me and nodded. "Yes. Do you know what convinced me?"

I shook my head.

"The snow," he said. "When we came in for our landing I saw the snow and I knew it was true."

"The announcement is going to the papers this morning," I said. "You have a luncheon date with Sinclair, twelve thirty at Twenty-One; at two thirty you have a staff conference to meet the department heads."

"Will you be there?" he asked.

"Not at lunch. But I will be at the staff meeting."

He nodded. "I'll clear everything with you."

"No," I said.

He was puzzled. "Who do I report to then?"

"Nobody." I looked at him. "You're head of the network now. It's your baby. You make the decisions. All I ask is that you keep me informed."

"Suppose I bomb?"

"Then it's your ass," I said. "But you won't bomb. You'll make mistakes. Sometimes you'll guess wrong. But I'm betting you'll be right more often than not."

"That's fair enough, Steve." He opened the briefcase he had brought with him and took out some papers. "I've been studying the schedule on the way in. I have some ideas. Want to hear them?" I nodded. "You won't like the first couple of things I'm going to tell you."

"Tell me, anyway."

"I'm canceling the rest of the specials. No matter how you look at it, they got to be losers. Until we develop a replacement show, I'm going to movies." He paused and looked at me.

I nodded. "What's the other?"

"Angel Perez," he said. "I know you don't like him. But he's bright and he's tough and ambitious. I want him to be my executive vice-president."

I was silent.

"I told you that you wouldn't like it," he said.

"I don't have to," I said. "You're the one who has to live with him. Just watch your rear at all times."

"If I can't take care of myself, then I don't deserve the job," he said.

"Good enough. What else?"

He then proceeded to tear apart three of my favorite programs. "They're old and tired. They've been on the air three to five years and they've had it. I'd like to dump them all right now, but I haven't enough replacements, so I'll phase them out one at a time, beginning with 'Hollywood Stardust.'"

"Hollywood Stardust" was our person-to-person show, only we went into the stars' homes and did it there. It was great when we started four years ago, but it had gone way down. There just weren't that many real stars around. "What are you putting in its place?" I asked.

"A teen-age rock show," he said. "Rock groups, dancing, light effects, lots of girls in minis, lots of crotch shots, big noise."

"That's primetime you're talking about," I said. "Not *American Bandstand* time."

"That's right. But if ABC can find a primetime show in *Lawrence Welk*, then we ought to be able to get to the kids. What do you think?"

"What difference does it make?" Then I grinned at him. "Like I said, you make the decisions."

"Okay," he said. "Now what about the Benjamin deal?"

"You'll find a copy of the proposal on your desk when you get into the office. You look it over and then we'll talk."

He got to his feet. "I'll get back to my hotel and clean up, then head for the office."

I walked to the door with him. "See you this afternoon. Good luck."

I stood there until he got on the elevator, then went back into the apartment and poured myself another cup of coffee. Suddenly I felt old. It wasn't that long ago I had stood where Jack stood now. All the enthusiasm, the hopes, the plans. I couldn't get excited about them anymore. Everything had become cut and dried. For the first time

I began to appreciate Spencer's role in the company. Somebody had to tear the ship apart once in a while in order to rebuild it.

"Has he gone?" Her voice came from the bedroom door.

I turned. She had it open a fraction of an inch and was peering through the crack. "Yes," I said.

"Good." The door opened wide and she came into the living room. She had a towel wrapped around her sarong-style and her skin was still wet from the shower. "I was beginning to think he would never leave."

"Want some coffee?" I asked.

"Do you have any pineapple juice?"

I nodded. "In the refrigerator."

She went behind the bar for a can of pineapple juice. She punctured it and poured some into a glass filled with ice. She took a bottle of vodka and filled the glass to the top. She stirred it quickly and tasted it. "That's good." She held the glass out to me. "Try some?"

I shook my head.

She shrugged and lifted the glass. "Bang, bang." She drank as she walked back to me. "What time is it?"

"About ten o'clock."

"Shit! I had an audition this morning and forgot it." She sat down and reached for the telephone. "Mind if I call my service?"

"Go ahead. I'll shave meanwhile."

When I came out of the bathroom she was back in bed. There was a fresh glass of pineapple juice on the table next to her. "My agent's pissed off because I missed the audition."

"Was it a good job?"

"A commercial. I wouldn't have gotten it, anyway. They were looking for a Sandra Dee type. And that's one thing I'm not."

I couldn't fault that.

She looked at me. "You going right in to work?"

I shook my head. "Not until after lunch."

"Good." She rolled over on her stomach. "Do you think I have a beautiful ass?"

I looked down at her. There was only one answer. "Yes."

"Then why are you standing there? Come over here and kiss it."

I walked over to the bed and bent over her. She jumped when I slapped her and rolled over. There was a strange look in her eyes. "What did you do that for?"

I said nothing.

She smiled slowly and rolled back on her stomach. "Do it again," she said. "I like it."

—

SPENCER WAS WAITING IN MY office when I returned from the conference room after introducing Jack to the department heads. He took one look at my face. "You could use a drink," he said.

We walked over to the bar and he fixed two drinks. "Cheers," he said.

We drank.

"How do you feel?" he asked.

"Like I gave away my first baby," I said.

He nodded. "Now you know how I felt."

SIX

"THEY WANT SIX MILLION DOLLARS for the package," Jack said. "I'm going to pass."

"Okay."

He looked across my desk. "Benjamin's not going to like it. He felt sure you were going to go for it."

"I don't know why. I never spoke to him about the deal."

"He says you made him a commitment when he was at the studio. That you still had an obligation to take them." He lit a cigarette. "He's up the wall, desperate for the money."

"That's his problem."

"Ritchie tells me that the lawyers have gone over the dissolution agreement and that if we don't arrive at a compromise, they'll sue."

"They won't sue," I said.

"What makes you so sure?" he asked.

"Sam's not about to admit that he's tight. He can bring the walls down around him if his creditors find out how bad the situation really is." I got to my feet.

"Some of the pictures aren't that bad," he said.

I got annoyed. "You're president of the network. Buy them or don't. Whatever you like. But you make up your mind. That's your job."

He thought that one over. "Okay," he said. He started for the door.

"Jack," I called after him.

He stopped and looked back at me. "I'm not angry with Sam," I said. "I like him. But I'm not going to be pushed around or threatened."

"I understand," he said and went out the door.

The intercom buzzed. I pressed down the switch. *"Miss Darling on four."*

I picked up the telephone. "Hello, Darling Girl."

"What are you doing for lunch?" she asked. *"I'm horny as hell."*

"Sorry, I have a date."

"Business or pleasure?"

"Pleasure."

"I'll kill you if you're going out with another girl," she said vehemently.

"My aunt is coming down from the Cape."

"Yeah," she said sarcastically. *"And I suppose you're taking her to the Four Seasons?"*

"That's right," I laughed. "How did you guess?"

"I hate you," she said and hung up.

—

I SAT THERE AT THE poolside table, drinking my third Scotch. Aunt Prue was late. I should have guessed. She never could resist Saks Fifth Avenue when she came to town.

I finished the drink and signaled the maître d'. A fourth Scotch appeared as if by magic. At this rate, by the time Aunt Prue got here I would be bombed out of my mind. I looked toward the long entrance hallway. It was empty. I felt a hand touch my shoulder then looked around.

"I hope she stands you up!" Darling Girl said in a fierce whisper.

Before I could reply, she followed the maître d' to a table and sat down facing my way. She ordered a drink. I grinned and she stuck her tongue out at me.

"Do you know that young lady?" Aunt Prue asked.

I jumped to my feet. I hadn't even seen her arrive. "Sort of," I said. I kissed her cheek.

The waiter held her chair and she sat down. "Extra dry martini, straight up and very cold," she ordered and turned to peer at Darling Girl. She turned back to me. "She's very pretty. But her hair is dyed and she's had a nose job."

I stared at her. "How can you tell?"

"The hair is easy," she sniffed disdainfully. "And nobody on earth was born with a nose that perfect."

I smiled. Aunt Prue had to be close to seventy and she didn't miss a thing. "I got smashed waiting for you," I said.

"I dropped by Saks." The waiter brought her drink and she picked it up and held it toward me. We clinked glasses. "Much love," she said.

"Much love," I answered.

She tasted her drink. "Very good." She took another sip and put it down. "Everything all right with you?"

"Yes," I said. "Why do you ask?"

"There was something in the paper about Sinclair TV having a new president. I thought maybe you got fired."

I laughed. "That's not the way it is. I had too much to do, so I put on another man."

"A company can't have two presidents," she said with irrefutable logic. "Even I know that. Now you better tell me the truth, young man, because if you're not there any longer, I am going to sell my stock."

"You don't have to do that." I explained it to her. After a while she understood.

"Good," she said. "I'm glad that you did it. You have been working too hard."

"Not really."

"You're too thin."

This I heard before. "I lost four pounds just waiting for you to arrive."

She sipped her martini. "You ought to get married again," she said. "What are you waiting for? You're not getting any younger, you know."

"I'm waiting for the right girl," I said. "Someone like you."

"That's a copout," she said disdainfully.

"Aunt Prue, where did you learn to speak like that?" I asked in surprise.

"We're not exactly isolated up there on the Cape. We have television too."

"Okay." I signaled for the menu. "Let's order."

The waiter came to the table. He put a folded piece of paper down next to me. "From the young lady," he whispered, with a sidewise gesture of his head.

I looked down at the note. *Dinner tonight? If you're not too angry. M.*

I scribbled my answer on her note and gave it to the waiter.

He went back to her table.

"Wouldn't it be simpler if you invited her to join us?" Aunt Prue said.

"If I wanted her to join us, she would have been at the table when you arrived."

"I'll have another martini," she said testily. "You don't have to snap at me like that."

"Okay. I'll ask her." I began to get up, but when I looked over, she had already gone.

"Now see what you've done," Aunt Prue said. Suddenly she was on her side. "You've probably ruined the poor child's lunch and driven her away."

I stared at her.

"Stephen," she said. "You haven't changed since you were a child. You're just as rude as ever."

I leaned back with a sigh and ordered another Scotch. "Make it a double this time," I said. There was no other way to go.

"Is she in love with you?" Aunt Prue asked.

"Who?"

"The girl you drove out of here."

"You think every girl I talk to is in love with me. Besides I didn't drive her out."

"I know your reputation, Stephen. We also read the newspapers up there."

I was getting annoyed. "I know. You also have electricity, gas, and telephones."

Aunt Prue looked at me. "You do like the girl!" There was a note of discovery in her voice.

"I didn't say that."

"You don't have to," she said positively. "I can tell."

I hid behind my whiskey glass.

"Stephen."

"Yes, Aunt Prue?"

"If you do like her, really like her, don't hold back." Her voice was very soft. "Don't be afraid."

—

IT WAS ALMOST ELEVEN O'CLOCK when Jack finally left my office. He had not wasted the afternoon. He came in with a format for the rock show that seemed to have great promise.

"I spent all afternoon on the phone with Angel," he said. "That boy knows the music scene. I told him to start coordination on the coast. The best American groups are out there, L.A. and San Francisco. I'm sending him to Nashville next week to look over the scene there."

"Okay," I said.

"That's about it." He began to fold up his papers. "I'll try to put on a contact man to stay in touch with the record companies and the music publishers so we can be on top of what's happening."

"You'll need a very hip producer, too," I said.

He nodded. "I've been thinking about it, but I haven't come up with a man yet."

"I might have one for you. Bob Andrews."

Jack was surprised. "He's not a producer. He's a disc jockey."

"The number-one disc jockey in the country," I said. "The kids love him. He was the first to play Elvis, the first to play the Beatles. And he has one great added value. He's under contract exclusively to us."

He was even more than that. Because of him we had the number-one radio station in New York. Before he had come to work for us, we had the biggest loser of all time.

"I like it," Jack said.

"I'll have him call you in the morning."

"What if he isn't interested?" Jack asked. "He's number one where he is, maybe he wouldn't want to change."

"He'll be interested," I said. "For two years he's been after me to go into the record business or buy a record company. If we're going to put music in primetime, maybe the whole thing makes sense now."

"We should have gone into it years ago," Jack said. "Do you know how much RCA is making on Elvis, how much Capitol is making on the Beatles?"

"I know."

"That's about it." He shoved the papers into his attaché case and got to his feet. "I'm beat. I'm going back to the hotel and get some sleep."

The telephone began almost as soon as he had gone. I let it ring a few times, until I realized that Fogarty had already gone home, and picked it up.

A blast of noise, voices, and music hit my ears.

"Steve?" Her voice was hushed and quiet.

"Yes, Darling Girl?"

"I'm stoned."

"So what else is new?" I asked.

"No. I really mean it. I'm all the way out," she said. *"I've been tripping all night."*

I didn't answer and for a moment there was silence. I could hear her breathing over the background noise. *"Steve,"* she said. *"Are you still there?"*

"Yes."

"Steve. Why didn't you take me to dinner tonight?"

"I had work to do," I said.

"I would have waited for you," she said.

"You seem to be doing all right."

"I missed you," she said. *"I was lonely. I was sitting home alone. Smoking pot and crying. I had to get out."*

"Sounds like a great party," I said.

"Will you come and get me, Steve? I want to be with you."

I hesitated.

"Please."

"Okay," I said, reaching for a pencil. "Give me the address."

—

IT WAS AN ANCIENT WALK-up tenement near Twenty-eighth and First Avenue and I could hear the noise from the street and smell the pot in the ground-floor hallway as I began to climb the stairs. The noise great louder and the fumes stronger by the time I reached the top floor. The last staircase was an obstacle course of couples involved in doing their own thing and paying no attention at all to each other or to me as I stepped over or around them.

"Man, you're late," the long-haired boy in the doorway said as I came up to him. "You have a lot of catching up to do. That will be five dollars, please."

I put the five-dollar bill in his outstretched hand. He gave me a twisted stick. "Light up and turn on," he said.

If I had thought the noise was loud, it was silence compared with the blast of sound I got when I stepped inside. I stood in the narrow foyer for a moment letting my eyes get used to the semidarkness. The big noise came from the room just beyond. I moved toward it. The sound stopped and the room went abruptly dark as I reached the doorway.

I could feel the hushed expectancy of the crowd flowing around me. I stood there waiting, trying vainly to see into the darkness.

The deep baritone voice came from the far corner of the room. "And now Don Rance presents his latest work in living art, Preview of the New Year. Done in Hershey's chocolate fudge, blueberry and strawberry jam, orange marmalade, peppermint candy, Reddi-whip and, of course, the fantastic bod of Marianne Darling!"

The blaring music and the lights came on together. I blinked my eyes a moment. Then I saw her.

She was standing on a table in the center of the room, holding a sign over her head, her back to me. Her body was covered with a wild mélange of colors made by the syrup and jams already beginning to melt. Slowly she began to turn around.

The crowd went wild. They burst into applause and roars of approval. They began to press closer around the table.

I heard her voice over the noise. "What's the matter with you people? Can't you read?" She was laughing wildly and moving with the music.

They leaped toward her, their tongues out, licking at her body. The colors began to smear, one into the other. The little table began to wobble as they tried to leap higher and higher.

Still laughing, she kept her balance and completed her turn. Now she was facing me. I stared at her.

Her breasts were painted into giant testes, red and purple, and from between them drawn in sticky chocolate-fudge syrup was an erect phallus pointing down and disappearing into her Reddi-whip-covered pubis from which appeared the hook end of an inch-thick, long, candy-striped peppermint cane. The sign she held above her head had just two words printed on it.

EAT ME!

Her eyes found mine and for a brief moment, they cleared. But she was too far out and she had already made her commitment. The clouds came back and she smiled at me. "Isn't it beautiful?" she yelled.

Just then a man reached up and pulled the peppermint cane from her and buried his face in her whipped-cream-covered crotch, his tongue licking the cream avidly. The table finally collapsed and she went down in the midst of the screaming crowd and was hidden by the mass of bodies pressing forward.

I closed my eyes and fought the nausea inside me. Then I turned and ran from the apartment. I didn't stop running until I had gone down the stairs and out into the street. Then I leaned my head against the cold stone of the gray building on the corner and retched out my guts.

It was Barbara. All over again.

SEVEN

"MR. BENJAMIN ON THE LINE *for you,"* Fogarty said.

I pressed down the button. "Hello, Sam."

His voice was filled with reproach. *"Why do you hate me, Steve?"*

I laughed. "What makes you think that?"

"You sicced Jack Savitt onto me. You know I never could communicate with him."

Sam had come up in the world. "Communicate" was a word I had never heard him use before. "I didn't sic him onto you. That's his job. He's network president now."

"So what's a title between friends?" Sam asked. "We always dealt direct. Face to face. Why not now?"

"I'm afraid it's not my job anymore, Sam. You wouldn't want me to go over his head, would you?"

"Yes," Sam answered flatly.

"I won't do it, Sam. That's not the way I operate."

He was silent for a moment. *"Okay,"* he said. *"Does that mean you won't come to dinner tonight if I ask you?"*

"Ask me."

"How about it? It will be like old times. Junior is down from school for the holidays and Myriam is honoring us with her presence. I'll even have Denise make brust flanken *for you, if you want."*

"You don't have to. Just give me the address."

"Seven hundred Fifth, eight o'clock."

Sam had come up in the world. Fifth Avenue was a long way from the Bronx. I hoped half the things I heard about his problems weren't true. It would be heartbreaking if he had to go all the way back.

The intercom clicked. *"Mr. Savitt and Mr. Andrews are here to see you."*

"Ask them to come in."

She opened the door and they came into the office. I waved them to seats in front of the desk and a moment later she came back with the coffee. By the time we finished shaking hands all around, the coffee was served and the cups were in front of us. She closed the door behind her.

"I see you and Jack got together. What do you think of the idea?"

"I'm flipped out," he said in his hip, resonant announcer's voice. "I've been waiting for something like this for a long time."

"I'm pleased," I said. "Did Jack also tell you about our plans to go into the music and record business?"

Andrews nodded. "He mentioned it but said that you would fill me in."

"It's simple," I said. "We're starting a separate division and I think you're the man to head it up. You know the business and have the respect of everybody in it."

"I don't believe it. It's like getting all the goodies at once."

"I was approached a few months ago by Joe Regan about taking over his company. What do you think of Symbolic Records?"

He thought for a moment. "It's not a bad company. Musically they're in all the grooves, they have a good library of standards which they acquired when they took over the old Eagle Record and Music companies. They get their share of hits and have fair distribution."

"What's on the flip side?"

He grinned at my use of his own language. "They have lousy administration and management. They're into the Mafia shylocks for their financing and the word is out that the squeeze is on them."

"Any idea how much they owe?" I asked.

"I hear between two and three million dollars," he answered. "And at thirty percent interest, they have no room to swing."

"Are they worth a shot?"

He nodded. "Worth getting more information on. The label is good in the trade."

I like the conservatism of his approach. Strange that you could know a man for so long and never really know him in depth. I would have been the last person in the world to give him credit for business brains. But then I suppose I should have known better. He had negotiated his own contract with us and it was a bitch. The best dee-jay deal in the world.

I pressed the Fogarty button. "Get Joe Regan at Symbolic Records in Los Angeles." I turned back to them. "Now about the show, what are your plans?"

"I thought Bob might go out to the coast after the first of the year and get it started," Jack said.

"I have a few dates over the holidays that I can't get out of," Andrews said. "I'm doing a New Year's rock show at the old Brooklyn Fox."

"That seems all right with me," I said.

The intercom clicked. *"Mr. Regan on the line."*

I picked up the telephone. "How are you, Joe?"

His voice had an echo. I sensed that he had me on the box so I could be heard by other people in his office. *"Couldn't be better, Steve. And you?"*

"Good," I said. "Thought I'd check and find out if there was anything new on that matter we spoke about a few months ago."

"Nothing much has happened, Steve," he said. *"We've had a couple of offers, but they weren't the kind of association we were interested in. Right now we're in pretty good shape. We got a couple of records on the charts."*

"Still interested in talking?"

"Could be," he said cautiously, then blew the whole thing with his next question. *"When would you like to sit down?"*

"I'll be back in California tomorrow. Why don't you come over to the studio for lunch with me?"

"Twelve thirty okay?"

"Perfect," I said and put down the telephone. "You heard the conversation. I'll meet him tomorrow." I got to my feet. "I'll keep you informed."

They left the office and Fogarty came on the intercom. *"Miss Darling called twice while you were in the meeting. Do you want me to get her for you?"*

"No." I clicked off, then put the switch back on.

"Yes, Mr. Gaunt?"

"If Miss Darling should call again, tell her that I have no interest in talking to her."

Fogarty was silent for a moment. *"Just like that?"*

"Just like that," I said and clicked off.

—

DENISE OPENED THE DOOR FOR me herself. "Stephen," she smiled. "It's been a long time."

I gave her the roses and kissed her cheek. "Too long," I said. "But you look younger than ever."

"Thank you," she said. "Now I know why I like seeing you. You're good for my ego."

I followed her into the living room. Outside the windows the snow covered the park, and the sound of traffic far below rose faintly to our ears.

"What would you like to drink? Sam is showering, he'll be out in a minute."

A maid gave me the drink. I tasted it. Good. "This is a lovely room."

"I'm glad you like it," she said, pleased. She gave the flowers to the maid. "You can't decorate in California the way you do here."

I nodded. California living was much less formal. "Happy to be back?"

"Yes," she said. "Sam is too. He never really liked California. He's a New Yorker through and through."

Junior came into the room. He was almost as tall as I, slim and slightly awkward, with long, evenly cut hair. He came over to me, his hand out. "Uncle Steve."

We shook hands. "Junior," I said. I grinned at him. "Either I'm growing shorter or you're growing taller. It has to be at least three years since I've seen you."

"Yes," he laughed. "At my *bar mitzvah.*"

I nodded. "That was a swinging affair."

He laughed again. "It sure was. My father had a ball."

Sam came into the room. "How do you like it?" he asked, gesturing grandly to the apartment.

"It's great," I said.

He turned to Denise. "Where's Myriam?"

"She'll be here," Denise said.

"It's after eight o'clock," he said. He turned back to me. "That daughter of mine has no concept of time. She's always late."

"That's okay," I said. "I've got time. I'm not leaving until eleven. I'm making the midnight plane."

"Going back to the coast?" Sam asked.

I nodded.

The doorbell rang. "That must be Myriam," he said. "I'll get it."

I turned back to Denise. We could hear his voice from the other room. "What kind of a way is that to dress?" he yelled. "If your skirt was any shorter you'd have to shave!"

We couldn't hear her reply.

Junior grinned. "Pop's at it again."

I turned to the door just as they appeared in it. Sam came right into the room, but she stood there staring at me. I stared back at her.

Sam stopped and turned around. "Myriam, you remember Uncle Steve, don't you?"

She hesitated a moment, then came toward me, her hand outstretched. "Of course I do," she said.

I took her hand. Her face was pale beneath her makeup. There was a strange frightened look in her eyes. "Myriam," I said.

Over her shoulder I could see Junior watching us with a peculiarly private form of amusement. I suddenly realized that he had been the only person in the room who had known in advance what would happen.

"But I think I'm a little too grown up to call you 'Uncle' anymore," Darling Girl said.

EIGHT

THE MAID RETURNED WITH THE roses in a vase. She looked questioningly at Denise.

"Put them on the piano, Mamie," Denise said.

Mamie crossed the room, put down the flowers, and turned to us. "Dinner is ready."

I was seated next to Darling Girl. She was busy playing games. "Are you going to be in town for awhile?" she asked.

"I'm leaving for the coast tonight," I said. Opposite me, Junior grinned. I saw him glance at his sister.

"Myriam was thinking of going to the coast," he said. "She says there's more work out there."

"Over my dead body, she'll go," Sam said. "I have enough trouble keeping track of her right here."

Mamie placed the soup in front of us. I took a spoonful and almost dropped it in my lap. Beneath the tablecloth, Darling Girl had put her hand on my cock.

"What do you think, Steve?" she asked in a falsely sweet voice. "Don't you think there is more work out there?"

"I'm not all that sure," I answered. "It would seem to me that if you have real talent one place is as good as the other."

"You'll go out there only if you have a firm job," Sam said.

She looked into my eyes, teasing. "Why don't you give me a job, Uncle Steve?"

"That's enough, Myriam," Denise said firmly. "Steve came here for dinner, not to be bothered."

"I don't mind, Denise, I'm used to things like that. I have a standard answer."

"What's that?" Darling Girl asked.

"Send in your picture. I'll see that it gets to the casting department."

"Then what happens?"

"They put it in the file-and-forget folder." I almost went out of my seat as she pinched me.

"I'm sorry I asked," she said in a cold voice.

—

I LOOKED AT MY WATCH. "Time for me to go. Thank you for a very lovely dinner, Denise."

"We enjoyed seeing you."

"Can you give me a lift?" Darling Girl asked. "I'm going to Ninetieth and York. It's on your way."

"Okay," I said.

"I'll go down to the car with you," Sam said. He went to the foyer closet for our coats.

"So long, Uncle Steve," Junior smiled. We shook hands. He glanced around quickly to see if anyone was near. "Myriam's been in love with you ever since she was a kid," he whispered. "That's why she was so shook up when she saw you."

I looked at him with relief. At least there were some things he didn't know. "So long, Junior."

We went out into the elevator. Sam looked at me. "What are we going to do about those pictures?"

Darling Girl was watching us with peculiar concentration.

I didn't answer.

The elevator door opened. "You go on to the car," Sam said to her. "I want to talk to Steve for a minute."

She kissed his cheek and ran out. I saw the chauffeur hold the door for her. When it closed Sam turned to me.

"That girl's a problem. She's running with all the bums in New York. I don't dare tell her mother."

"She's young yet."

"I hope she finds some nice boy and settles down," he said.

"She will. Give her time."

The words seemed to come reluctantly to his lips. "We've always been friends. I'll lay it right on the line for you. If we don't make a deal and make it quick, I'm bust."

I saw Darling Girl looking back through the window of the car at us. I turned to him. "How much do you need?"

"Four million dollars."

"What about Dave Diamond?"

"I can't go to him. I'm into him for ten million now and he's hollering." He took a deep breath. "I had a run of bad luck, but I got a couple of pictures almost finished that I think will be winners."

That was film talk. Nobody ever made a picture that wasn't going to be a big winner. I looked out at Darling Girl. She was still watching us.

"What have you got that isn't in hock?"

"Nothing." He thought for a moment. "Except the stock in my company."

"What can you get for that?"

"Right now?" He didn't wait for my answer. "Not a penny. But if I had the room to operate with the four million it would be worth twenty-five million in a year."

"Okay," I said. "I'll take twenty-five percent for four million dollars and give you an option to buy it back within one year for the same money or book value, whichever is higher."

"You mean Sinclair will buy twenty-five percent of my company?"

"No. Sinclair won't," I said. "I will."

He took my hand and gripped it hard. For the first time since I knew him, he was speechless.

"Tell your lawyer to call me at the studio tomorrow," I said and went out to the car.

It was a hell of a price to pay for fucking his daughter.

She moved to the far end of the seat as I got into the car. "Ninetieth and York," I said. "Then American Airlines at Kennedy."

"No. That was just an excuse to get out of there. I'll go to the airport with you."

"What for?"

"I want to talk to you."

I was silent.

"You could at least listen," she said.

"Skip York Avenue," I said to the chauffeur. "We'll go right to the airport."

She pressed the button near her and the glass partition went up, blocking the chauffeur from us. I took a cigarette and lit it. She looked at me. I held the pack toward her.

She dragged on the cigarette and leaned back in the seat. She looked at the chauffeur's head, not at me. "I love you."

The car went two blocks.

"You don't believe that, do you?" She still wasn't looking at me.

I didn't answer.

"I'm not a child," she said. "I'm not crazy. I got hung up on you when I was a little girl. It's always been like that?"

"Why didn't you tell me who you were when you came in that night?"

"At first it was a big joke," she said. "Then I was afraid. Afraid you'd be angry and stop seeing me."

Suddenly I was tired. I leaned my head back and closed my eyes. "It doesn't matter now," I said wearily. "It's over."

I heard her move on the seat and opened my eyes. "Because of last night?"

"No," I said.

"Then why?"

"Because I'm too damn old to start teaching kindergarten to emotionally disturbed children."

"Is that what you think I am?"

"What do you think you are?"

Her eyes filled with tears, but she kept looking at me. "Like everyone else," she said. "A little mixed up, a little frightened. Trying to grab it all in before the bomb. What makes you think I'm so different from every other girl you've been balling?"

"Maybe that's just it," I said bluntly. "You're no different."

"Oh!" She gasped as if I had physically hit her. She closed her eyes. We didn't speak until the car came off the Van Wyck Expressway into the airport. He turned onto the ramp at the terminal.

"Steve," she said.

I looked at her.

"Take me with you," she asked.

"No."

She seemed to shrink at the coldness in my tone. Her voice grew very small and very tight. "Don't close me out, Steve. I've nowhere else to go."

The car stopped and I got out. I leaned back into the car. "Myriam," I said. "Would you like to do yourself a favor?"

She just looked at me with wide dark eyes.

"Do what your father wants. Find yourself a nice boy and settle down." I started to close the door.

She put her hand on the door and held it open. "Steve. Please."

"Turn it off, Myriam. You're a big girl now," I said wearily. "Can't you see it just won't work?"

I pushed the door shut and walked into the terminal without looking back.

NINE

MY FIRST STOP IN THE morning was Dave Diamond's office on the second floor of the California Consolidated Bank's head office on Wilshire Boulevard. He came out from behind the walnut executive desk that made him look half his size and held out his hand. "This is a surprise."

I took his hand. Over in the corner of the room a small television set was running the latest market figures. It was one of the services of our UHF station. It was amazing how big an audience it pulled. Everybody was interested in money.

"What can I do for you?" he asked, as his secretary put a cup of black coffee in front of me.

"Two things," I said. "First, I want you to give me a complete rundown on Joe Regan and Symbolic Records."

"You'll have that in ten minutes," he said. "We keep a current file on all companies we do business with." He spoke a few words into the telephone and turned back to me. "What's the second?"

"I want to borrow four million dollars."

"Personally?" he asked.

"Personally."

"Money's very tight," he said.

"I know. That's why I'm here. This is where you come when it's hard to get."

He laughed. "You guys must think I print it."

"Don't you?"

He laughed again and became serious. "What's your collateral?"

"Sinclair stock," I said.

"Good collateral, but do you have enough stock to cover the loan? We're allowed to lend seventy-five percent of the market value."

"I have enough."

"Okay," he said. "When do you want the money?"

"As soon as I can get it."

"I'll put it in the works." He picked up the telephone again and spoke a few minutes to his loan department. "See how easy it is? Just visit your friendly neighborhood banker."

I smiled.

"If it's not a secret," he asked delicately, "what do you want the money for?"

"I'm buying twenty-five percent of Samarkand."

He stared at me incredulously. "Sam Benjamin's company?"

I nodded.

"I don't believe it. You gotta be too smart for that. Do you know how much he owes us that he can't pay back?

I had nothing to say.

"Eight million dollars!" he said vehemently. "And I was the world's prize shmuck to give it to him!"

I smiled. Sam even had to exaggerate his disasters. "Well, now you don't have to feel so bad. You've got company."

"It may sound crazy to you," he said. "Like I'm talking against myself. Your loan is good business for us, we charge the highest interest rates in town. Besides that, we'll grab a million dollars of that money right off the top before he even sees it because that's what's due right now. So you see we can't get hurt by it and still, I'm telling you just one thing—" He paused to catch his breath. "Don't do it!"

His secretary came into the office and put some papers on his desk. "The report on Symbolic Records that you asked for, Mr. Diamond."

He nodded and she left the office. He looked down at the report and then back at me. "Now if you wanted to but this company I would say it's a smart thing. They're doing good business and once you get rid of the shylocks and put in proper management you got a chance. But the other's like throwing the money into the sewer."

"I appreciate your honesty, Dave," I said. "But I'm committed."

"Nothing's committed until the money is passed," he said. He saw I wasn't going to answer. "Okay. But I'm your friend. At least you can tell me why."

"Let's put it this way," I said. "Everybody has to pay his dues. I'm paying mine."

BY THE TIME I COMPLETED the arrangements at the bank, signed the papers, had the stock certificates brought up from the vault, it was almost twelve o'clock.

"Everything's clear on this end," Dave said. "I'll credit Sam's account as soon as you notify me."

"I'll call you from the studio."

Joe Regan was waiting by the time I reached my office. "Give me ten minutes," I said. "And we can go right over to the commissary."

"Take your time, Steve," he said.

I went into my office and placed a call to my attorney in New York and another call to Sam. The attorney's call came through first.

"It's a simple transaction, Paul." Briefly I explained it to him.

"I understand," he said.

"I'll arrange for Sam and his attorney to go over to your office," I said. "As soon as I hear from you that they have delivered the stock and signed the repurchase option, I'll have the money transferred to his account."

"It would be preferable if the money could be paid over at the time of the closing," Paul said.

"All right. Notify me when you set the closing and I'll have Dave Diamond at the bank on a conference hookup."

"That's better," Paul said. "I'll get back to you."

Sam was on the line as soon as Paul got off. "The money is ready for you," I said. "Have your attorney get in touch with Paul Gitlin. He'll handle the closing for me."

"Why Paul Gitlin?" Sam snorted. "I've done business with him before. He's a monster. Certifiable."

"For four million dollars you can afford to love him," I said.

"Can I get the money today?" Sam asked.

"He says all you have to do is deliver the stock, sign the agreement, and you've got the money."

"I love him already," Sam said.

I put down the telephone and had my girl bring Joe Regan into the office. "How about a drink before we go over to lunch?" I asked. "There's no hard liquor sold in the commissary."

"Bourbon and water," Joe said quickly.

I nodded to the girl and she went to the bar and fixed our drinks. She brought them to us and left the office.

"Cheers," I said.

He nodded and we drank. "Ah, that helps," he said. "I'm glad you called. I really couldn't speak the other day. I had some people in the office and I had to put you on the box."

"I guessed as much."

"They're beginning to squeeze," he said. "They want to move in the way they did on that company back East."

I let him talk.

"I was getting ready to turn it over to them. It's getting so that I can't sleep nights." His glass was empty. "Can I have another?"

I got up and walked over to the bar. I refilled his glass and went back behind my desk.

He took a swallow of the drink. "I was going to give it to them and walk away from it. Can you imagine that? Fifteen years of my life and I'm ready to chuck it."

"What does it take to get them out?"

"Just pay them what I owe them," he said. "They don't own any stock—yet. That was the next step. They offered to knock off half the loans for fifty percent of the company."

"How much do you owe them?" I asked.

"About a million seven."

"That's not bad."

"To you," he said. "But not to me. As much money as we make, I can never seem to catch up."

"Relax," I said, putting down my empty glass. "Let's put our heads together. We ought to be able to work something out."

I started to get up and the phone rang. It was Paul on the line from New York. "I just heard from Benjamin," he said. "They'll be over at my office at five o'clock. If you set up the conference call for five thirty, everything should be in order. That's two thirty your time."

"Will do," I said.

"Steve," he said.

"Yes."

"It's none of my business, I know, but have you thought about this?"

"What do you mean?" I asked.

"Speaking as an attorney," he said, "I'm not familiar with your employment contract, but there could be a clause in it that prohibits you from doing something like this."

"There isn't."

"There's also a question of ethics," he said. "After all, they are a company with whom your company does business. There could be a question of conflict of interest."

"It can never come to that," I said. "It's actually nothing but a loan; I'm taking the stock merely as a form of security. That's why the repurchase agreement."

"Then why don't you let me draw it up that way?" he asked. "It might not help much, but it will look a little better if anything does come up."

"You're the lawyer, you do it any way you think right. Just have it ready for him today, please."

"I will," he said. "I feel better about it already."

"So do I, Paul. Thank you." I put down the phone and turned to Joe. "Come on, let's go to lunch."

"I could just as well sit here and drink," he said.

"That's not a bad idea," I said. "I'll have something sent in."

He was smashed by the time he left. But I had a hunch that it wasn't the liquor as much as it was relief. He was going to get two and a half million dollars of Sinclair stock for his company and we were going to pay off the debt.

The conference call came through almost as soon as he had left. Sam was on the line as soon as the formalities were completed. "I just wanted to thank you."

"You don't have to," I said. "Just make it work and you get your stock back."

"I will. Everything will be all right now. It really will be a happy New Year."

That was the first time I realized that it was New Year's Eve.

—

IT WAS TOO LATE TO make any plans. Besides I wasn't in much of a mood to hit any of the parties. I was tired and all I wanted was to go back to the hotel, take a hot bath, have some dinner, watch a little television, and go to bed. I made only one mistake. I never should have turned on the television set.

Television on New Year's Eve is filled with nostalgia. I began to drink. At nine o'clock, I watched the lighted ball drop down the Times Building at midnight in New York while Guy Lombardo played. At ten o'clock, I caught Woody Herman at midnight in Chicago. By that time I had killed almost a bottle of Scotch and I stumbled into bed.

I thought I would go right to sleep, but the whiskey was working on me. I was too high to drift off. I lay there half in and half out of the world while the sounds of the approaching midnight grew louder around the hotel.

It was five minutes to twelve when the front doorbell of the bungalow began to ring. I waited a few minutes, hoping whoever it was would realize their mistake and go away. They didn't. The bell kept ringing.

Finally I got out of bed, slipped on my robe. I threw the door open angrily, ready to blast anyone who stood there.

She was there, looking up at me with wide, timid eyes. "I was—I was afraid I wouldn't get here in time," she said in a soft voice. "Happy New Year."

I opened my arms and she came into them.

TEN

I ROLLED OVER IN THE bed and looked at her. She opened her eyes. "Good morning," I said.

She smiled. "Happy 1965."

I kissed her. "Happy 1965." I picked up the phone and asked for room service. I looked back at her. "What would you like for breakfast?"

She made a face. "Just coffee."

"I'm starved," I said and ordered the works.

"You're not going to be able to eat all that," she said.

"Watch me," I said. I rolled on top of her pressing her into the bed with my weight. Her arms went up around my neck and pulled my face down to her. Her mouth was morning sweet.

"What would you have done if I hadn't come out?" she asked.

"Nothing," I said. "Been lonely."

She held my cheek close to her face while she whispered, "My cunt feels so good. So warm and loved." She drew back and looked into my eyes. "I'm still full of you. You poured. Man, how you poured."

"You keep on talking like that," I said, "and you might have to go through the whole thing over again."

"You don't frighten me," she smiled. "I love it."

I started to kiss her again, but the doorbell rang. "Damn," I said.

She slipped out of bed. "You wanted breakfast." She started for the bathroom. I called her and she turned in the doorway and looked back.

"You're beautiful. Do you know that?"

"Go get your breakfast," she laughed. "I don't want to be responsible for your starving to death."

I slipped into my robe and went to the front door. I was drinking the orange juice before the pink cloth-covered table came to a stop.

I had almost finished my ham and eggs by the time she came out of the bedroom, wrapped in a towel, her hair still wet from the shower. I looked at her with my mouth full and gestured to the chair.

She sat down, poured herself some coffee, and didn't speak until I had finished mopping up my plate with the last piece of English muffin.

"You weren't kidding," she said when I put down my knife and fork.

"I told you I was hungry." I poured myself more coffee. "I feel better now."

She picked up her coffee cup.

I got up and pulled the venetian blind. The sunlight flooded into the room. "It's a beautiful day out and we have a long three-day weekend in front of us. Why don't we take off?"

"And go where?" she asked.

"Palm Springs?"

"Too dull," she said.

"Las Vegas?"

"Too busy," she said.

"The ocean? We can go down to La Jolla and charter a boat."

"I get seasick just looking at the waves," she said.

"What would you like to do then?" I asked.

"Why do we have to do anything?" she smiled up at me. "Why can't we just stay in and fuck?"

"Can't top that," I said. "Okay, if that's what you want, go get dressed."

Her surprise showed in her voice. "What for?"

"If that's all we're going to do this weekend," I said, "I've got a much more romantic place to do it."

—

I TURNED THE CAR INTO the driveway and went on into the carport. I got out of the car. "Come on."

She followed me to the front door and I took out a key and opened it. "You walk down," I explained.

We stopped at the bedroom on the first level and I put away the valise into which we had tumbled enough things for the weekend. I hit the button and the ceiling rolled back.

She threw herself on the bed and looked up. The overhead sun bathed her in gold. "I don't believe it," she cried.

"That's only the beginning," I said. I hit the other button and the bed began to move and the television sets came up and down around the room. I turned the switch off and everything stopped.

"Enough for now," I said. "Let me show you the rest of the place."

We went on down the steps into the living room. I pressed a wall switch and the drapes moved back. All Los Angeles lay there at our feet. I moved back the sliding glass door and we stepped outside. The small oval pool sparkled in the sunlight.

"It's beautiful," she yelled, kicking off her shoes and pulling her dress over her head. She dove into the pool and came up sputtering water. She squinted her eyes and turned her face toward me. "Whose place is this?"

"Mine," I answered.

She swam back toward me, her naked body gleaming even more whitely in the blue water. She rested her arms on the edge of the pool. "How long have you had it?"

"Five years about."

"Who lives here?"

"Nobody," I said.

She was silent for a moment. "I don't get it. With a place like this, why keep living in the hotel?"

"I'm not ready for it, I guess. Besides I get service in the hotel." I began to take off my shirt. "I tried it for one night."

"And?"

"It was too empty." I stepped out of my shoes and slacks and pulled off my shorts. I ran naked to the diving board and held my hands over my head.

"Yum, yum, yum," she laughed, looking up at me.

I dove into the water. Between the pool heater and the sun, the water was warm. I came up looking for her. I didn't see her.

She was a white streak under the water as she caught me around the waist, her mouth nibbling at my loins. We sank into the pool and came up blowing water.

"Hey," I asked laughing, "do you know you can drown trying to do something like that?"

"Do you know a better way to die?" she asked.

—

WHEN THE SUN WENT DOWN we had steaks and baked potatoes that I had picked up at the market on Sunset on our way over. Afterward we turned on the stereo and stretched out in front of the fireplace.

"How do you feel?" I asked as I turned to her with the brandy warmed by the hearth.

"Fantastic," she said. She sipped her brandy. "Am I anything like your wife?"

I was startled. "What makes you ask?"

"Once, last night, when you were inside me, you called out her name. Barbara, wasn't it?"

"Yes," I said. "Barbara."

"Do I remind you of her?"

I looked into my brandy glass. It was dark and golden. I swished the liquor around. "In a kind of way."

"How?"

"Attitudes mostly. Nothing I could put my finger on. The way you both looked at life and approached it. Barbara was a very physical person. She, too, wanted to feel everything, taste everything."

"Did she?"

"No," I said. "But then, no one ever does."

She was silent. Then she took another sip of the brandy. "I will," she said.

—

LATER THAT NIGHT WHEN I was lying on her and in her and our skins were like extensions of each other, she looked into my eyes. "I want to see the sky," she said.

"It will be cold, the nights are cold," I said.

"I don't care," she said. "You'll keep me warm."

I reached across then hit the switch. The cool night air came rushing down over us. The moon painted her face a pale white.

She pulled my head down to her breast. "Don't move," she said. Then she pulled the sheet over us up to our shoulders. "Now turn your head and look up."

It was beautiful. The moon and the stars filled the midnight-blue velvet of the sky.

"It's like flying, isn't it?" she whispered.

"Yes," I said.

I could feel her tighten around me. "I love you."

I thrust myself deeply into her until she groaned trying to absorb all of me. "More, I want more," she said huskily. "Put all of you inside me. Your balls, your whole body. All of you."

It was like that the whole weekend. We never left the house except to go to the market for food, the liquor store for wine and whiskey, and the Strip for grass.

On Monday I brought the rest of my things from the hotel and we moved in.

ELEVEN

"I'LL HAVE TO FIND AN apartment," she said.

"Why?"

"You know why. How would it look if Mother or Daddy called me and the service answered, 'Gaunt residence'?"

"That's simple," I said. "We'll have a separate line put in. Only you will answer it."

"And the address?"

"Nobody knows this place. That wouldn't make any difference."

She shook her head. "It wouldn't work. The first thing they'll want to do if they come out here is see my apartment. Just to make sure that I have a comfortable place to live."

"Okay," I said.

"Don't look so hurt," she laughed. "I'm not moving out. It's just a cover."

"Try to find a place nearby."

"I'll need a car too."

"I've arranged for that already. A Mustang convertible will be delivered here for you tomorrow."

"White with red leather?" she asked.

I nodded.

She flung her arms around me like an excited little girl.

That was on Monday. When I came from the studio Tuesday evening, she was pacing up and down the living room. "They didn't deliver the car yet."

"I'll check them tomorrow," I said casually. "I'll get into a pair of slacks and we'll go out for a bite to eat."

"I'm not hungry!" she said petulantly and went up the steps to the bedroom. I could hear the door slam.

I went over to the bar and poured myself a drink. I wondered if there was anything I had done to upset her. I looked down at the ashtray behind the bar.

It was filled with cigarette butts, half of them roaches. It all began to make sense. She had been bored with nothing to do all day and now she was coming down from her high.

I swallowed some of my drink and sat there. I heard her footsteps on the stairs and turned around. She had put on a pair of pants.

She came toward me and took a cigarette from the bar. I held the light for her. She looked slightly pale, blue shadows under her eyes, and there seemed to be faint beads of perspiration on her forehead.

"Are you feeling all right?" I asked.

"No," she answered shortly. She dragged on the cigarette.

"What is it?"

"You wouldn't understand," she said antagonistically.

"I think I might. Is it a female thing?"

For a moment I thought I detected a kind of relief in her eyes. "Something like that," she admitted.

I didn't speak.

"Ever since I began to take the pill," she said. "There are times when I go out of whack."

"Why didn't you say so? Is there anything I can do?"

She shook her head. "No." She dragged on the cigarette, then looked at me. "Can I borrow the car for a few minutes?" she asked. "I'll run down to the drugstore. Maybe I can find something there that'll help me."

"I'll drive you down if you like."

"No. You don't have to bother," she said. "You take your shower and change. I'll be back in a few minutes."

"Okay. The keys are in the car."

She kissed my cheek. "Thanks." She ran up the steps. I heard the motor start and the car move out of the driveway. Then I took my drink from the bar and went up to shower.

It was over an hour and I was on my third drink by the time she got back. I heard her footsteps on the stairs crossing over to the bedroom, then I heard the bathroom door close. I made myself another drink and waited. It was another fifteen minutes before she came down.

"How do you feel?"

"Better," she said.

"You look better." It was true. Her color was more normal and the blue shadows seemed to be disappearing from beneath her eyes. "What did the druggist give you?"

"I don't know," she said. "But he made me take it there and wait to see if it worked. That's what took so long."

"I'm glad it worked," I said. "Would you like a drink?"

"No," she smiled, taking my arm. "You must be starved. Let's go out to eat."

"Okay," I said, putting down my drink. "But you might have to drive. I think I'm a little smashed."

"My poor baby," she smiled. She pulled my face down to her and kissed me. "I'm sorry I gave you such a hard time."

—

SHE FOUND A SMALL APARTMENT on the hill just below the house. She put a telephone into the apartment and an extension line to the house. That way whenever the telephone rang in the apartment, it would also ring at the house. It worked very well.

She was generally awake and on the phone to her agent by the time I left in the morning. She spent a good part of the day running around town on interviews. Once I asked her how she was doing.

"It's a drag," she said. "All most of them want is to get laid."

Another time when I came home, she was sitting in the fading light in the living room, dragging on a reefer.

"Aren't you turning on a little early?" I asked.

She didn't answer.

I went over and kissed the top of her head. "You can talk to me. I'm your friend."

"I have to get a job," she said. "I have to."

"Why the blues?" I asked. "You're only out here a few weeks. It takes time until you get established."

"Daddy's raising hell," she said. "He says if I don't get something within a month, he wants me to come home."

"You spoke to him?"

"Just before you came home," she answered. "He and Mother called me."

"Keep on making the rounds," I said. "Something will turn up. They're beginning to cast next fall's shows."

"So what?" she asked. "I keep losing the job to somebody's girlfriend. Maybe I'm using the wrong approach."

"No, you're not," I smiled. "You've got a friend at Sinclair."

She looked up, a hope in her eyes. "You mean you'll do something to help me?"

"I might," I put on a false leer. "Of course you know what that means. You'll have to show your appreciation. You might even have to sacrifice your honor."

"I'm willing." She laughed, got to her feet and pulled off her dress. "Now?"

"It's as good a time as any," I said, pulling her to me.

The next morning I heard they were looking for a new girl in one of our Western series. I had her go up for it. It wasn't much of a part, but it was good exposure. She got it.

—

AT THE END OF THE month I had to go into New York for the board meeting. Besides, the rock show was ready and I wanted to see how Jack would juggle the schedule to accommodate it. She drove me out to the airport.

"You hurry back," she said.

"I will," I promised.

"And stay away from the New York girls. I'm a very jealous woman."

"I know that," I laughed. I kissed her and went into the terminal as she drove off. But the airport was socked in by fog and at one o'clock in the morning when they announced that all flights were canceled for the night, I caught a taxi and went home.

She was fast asleep, curled in a ball, the sheets kicked down around her feet. There was a kind of childlike defenselessness about the way she lay there that made me smile to myself. A dozen burglars could have come and gone and she wouldn't have known the difference. Gently, I picked up the sheet and covered her.

I undressed in the dark and went into the bathroom, closing the door before I turned on the light so that I would not disturb her.

I went over to my washbasin and turned on the water. As usual, it ran cold and I waited for the hot water to come through the pipes. I glanced over at her washbasin and forgot all about the hot water. The two washbasins were built into the same marble counter. Her side was normally cluttered with her makeup and hairpins and combs and brushes. Tonight there was something added. A teaspoon, some burnt wooden matches, and a hypodermic needle.

There was a small envelope lying beside the hypo. I picked it up and opened it. There were several small packets inside. I took one out and opened it. It was filled with a fine, white, crystalline powder. I put some on my finger and tasted it. The sickly bittersweet taste of "shit" lingered on my tongue.

Suddenly it all made sense to me. Her peculiar attack of nervousness the day the car didn't arrive. The strange glazed look in her eyes that night in New York I went to pick her up at the party. The funny way she slurred her speech at times as if her tongue were too thick to say the words. No one ever traveled that far on pot.

But I still couldn't believe it.

I took a washcloth from the rack and held it under the hot water until it was soaking wet. I squeezed it out and went back into the bedroom. I pulled the sheet away from her and hit all the lights.

She came awake with a start. "Steve!"

I grabbed her by the wrist and pulled her arm out straight. I began to rub the inside of her elbow with the washcloth.

She tried to pull her arm away. "Steve! Have you gone mad?"

I held her arm tightly without answering. The makeup came off all over the washcloth. I looked down at the suddenly naked white flesh. The needle marks were there. All around the purple-blue veins.

I flung the washcloth angrily across the room. "Damn you!" I said. "Damn you for a stupid bitch!"

My Darling Girl was a first-class addict.

TWELVE

I SAT AT THE BAR in the living room, swirling the Scotch in the glass. I heard her footsteps on the staircase behind me. I didn't turn around.

She crossed the room and sat down at the bar beside me. "Steve."

I didn't look at her. "Yes?"

"I'm not on the stuff. Really. It was only because I was lonely. I missed you and I couldn't sleep."

"Don't lie to me, Myriam," I said. I turned to look at her. "I counted at least six punctures on your left arm. How many have you got on your right?"

"I can kick it anytime I want."

"Who are you kidding, Myriam?" I asked. "Did you ever try?"

"I'll prove it," she said. "Look." She opened her hand and showed me the small packets. She got down from the stool and went behind the bar. She turned the water on in the sink and began to open the packets one by one and empty them.

I reached over the bar and took one packet from her hand. I opened it and tasted it. Bicarbonate of soda. I gave the packet back to her. "I never knew a junkie yet who could pour the stuff down the drain."

She stared up at me. Slowly, she turned off the tap. "I love you," she said. "Do you know that?"

"Sure," I said sarcastically. "I would not love thee half so much, loved I not heroin more." I put Scotch in my glass and walked away, leaving her. I sank into the couch facing the window. Los Angeles lights were out there in the night. But somehow it didn't look all that beautiful anymore.

She came from behind the bar and stood in front of me. "What are you going to do?"

"Nothing." I looked up at her. "It's your problem, not mine."

The tears began to well into her eyes. "Don't turn me off like that, Steve." She sank to the floor in front of me, clasping me around the knees. The racking sobs shook her entire body. "Help me, Steve. Please help me."

She grabbed at my hand and began to cover it with quick tiny kisses. The hot tears burned my skin. "Help me, help me, help me," she kept murmuring over and over.

I looked down at her. For a moment I could have cried. After all, it wasn't that far back that she was a little girl. I stroked her hair.

She caught my hand and held it to her cheek. "What am I going to do?" she asked, her voice filled with despair.

I was silent, looking at her.

"Tell me, Steve," she said insistently, almost fiercely.

"There are three things that I can think of that you can do," I said. "But I don't think you'll do any of them."

"Tell me," she said again.

"One, you can go back to New York and tell your parents. Have them help you."

"No," she said. "It would kill my mother."

"Second," I said, "you can go to England and sign on. At least that way you'll get the stuff under medical supervision."

"No. That would take me away from you. I'll be over there and you'll be here. And I couldn't come back."

"The third is the roughest," I said.

She didn't speak.

"Sign yourself in at Vista Carla." It was probably the best private narcotics rehabilitation center in America. And the most expensive. But they had every modern technique that was needed. Medical and psychological. "In the morning."

I felt the cold shiver run through her. Fear was a very real thing. "Is there anything else?"

"Sure there is," I said harshly. "Don't do anything. Just keep on the way you're going and slide into the shithouse."

She was silent for a long while. I lit a cigarette and gave it to her, then lit another for myself. I watched her. There were lines on her face that had never been there before.

The cigarette had burned almost to her fingers before she spoke. "If I do that," she asked, "you won't leave me?"

"No," I said.

"You'll come and see me?"

"Yes."

"You mean it?"

I nodded.

"I won't make it without you," she said. "I know that."

"You'll make it," I said, drawing her up into my arms. "I'll help you."

—

VISTA CARLA WAS SET IN the rolling hills just back of Santa Barbara. We got there about noon. If it weren't for the ten-foot iron fence around the ground and the uniformed guard at the big gate, it could be mistaken for a rich man's country mansion.

I stopped outside the closed gate and gave the guard my name. He went back into the gatehouse and came out with a small book.

"Is that the patient with you?" he asked.

"Yes," I answered. "Miss Darling."

He peered into the car at her for a moment. She didn't look at him, just down at her nervously twisting hands. He nodded and stepped back. "You go on up the driveway," he said. "Turn left at the top and stop at the main entrance. You'll find a place to park there. Dr. Davis will be waiting for you."

He went back into the gatehouse. Through the window I saw him press a button. The large iron gates began to swing open. He picked up the telephone as we drove in. The gates swung closed as soon as the car had passed.

An attractive young woman was waiting for us on the steps leading to the entrance. She was wearing a white smock over her short dress. She came down the steps as soon as I had parked the car.

"Mr. Gaunt?" she asked, her hand outstretched.

Her grip was firm and businesslike. "I'm Dr. Shirley Davis."

"Good to meet you," I said.

She turned toward Myriam as she came around the car. "Miss Darling? I'm your doctor, Shirley Davis."

Myriam nodded. She looked at me questioningly.

Dr. Davis laughed. It was a pleasant laugh. "In case you're wondering about it, I really am a doctor. I'll show you my diplomas and certificate when we get to my office."

Myriam laughed. She held out her hand. "Happy to meet you, Dr. Davis."

I looked at Dr. Davis approvingly. Score one for her. For a moment, Myriam almost sounded as if she meant it. We went up the steps. Dr. Davis took a key from her pocket and opened the door. We went inside and the door swung shut automatically behind us.

"The foyer is furnished in genuine Mexican-Spanish antiques of the nineteenth century," Dr. Davis explained as she led us through it to her office. "It was donated to Vista Carla by a foundation."

We paused in front of a dark oak-paneled door. Again Dr. Davis took a key from her pocket. Again the door locked automatically behind us.

The room was comfortably furnished. The only sign that it was a doctor's office was a small wooden cabinet behind the desk, through the windows of which I could see various colored vials of medicine.

"Why don't you sit here on the couch, Mr. Gaunt," Dr. Davis said, "while Miss Darling and I attend to the necessary routines? There are some magazines on the table if you care to read."

I sat down as they went to the far end of the room. Dr. Davis took out some forms. She began to read the questions in a low voice.

I picked up the magazines. They were back issues of medical journals. I imagined they would be very interesting if you were a medical historian. I put them down and looked out the window.

An occasional patient went by, always accompanied by a nurse. Other than that, the green rolling lawns seemed almost pristine in their virginity.

"I guess that about completes the forms," I heard Dr. Davis say. I turned back into the room from the window.

The doctor was standing, holding a large manila envelope. "If you'll place all your valuables in this," she said, "we'll keep them in the safe for you. They will be returned when you leave."

Silently Myriam took off her rings, a bracelet, and the gold chain she wore around her neck. She dropped them into the envelope.

"Your wristwatch also," Dr. Davis said.

Myriam unclasped her watch and dropped it into the envelope. The doctor sealed it and placed in on the desk. She pressed a button.

A gray-haired motherly nurse came through the door behind the desk. She stood there waiting.

"Mrs. Graham will show you to your room," Dr. Davis said. "You will take off all your clothes and put on a hospital gown. Then we'll begin our examination and tests."

"This way, my dear," the nurse said in an agreeable voice. She held the door open behind her.

Myriam got to her feet. She glanced apprehensively at me.

"Don't worry," Dr. Davis said quickly. "Mr. Gaunt will be in to see you in your room just as soon as we get you comfortable."

I smiled reassuringly at Myriam. She tried to return the smile, but she didn't quite make it. She turned and followed the nurse through the door. I walked over to the desk.

Dr. Davis sat down again and gestured to the seat that Myriam had occupied. I sat down. It was still warm.

"Do you know when the patient had her last shot?" Dr. Davis asked in a cool, businesslike voice.

"As far as I know—last night," I answered.

"Do you know how long she's been taking drugs?"

"No."

"Do you know about how often she takes drugs?"

"No."

While she had been asking questions she had been studying the papers in front of her that had the information she had gotten from Myriam. Now she looked up at me. "Did the patient come here voluntarily, or under coercion?"

"Voluntarily."

"Do you think she has a genuine desire to rehabilitate herself?"

"Yes."

"She's a very pretty girl," she said. "I hope we can help her."

I didn't answer.

"You know, in cases like this, more depends on the patient than ordinarily."

"I understand," I said.

She took out a form. "Please let me know where you can be reached in case of any special problems."

I gave her all the numbers, including the apartment in New York.

"I hope it won't be necessary to disturb you," she said. "But one can never tell. While, as you see, we do observe maximum security precautions, this is a clinic not a prison and sometimes patients do manage to elude us."

I nodded. "When do you think I will be able to visit?"

"With luck, in one week," she said. "More probably sometime near the end of the second week. The first two weeks are the most difficult for the patient." She got to her feet. "I will call you just as soon as I feel she is able to have you visit her."

I rose. "Thank you, Doctor."

"Now, if you'll follow me, I'll take you to her room. She should be ready for us."

I followed her out through the door that Myriam used. Now I knew we were in a hospital. The corridor was green and sterile. We went up a flight of stairs and down another corridor. She stopped in front of a door and knocked.

"Come in." The gray-haired nurse opened the door. She turned to Myriam. "I'll be back in a few minutes, dear." She walked out past me and I went into the room. The door snapped shut and locked.

Myriam looked like a child in the white hospital gown, propped up in the bed with pillows. I glanced around the room. It was pleasant enough, but the only window in it was high on the wall, near the ceiling.

"How do you feel?" I asked.

Her lower lip trembled. "Frightened."

I sat down on the bed and took her in my arms. I kissed her. "You're doing the right thing," I said. "It will be all right."

The door opened and the nurse came back in, wheeling a small table on which various instruments were laid out. "Time for us to begin our work, dear," she said cheerfully.

Myriam looked at me. "When will I see you?"

"The doctor says I can probably come up next week."

"That's a long time," she said. "Why can't you come before that?"

"I'll try," I said.

She held her arms out toward me. "Kiss me again, Steve."

I kissed her and held her for a moment, then went outside into the corridor. The doctor was waiting there for me.

We began to walk down the hall. "How does she seem to you?" the doctor asked.

"Okay," I said. "A little frightened."

"That's normal enough," she said. "It's a big step she's taking."

We went down the stairs and at the bottom she turned to me. She held something in her hand. I looked down at it.

"By the way, she had these hidden in the lining of her handbag," she said.

I nodded. "I kind of expected something like that." Now I knew where the heroin had gone.

"Do you think she might have any more on her?"

"I wouldn't know."

"Then don't worry, Mr. Gaunt," the doctor smiled. "If she has, Mrs. Graham will turn it up. She's very good at that sort of thing."

I thanked the doctor and went outside to my car. I drove down to Los Angeles International Airport and got aboard the three o'clock plane to New York.

The worst part of the whole thing was yet to come. Telling Sam and Denise about their daughter.

THIRTEEN

I WAS IN THE OFFICE early. Fogarty followed me with the coffee. She waited until I had taken my first sip. "There was a big panic here yesterday," she said. "They didn't know whether you'd be in time for the board meeting today and they couldn't find you."

I had some more of the coffee without answering.

"We were wondering whether to call Sinclair. It wouldn't make much sense to have a board meeting without either of the executive officers present."

Spencer was on vacation in the Caribbean. He had been gone almost a month. I look up at her. "I'm here."

I knew she was curious about where I had been yesterday, but I volunteered nothing and she didn't ask. She knew better. She began to run down the list of calls.

"Mr. Savitt wants to see you before the meeting. He would like to go over the new lineup before he presents it to the board for approval."

"Ask him up as soon as we're finished."

"Mr. Regan called from the coast. He asked me to tell you that his board formally approved the sale of Symbolic Records stock to Sinclair. He asked that you call him as soon as our board approves so that the press release can be coordinated on both coasts."

I nodded.

"Mr. Benjamin called. He asked me to express his satisfaction to you on the conclusion of the new deal. You don't have to call back."

"What deal?"

"Mr. Savitt tried to reach you yesterday and tell you. He bought a package of feature films from him." She checked her notes. "That's another thing he wanted to talk to you about."

"Any other calls?"

"All routine. Nothing special."

"Okay. Ask Mr. Savitt to come up."

"Will do," she said. She placed a folder on the desk in front of me. "There's your copy of the agenda for today's board meeting."

I thanked her and looked through it as she left the office. But it was just a blur of words to me. Darling Girl's face kept intruding between the paper and my eyes. The fear somehow mixed with trust in her young face.

Jack came into the office. We shook hands while Fogarty placed his coffee in front of him. He waited until she had left the office. "You don't look well."

"I'm all right," I said. "I'm just tired."

He was silent for a moment. "Maybe you can grab a vacation after the meeting."

"When Spencer comes back," I said. "The bylaws of the company state specifically that one of us must always be around."

"When is he coming back?"

I shrugged. "The end of March, beginning of April. Sometime like that."

"That's two months off."

"I'll make it, all I need is a good night's rest." I changed the subject. "Bring me up to date on the Benjamin thing. I thought you were dead set against it."

"I was," he said. "But Sam came in himself last week without Dan Ritchie and offered me a whole new proposal. He gave us our choice of the package for three million dollars. I got him down to two and a half and then skimmed the cream. I picked the twelve best of the lot. That's a million and a half less than he had asked before."

I didn't say anything. Sam was no fool. With the additional financing he had gotten from me, he didn't have to be sticky. Between the two, he had managed to put together six and a half million dollars.

Jack mistook my silence for disapproval. "You don't like it?"

"It's fine." I said. "What happened to Ritchie?"

"I don't really know," he answered. "I heard they had a fight. Ritchie was supposed to come with the money from the sale of films to television and he struck out. Meanwhile Sam got financing somewhere so he canned him. Ritchie's pissed off and threatening a suit. But, as far as I know, that's all scuttlebutt."

"New York is a fun city."

"Yeah. Something going on all the time," he answered. "Can you go over the scheduling now?"

"Yes."

He took out the charts and schedules. I looked down at them. The same old shit. The headings across the top of the page were always the same. NBC, CBS, ABC, and SINCLAIR. I was bored with it.

—

IT WAS AFTER FIVE O'CLOCK by the time the board meeting was over. I went back to my office and put in a call for Sam.

He came on the phone in high humor. "I'll make a rich man out of you yet," he said. "By the time I buy the stock back from you it will be worth double what you loaned me for it."

It was the first laugh I had that day. "You can ruin my tax picture for ten years with something like that."

"In that case you better be nice to me," he said. "Or I'll pay you what I owe you."

"I'd like to see you," I said, turning serious.

"Why don't you come to the house for dinner? Only Denise and Junior will be there."

"I thought Junior was away at school?"

"He just got kicked out," he said. "They caught him smoking marijuana or masturbating or maybe both in the men's room. You know how kids are nowadays."

"I know," I said. For a moment I almost canceled out. But it was his daughter and he was entitled to know. Now. "I can't make dinner because I'm catching the nine o'clock back to the coast. How about a drink?"

"Where would you like to meet?" he asked.

"I'll be at your apartment at six thirty if that's all right with you."

"Okay," he said. "I'll see you then."

—

I GOT OUT OF THE limo in front of the apartment house. "Don't go away," I said to the chauffeur. "I don't know just how long I will be."

He nodded and I went into the building. I lit a cigarette going up in the elevator and dragged on it. It wasn't going to be easy. There were a million other things I'd rather tell them.

The maid, Mamie, let me in and I followed her to the library. Sam and Denise were already there and the maid brought me a Scotch on the rocks without my having to ask for it.

"You look so serious," Sam said as I took it. He laughed. "I don't know whether I didn't like you better when you were on martinis."

I forced a smile. "Cheers," I said. Even the whiskey tasted lousy.

Junior came into the room. "Hi, Uncle Steve."

"How are you?"

"Don't ask him anything," Sam said. "He's a bum." But there was tolerant humor in his smile. "Imagine a son of mine getting caught doing a stupid thing like that." He turned to Junior. "What was such a big rush? Why didn't you wait at least until you got back to your own room?"

"Oh, Father," Junior said in a disgusted voice. He looked at me. "I wasn't the only one that got busted. There were four of us sharing one lousy little joint."

It wasn't getting any easier.

Denise started from the room. "Come, Junior. We'll leave them to talk business."

"Don't go," I said.

She stopped almost at the door and looked at me. There was an expression in her eyes that made me think of her for the first time as Myriam's mother.

"This concerns you too," I said.

She came slowly toward me. "Has it got something to do with Myriam?"

I nodded.

Instinctively she moved toward Sam. I saw her hand search out and find his. She didn't speak. Just looked at me with a secret fear in her suddenly white face.

I took a deep breath. "Myriam signed herself into Vista Carla sanitarium yesterday morning."

Sam still didn't get it. "Is she sick?" he asked in a puzzled voice.

"Yes," I said.

"Why didn't she let us know? After all, we are her parents." He was beginning to get angry. Suddenly he stopped and looked at me. "What's the matter with her? Is she pregnant?"

"No," I said. They were probably the most difficult words I ever spoke in my life. "Myriam's on drugs. She's addicted to heroin. She went into Vista Carla to try to break the habit."

"Goddamn it!" Sam roared. He turned to Junior. "Samuel, go to your room!"

"No," Denise said. "She's his sister. Let him stay."

"You and your ideas," Sam yelled angrily. "Let her become an actress. That's what she wants. Didn't I tell you that they're all nothing but whores and bums? Now I hope you're satisfied."

Denise stood there silently, the tears welling in her eyes. I watched her fight to control herself. After a moment, she turned to Sam. "I'll pack a bag."

"No!" Sam roared. "You're not going anywhere."

"But she's still my baby," Denise said. "And she needs me."

"She didn't need your help to get into it," he snapped. "Let her get out of it the same way."

Denise stared at him for a moment, then walked from the room. He turned to me. "How did you find out about it?"

"She was at my house the night before last," I said. "I went into the bathroom and found the hypo."

I saw the blood climb into his face. His eyes were suspicious narrow slits behind the shining glasses. "What was she doing at your house?"

I didn't answer.

He gripped my lapels with strong fingers. "Answer me, Goddamn you!"

I stared deep into the anger in his eyes. I pushed his hands away. "She was staying with me," I said.

I never thought a man of his size and bulk could move that quickly. Too late, I saw the blur of his arm, then the pain exploded in my stomach and I bent almost double. I twisted trying to avoid the blow coming down at me. I caught it between my neck and shoulder and pitched forward to the floor. Another sharp pain exploded in my ribs as he kicked me. I tried to roll away from him.

"Papa! Papa!" Junior screamed, grabbing at him.

"Keep out of this!" He pushed Junior away violently. "I'm gonna kill the son of a bitch!"

I grabbed the edge of the couch and began to pull myself to my feet. Sam came toward me. I stared up into his face, almost unable to move.

Junior flung himself at his father again. "She was in love with him, Papa! She was always in love with him!"

This time Sam half turned and struck him. The boy slammed back against the library shelves. The books began to tumble and fall around him. "I said, keep out of it!"

The boy stared at him with horror-stricken eyes as he turned back to me. I was on my feet now, but I still had to hold onto the couch to keep from falling again.

"You sick bastard!" Sam said, staring at me. "You had to have her, too. All the cunts in the world aren't enough for you!"

I saw his arm go back, but there was no way in the world I could lift my arms to block him. I just didn't have the strength.

Then, suddenly, Denise was between us. "Sam!"

He stood there, frozen, his fist still cocked.

"She's twenty-two, Sam. And she's a woman, not a child," Denise said. "Steve didn't have to come and tell us anything if he didn't want to."

He kept staring into her eyes. "Get out of my way," he said harshly.

"She's my daughter, not yours, Sam," she said quietly. "Leave him alone!"

He blinked as if he had been hit. Slowly his hands fell to his sides. In spite of the pain, I felt pity for him as he seemed to shrink before my eyes. He walked to the door and then turned back to us.

But it was only Denise he spoke to, I did not exist for him anymore. "If you take one step to go to her," he said in a shaking voice, "neither of you have to come back!"

FOURTEEN

I FOLLOWED DR. DAVIS INTO her office. "It's not been easy for her," she said. "She's having a very difficult time."

I didn't speak.

"I'm not quite sure that you should see her even now."

"It's two weeks since she's been here," I said.

"We can't work miracles," she said. "We can only try. After all, she's been hooked for more than three years now and it's not that easy to get out of her system."

"That long?"

"Yes," she said. "Up to now we have had all we could do to cope with her physical problems. We haven't had a chance to delve into her psychologically. And four times out of five that's where we find the key to any kind of a cure."

"What do you suggest I do then?"

"I would like you to see her," she answered. "She loves you very much and you're the only person she seems to want to see. But—"

I noticed her hesitation. "But what?"

"That could be because she thinks she might be able to convince you to take her out of here."

I listened.

"You have to understand that, for the moment, she's not the same girl you brought here. She's like an animal driven by the demands of her addiction. She'll do anything to get out and get the drug she needs. She's already made two attempts to escape."

"I wasn't told about that."

"I didn't bother to mention it in our telephone conversations," she said. "We accept that almost as normal. If I do let you see her, she'll play on your sympathy in every way she can.

"What she needs from you more than anything else right now is love and understanding. But you have to draw a very fine line. You can't afford to oversympathize. If you do, you'll only raise her hopes that she can get out.

"It's not an easy thing to do. Do you think you can?"

"I don't know," I said. "What do you think?"

"If it goes right, the visit can be extremely helpful. It can give her an even greater motive to get well."

"Then I should try." I put out the cigarette and got to my feet.

Dr. Davis nodded and I followed her into the corridor. "Do not appear surprised at the way she looks," she said as we went up the steps to the second floor. "She's lost a considerable amount of weight. Compliment her if you can. Try to make her feel attractive. That can be a big help."

We stopped in front of Myriam's door and she knocked on it. The same nurse who had been here the day we first came opened the door.

She turned back into the room. "Now, isn't that nice, dear," she said. "We have a visitor. Your young man has come to see you."

"Steve!" I heard her voice. Then she came running to the door and flung herself into my arms. The door snapped shut as the nurse left the room.

"Steve," she said, beginning to cry. "Steve, Steve, Steve."

I held her tightly to me, stroking her hair. "Darling Girl," I whispered.

She looked up into my face, trying to blink away the tears. "I must look horrible. They won't let me have any makeup."

"You're beautiful," I said. I felt the pang inside me. She was all skin and bones and her eyes were sunken hollows in her face.

"I know better. Even if there isn't a mirror in the room that I can look into."

"You look fine."

She walked over to the bed and sat down. "Come over here and sit next to me."

I sat down next to her.

She took my hand and put it inside her gown on her breast. "I'm so horny," she said, looking into my eyes.

I couldn't speak. I had all I could do to keep from weeping.

"You know I've kicked it, don't you?" she asked. "They say you don't want sex until you've kicked it."

"I don't know."

"It's true," she said earnestly. "Feel my cunt. It's all wet, I'm so horny."

I shook my head. "The doctor says you're not strong enough for sex yet. You're still run down."

She was suddenly angry. "She would say that. All they care about is keeping me here so they can collect more money. I suppose she didn't even tell you that I kicked it?"

"She told me you've made good progress," I said cautiously.

"They're crazy!" she said. She got to her feet. "I could tell you things about this place and the way they treat their patients, you wouldn't believe."

She glanced around quickly as if to make sure there was no one else in the room with us. Her voice lowered to a conspiratorial whisper. "You know that nurse, Mrs. Graham?"

I nodded.

"You think she's nothing but a nice old lady, don't you?" She didn't wait for my answer. "Well, she's not. She's a sadist. She's beaten me up several times. I'll show you!"

She pulled her nightgown down from her shoulders and let it fall to the floor. She stood naked. "See the bruises?"

There wasn't a mark on her. All I could see were her ribs pressing against her flesh and the pale, almost translucent quality of her skin.

She made no move to pick up her gown from the floor. "Besides that, she's a dyke. More than once when I was asleep I felt her eating me."

I picked up her gown. "Put it on," I said. "I don't want you to catch cold."

Silently she let me slip the gown around her. She went back to the bed and sat down, looking up at me. "And that Dr. Davis, with her degrees and her high and mighty airs. Do you know what she does? She takes a couple of patients and a couple of orderlies into her room and has orgies every night. She's cock crazy. She takes it in the mouth, cunt, and ass, all at the same time. Then during the day she puts on her airs and fools everybody. But she doesn't fool me. I know better.

I just looked at her.

She was still for a moment, then she threw herself into my arms, sobbing. "You've got to take me out of this horrible place, Steve. I'll go out of my mind if I have to stay here any longer!"

I held her tightly, she was shivering.

She looked into my eyes pleadingly. "You can take me out. Really. I've kicked it."

"In a little while, Darling Girl. First we have to build up your strength again."

She tore herself away from me and flung herself across the bed. Her sobs racked her whole body.

I went over and placed my hand on her shoulder. Angrily she pushed it away. "Go to hell!"

I stood there, looking down at her for a moment, then started for the door.

"Steve!" she screamed.

I turned and she was on the floor, her hands clasped around my knees. Her eyes were swimming in tears. "Take me out of here, Steve. Please. I'll be good. I'll do anything you want. Only take me out!"

I raised her to her feet and held her against me. "It won't be long now, Darling Girl," I said.

Her hand went inside my jacket. Before I realized what she was doing, she had pulled my pen from my pocket. She held if over her head like a dagger. "If you don't take me with you," she screamed, "I'll gouge out your eyes!"

I looked at her. She was wild and she seemed perfectly capable of carrying out her threat. "Okay," I said as calmly as I could. "But how am I going to open the door? I haven't got a key. I'll have to call the nurse."

Her eyes drifted for a moment to the call button beside the bed. That was all I needed. I grabbed her arm and got the pen away from her. She looked at me, then at her empty hand with unbelieving eyes.

"You tricked me!" she said in a child's voice. Then she put her hands up to her face and began to cry.

I took her into my arms and soothed her. "I know it's not easy, Darling Girl," I said. "But you keep on trying. The sooner you get better, the quicker we'll be together again."

"I am better," she cried. "I am better."

Then the door opened and the nurse came into the room and the visit was over.

The doctor was waiting for me. "Come into my office," she said.

I followed her and the door closed behind us. She looked at me. "You could use a drink." She opened the medicine cabinet behind her and took out a bottle of Scotch and a glass. She gave me about two fingers of the whiskey.

I drank it like water. It burned all the way down, but I began to feel better almost immediately. "It wasn't easy," I said.

"I know. We were listening. We have a microphone in every room. It's the only way we can keep on top of all the patients. You did very well."

"I hope so." But I had the feeling that she was just saying that to make me feel better.

She came out to the car with me.

"Mr. Gaunt."

I stood there. She squinted at me in the sunlight. "I'm not trying to pry into your personal life. But a few answers from you might be very helpful to me."

"Ask."

"Exactly what is your interest in her?"

"I've known her since she was a child. Her parents and I have been friends for a long time."

"But you were having an affair with her, were you not?"

"Yes."

"How long did that last?" she asked.

"About one month at the time I brought her here."

"One more question, Mr. Gaunt. Are you in love with her?"

I thought for a long time. Finally I answered. "I don't know."

She looked into my eyes for a moment. Then she dropped her gaze. "Thank you, Mr. Gaunt," she said quietly.

I got into the car and started the motor. When I looked up again, she was walking back to the building.

FIFTEEN

SHE REFUSED TO SEE ME the next visiting day. "She didn't tell us until this morning," Dr. Davis said. "I tried to call you, but you had already left your home."

"I don't understand it."

"It's all part of the game she's playing," the doctor explained. "She's punishing you for not taking her away. Either that or she has some idea about convincing you to take her out."

I didn't answer.

"I'm sorry you had to drive all the way for nothing," she said.

"That's all right," I said.

"In spite of how it appears, we are making progress," she said. "It's a month now and her physical reaction to drug deprivation is considerably less. She's even managed to gain a little weight. But she still refuses psychiatric guidance. She won't even speak to the therapist."

"How do you get her to do that?"

"We just keep on trying," she answered. "Sooner or later she'll want to talk to someone. If only to get a sympathetic ear. They all do, but right now she is still hostile toward us.

Mrs. Graham came into the office. She placed an envelope on the doctor's desk. "She gave me this letter to mail for her."

She looked at me and smiled. "Oh, how do you do, Mr. Gaunt? Our patient is being a little stubborn today, but don't you worry. We'll bring her around all right."

She left the office and Dr. Davis looked down at the envelope. She gave it to me without speaking.

It was addressed to me. I opened it. It was written in pencil in almost childish scrawl.

Dear Steve,

When you came up to see me yesterday they told you that I did not want to see you. They were lying. They are holding me prisoner here and beat me every day and abuse me. All they want to do is collect the money every week. I have kicked the habit and still they are not satisfied. This letter ought to convince you. I want to see you very much. Come and get me out. Love.

Your Darling Girl.

"Read that," I said, giving the letter back to her. "I guess you were right."

She looked at it without comment. I got to my feet. "I have to go to New York next week for a board meeting," I said. "So it will probably be at least ten days before I can come up again."

"Go right ahead, Mr. Gaunt," she said, rising. "I'll call you if any problem should arise. But I really don't expect anything to happen."

But this was one time the doctor was wrong.

Dan Ritchie had filed his suit against Sam the day before the board meeting. He was asking for two hundred and fifty thousand dollars as his ten percent commission on the package sale of films to us, plus damages and legal costs. And to make the cheese more binding, he included us in the suit. Specifically he charged Sinclair Broadcasting, the corporation, and me, personally, as coconspirators with Sam in an attempt to defraud him of his rightful commissions.

In his statement to the press accompanying his lawsuit, he said that unless his demands were met promptly he would expose what he called "the incestuous practice of business that exists between Sinclair and Samarkand and certain of their executives."

I arrived in New York the day of the big board meeting and Jack was waiting in my office.

"I told you we couldn't trust the son of a bitch," he said.

I grinned at him. "Which one?"

He stopped and stared at me. "You're right. I never thought of that. There's not much difference between Sam and Ritchie. They're both greedy bastards."

"Better not say that in public where anybody can here you," I laughed. "That's no way to talk about our codefendant."

"I don't get it," he said, shaking his head. "You have the weirdest sense of humor."

Fogarty brought in the coffee. "Mr. Sinclair would like to see you at your earliest convenience, Mister Gaunt."

"Is he in already?"

She knew everything. "He's been in his office since eight o'clock this morning."

Jack waited until she had left. "He's probably going through the roof."

I sipped my coffee without answering.

"Aren't you going up there?" he asked.

"Sure," I said. "In time. Right now we've more important things to do than my going up there to hold his hand."

"Do you think you can stand a little good news?"

"That would be a pleasant change."

"The rock show is a solid hit," he said. "We're getting almost a forty percent share of the audience and the sponsors are killing themselves to get aboard."

"Good."

"I was thinking of going to twice a week with the show."

"Don't," I said. "Too many guys get nailed at home plate trying to stretch an extra-base hit into a homer."

"We need something to pick us up toward the end of the week."

"You bought those films from Sam," I said. "Use them."

"I was saving them for next fall."

"You have eight months to plan for next fall," I said. "And only eight weeks left in this season before you go to reruns."

He looked down at his programming schedule without speaking.

I finished my coffee and got to my feet. "I'll let you in on the only thing I've learned in the years I've been in this business. All the sponsors buy is performance. The ratings they see today, they buy for tomorrow. And they're for yesterday's show."

I left him and went up in the private elevator to Spencer's office. He was sitting behind his desk fresh from his Caribbean trip.

We shook hands. "How was your flight?" he asked, in his ever polite manner.

"Another plane ride," I said. "And your vacation?"

"Fine," he answered. "I'm thinking of buying a winter place down there for when I retire. I'm a little bored with Palm Beach."

"Not a bad idea," I said, sitting down opposite him.

"The directors have been calling me all morning about this suit of Dan Ritchie's."

"I've had the calls, too."

"I don't know anything about Benjamin's case," he said. "But I've talked to Harley. He assures me that we have no legal liability in the matter."

Harley Garrett was our general counsel. A staid, very conservative attorney.

"I'm not as concerned about the lawsuit as I am about Ritchie's allegations," he said. "Is there anything you know that I don't?"

"Perhaps," I said. I told him about my loan to Sam, secured by the stock.

He listened attentively without speaking until I finished. Then he nodded thoughtfully. "That wasn't very wise," he said.

I was a little surprised. The Sinclair I had met when I came to work here ten years ago would have exploded. "But my relationship with Sam had no bearing on the purchase of those films. Jack bought them without my knowledge. I only learned about it after the deal had been completed."

"You'll have to explain that to the board," he said.

I got to my feet. "I intend to."

The directors weren't quite as calm about it as he had been. They began to drag up all the bugaboos. The FCC, the SEC, antitrust, and internal revenue. After a while they fell to wrangling among themselves as to the proper reply to make.

"Perhaps we should try to negotiate a settlement," Harley said finally. "The publicity can't help our image if we have to go into court."

"I'm against it," I said.

"You won't be able to keep them from intimating that you personally approved the deal because you would profit from it due to your equity in Samarkand."

"At the moment I have no equity in Samarkand," I said. "I only hold the stock as security for a loan."

"Do you think there's any chance of his repaying the loan?" Harley asked.

"I haven't the faintest idea."

"Even the repayment can be misconstrued to your benefit," he said. "I think we should settle. It doesn't involve that much money."

"No," I said flatly. "It's blackmail and I don't like it. Once you open yourself to blackmail, you'll find a thousand nonsense things like this coming up to haunt you."

There was a silence around the table. I looked at Sinclair. His face was expressionless. The telephone next to me began to ring.

"Excuse me, gentlemen," I said, picking it up.

Fogarty was on the line. "I wouldn't disturb you, Mr. Gaunt," she said. "But I have a Dr. Davis on the line from Santa Barbara, California. She says it's an emergency."

"Put her through," I said. There was a click on the line. "Dr. Davis?"

"I'm afraid I have bad news, Mr. Gaunt," she said. "The patient got away from us this morning."

"How?" I asked.

"We don't know," she admitted. "When Mrs. Graham went to her room after breakfast, she was gone. We've made a thorough search of the grounds, but she's not on them." She paused for a moment. "Do you want us to notify the police?"

I thought for a moment. That was all we needed right now. I could see the headlines. "No," I said. "Don't do anything. I'll catch the next plane out."

I looked around the table. They had been talking among themselves while I had been on the telephone.

"I think we ought to put the matter to a vote," Harley said. "I make a motion that we negotiate a settlement in the case of Daniel Ritchie vs. Sinclair Broadcasting Corp., Stephen Gaunt, et al."

I got to my feet and walked toward the door.

"Wait a minute, Steve," Harley said. "I put a motion before the board. You have to vote on it."

I stared down at him. "You vote on it," I said. "I don't give a damn."

SIXTEEN

DR. DAVIS WAS WAITING IN the terminal when the plane landed. She came toward me. "Your secretary gave me your flight number."

"You didn't have to come down. I would have come straight there."

"I felt I should," she said simply, looking straight at me. "Besides I have some information that might lead us to her."

"You found out how she escaped?"

She shook her head. "No. But we do know she's in Los Angeles."

"How?"

"We work with a private detective agency that has been very helpful to us in cases like this. I put them on."

She led the way to the cocktail lounge and stopped before a table in the far corner. The young man sitting there over a glass of beer got awkwardly to his feet.

"Nick Jones, Stephen Gaunt," she said. "Nick is top man at the agency."

He held out his hand. "Howdy, Mr. Gaunt," he said with a distinctly western twang.

He looked like no private detective I ever imagined. But then, all the conditioning I ever had was from motion pictures and television.

He stood at least six foot four, string-bean thin. He wore a white, western cowboy hat, curled tightly at the sides, slanted low over his face, a nondescript work shirt under a dirty brown, fringed suede jacket, and faded Levis. He had long brown hair falling halfway down his neck and a long drooping moustache flowing along his lantern jaw. He looked like Buffalo Bill come to life.

"Mr. Jones," I said.

"Yew cawl me Nick," he drawled.

We sat down. Dr. Davis ordered a Scotch and water and I had my usual Scotch on the rocks.

"Tell Mr. Gaunt what you've found out," she said.

The western accent suddenly disappeared. The tone was businesslike and professional. "We learned that the subject hitched a ride on a truck at eleven this morning on the Pacific Coast Highway. She left that truck in Santa Monica at a gas station near Sunset Boulevard and got another truck going into Los Angeles. We haven't been able to locate that one yet so we don't know where she got off."

"How did you find out about the first truck?" I asked.

"Many of the big interstate haulers have two-way radios," he said. "I spoke to the driver myself."

"Did she have any money on her?"

Dr. Davis answered. "Not when she left. Everything's still in the safe."

"She'll need money," I said. "I never heard of a pusher who gave credit."

"She has money," Nick said flatly.

"How do you know?"

"She got it from the truck driver," he said.

"Why the hell would he give her money?"

He looked at me without answering.

The waitress came back with our drinks. I swallowed half of mine in one gulp.

"You've got to understand," Dr. Davis said sympathetically. "She's a very sick girl."

I didn't speak.

"It's ten thirty now," the detective said. "On Friday nights, the Strip turns on by eleven o'clock. If she hasn't made a contact yet, chances are she'll be around there. I alerted some of my friends in the sheriff's department to keep an unofficial eye out for her."

"Good," I said.

"Meanwhile it wouldn't do no harm if we ambled over and sort of looked around ourselves, you know?"

I finished my drink. "I'm ready when you are. I've got my car in the lot."

"Okay," the detective said. "I'll be on the corner of Sunset and Clark when you get there."

"I'll go with you," Dr. Davis said. "Nick's isn't exactly the most comfortable transportation I ever had."

"It gets me around," he said dryly. "Besides it's just right for my image."

I looked at him. It was the second time that day I had heard that word. The whole world was concerned with its image. But I didn't know what he was talking about until I saw him get into his car and drive off.

It was a dark green Ford ranch wagon.

—

THE STRIP WAS THAT PORTION of Sunset Boulevard running through West Los Angeles, bound on the west by the City National Bank as it turned off toward Beverly Hills and on the east by Schwab's Drugstore, just past Lytton Center. During the day it was a dreary street, lined mostly with old buildings filled with hamburger joints, nondescript shops, and an occasional new, towering office building. It served mainly as a conduit for the traffic between Beverly Hills and Hollywood.

At night, it was another story. Then it came to life with bright neon signs. Restaurants, discothéques blaring the sound out into the street. And more than anything else, the kids were there. Thousands of them. All shapes, sizes, ages, and colors, walking, talking, looking, or just standing around. The faintly sweet odor of pot hung like a miasma over them, and from their slowly moving patrol cars, the white crash-helmeted sheriff's deputies watched them, praying each night that nothing would erupt and turn the street into a churning volcano.

He was standing under the Clark Street sign of Whisky A GoGo just where he said he would be. We started toward him, but he made a faint negative gesture of his head and began to walk away.

He was an easy man to follow. He stood head and shoulders over the crowds. He seemed to know everyone there, kids as well as adults. Occasionally he stopped to talk to someone but it would only be for a moment, then he would walk on.

He went as far as the Gaiety Delicatessen on the 9000 block and then backtracked. "Nothing up here," he whispered as he walked past us. "We'll try down the other way."

We waited until he had gone about twenty feet behind us before we turned back. He paused in front of Whisky. The music blared out into the night and the kids were lined up waiting their turn to get in. We paused in front of Sneaky Pete's and watched him.

I looked up at the sign. There wasn't any pleasure in recognizing that the group inside was the lead group on our rock show this week. He moved on and we trailed after him.

We wound up in front of the Body Shop, footsore and weary at two o'clock in the morning. He nodded toward a darkened building across the street and we followed him.

He stepped into the shadows. "The pushers aren't out," he said, his eyes hidden under the cowboy hat. "They're all uptight and laying low. Something's got them scared shitless, but I can't find out what it is."

"What do we do next?" I asked.

"I got a few places to go," he said. "But you can't come with me. Where can I contact you if I learn anything?"

I looked at Dr. Davis. "How about my place?"

She nodded.

I gave him the telephone number and he ducked out of the shadows into the street. We waited a few minutes to give him a start and then went back to my car.

—

"THIS IS REALLY LOVELY," DR. Davis said as we came down the stairs to the living room.

"I can use a drink," I said, going to the bar.

"It wouldn't hurt me a bit," she said.

I made two Scotches and gave one to her. We drank silently. After a moment she walked over to the giant glass doors and looked out.

"Can we go outside for a moment?" she asked.

I pressed the buttons to roll back the doors. The night air was cool in the hills. It felt good. Down below us, the lights twinkled. In the distance, almost level with our eyes, we could see the blinking green and red lights of a plane on its approach to the airport.

"It's so quiet up here," she said.

"That's why I built it. And yet, in five minutes you can be right in the center of the action."

She looked at me. "Is that important to you?"

"I used to think so," I answered. "Now I don't know anymore."

"Strange, how time alters our values," she said. "When I graduated from medical school, I thought I knew everything. Now I realize how little I do know."

"I think that's part of growing up, Doctor."

"I'm a little tired of hiding behind that title."

"How do you like Doctor Girl?" I asked.

"I *am* a girl. You know that, don't you?"

"You can't miss it," I said.

I don't know how it happened but she was in my arms. Then it was like an atomic fire searing through us. We couldn't wait to get at each other.

Our clothes made a trail up the stairs to the bedroom. We fell naked on the bed, tearing at each other like raging animals.

Then we exploded and fell backward on the bed, gasping for breath. We watched each other quietly for a long time; finally she spoke.

"That wasn't very professional of me."

"You came out from behind your title," I said.

Her eyes fell for a moment. "Are you glad?"

"Yes," I said.

She laughed and kissed me. "So am I." She rolled away and got out of bed. She stopped at the bathroom door. "I could use a shower."

I nodded.

She turned and went into the bathroom, closing the door behind her. A moment later, she was back. She held on to the frame of the door, her face white.

I stared at her.

"Do you have another bathroom?" she asked, in a faint voice. "I think I'm going to be sick."

"Downstairs. Next to the bar."

She ran across the room and I heard her naked feet on the steps. I got out of bed and went into the bathroom.

Darling Girl was there. Curled on her side in a fetal ball, her head on the floor between the toilet and the bathtub, her eyes open and staring, her right fingers touching the needle still in the crook of her left arm.

She had been there all the time we had been looking for her on the Strip, all the time we had been balling on the bed in the next room.

Now it all made sense. Where else did she have to go but home?

I heard the sound of the toilet flushing downstairs and went back into the bedroom. I picked up the telephone and called the police. Slowly I gave them the information they required and started to put down the receiver.

Suddenly I was angry. I slammed the receiver down, shattering the instrument. It fell to the floor, all the red and yellow and white and green and blue and purple wires running everywhere in and out of the tiny silver and brass screws like the threads in a mechanical brain.

I stared down at it and closed my eyes. I could hear Sam's voice in my head all those many years ago.

What was that prayer? What did he call it? I couldn't remember. But I could remember the words. I said them aloud.

"Yisgadal, v'yiskadash sh'may rabbo—"

I felt the hot tears burn their way into my eyes.

It was time I got off the plane.

THAT DAY LAST SPRING

NIGHT

A MAN IS A THOUSAND parts. All of them other people. Those he loved, those he did not, those who merely passed through his life. And the total of him is the sum of all of them added together, divided by each other, subtracted from each other and multiplied individually and cumulatively. I looked around the room. And there I was.

Spencer and Johnston were talking quietly in one corner, Sam and Dave in the other. Outside on the terrace, Lawyer Girl was looking down at the city while, upstairs in my bedroom, Denise and Junior had closed the door and the world behind them.

I walked out on the terrace and stood next to Lawyer Girl. "What do you think?" I asked.

"You're too high for me," she said. "You're flying jets and I'm still trying to get a Piper Cub off the ground."

"It's simple," I said. "So simple I'm surprised they didn't think of it themselves. All of them get exactly what they want. Period. Happy ending."

"Not that simple," she said. "They get everything they want except the one thing they all seem to want the most. You."

I looked at her. "They don't really want me. I'm an illusion they all carry in their heads. They'll find that out as soon as they examine themselves."

"Is that what you are to me too, Steve?" she asked. "An illusion in my head?"

I didn't answer.

"I remember reading in the paper after I went back to San Francisco about the girl. The one who died. I cried for you, Steve. You must have loved her very much."

I looked at her without answering. Sure, I loved her so much that I was fucking another girl while she lay dead in the next room. I remembered the evening I went to the apartment on Fifth Avenue the day after her funeral to pay my condolences.

—

MAMIE OPENED THE DOOR AND took my coat. Her warm black face was swollen with sorrow. "Evening, Mr. Gaunt," she said.

"Good evening, Mamie," I said.

"They're in the living room," she said.

I walked through the apartment, noticing the mirrors covered with sheets and the pictures in the frames turned to the wall. The wide doors to the living room were open and I stopped in the doorway.

The room seemed filled with people, sitting uncomfortably on wooden crates and boxes. A sudden silence fell over them and all faces turned toward me.

I stood there awkwardly, not knowing whether to go in. Jewish ritual was something I knew nothing about.

Denise came to my rescue. She rose and came to the door. She let me kiss her cheek and then, taking my hand, drew me into the room. "I'm glad you came," she said. "I never had the chance to thank you for all you did."

The hum of conversation began again as quickly as it had stopped. But I could still feel the eyes on me. Sam rose clumsily from the wooden box as we approached him. He held out his hand.

I took it. "My deepest sympathy, Sam."

He stood there blinking his eyes without letting go of my hand. "Yes," he said. "Yes." He looked up at me, then, letting my hand go, took off his heavy black-rimmed glasses and polished them with a handkerchief.

"She was a good girl, Steve," he said heavily. "She was sick."

I nodded. "Yes, Sam."

"That was it," he said. He returned the handkerchief to his pocket and put his glasses back on. "She was sick," he repeated, almost to himself.

I saw Junior watching us from across the room. His face was drawn and pale and his eyes were red-rimmed. He nodded to me, without moving from the wall against which he leaned. I nodded back.

"I'd like to talk to you, Steve. Privately," said Sam. "Let's go into the library."

I followed him into the other room. He closed the door. He turned to me. "Would you like a drink?"

"Yes," I said.

He went to the door leading to the foyer. "Mamie!" he called.

He didn't have to tell her anything. She came with two drinks. He thanked her and she went out.

We sipped at our drinks. He walked over to the desk and put his glass down. The words were not easy for him. "I don't know how to do this—say this. I never had to do anything like it before."

I watched him without speaking.

"I had a long talk with Dr. Davis," he said. "She told me everything you tried to do for Myriam."

I was silent.

"What I want to say… I mean… I'm sorry." He picked up his drink again. "I don't know what came over me. I went crazy. Out of my head. But I'm sorry. I wanted you to know that."

I took a deep breath. "It's over, Sam. I'm sorry too. Sorry that it didn't work. For her sake. Now there's nothing we can do except leave it behind."

He nodded. "It won't be easy. I don't know whether we'll ever really get used to it."

I was silent.

"And now there's something else," he said. "Junior. He hasn't spoken to me since that day you were here. Even now, he turns away whenever I come near him."

"He'll get over it."

"I'm not so sure," he said heavily. "I'm not so sure." He took a deep breath. "But that's my problem. Let's go back into the other room."

He stopped, his hand on the doorknob. "Someday, I'll make it all up to you, Steve," he said. "For everything. You've always been a good friend."

—

GOOD FRIEND. I REMEMBERED HIS promise. But that had been three years ago and I hadn't heard from him until this morning. I also remembered his promise two weeks after he made it, the day I sat in Spencer's office.

—

SPENCER LOOKED AT MY RESIGNATION on his desk, then up at me. "You don't have to do this."

"I think it's the best thing under the circumstances."

"All you have to do is to persuade your friend not to go into court with Ritchie."

"How can I do that?" I asked. "When in all honesty I think he's doing the right thing. I said at the board meeting I didn't believe in blackmail. I still don't."

"But the board voted for a settlement. Now the only thing that's holding it up is Benjamin's refusal. We're even willing to pay off the entire liability in order to get it behind us. Then we can forget it." He paused for a moment. "And you can forget about this."

"No," I said. "I think you're going to win in court. But whether you do or not, it doesn't matter. That stands."

He got to his feet and walked over to the window and stood there looking out, his back to me. "Would it make any difference to you if I were to retire now and you were to take over my job?"

I felt an actual physical pain in my throat. I knew what he was offering. He would be the scapegoat in my place if he were to leave now.

"No," I said.

He came back from the window of my chair and looked down at me. "Why, son?" he asked gently.

For a moment I couldn't speak. Then I found my voice. "Because I let it fuck up my life, Dad. And it's not fun anymore."

"What are you going to do then? You're still a young man. Not even forty."

I got to my feet. "Go back to my house on the hill," I said. "And see if I can find a way to live with myself."

—

A WAY TO LIVE WITH myself. I guess that had always been the key. But it was not that easy to find the key when you lived in a vacuum. And that was where I had spent the last three year years. Waiting for something. I don't know what.
Something to give me purpose.

I turned and looked back into the house. Denise came down the stairs into the living room. She went over to Sam and said something to him. He nodded and went up the stairs.

She came out onto the terrace and looked at me. I saw the tears in her eyes. Suddenly she leaned forward and kissed me. "I think it will be all right now."

I smiled at her. "I'm glad."

"Junior's coming home with me," she said. She went back into the house and up the stairs.

A few moments later, Junior came down the stairs and out on the terrace. I stared at him in surprise.

"For a minute there, I almost didn't recognize you."

He self-consciously rubbed his hand over his freshly shaven face. "It does feel strange," he admitted. Even his hair was sort of combed. "I'm not selling out," he said quickly.

"I know," I said.

"I'm going back to college," he said. "That's where it's at now. You see those pictures on TV? You gotta be active, man, if you want to contribute. There just ain't no room no more for dropouts."

"Right," I said.

"I'm goin' back to the hotel with Mom." He stuck his hand out toward me. "Thanks for everything, Steve."

I shook his hand. No more "Uncle Steve" I noticed. "You're welcome," I said.

"Thank you too, Miss Kardin," he said, turning to her.

She smiled, nodding, and he ran back inside. He disappeared up the stairs. A few minutes later I heard a car pull from the driveway and Sam came back into the room.

The four men sat together and talked. A few minutes later, Dave came out on the terrace. He smiled at me. "They all like your idea."

"Good."

"It will work," he said. "They'll fit it all together. Sinclair will put in the broadcasting and record companies, Sam will put in Samarkand, and Johnston will put in his publishing and tape manufacturing companies and supply the overall financing and corporate shelter. When it's all done, it will be spun off into a completely autonomous tandem corporation with no more than twenty-five percent of the stock to remain in their hands, the balance to go to the public. They even like the name you suggest for the new company: Communications Corporation of America. It'll be the biggest thing to hit the market since Ford went public."

"That's fine," I said.

"There's only one hitch," said Dave.

I looked at him.

"It's your idea. And they feel that you're the only man that can make it work."

I didn't speak.

"They sent me out here because I'm the only one in there who is impartial."

I grinned at that. He was about as impartial as a fixed jury. He had nothing to gain from this but big deposits.

"I think you ought to do it," he said. "After all, you're goin' to have a big stake in this when you convert your twenty-five percent of stock in Samarkand and your fifteen percent of stock in Sinclair. You owe it to yourself to make sure it works.

I still didn't speak. They didn't call him "The Shtarker" for nothing.

He sold like crazy.

"You said you were looking for fun. It'll be all new and if you don't find it there, it's no place." He paused for breath. "They want you to think about it. You don't have to rush. They'll wait inside for your answer."

I watched him walk back and turned to Lawyer Girl. Silently I took out a cigarette and lit it.

I glanced into the room over my shoulder. The four men had their heads together. "Look at them," I said. "Already they're plotting to take over the world."

"At least they're not dull," she said.

"They're all tough, hard, selfish men, you know that."

"Yes," she said. "But I know two of them, maybe even three who love you."

I looked at her.

"And you love them, too," she said. "Even if you don't admit it to yourself."

"They'll fight each other and scratch and claw and try to eat me alive," I said. "They're savages."

"You can take care of yourself. Like Junior said. 'You gotta be active, man, if you want to contribute. There just ain't no room no more for dropouts.'"

"Then you think I ought to take it?"

She didn't answer, just looked at me.

I turned and looked out at Los Angeles. It was late. Or rather it was early in the morning. In the east the first faint signs of dawn began to appear.

"And what about you?" I asked.

"I'll go back to San Francisco and read about you in the papers," she said.

I turned to look at her. "And if I asked you to stay?"

Her eyes looked into mine. "For two or three days?"

"Maybe more," I said.

"I can be tempted."

I looked at her for a long silent moment. "Don't go away. I'll get rid of them."

Then I went back into the house and bound myself over to the Philistines.

AFTERWORD

BY HAROLD ROBBINS

Prestel Museum Guide

Pinakothek der Moderne, Munich

by Melanie Klier

Prestel

Munich · Berlin · London · New York

Front cover: The Rotunda of the Pinakothek der Moderne, Munich
Back cover: Staircase to the Rotunda

All works are part of the collection at the Pinakothek der Moderne, Munich

Image credits: Front and back cover, pp. 4/5, 8, 10/11, 15, 16: Ulrich Schwarz, Berlin; pp. 1, 12/13: Tom Vack; pp. 2, 6, 18/19, 22–52: Artothek, Weilheim; p. 53: Courtesy Galerie Barbara Thumm; pp. 54/55, 58–68, 69 (Courtesy Matthew Marks Gallery, New York): Staatliche Graphische Sammlung, Munich; pp. 70/71, 74–83, 84 (photo: Herzog and Partner), p. 85: Architekturmuseum der Technischen Universität München; pp. 86/87, 93, 95, 97, 101 (photo: archive of Die Neue Sammlung, Munich), pp. 90–92, 94, 96, 98, 100 (photo: Angela Bröhan, Munich), p. 99 (photo: Lepowski, Berlin): Die Neue Sammlung, Staatliches Museum für angewandte Kunst, Munich

Library of Congress Cataloguing-in-Publication data is available

Die Deutsche Bibliothek lists this publication in the Deutsche Nationalbibliografie; detailed bibliographic data is available on the Internet at http://dnb.ddb.de

Prestel Verlag
Königinstrasse 9, 80539 Munich
Tel. +49 (89) 381709-0
Fax +49 (89) 381709-35
www.prestel.com

4 Bloomsbury Place, London WC1A 2QA
Tel. +44 (20) 7323–5004
Fax +44 (20) 7636–8004

175 Fifth Avenue, New York NY 10010
Tel. +1 (212) 995–2720
Fax +1 (212) 995–2733

Prestel books are available worldwide. Please contact your nearest bookseller or write to any of the above addresses for information concerning your local distributor.

Pinakothek der Moderne
Kunstareal München
Barer Strasse 40
80333 Munich, Germany
Tel. +49 (89) 23 805-360
www.pinakothek-der-moderne.de

Opening Hours
Tuesday – Sunday 10 a.m. to 5 p.m.
Thursday, Friday 10 a.m to 8 p.m.
Closed on Dec. 24, Dec. 31, Shrove Tuesday, May 1

Translated by Paul Aston, Dorset
Copy-edited by Michele Schons, Munich
Designed and Typeset by WIGEL, Munich
Lithography by ReproLine, Munich
Printed and bound by Passavia Druckservice GmbH, Passau

Printed in Germany on acid-free paper

ISBN 3-7913-2880-8

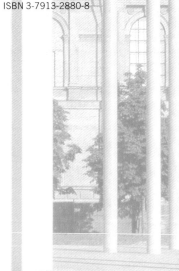

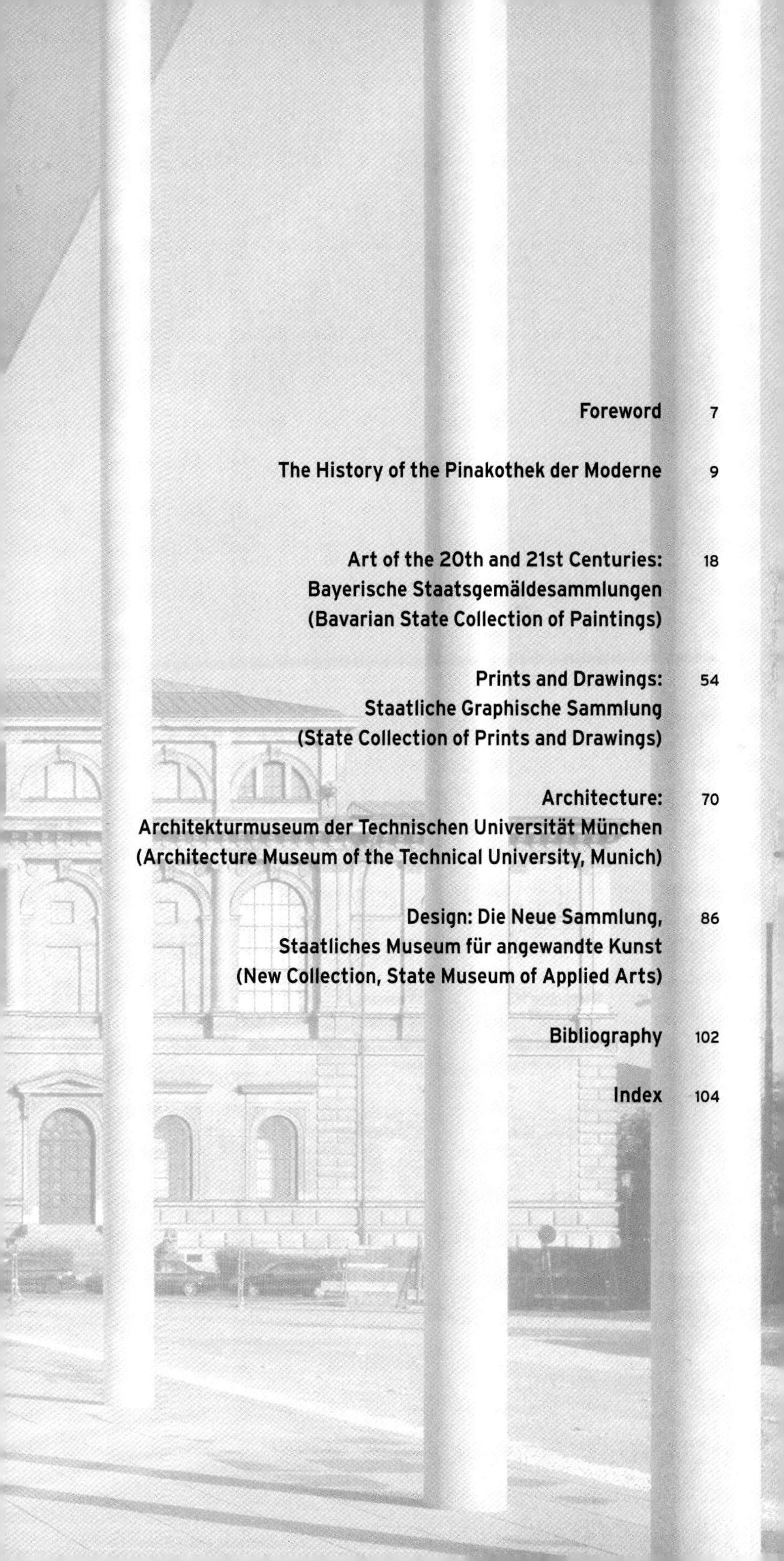

Foreword

Freely translated, the Spanish phrase *buscando la luz* means 'seeking the light'. It is also the name of a sculpture commissioned specially for Munich from the great Basque sculptor Eduardo Chillida, who died on 19 August 2002. A sensitive, handcrafted statement on the subject of volume and space and the interaction of inside and outside, it is above all one thing: an impressive symbol of Munich's three most important art museums (the Alte and Neue Pinakothek and the Pinakothek der Moderne), and an aptly sited manifestation of the link between tradition and modernity. Three elements of rolled, undulating steel seek the light, an elegant U-shaped arrangement outside the Pinakothek der Moderne soaring eight metres high towards the sky, defying the sheer weight of the material.

This book presents the Pinakothek der Moderne, one of the largest museums in the world devoted to 20th and 21st-century art, housing not one, but four major museums. Occupying the 12,000 m^2 of floor space beneath its roof are the former Staatsgalerie moderner Kunst (State Gallery of Modern Art) from the Bayerische Staatsgemäldesammlungen (Bavarian State Collection of Paintings), the Staatliche Graphische Sammlung (State Collection of Prints and Drawings), the Architekturmuseum der Technischen Universität München (Architecture Museum of the Technical University, Munich) and the Neue Sammlung, Staatliches Museum für angewandte Kunst (New Collection, State Museum of Applied Arts). With a single ticket the visitor has access to a variety of art forms that cater for a wide range of interests and are likely to lead to new discoveries. Having come to experience computer culture or automotive design, you may well find yourself discovering contemporary architecture that may lead you to want to look at the architectural collection too. Video art buffs or fans of Max Beckmann, Pablo Picasso, Cy Twombly or Georg Baselitz might likewise go for a stroll round the Graphische Sammlung to catch a glimpse of the full range of high-quality prints and drawings the collection has to offer.

Like Chillida's sculpture, Stephan Braunfels's fantastic building is driven by the concept of transparency. Designed on a generous scale, the open building presents glimpses, overviews and interconnections within a spectrum of art that reaches across the turn of the millennium and beyond. The stunning design of the building in which the Pinakothek der Moderne is housed impressively brings out the individuality of the various collections and, despite the wealth and variety, enables visitors to gain ever-new insights into the works exhibited

MK

Eduardo Chillida (1924–2002)
Buscando la Luz 1997
Three pieces of rolled steel,
H each 798 cm, base dimensions each approx. 150 × 140 × 150 cm
Inv. no. B 900, purchased in 2002 with funds from Kunst am Bau and from a private donation

The History of the Pinakothek der Moderne: Stephan Braunfels's Architecture

Preconditions: Requirements, urban planning, prerequisites

Just imagine everything that has to be borne in mind in order to build a museum for 20th and 21st-century art. Let's take a quick look at a few basic points, starting with the prehistory of the site and the urban planning context.

The site was one of the last undeveloped plots of land in downtown Munich, a block measuring roughly 33,100 m^2. The museum is located on the southern part of the block, which lies between Gabelsbergerstrasse, Türkenstrasse, Theresienstrasse and Barerstrasse. The site used to be part of the former Türkenkaserne, a barracks built in 1826 to house the 1st and 2nd Royal Bavarian Infantry Regiments, but destroyed during air raids in the Second World War. Apart from the gateway on Türkenstrasse, none of the buildings is left, for what survived the war was later demolished. To most Munich residents, the southern part of the block was more familiar as an undeveloped site used for parking and later called Roncalli-Platz, because the Roncalli Circus set up its Big Top here between 1977 and 1996.

The design had to take into account that the area is a link between the rectangular grid of the planned Maxvorstadt area of Munich and the irregular street plan of the old city. Moreover the existence of the other cultural institutions in this part of town needed to be acknowledged. From a planning point of view, the positioning of the projected museum relative to the isolated grandeur of the Alte Pinakothek and its setting also needed to be borne in mind.

In the competition for the design of the new building—under these conditions—the key questions asked were: Could a link be created via the new building to the museum ensemble of the Alte Pinakothek and Neue Pinakothek, the Antikensammlung (Antiquities Collection) and Glyptothek (collection of Greek and Roman statuary) on Königsplatz and the adjacent Städtische Galerie im Lenbachhaus? As a free-standing building should the new museum form an extension of the row of Munich's great museums? Should the Pinakothek der Moderne be oriented to the old city or to the newer area of the Maxvorstadt? Or should it fit in with the mainly residential buildings of the surrounding area? And, last but not least, how should four separate Munich collections, which could hardly be more different from each other, be united under one roof? These four institutions had hitherto been in separate locations, to some extent in rather unsatisfactory accommodation?

A museum building as a work of art: The realisation of the diagonal and the rotunda

These were the questions Munich architect Stephan Braunfels found answers to. His was the design that won first prize from among 167 proposals. His Pinakothek der Moderne, the third largest of the Bavarian art collections in Munich after the Alte and Neue Pinakothek, came up with some impressive solutions.

In an interview, he was asked what the principal ideas were that had influenced his design: 'The key aspect was not, as is always asserted, the diagonal, i.e. opening up the museum on two sides, but the way the huge overall complex breaks down into several separate buildings. Thus the first section of building constitutes the core around which the second section of building can be wrapped in several stages of construction, like a skin.' Opening up diagonally from south-east to north-west was, as he said, much more an opportunity to bring out the internal relationship between the three Pinakotheks without diminishing the central prominence of the Alte Pinakothek.

Nonetheless, the Pinakothek der Moderne can be entered both from the city centre and from the Maxvorstadt side. On the south side, entry to the Museum is via the tall glazed loggia of the conservatory with its café. On the north side, visitors enter the Museum via an imposing pillared hall and glazed lobby. From either entrance, one passes into the spectacular 24.5-metre-high central hall shaped like a rotunda. This forms the starting point of all 'tours' of the Museum. The view upwards into the 30-metre-wide dome, where the incoming light is broken up as in a prism, is breathtaking. Here it is easy to understand why the Pinakothek der Moderne was described as a 'cathedral of light' even before it was opened to the public. Here in the 'core', the pivot and centre-point of the whole complex, is Braunfels's answer to the fundamental question in museum architecture as to whether the architecture should serve as a mere handmaiden to art or itself be approached as a work of art.

The architect opted for a two-part solution: 'The size of the whole complex and the specific planning problem provoked by the diagonal cutting through the building enabled the "social" areas of the Museum, such as the rotunda, entrance loggia, winter garden and grand staircase, to be

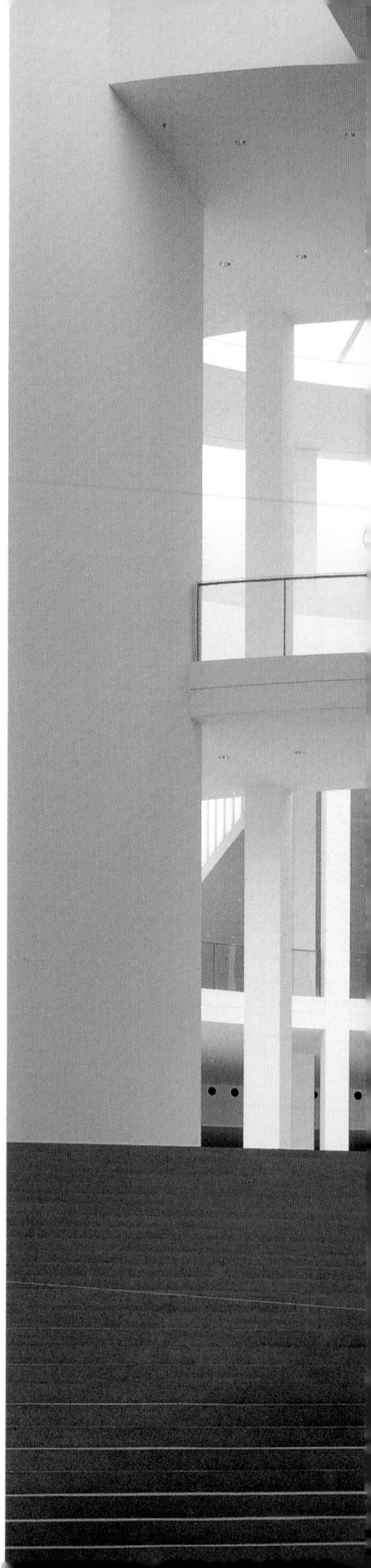

developed as a composition of exciting spatial sequences offering diverse perspectives. In the exhibition rooms proper, the architecture must take a secondary role, with clear, simple rooms lit from above, square or rectangular in varying proportions as the works of art require, with white plastered walls, a minimally obtrusive stone floor, so that in the exhibition rooms the focus is on the art, not the building.'

Realisation: Staircase, lighting and spatial requirements of the collections

The ground plan of the Pinakothek der Moderne is rectangular. All exhibition rooms are grouped around the central rotunda and follow a square grid pattern. In this purist setting, the various museums are not simply stacked one above the other on three floors; the solution is more elegant. Though the rooms devoted to the Neue Sammlung are in the basement, those of the Graphische Sammlung, the Architekturmuseum der Technischen Universität München and temporary exhibitions are on the ground floor and the selection of 20th and 21st-century art from the Bayerische Staatsgemäldesammlungen is displayed on the upper floor, the various areas of the Museum are also linked vertically. Braunfels achieved this, as he says, with the 'large staircase funnelling upwards and downwards, allowing visitors to pass diagonally through the whole building from the Neue Sammlung in the basement to the former Staatsgalerie moderner Kunst on the upper floor. Integrated into the rotunda, this staircase forms an extraordinary interior sculpture that over a distance of 100 metres and a height differential of 12 metres links every part of the building.'

Braunfels's design for the Museum was conceived on a supra-disciplinary basis. Externally a fair-faced concrete block (made of concrete, glass, steel), internally the building endeavours to accommodate the diverse spatial requirements of the four departments, allowing for numerous perspectives and optical links as well as conveying openness and transparency.

Particularly in the display surfaces for art on the entire upper floor, Braunfels has created a bright, light-filled space by installing a 'light ceiling combining a maximum degree of both homogeneity and variability'. The square, 1.5-metre-high light cassettes are above the 5.8-metre-high room. Contemporary installation art, current large-scale artefacts and video art can be presented in large, darkened rooms at the end of the staircase and in the temporary exhibition area on the ground floor. 'The encircling gallery linking the first and second circuit of the painting collections provides the rotunda with another exhibition area, whence you can look down into the central foyer of the ground floor from a height of 14 metres. ... Being integrated into the double skin of the rotunda, the staircase allows visitors to break off after one of the two circuits or to take all sorts of short cuts during a circuit' (Braunfels).

Because of their sensitivity to light, the works from the Graphische Sammlung and the Architekturmuseum der Technischen Universität München have been housed in north-facing rooms on the east side of the ground floor, lit by artificial or indirect light. The objects in the Neue Sammlung, the Museum für angewandte Kunst, vary greatly in size—ranging from automobile designs to designer furniture or miniatures. The rooms therefore likewise vary in size and are optimally located on the ground floor, where they show off the design exhibits to best advantage, such as the Thonet amphitheatre.

The Pinakothek der Moderne is also a place for the exchange of new artistic ideas and for discussion and debate. The lecture theatre is the venue for this, a tiered structure reaching from the depths of the basement to the ground floor. We can also look forward to the planned Danner Rotunda, the 'jewel' of the basement and a showroom of the Neue Sammlung. This will be a walk-in, two-storey display measuring over 600 m^2 and presenting the whole spectrum of design exhibits.

Chronicle

1990
In spring the Bavarian government decides to use the site of the former Türkenkaserne, previously reserved for the Technische Universität, as the site on which to build museums instead. The ministerial council decrees that a building for four museums should be erected—the Staatsgalerie moderner Kunst, the Neue Sammlung, the Staatliche Graphische Sammlung and the Architekturmuseum der Technischen Universität München.

1992
In February 167 architects submit plans for the site. First prize is awarded to Munich-based architect Stephan Braunfels.

1993
In summer Bavaria's Minister President Edmund Stoiber declares the museum to be 'desirable but not necessary'. Minister of Culture Hans Zehetmair saves the day by adding that if 10 per cent of the construction costs were raised in donations, the building could proceed. The Wormland-Stiftung, long an active supporter of the Staatsgalerie, calls for an initiative to be taken up and makes the first contribution itself.

1994
The Stiftung Pinakothek der Moderne is founded. So far over DM 30 million have been raised. In July the Bavarian government agrees to build the museum with monies earned by privatisation measures. It imposes an unrealistic cost cap of DM 200 million.

1995
In December Minister President Edmund Stoiber announces the decision to go ahead with construction.

1996
On 9 September the first sod is turned for the 'Pinakothek der Moderne: Art—Architecture—Design'. The target date for completion is the millennium.

1998
July brings the topping-out ceremony. Johann Georg, Prince of Hohenzollern and Director General of the Bayerische Staatsgemäldesammlungen, retires. He had vigorously campaigned for the Pinakothek der Moderne. His successor is Peter-Klaus Schuster.

1999
Peter-Klaus Schuster is appointed Director General of the Staatliche Museen zu Berlin. Reinhold Baumstark,

who is Schuster's successor, and his team drive planning forward.

2000
Over the following months a dispute between Braunfels and the construction authorities comes to a head. Having never been allowed control over construction, Braunfels has already resorted to legal action, owing to the use of inferior materials, for example. The architect is accused of incurring additional costs of DM 30 million. Following a stormy debate, parliament's Budget Committee approves additional funds.

2001
Construction defects are remedied, such as on the roof of the Museum, but a plague of rats also has to be dealt with.

2002
In March the Pinakothek der Moderne—bare of exhibits—is presented as 'pure architecture', to great acclaim from the specialist press. In June, the National Audit Office provides a bit of excitement once again, declaring the cost cap to be illusory and stressing that the total cost of DM 237.5 million will still be exceeded (recourse claims etc). The opening date is postponed several times before being set definitively for 16 September. Germany's Federal President, Johannes Rau, and Bavaria's Minister President, Edmund Stoiber, and Minister of Culture, Hans Zehetmair, inaugurate the Pinakothek der Moderne.

The Pinakothek der Moderne in figures

Building:
length 143 m
width 68 m
gross volume 258,527 m^2
usable floor area 20,105 m^2

Exhibition space:
art 5,262 m^2
prints and drawings 219 m^2
architecture 424 m^2
design 2,587 m^2
temporary exhibitions 1,013 m^2
Staircase: 100 m
height differential 12 m
Rotunda: height 24.5 m
diameter 24.75 m

Total cost: € 121,431,820

The museums and their holdings:
1. 3,000 paintings from the Bayerische Staatsgemäldesammlungen zur Kunst des 20./21. Jahrhunderts, of which some 350 are on show at any given time
2. 400,000 works on paper from the Staatliche Graphische Sammlung, of which some 100 are exhibited at any given time
3. 350,000 drawings, 100,000 photographs and 500 models from the Architekturmuseum der Technischen Universität München, of which some 380 items are on display at any given time
4. 60,000 objects from the Neue Sammlung, Staatliches Museum für angewandte Kunst, of which 1,000 items are on show at any given time

Art of the 20th and 21st Centuries: Bayerische Staatsgemäldesammlungen

August Macke (1887–1914)
Girls Beneath the Trees 1914
Oil on canvas
119.5 × 159 cm
Inv. no. 13466
Gift of Sofie and
Emanuel Fohn 1964

August Macke and Robert Delaunay are two names that have come to be associated with each other. Macke's development of his own personal idiom would be inconceivable without the encouragement and impetus he received from Delaunay and his notions of art, such as the concepts of Orphism and Synchromism. Delaunay's window pictures had impressively demonstrated to the Blaue Reiter painter what could be done with 'living' colour or colour prismatically fragmented—and how light in painting can glow from within to create an undertow of spatial depth by means of colour contrast. The present Expressionist picture by Macke depicts two sets of three girls in a park. We are drawn into a geometric arrangement of surfaces with and alongside polished colour harmonies. What is essentially an ordinary walk in the park is stylised here as an idealised, well-nigh Elysian portrayal of nature. Everyday life is seen here as a sunny, relaxed, fragrant riot of colour.

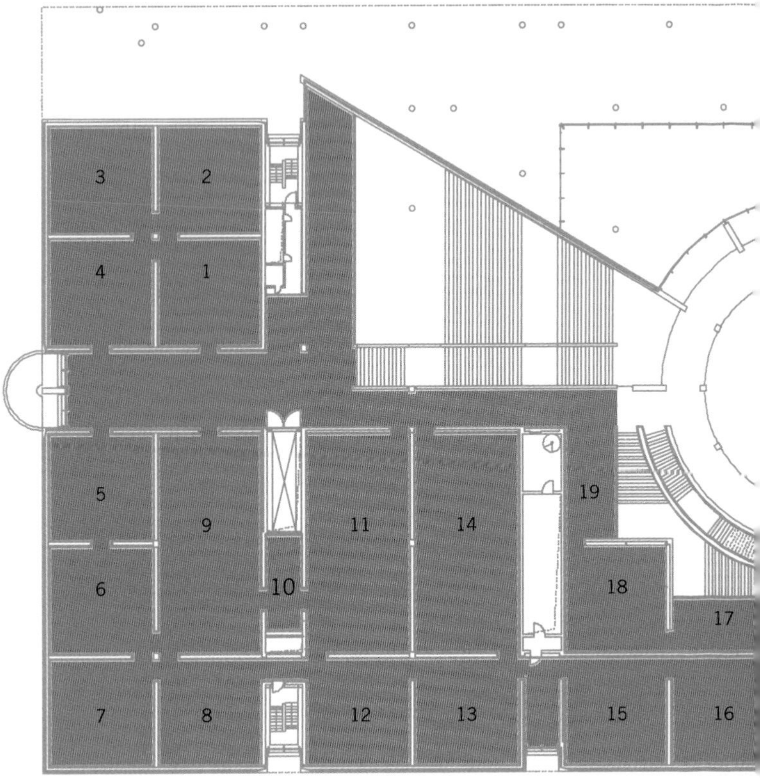

'What we exhibit is based on the biography of the collection and a certain art-historical credo. ... We are strong mainly in Beckmann, Beuys, Warhol and Baselitz. It would be completely wrong to try to show everything.' This is how Carla Schulz-Hoffmann, Deputy Director General of the Bayerische Staatsgemäldesammlungen, describes the exhibition of 20th and 21st-century art. It comprises the static exhibits of early modernist art in the West Wing, and art from 1960 onwards in the East Wing. Temporary exhibitions of contemporary art, which encompass installations, object art and video art, keep visitors abreast of the latest artistic trends.

Stephan Braunfels's architecture opens up many perspectives, allowing the visitor to make unexpected cross-references between rooms within the exhibition, particularly on the upper floor. The advantage of this open matrix is that we are thereby confronted with both connections and contrasting positions in 20th and 21st-century art. The classic museum circuit is thus broken up and imperceptibly instructive. For example, in the West Wing Max Beckmann and Pablo Picasso are juxtaposed. Post-1950 art is presented on a one room, one artist basis. Thus Lucio Fontana's slashed canvases immediately precede Arnulf Rainer's overpaintings, his crucifixions. No one familiar with the way these works were hung in the old Staatsgalerie moderner Kunst would recognise the same pictures in the Pinakothek. Today one of the world's leading collections of painting, sculpture and new media, the Staatsgalerie in 1945 contained only six works of art of great significance—those of Henri Matisse, Franz

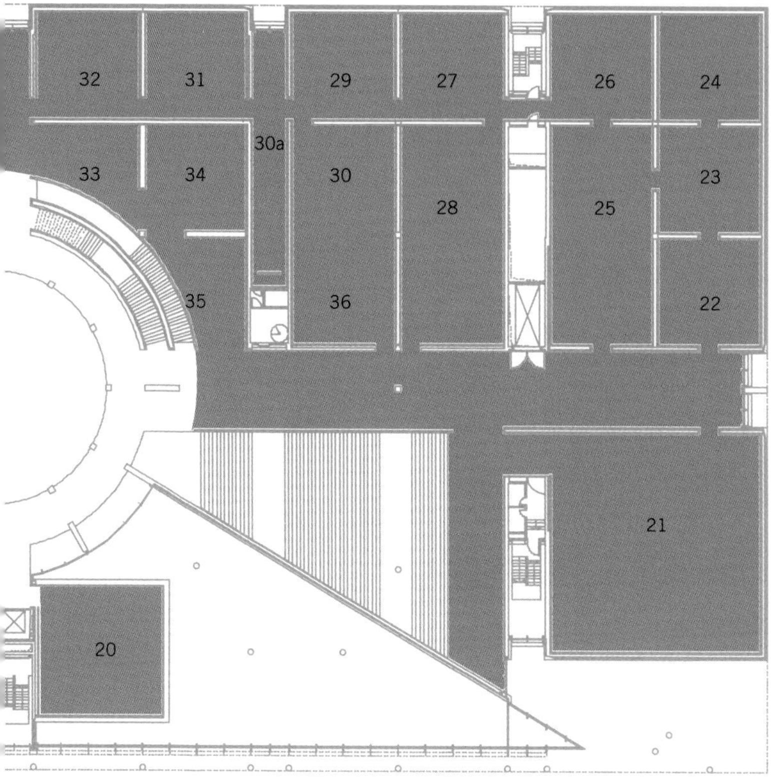

Marc, Oskar Kokoschka and Lovis Corinth. Its present rich offerings are the result of donations and bequests made since then, notably by Sofie and Emanuel Fohn in 1964 (works of German Expressionism), Theodor and Woty Werner (early modernist art), the Stiftung Günther Frankes (paintings by Max Beckmann) and Markus Kruss (works by the Brücke artists) in the 1970s and the Theo Wormland Collection (Surrealist art) and Prince Franz von Bayern Collection (German art after 1960) in the early 1980s. Since the mid-1960s the former association of art galleries, the Galerieverein München e.V. (now called PIN), has also helped build up the collection.

Upper storey, West Wing: Early modernism

Room 1	Fohn Collection
Room 2	Die Brücke
Room 3	Kirchner
Room 4	Müller, Nolde, Schmidt-Rottluff
Room 5	Cubism, Futurism
Room 6	Der Blaue Reiter
Room 7	Bauhaus
Room 8	Between Expressivity and Neue Sachlichkeit
Room 9	Braque, Corinth, Kokoschka et al.
Room 10	Klee, Lehmbruck
Room 11	Beckmann
Room 12	Theo Wormland Stiftung I
Room 13	Theo Wormland Stiftung II
Room 14	Picasso
Room 15	Early Abstraction
Room 16	Appel, Burri, Jorn, Saura et al.
Rooms 17–19	Figurative Painting of the 1960s and 1970s

Upper storey, East Wing: Art from 1960 onwards

Room 20	Beuys
Room 21	Temporary exhibitions
Room 22	Fontana
Room 23	Rainer
Room 24	Beuys
Room 25	Judd
Room 26	Polke, Richter
Room 27	Twombly
Room 28	Baselitz
Room 29	Flavin
Room 30	Wall
Room 30a	Grimonprez
Room 31	Palermo
Room 32	Warhol
Room 33	Wall
Room 34	Bacon, Richter, Segal et al.
Room 35	Johns, Rauschenberg, de Kooning

Second upper storey: Sculpture gallery
Basement: Temporary exhibitions

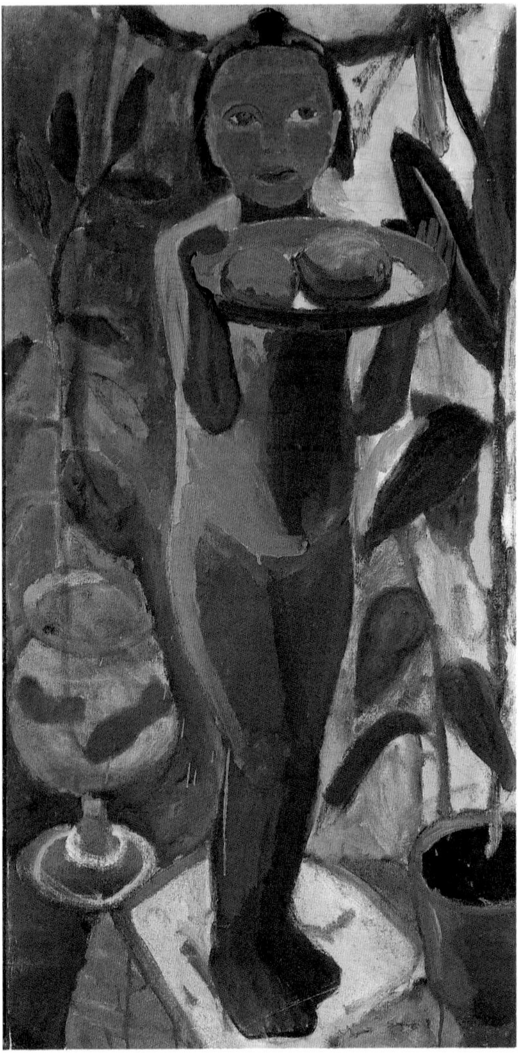

Room 1—Sofie and Emanuel Fohn Collection

Paula Modersohn-Becker (1876–1907)
Child Nude with Goldfish Bowl
c. 1906/07
Oil on canvas, 105.5 × 54.5 cm
Inv. no. 13468, Gift of Sofie and Emanuel Fohn 1964

'Paula hates the conventional and is now making the mistake of making everything angular, ugly, bizarre and wooden.' Even Modersohn-Becker's husband, Otto, thought this, according to a diary entry of 1903. Yet the artist did not make everything merely 'ugly'; there was something to be said for the wooden and the bizarre. As an artist, her thinking was always oriented to avant-garde trends in Paris and had nothing in common with the initial views of the Worpswede artists' colony, which she had joined. The child here resembles a clay sculpture, in a style influenced by Van Gogh or Gauguin, and reveals the artist's particular predilection for the use of symbolism. Compositionally reduced to simple forms and earthy colours, the figure of the girl would seem to have been inspired from 'primitive' art, while the motifs of fruit (fertility) and plants (growth) indicate a transitional stage between child and woman. It is an irony of fate that her preoccupation with the subject of growth and death in the year this picture was painted coincided with the artist's own death from childbirth.

Room 2—Die Brücke

Emil Nolde (1867–1956)
Dance around the Golden Calf 1910
Oil on canvas, 87.5 × 105 cm
Inv. no. 13351, purchased 1963

'To be both a child of nature and a cultivated person, to be both divine and a beast, ... that is the gifted artist who does not cling one-sidedly to one thing but creates the greatest art.' This was Nolde's view, even in his early days, and throughout his lifetime dance in particular served as subject and means of expression in both his art and his personal life. 'Expressive' dance (Nolde had been acquainted with Mary Wigman and Loïe Fuller's serpentine dances) applies especially to this picture. The biblical subject is presented without any moralising finger-wagging. By means of burning coloration and sharp, complementary contrasts (yellow-blue), the Brücke artist kindles an emotionally unbridled fire, a Dionysian intoxication. The relaxed, sensually uninhibited wildness of the spontaneous dance movements sends skirts whirling and unbound hair streaming. The stamping feet—whether barefoot or in red shoes—suggest drum rhythms. Nolde was an enthusiastic frequenter of vaudeville theatres and café dance floors.

Room 3—Ernst Ludwig Kirchner

Ernst Ludwig Kirchner (1880–1938)
Self-portrait as a Sick Man 1918
Oil on canvas on plywood
59 × 69.3 cm
Inv. no. L 2334, purchased in 2002 with the support of the Kulturstiftung der Länder, the Ernst-von-Siemens-Kunstfond and the Bayerische Landesstiftung

In 1905 Kirchner founded the artists' group Die Brücke together with Erich Heckel, Karl Schmidt-Rottluff and Fritz Bleyl. At first the four students lived and worked together in shared premises in Dresden, but later moved to Berlin. Like many of his Expressionist contemporaries, Kirchner was fascinated by city life. He became a chronicler of it, painting elegantly elongated cocottes and numerous colourfully explosive, boldly composed street scenes. *Self-portrait as a Sick Man* shows a different Kirchner—the broken man. After the horrors of the First World War—of which he, like many of his generation, had initially hoped for cathartic effects—he fled to the Swiss Alps. This is where we see him: the prodigal son trapped in a confined, wooden room with a small, barred window. Exhausted, with a sickly green countenance, he props himself up on his bed, which seems to glow in its redness.

Corridor

Wilhelm Lehmbruck (1881–1919)
Fallen Man 1915/16
(cast posthumously)
Bronze, 78 × 239 × 83 cm
Inv. no. B 397, purchased 1963

Lehmbruck found the war unbearable—so much so that in the end he took his own life. Still a young man, a good two years after he had produced his memorial to the youth of Europe killed in the war, he himself fell, just like his sculpture. His *Fallen Man* is at floor level in the corridor forming a 'bridge' between the art of the Expressionists and the Pinakothek's Cubism and Futurism Room. The Expressionist sculpture reiterates the bridge motif in the way the body of the defenceless man has been shaped, as an appeal to 'build bridges' of understanding between people of different nations. Moreover, the *Fallen Man* lends poignant expression to the general suffering of humanity. With his strongly simplified composition focusing on the principal subject of the 'fallen man', Lehmbruck breaks with the ideology of heroic warrior memorials of the 19th century. His contemporaries reacted with hostility. After all, they were accustomed to seeing fighting soldiers in such memorials, as far as possible in heroic poses high up on a plinth. With its floor-level positioning and the all-too-obvious depiction of the 'all to pieces' state of human dignity, corporeality and spirituality, the fallen man does not even provide historical allusions. There is no uniform, no inscription referring to battle, just the stump of a sword in the youth's right hand. Lehmbruck records the figure actively falling rather than simply 'in a state of collapse or prostrated. … The fallen man has just enough strength to prop himself up on the ground with his knees, head and arms' (Kurt Badt).

Room 5—Cubism and Futurism

Georges Braque (1882–1963)
Woman with Mandolin 1910
Oil on canvas, 91.5 × 72.5 cm
Inv. no. 13824, purchased 1967

Braque's oval *Woman with Mandolin* makes a good comparison with Boccioni's Futuristic portrait *Volumi orizzontali*. The juxtaposition may seem odd, as normally Braque's style is associated with Picasso's Cubist phase, from 1907 to 1914. But the confrontation of Braque and Boccioni clearly brings out the differences between the formal idioms of Analytical Cubism and Futurism. Braque's portrait does not aim at reality in the sense of imitating life. He is more concerned with depicting nature as a formal structure. Sculptural multiple perspectives are arranged in a flat, two-dimensional picture. The geometric forms of woman and mandolin are deliberately kept brownish grey. There is no garish coloration or even clear perspective to detract from the formal vocabulary. The compositional procedure emphasises the notion of the autonomy of art.

Umberto Boccioni (1882–1916)
Volumi orizzontali 1912
Oil on canvas, 95 × 95.5 cm
Inv. no. 14611, purchased 1979

Boccioni likewise juggles with realistic and abstract elements in his composition. But he and his Italian artist colleagues Giacomo Balla, Carlo Carrà, Luigi Russolo and Gino Severini favoured *dinamismo*—speed and visible motion—and 'simultaneity'. Boccioni depicts his mother wholly in the spirit of the technology-inspired philosophy that Filippo Tommaso had proclaimed in the Futurist Manifesto of 1910. Though the figure here is shown on the pictorial axis in a reposeful, seated pose with hands folded in her lap, dynamic forces are at work in the depiction of the body. The arms are twisted into an oval, and a flurry of spiralling lines criss-crosses the body, neck and head. The face is seen from a double perspective—frontally and in profile. The background is likewise in motion: walls and roofs are fragmented as in a kaleidoscope, appearing to push the figure forward.

Room 6—Der Blaue Reiter

Franz Marc (1880–1916)
Fighting Shapes 1914
Oil on canvas, 91 × 131.5 cm
Inv. no. 10972, purchased 1949

Like Kandinsky, Franz Marc dreamt of a better, ideal world. For him, animals were synonymous with and a medium of this purity. In this picture, the animal recalls the shape of a bird of prey but is at the same time virtually abstract. Previously Marc had stylised his animals in complicated, simultaneous perspectives and colour zones. Here, two dynamically whirling, circular shapes dominate the picture, dividing it diagonally into aggressive red and blackish blue shapes. The fire-red shape is attacking the blackish blue whorl with claws, beak and pinions. Among the many interpretations of the picture, it seems most sensible to see the act of violence as a cathartic new beginning that will lead to the hoped-for better, more 'spiritual' world. Marc's *Fighting Shapes*—one of a four-part group of pictures—dates from just before the outbreak of the First World War. The artist had longed for war as a necessary, violently purifying step towards the world of which he dreamed. When you recall other bird pictures by Marc, there is no longer anything here of the angular, fragmented triangles. The dynamism is discharged in circles that break up and explode of their own accord. Marc commented aphoristically: 'These days we take chaste, ever-deceptive nature apart and reassemble it as we will. We look through matter, and the day is not far off when we shall reach through its vibrating mass as through air.'

Room 6—Der Blaue Reiter

Wassily Kandinsky (1866–1944)
Dream Improvisation 1913
Oil on canvas, 130 × 130 cm
Inv. no. 14091, purchased in 1969
with the support of PIN. Friends of
the Pinakothek der Moderne

Kandinsky's *Dream Improvisation* is an important work, for it is a plausible rendering of what the head of the Blaue Reiter considered a visual realisation of an abstract, 'resounding cosmos'. If you try to describe the picture from a musical point of view (as Kandinsky's classification of many works into 'compositions' and 'improvisations' might suggest), you find the following homogeneous and disparate elements that correlate with the realisation of this floating state of consciousness and freely shape it: the tonic keynote—the ground of the picture—vibrates in diffuse shades of brown. Overlying this, around a blue-white colour core in the middle, is a counterpoint of diverse colour shapes that mingle, overlap or stand for themselves. Black lines and graphic symbols interpret the musical vision, marking accents, standing out or blurring into the background. Thus Kandinsky's picture is a multi-layered, multi-referential polyphony of liberated shapes and colours organised subconsciously or 'spiritually'.

Room 7—Bauhaus

Lyonel Feininger (1871–1956)
Market Church in Halle 1930
Oil on canvas, 100.7 × 85 cm
Inv. no. 12013, purchased 1954

If we look at Feininger's market church picture, an echo of Romantic thought is immediately perceived. For the head of the graphic art studio at the Bauhaus, the church was an architectural, utopian symbol of the upward striving for spirituality. Three elements make up the composition: overlapping and interlocking cubic, crystalline shapes; a transparent, prismatically fractured colour idiom (even in the black areas); strictly regimented structural blocks. Despite its monumentality (the staffage of human figures in the marketplace is tiny, almost self-effacing by comparison) and weighty compactness, the church reaches beyond the picture edge into the blue of the sky, forming a giant vertical. The transparency of the picture structure has a musical quality. The son of musicians, Feininger was also a fine interpreter of Bach and fugues.

Room 8—Between Expressivity and Neue Sachlichkeit

Alexander Kanoldt (1881–1939)
Half-nude II 1926
Oil on canvas, 90.5 × 71 cm
Inv. no. 14157, purchased 1971

This is the gaze of a disillusioned woman, portrayed against a bare background. Is she a prostitute? Or is she just a woman undressed and exposed, who clams up and literally stiffens under the cool, dissecting gaze of the artist? 'New objectivity' renders the mature woman with exaggerated precision—a lost, de-individualised, ruthlessly bared object paralysed by the cold surroundings. Rather in the style of Otto Dix, the severe composition hardens the unerotic sight into a *veriste* portrait of oppressive confinement, ageing and finiteness. This is not a sensual, voyeuristic peek behind the curtain of a *chambre séparée*. What we are confronted with here are accentuated aspects of an attitude to life prevalent in the 1920s. In Kanoldt's *Half-nude II* we see not a glittering world but dour pessimism and the asperity of loneliness.

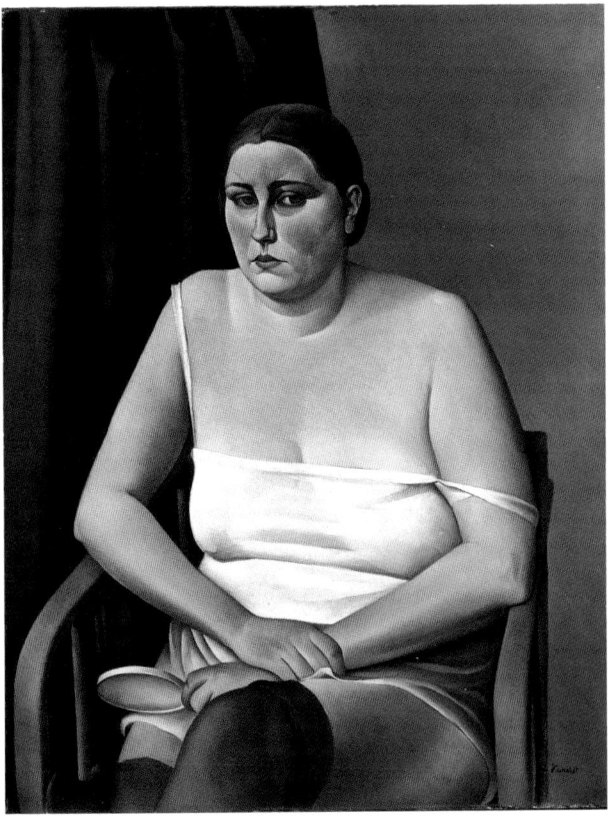

Room 9—Georges Braque, Lovis Corinth, Oskar Kokoschka et al.

Lovis Corinth (1858–1925)
Large Self-portrait at Lake Walchen
1924
Oil on canvas, 137.7 × 107.7 cm
Inv. no. 11327, purchased 1952

Corinth loved the mountains, particularly the Bavarian village of Urfeld beside Lake Walchen. The air and the light here were different from Berlin. Here he could paint out in the open outside his own house, which was built on a slope with a fantastic view across crystal-clear water to the Karwendel mountains in the distance. Here nature was constantly changing moods, as reflected in the weather. Corinth's self-portrait is a *plein air* portrait with a remarkable background. Like many predecessors, it was painted on his birthday, and is his last self-portrait. As if aware of this, on this hot July day, the 66-year-old artist shows himself to the viewer in three-quarters profile in a strangely unreal-looking landscape. The light illuminates trees, meadow and lake, creating a reality apart, and

conspicuously lights up the painter's head. The *contre-jour* of the glaring noonday sun throws the artist's face and the front of his body into shadow.

Room 11—Max Beckmann

Max Beckmann (1884–1950)
Temptation (Temptation of St Anthony) 1936/37
Oil on canvas
Centre picture 200 × 170 cm
Side pictures each 215 × 100 cm
Inv. nos. 14486–14488,
purchased 1977

'A defect of the book—not much character in St Anthony, lots of background information and yet not enough', said Beckmann critically of Gustave Flaubert's eponymous novel, which he had used as source material for his triptych on the Temptation of St Anthony. The painter thought 'enchainment' was the appropriate motif to convey the notion of the saint's entanglement and sacrifice of passion in this three-part pictorial drama. In the centre painting the figure of St Anthony is shown sitting on the floor in front of a goddess. Two side pictures show temptations of different kinds in the oppressed figures: on the left an erotic figure of a woman chained to a spear on a raft (Helen/Ennoia) in front of a sailor; on the right a seductress (the Queen of Sheba) in a cage on a boat. On the left is an androgynous knight vanquishing mortal lust, on the right a sexless page-boy house-training a woman like a dog. A remarkable aspect of the paintings is the contrast of content and form. Though the figures accept their lack of freedom, they do not all seem spiritually bowed. The scenes of enslavement in the side pictures are set in the open air, whereas the youth in the middle is depicted indoors.

Room 12—Surrealism—
Theo Wormland Stiftung I:
René Magritte, Salvador Dalí,
Pablo Picasso, Giorgio de Chirico

Renée Magritte (1898–1967)
The Acrobat's Exercises 1928
Oil on canvas, 116 × 80.8 cm
Inv. no. 14252, purchased 1971

Magritte's Surrealist painting aims to shake our perception and challenge our view of what art does. Here the picture also acts as a mind game. We follow the acrobat going about her exercises as if she were on stage, performing against a backdrop of the sky. The sequences are truncated cut-outs seen from different view-points, at different times. In the picture a metamorphosis takes place in the serpentine movements of the artiste as much as in the spectator's point of view. The exercising legs, neck, head and arms wind and contort themselves, and our thoughts are spurred into action by fragmentary chains of association and pictures requiring completion. We discern a trumpet and a gymnastics costume, and think of vaudeville. The grey stage opens up horizons. But isn't the sky in fact a mirage? Even if title and picture do match, the existence of the artiste is 'at the frontier. She balances between the real and the fictive' (Wieland Schmied).

Room 12—Surrealism—
Theo Wormland Stiftung II:
René Magritte, Salvador Dalí,
Pablo Picasso, Giorgio de Chirico

Salvador Dalí (1904–1989)
The Enigma of Desire, or
My Mother, My Mother, My Mother
1929
Oil on canvas, 110 × 150 cm
Inv. no. 14734, purchased in 1982 with the support of the Theo Wormland Stiftung

The Surrealist Dalí was an exhibitionist and an eccentric. He applied what he called the 'critical-paranoid' method, supposedly based on Freudian psychoanalysis, to make exact reproductions of his meandering fantasies. Absurdity elevated to a principle is shown realistically in this fantasy image. A brain-like formation full of excrescences labelled 'ma mère' is placed in a desert, melting into a sleeping skull. This phantasmagory with ants, cannibalistically embracing figures and lion heads has frequently been interpreted as a 'mental landscape with family obsessions' and architectural quotes from Antonio Gaudí have been identified in the detailed realism of perversion. What is certain is that, like all Dalí's delirious artistic flights of fancy and neurotic delusions, this vision follows the laws of dreams. The relationship between the individual objects is incomprehensible.

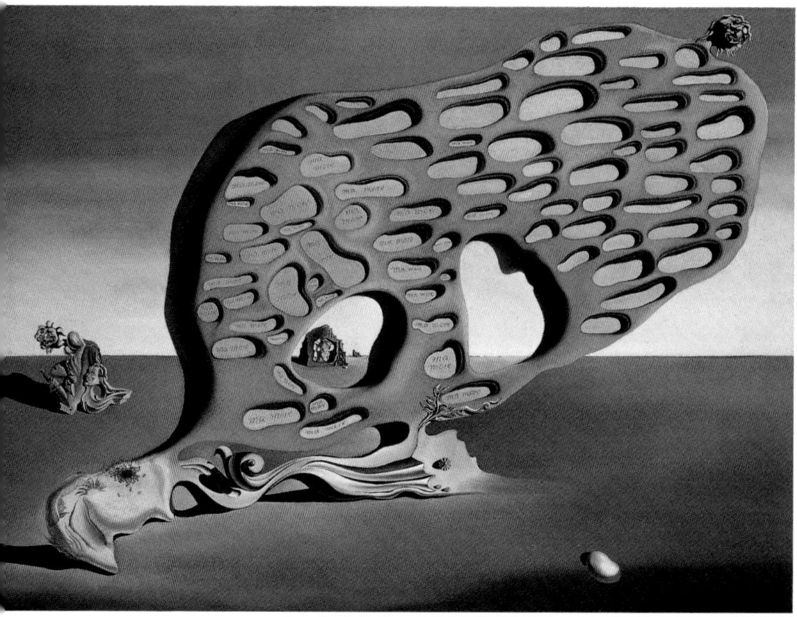

Room 12—Surrealism—
Theo Wormland Stiftung I:
René Magritte, Salvador Dalí,
Pablo Picasso, Giorgio de Chirico

Giorgio de Chirico (1888–1978)
Self-portrait 1920
Oil on panel, 50.2 × 39.5 cm
Inv. no. 14682, purchased 1981

Pittura metafisica means for painter and viewer uncertainty about everything, experiencing alienated, enigmatic reality and looking far beyond what you see. Greek-born painter Giorgio de Chirico was a master of metaphysical puzzles, as his programmatic self-portrait makes clear. Against the background of a black, claustrophobic space he poses for himself as an enigma in a picture of emblematic quality. He presents himself in the traditional way as a painter, but holds up a Latin inscription asking: 'And what shall I love apart from the metaphysical aspect of things?' Is this an explanatory inscription or a reference to a picture within a picture, the receding space in the upper right-hand corner? Is the architectural prop of the Uffizi in Florence a false perspective or an interior view? Does it describe an enigmatic, imaginary building, the moment of inspiration that struck de Chirico in Florence just before he embarked on his most celebrated period of work?

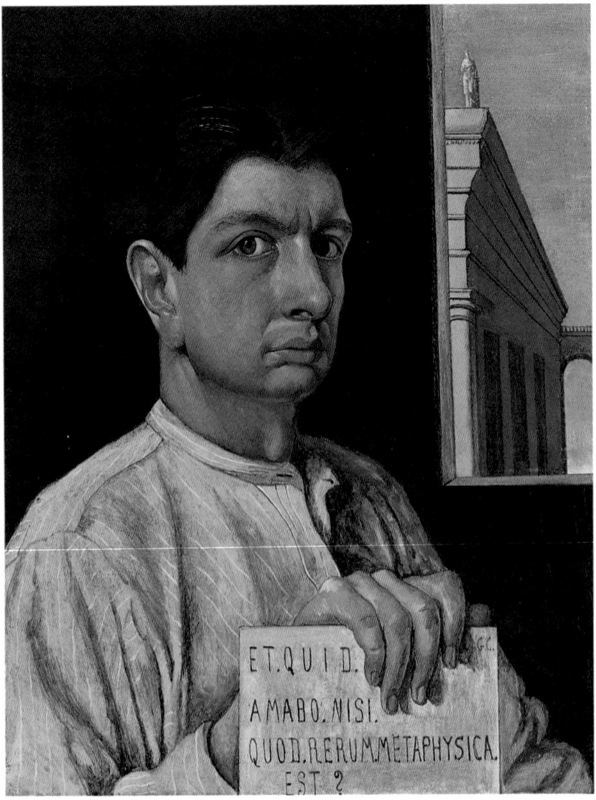

Room 13—Surrealism—
Theo Wormland Stiftung II: Max Ernst

Max Ernst (1891–1976)
Fireside Angel (L'ange du foyer)
1937
Oil on canvas, 54 × 74 cm
Inv. no. L 1944, on loan from the Theo Wormland Stiftung since 1983

'Evil is ... a fallen angel. Evil is a part of man whose monstrosity comes even from banality' (Hartwig Garneus). Ernst's paintings don't need any armies or gods of war to illustrate approaching disaster and the horrors descending on the world. Max Ernst's reaction to Franco's Fascism was what he called a 'clumsy brute', a politically surreal picture of the Spanish Civil War (1936–39). Ernst's fiend from the abyss of horror, a flapping bogey, is beside itself. It dances a destructive St Vitus's dance to the screeching obbligato of a green-beaked lizard creature. Evil rages over the landscape, threateningly flapping its fatigues-coloured outfit and blood-red cloak. (If you see it as the red flag of the Republicans, it is already torn in the clutches of evil.) What is more dangerous—the carnassials of the dragon-man? The battle axe that the material has wound itself into? The claw foot? Or even the carpet slipper, the token of petty bourgeois cosiness that will trample everything beneath it? In 1946 Paul Eluard wrote a poem for Ernst that reads: 'The man that tastes/Of carpet slippers/His head is always/On the reverse of everything/ My domain/Remained Night alone/ Heaven has/Turned away from man.'

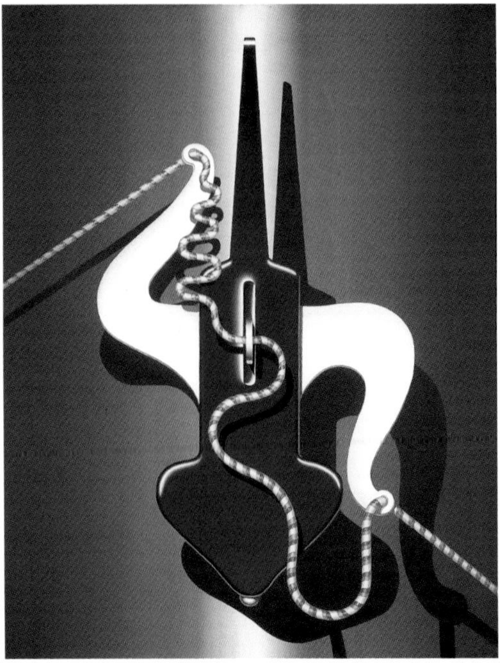

Room 19—Figurative Painting of the 1960s and 1970s

Konrad Klapheck (1935)
The Decision-taker, or
The Boaster 1965
Oil on canvas, 100 × 80 cm
Inv. no. L 1971, on loan from the Theo Wormland Stiftung since 1983

The works of Konrad Klapheck from the Bayerische Staatsgemäldesammlungen zur Kunst des 20./21. Jahrhunderts along with the paintings of Horst Antes and Fernando Botero are important examples of the so-called New Figuration of the 1960s and 1970s. Klapheck resists the broad trend towards arbitrary abstraction. Instead he distils the styles of Surrealism and the Neue Sachlichkeit into a unique kind of figurative painting. The original German title of the present piece is *Der Angeber*, which can mean a variety of things, including someone who takes a decision and a boaster. Of his work the artist remarked: 'All interpretations are permitted. … The object is like a radiator mascot on a car. … I can see the phallic element with a vagina in the dark shape as well, but at the same time a man in shirt-sleeves also springs to mind. … The figure … decides how and in what tempo the cord passes through its hands. But an *Angeber* is also a show-off, someone who claims capabilities that he ultimately doesn't have.'

Room 14—Pablo Picasso

Pablo Picasso (1881–1973)
Mother and Child 1921
Oil on canvas, 154 × 104 cm
Inv. no. 14635, purchased 1980

A compact figural group in reddish brown coloration, Picasso's monumental, heavily outlined *Mother and Child* is almost sculptural, and timeless. The folds in the garment on her left knee ossify into the fluting of a column. Picasso's idiom now exhibits classicising tendancies, reducing subjects to simple forms rather than fracturing them as in Cubism. Within the artist's sheer inexhaustible stylistic diversity, the painting documents his so-called Neoclassicist phase. The style determines the choice of such timeless subjects as 'mother and child'. The picture is not a record of fatherhood (though his son Paul was born on 21 February 1921). Picasso does not even endow the young boy with typical features. Instead, he transposes the child 'into the model that was made available to him by the muses; ... he turns this into a picture of the Christ Child in the Virgin's lap' (Werner Spies).

Lucio Fontana (1899–1968)
Concetto spaziale, Attese (59 T 132) 1959
Blue ink on canvas, 82 × 116 cm
Inv. no. 14976, purchased 1986

In Europe artists reacted to Action Painting, Abstract Realism and art as an excess of stimuli by emphasising light, using different tonal values of the same colour or stylising and processing monochrome surfaces Lucio Fontana followed a similar path. His canvases are conceptual art, leaving room for the idea of space. Even if the notion of transformation reigns supreme in his work, Fontana's ideas possess the power literally to penetrate, to which the four horizontal gaping gashes made from behind the support of the picture attest. These gashes (*tagli*), to which *Attese* (which signifies 'expectation' in Italian) belongs, thus disclose—without intending to destroy—the radical notion of space behind, between and in front of the canvas.

Room 20—Joseph Beuys

Joseph Beuys (1921–1986)
The End of the 20th Century 1983
Basalt, clay, felt, 44 stones
Each approx. 48 × 150 × 40 cm
Inv. no. GV 81, on loan from PIN.
Friends of the Pinakothek der Moderne since 1983

With this room sculpture, Beuys takes up his notion of the 'universal communicative capacity of nature and man' with the intention of reanimating our lost creative visual faculties. Forty-four basalt columns are spread out in an apparently random arrangement on a large floor, side by side or resting on each other. Cylindrical shapes have been milled out of the blocks of basalt and remounted in the resulting holes. Regardless of whether they are eyes or hearing devices, the telescope-like character of the shapes recalls detection devices. Is nature ready to receive, ready to communicate with us and with itself? What does it wish to communicate? Are we looking at a theatre of war with petrified corpses, or primeval, fish-like creatures? The polarisation of life and death is not least substantiated by the materials used. This monumental work was the Pinakothek's first work of art.

Room 26—Sigmar Polke, Gerhard Richter

Sigmar Polke (1941)
Skaters *c.* 1966
Dispersion on canvas
180 × 195 cm
Inv. no. 14484, purchased 1976

Polke's half-tone pictures of 1963–69 combine three basic aspects: the artist's play with and subversion of Pop-art traditions; dot-by-dot painted sections; and well-aimed punch-lines. *Skaters* is an excellent example of this. Polke's wintry scene is not a jolly, exaggerated Christmas card reproduction of quiet pleasures, even if trivial things are the starting point of the picture. Polke doesn't break up his pictures into screened images by copying a photo on to a canvas. This is a handcrafted, specially set-up 'solution'. The dots are deliberate, and to some extent function like dots of colour to create a pictorial reality in which individuals ultimately blur into something diffuse in the viewer's eyes. His skaters pale in the trenchant reality of a genuinely colourless subject.

Room 28—Georg Baselitz

Georg Baselitz (1938)
Two Meissen Foresters 1967
Oil on canvas, 251.2 × 200.7 cm
Inv. no. 15331, purchased 1992

Baselitz does not invert figures in this picture. In his endeavour to find a style eschewing traditional rules and moving towards an idiom that is art for its own sake, Baselitz tears the scene apart. This tearing involves the objects in the picture, the pictorial idiom he uses, the concept of a hero, the viewer's expectations—in short, everything that is usually firm and fixed. All elements of the narrative have lost terra firma. Two sawn-down trees float past horizontally, one above the other, in the top left corner. The mangled, bloody bodies of two dogs hacked apart 'fly' down from top right diagonally across the picture. Even the figures of the two forest workers are fragmented and 'transparent'. Parts of the undercoat show through beneath the green forester uniform or the decomposing blue of the sky, and thus we can see the background passing in the two men. The artist systematically invests the unthreatening, unprepossessing subject of two forest workers with extreme fragility by introducing uncertainty at every level. Nothing stands firm here. The figures on the right even lack legs.

Room 29—Dan Flavin

Dan Flavin (1933–1996)
'monument' for V Tatlin 1969
7 white fluorescent tubes
305 × 71 × 11 cm
Inv. no. GST 6, on loan from the Museumsstiftung since 1999

The 'monuments', i.e. lights, of New York minimalist artist Dan Flavin are special in that they represent just themselves, devoid of any psychological overlay. No underlying artistic intention, childhood trauma or any cryptic political overtones lurk, or demand to be taken into account. Flavin's sober intent is inconspicuous art, art you might fail to notice. The individual objects—in this case, corresponding to the subject of electric light, seven fluorescent tubes—consist of identical, everyday working materials. The mastery involves placing them in relation to one another and within the installation space. The labour involved is simple: to erect or dismantle the work, the tubes are clipped on or unclipped and put up somewhere else. Nothing detracts from the object—there are no flourishes and no decorations. And yet Flavin's work in honour of the Russian Constructivist is almost decorative in its effect.

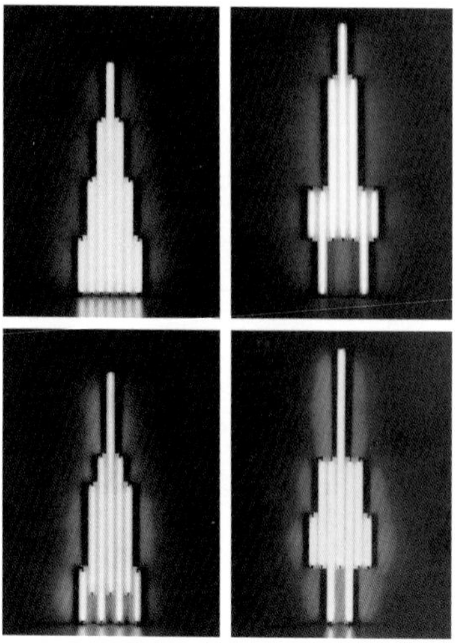

Room 30—Jeff Wall

Jeff Wall (1946)
Eviction Struggle 1988
Large transparency in a light box
249 × 434 cm
Inv. no. 15319, purchased in 1992 with the support of the Siemens-Kulturprogramm

One could describe Jeff Wall's photography as visual training. His gesture is that of subtle demonstration. As the large-scale light-box transparencies *Eviction Struggle*, and *Fight on the Sidewalk* of 1994, show, the artist deliberately deceives our conditioned way of seeing. Initially the viewer sees

the scene he is presented with as authentic : in an American suburb two policemen arrest a man outside his house. A woman rushes out at the sound of the dramatic struggle, evidently with the intention of helping the detainee. Drivers and passers-by look on, fascinated by the scene, stopping to watch by their cars or on the sidewalk. Yet, though apparently a real-life drama, the entire event is staged. Following the gaze of the bystanders and the ring of parked cars, our gaze gradually arrives at the staged reality taking place in the background. The struggle is a polished pose, synthetic violence. The frontiers of our perception of the environment thereby become blurred, just as the blurred demarcation of private and public space in the photograph is conveyed by the successive reduction from the wall bottom right, to the enclosing railings and finally the unenclosed front gardens.

Ultimately, Wall's photography is self-referential. It is not in the least a one-to-one mimesis, as we are intuitively wont to expect from photography. Wall's pictures are settings of the grotesque, presenting the absurdities of everyday actions. Wall states that neither beauty nor the sublime apply to his work. His element is the grotesque. 'Grotesque means a more dramatic condition, the condition of not being perfect and suffering deformations because of social, political or psychological circumstances.'

Blinky Palermo (1943–1977)
Pinball 1965
Oil on canvas, 89 × 69.5 cm
Inv. no. WAF PF 55, on loan from the Wittelsbacher Ausgleichsfond, Collection of Prince Franz von Bayern, since 1985

The work of Beuys's pupil Blinky Palermo demonstrates how sensitivity and design form a unity in minimalist art. As the title suggests, the subject matter is the reproduction of a pinball machine or, more precisely, the ordinary pattern on the side of a machine. Two ideas of art are shattered: that of a source from everyday life, and the idea of uninterrupted geometry. This effect is achieved through the careful, concentrated painting process, which dispels the assumption of a completely even grid of a geometric structure, instead conveying a strictly subjective painting gesture. The 'late Palermo', if one can say this about a man who died at the age of 34, systematically

rejected figurative painting. The principle of reduction determined his stylistic means, choice of colours and pictorial message.

Room 32—Andy Warhol

Andy Warhol (1928–1987)
AIDS / Jeep / Bicycle 1985 or 1986
Synthetic resin paints on canvas
294.5 × 457 cm
Inv. no. 15555, purchased 2001

This work shows how differently American Pop artist Andy Warhol treated the subjects of consumer society, advertising and superstars in his mature work compared with the early work. Nothing here is reminiscent of the series of garish portraits of himself (*Self-portrait*, 1967) and celebrities, whom Warhol had reduced to multiple copies by the silkscreen process and stylised into interchangeable publicity images. In this picture the much-exposed popular icons give way to such prestigious consumer goods as a racing bike and a Jeep. Frank Sinatra's eulogy of 'New York, New York' in the form of block lettering replaces the legendary film stars. The association of unlimited possibilities and hopes ('If I can make it there, I'll make it anywhere') is challenged, as the word 'AIDS', the most prominent feature of the picture, overlaps the consumer products, as does the red bar.

Room 34—Francis Bacon, Georg Baselitz, Gerhard Richter, George Segal

George Segal (1924–2000)
Alice, Listening to her Poems and Music 1970
Plaster, wood, glass, cassette recorder
240 × 240 × 82.5 cm
Inv. no. B 657, purchased 1973

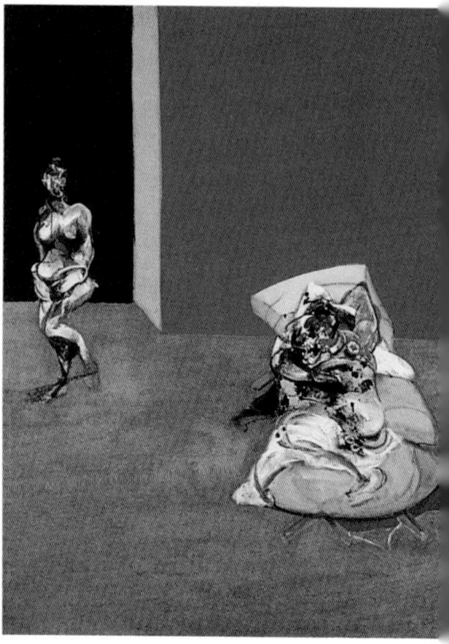

Alice sits alone. Hunched up, with arms crossed in front of her, the white plaster figure has pulled her chair up to the table by the window. Her stylised features are generalised, visible in the window reflection against a black background. New York artist Segal integrates real objects into this everyday situation (transistor radio, table, chair) to create room-object art. Has the curtain been drawn back for a frozen scene of isolation and one-dimensional communication? Is the poet Alice Notley as injured or feeling as bad as the hardened plaster suggests? We are observers of the tableau, in which every object has an existence of its own. And yet the question arises as to whether we should focus our attention on the bandaged figure or

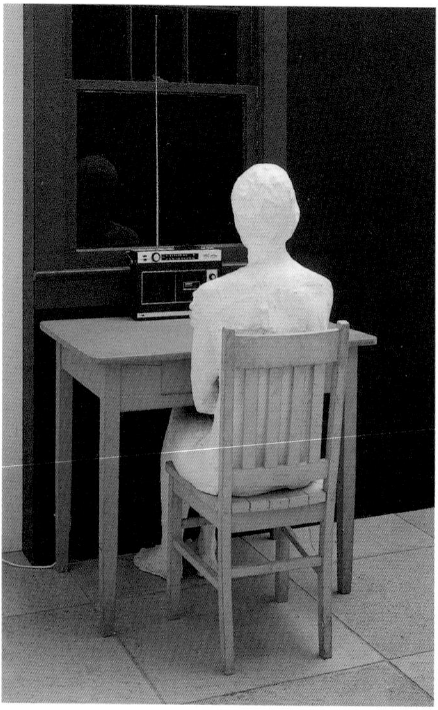

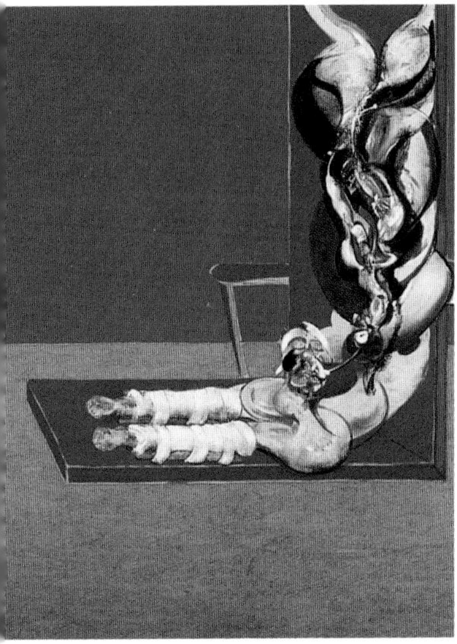 

the incomprehensible noises of the cassette recorder, which stands as pars pro toto for a typical situation of loneliness.

Room 34—Francis Bacon, Georg Baselitz, Gerhard Richter, Georg Segal

Francis Bacon (1909–1992)
Cruficixion 1965
Oil on canvas, each 198 × 147 cm
Inv. no. GV 1–3, on loan from the Museumsstiftung since 1967

For Bacon, the subject of the crucifixion is undeniably linked to 'pictures to do with slaughterhouses and meat' (1962). When asked why, the expressive painter said the cross was a peg on which to hang feelings about human behaviour. This 1965 triptych is a condensation: it shows, from left to right, a man as a mutilated, bloody carcass with skin flayed from his skull, on a hospital bed. In the middle, we see him as a chained, sacrificed and disembowelled beef carcass, on the third panel as a muscular desecrator wearing a swastika armband and acting the voyeur. Formally, the Irish artist sets the suffering of the flesh against a background of sterile colour geometry. Thus he deliberately targets the aesthetics of pain: the abstract, expressionist narrative event affects the viewer directly, like the abattoir scenes of Rembrandt, Francisco de Goya or Lovis Corinth.

Room 35—Jasper Johns, Robert Rauschenberg, Willem de Kooning

Willem de Kooning (1904–1997)
Detour 1958
Oil on paper on canvas
150 × 108 cm
Inv. no. 14614, GV 57, purchased in 1979 with the support of PIN. Friends of the Pinakothek der Moderne

Willem de Kooning, who with Jackson Pollock is considered a representative of Action Painting, is grouped with the American Abstract Expressionists, even though the Dutch-born artist deliberately sought to shake off the label by doing figurative painting. His art focuses on the non-perspectival, the process of painting, on the action involved. The broad brushstrokes of this painting take a 'detour'. The triangle overlaid on the other broad lines of colour and surfaces bursts the frame, only to return into the picture as a whitish brown gesture. If you want to see a realistic pictorial idiom in and behind this allover technique, you need to pay attention to the palpable toing and froing of the brushstrokes: these evoke an impression of street networks, altered routes and directions. The actual 'detour', however, is marked by de Kooning's handling of paint and brush.

Rotunda—Mario Marini, Henry Moore, Toni Stadler

Marino Marini (1901–1980)
Rider 1947
Bronze, traces of firestone
100.5 × 67 × 49 cm
Inv. no. B 702, Marino Marini Foundation 1976

Marino Marini was one of the leading sculptors of the 20th century. His style revitalises the tradition of the equestrian monument in both form and content. His bronze sculpture *Rider* is an example of a clown-like congruence, a humorously carefree, balanced unity. Later, Marini would increasingly allow the rider motif—which he constantly varied, as he saw it as an expression of his hopes and fears for his time—to take different directions. But here the man sits relaxed on the horse. Gazing upwards, he takes no notice of the horse, which would prefer to graze. The solidly upright group masters two complementary yet contrasting elements: the body weight of rider and horse in relation to the fragile legs of the animal and the upward and downward movements of man and beast.

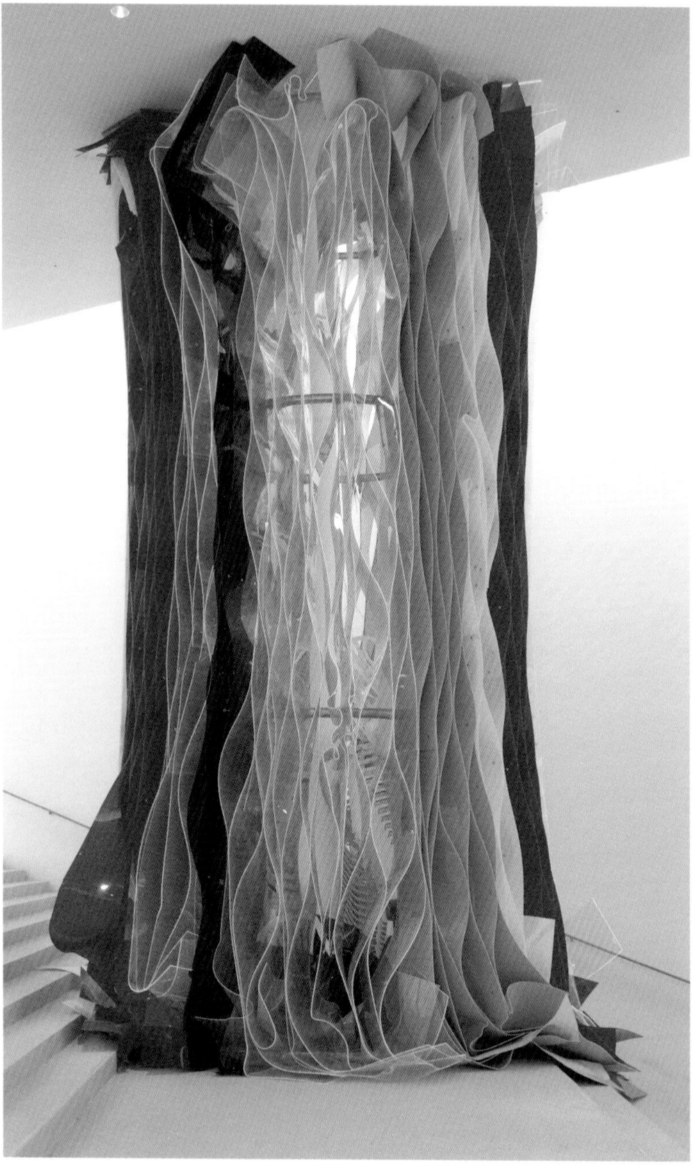

Staircase—Olaf Metzel, Sigmar Polke

Olaf Metzel (1952)
Musical Chairs 2002
Column clad in Plexiglas, plastic chairs, stroboscope, h. 7 m, diam. 3 m
Purchased 2002

Olaf Metzel's sculpture was done specially for the opening of the Museum. The seven-metre-high installation occupies a choice location—the column on the middle landing of the grand staircase leading to the East Wing of the upper storey. The staircase is 25 metres wide there, and provides a theatrical setting for the splendid presence of the abstract piece. The column is girt with brightly coloured Plexiglas strips and piled-up chairs.

In the context of a showroom, closely associated with the architecture and yet autonomous, it triggers various speculations: is this a glamorous film star about to descend the staircase? With this glowing whatsit behind you, can you sit at ease on the steps? The final thought comes when the illumination of the sculpture unexpectedly goes off. As in the party game of musical chairs, when to get a seat you have to sit down suddenly when the music stops, there is existential disquiet here, too.

Ground floor—Temporary exhibitions

Teresa Hubbard (1965) and
Alexander Birchler (1962)
Eight 2001
High-definition video on DVD with sound, 3 min., 35 sec., in a loop, ed. 8/10
Inv. no. GV 132, on loan from PIN. Friends of the Pinakothek der Moderne since 2002

Eight begins the rotating exhibition of contemporary videos shown on the ground floor. Hubbard and Birchler's video tells the emotional, atmospheric story of the rained-out birthday celebrations of an eight-year-old girl. The camera glides without breaks from plot to plot in a synaesthetic interaction of interior and exterior. The looped succession of scenes is so intricate that you do not notice the transitions between alternating spatial levels. For example, we hear and see pouring rain from a cosy room. We see the girl at the window looking at the rainy scene in the garden. In the inhospitable world outside, she stands dripping wet, by herself, cutting a slice of cake. Back in the room, acoustics are used again, while the girl looks pensively out the window.

Prints and Drawings: Staatliche Graphische Sammlung

Franz Marc (1880–1916)
The Tower of the Blue Horses 1912
Ink, opaque watercolour, 14.3 × 9.3 cm
Inv. no. 13550, Gift of Sofie and Emanuel Fohn

'What a lovely card—I always wanted some horses in my favourite colour with my greys. The crescent moons are terrifically arty, Egyptian crown prince daggers in the skin of the whinnying legends. How can I thank you!' These words are from a thank-you letter dated 3 January 1913 written by poet Else Lasker-Schüler to Franz Marc, who had sent her a New Year's card in the form of a painted postcard. The enthusiastic reference to 'crescent moons' and 'Egyptian crown prince daggers' carries weight on both a biographical and an artistic level. The cosmological sign language was equally important to both poet and painter. Marc had been familiar with Lasker-Schüler's poems even before he met her, after they were published in Herwarth Walden's magazine *Der Sturm*. Artistically Marc was exploring here the visual notion of animals as spectral beings, which he later developed into a major composition. This famous New Year's card is the only surviving study for the lost painting *Tower of Blue Horses*, which the Blaue Reiter artist painted in Sindelsdorf, in the foothills of the Bavarian Alps, in 1913.

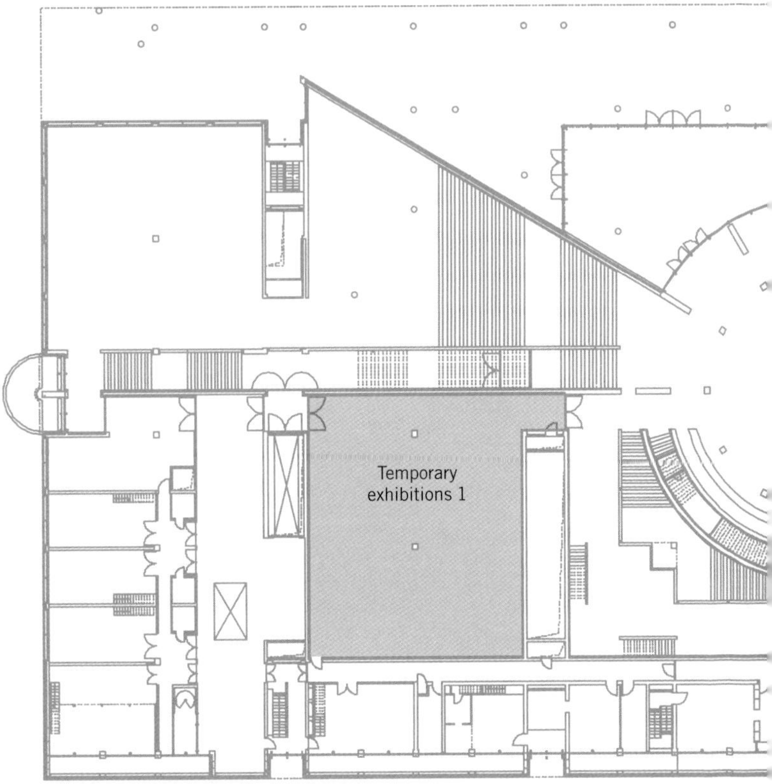

Although 'spotlighting works on paper' is not possible owing to their sensitivity to light, figuratively speaking that is what has happened as a result of the Staatliche Graphische Sammlung's move to the Pinakothek der Moderne. After being hidden away at 10 Meiser-strasse since 1949, the collection of prints and drawings at last has a worthy public platform.

The rooms for the light-sensitive sheets exhibited must be sparingly lit with indirect or artificial light. Braunfels therefore opted to create a separate section for what is the oldest of the Museum's four collections. It is, if you like, a modern 'cabinet of drawings' on the ground floor. The exhibition rooms devoted to the Graphische Sammlung include a vestibule, an atrium and 12 wall showcases. The principal concern of director Michael Semff is to use the space such that the juxta-position of works is in itself inspiring, while devoid of any didactic intent. And precisely because the works cannot be exposed to light for very long, the display is changed every three months.

The selection here was taken from the opening display, which provides a representative sample of the total holdings (400,000 works on paper from periods ranging from the 15th century to modern times, some 45,000 of which are drawings and 350,000 prints). The artists represented range from Old Masters, such as Schongauer, Titian and Rembrandt, via the precursors of modernism (Marées, Cézanne, Van Gogh) and exponents of early modernism (Marc, Klee) to such inter-nationally celebrated artists as Georg

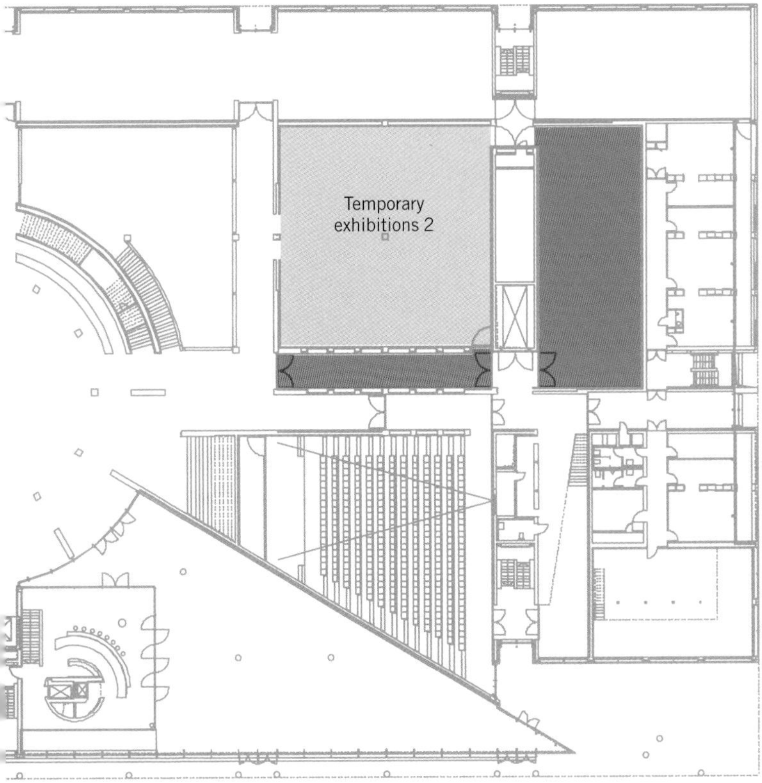

Baselitz, Brice Marden and Wols. In the following pages selected works are deliberately chosen to contrast old and new on the basis of common subject matter, to highlight the modernity of the collection of prints and drawings in the context of its integration into the Pinakothek der Moderne.

The origins of the collection go back to works amassed by Elector Carl Theodor at Mannheim Palace, where students of the Academy were encouraged to cultivate "good taste" by studying and imitating fine specimens of art. Catalogued by Johann Georg Dillis, the 80,000 items in the collection reached Munich towards the end of the 18th century. The history of the collection is closely associated with King Ludwig I and with the founding of the Prints and Drawings Department in the Alte Pinakothek in 1746. In the 1920s the collection (then called the Royal Collection of Graphic Art) was moved to the Neue Pinakothek.

The collection suffered heavily under the Nazis. Major works, both old and modern, were branded as degenerate and confiscated. Without bequests and donations such as those from Ludwig Gutbier, Sofie and Emanuel Fohn, Wothy and Theodor Werner, the Kruss Collection, the former Galerie Verein (PIN. Friends of the Pinakothek der Moderne) and the Erika und Karl Rössing-Stiftung, the Staatliche Graphische Sammlung would certainly not be the one we marvel at today.

Modelling the male body

El Greco (Domenikos Theotocopoulos; 1541–1613)
Study of Michelangelo's *Giorno*
c. 1570
Black pencil, with white highlights, on blue paper edged by Vasari with pen and brush in brown ink and given a blue wash, 59.8 × 24.5 cm
Inv. no. 13756 Z

El Greco's Munich drawing is unique in a number of ways. It is the only surviving drawing from his Italian period. As far as provenance is concerned the drawing can, despite the erroneous conclusions drawn by some scholars, definitely be attributed to him. No less an authority than art historian Giorgio Vasari inscribed it and included it in his own collection. The size of the drawing suggests that El Greco may have executed it *c.* 1570 directly in front of Michelangelo's sculpture (in San Lorenzo). In 1567 he travelled to Venice, and three years later to Rome. A spell in Florence is therefore quite likely. El Greco's version would seem to illuminate Michelangelo's *Day* from the inside out. The massive body glows not least owing to the subtle highlighting of the light and shaded areas.

Giorgio de Chirico (1888–1978)
Il Condottiere 1917
Pencil, 31.7 × 21.7 cm
Inv. no. 1966:100, private collection

De Chirico titled his drawing *Il Condottiere*—the commander. Actually armoured, mathematically combined, screwed and carpentered together from wooden triangles and calculating devices, this jointed puppet or *manicino* stands for de Chirico's concept of a robot. The 'metaphysical' model resembles a prop from and for his menacingly depopulated Italian piazzas. The head and posture of this study for a tailor's dummy is unmistakably reminiscent of the faceless hero in the oil painting *Hector and Andromache*. Because of the absurd, surreal combination of mechanical coolness and weird objectivity in the bizarre machine bodies, de Chirico's machine men are frequently taken to be mocking 'technical functionalism'. Basically we perceive them via the medium of dream, as 'products of an all-consuming rationalism' (Patrick Waldberg).

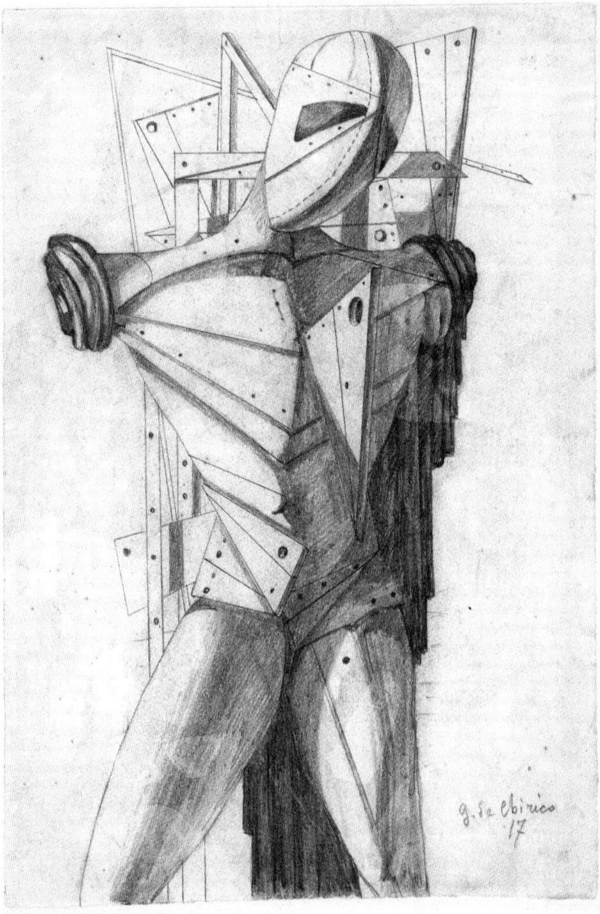

Salvador Dalí (1904–1989)
Gradiva 1932
Pen on smoothed glasspaper
63 × 45.5 cm
Inv. no. 1975:26 Z

This pen drawing shows all too extravagantly how picture, text and life can blend to evoke different views. Dalí's *Gradiva* has a biographical background. It is a reflection of Dalí's reading of Freudian psychoanalysis and the literature cited by him. The naked woman with her back to us holds a skull in her right hand and appears to be talking to it and breathing on it tenderly. In the background is a rocky landscape. Gala Eluard had indeed breathed new vitality into the eccentric Catalan in 1929 and helped him out of massive bouts of depression. However, *Gradiva*, or 'the forward-stepping woman', depicts not only Dalí's wife as a multiply varied, surrealist, hallucinatory figure of myth. Freud had used the story of *Gradiva* by Vilhelm Jensen as the subject of an analytical essay about delusions, and Dalí was familiar with this.

Psychological dimensions

Georg Baselitz (1938)
Girl from Olmo 1982
Black Indian ink and oil on paper
86 × 61 cm
Inv. no. WAF PF 42 Z, on loan from the Wittelsbacher Ausgleichfond, Collection of Prince Franz von Bayern

Baselitz's ink drawing is in contrast devoid of any interpretative approach or biographical background. His cycling *Girl from Olmo* is upside down. She is deliberately a 'symbol' of a picture that is just a picture. The content is only a framework to give the viewer some kind of formal orientation. The sketchy 'scene' can thus be seen as an illustration of a general, free painting process involving elements of equal status. Nothing is really denoted, explained or interpreted here. It is just a painting gesture that goes beyond the traditional rules of painting. The drawing is 'black and white painting' daubed with colour that is no longer painting—a jumble of visual habit, compositional considerations and an emphasis on 'pure painting'.

Expressive gestures in portraiture

Matthias Grünewald
(*c.* 1470/80–1528)
Half-length Figure of a Praying Woman (verso) *c.* 1515
Black chalk, 39 × 29.9 cm
Inv. no. 1983:85 Z

Grünewald's origins remain a mystery. When he was born and where he settled are not known for certain. His real name is also not established conclusively. However, there is no doubt that the great German Renaissance painter meticulously prepared all his compositions with sketches. His half-length figure of a burgher's wife can be associated with his masterpiece, the famous Isenheim altarpiece, on account of its subject, a devoutly praying woman or a woman suffering vicariously through Christ's pain. This highly expressive chalk drawing of an internal state has two particularly notable features—the hands redolent of emotion and the face that clearly betrays the feelings of an elderly, maternal burgher's wife in her simple, quiet contemplation.

Expressive gestures in portraiture

Ernst Ludwig Kirchner (1880–1938)
Head of a Woman *c.* 1913
Pencil, 40 × 26.8 cm
Inv. no. 1978:2 recto Z

In the period when this drawing was completed, Kirchner made repeated visits to the Baltic Sea island of Fehmarn, the Brücke group having fallen apart by then. While he was there, Kirchner carved figures from beached oak jetsam. Even though the influence of sculptural work can often be detected in the drawings and paintings he did, other characteristics should be noted here. The anatomy of the woman's face is severely articulated and elongated, almost like a preliminary study for his elongated Berlin cocottes. The heaviness of line in the hair, cheeks and neck cannot be overlooked. The rendering of the large, grave eyes and distinctive, narrow nose identify her as his partner, Erna Schilling. An interesting aspect is the artist's use of cursory gestures. Commenting in his diary (though much later, in 1925), Kirchner wrote: 'How stupidly and superficially people judge; they don't see that the cursory parts of my drawings are the most important because that is where I capture the first fine feelings.'

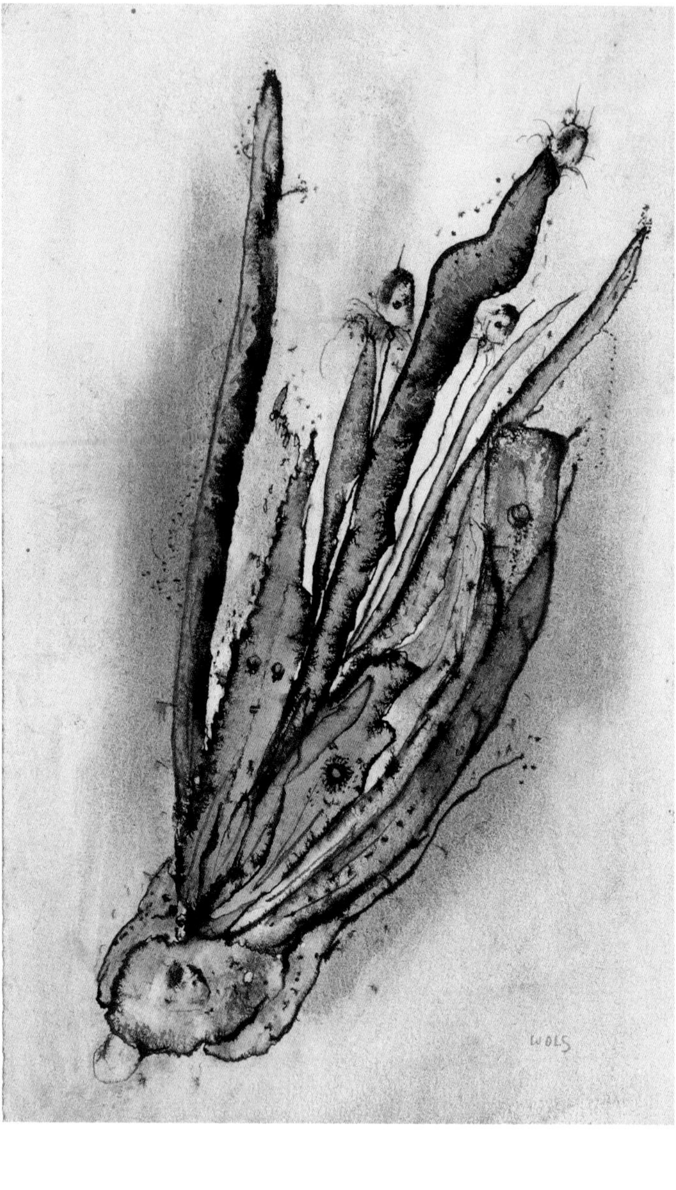

Capacity for abstraction

Wols (Alfred Otto Wolfgang Schulze; 1913–1951)
Untitled 1942/45
Mixed media, Indian ink, watercolour
22.2 × 13.8 cm
Inv. no. WAF PF 167 Z,
on loan from the Wittelsbacher Ausgleichfond, Collection of Prince Franz von Bayern

This drawing in ink and watercolour provides food for thought. You can identify an animal-like head, or an insect, or a piece of old bark with excrescences—and still you have not exhausted the possibilities. Every time you look at it, you discover something new in the plant-like, jellyfish-like thing, perhaps a slipper animalcule, leaves, thread, tentacles or bark. Even if the concepts are mutually exclusive,

Wols's subject is abstract and biomorphous at the same time, the shape and concretisation of a hallucinatory form. An in-between state, both in substance and appearance. Even the ink outlining and defining the figure runs and vanishes into the watercolour. Conceived in a free, formal language, Wols's picture illustrates an extract from the life of a multi-talented genius who suffered both psychologically and physically. It is a lyrical, abstract 'drawing' by someone still stigmatised by the Second World War, subsequent internment and alcoholic excess, who would die while still only 37.

Capacity for abstraction

Henri Matisse (1869–1954)
Reclining Female Nude *c.* 1928
Charcoal and brown pencil, smudge marks, on yellowish Ingres d'Arches
48 × 62.7 cm
Inv. no. 2000:3 Z

The exciting thing about this nude, the exact date of which is not known, is the singular drawing technique in which different areas engage the viewer's capacity for abstraction. Though the figure is sculpturally rounded, there are nonetheless various 'decorative' zones: the young woman is lying, for example, on a soft, florally patterned cushion like an odalisque or Venus. Yet there are strikingly different qualities of softness in the fabric, blurred facial expression, hair, skin and body. Though the reclining figure is clearly outlined, the hatching is subtle. The smudged areas accentuate tonal values, suggest and invite the viewer's eye to complete the picture—particularly around the eyes and feet. Scholars have identified in the figure parallels to studies for a sleeping bronze nude from the late 1920s.

Horse and rider

Peter Paul Rubens (1577–1640)
Equestrian Portrait of the Duke of Lerma 1603
Black chalk, pen and brush in brown ink, wash, white heightening
67.3 × 41 cm
Inv. no. 1983:84 Z

He was victorious, he had power and influence—and that was what he wanted shown. In 1603 the Duke of Lerma commissioned the Antwerp artist Peter Paul Rubens to undertake an equestrian portrait of him. This picture from 1603 is a study for the painting. The duke is shown high on horseback in the manner of a glorifying imperator image, in the tradition of the equestrian statue of the Roman emperor Marcus Aurelius. The horse is a plinth for the successful man of deeds (a battle rages in the bottom pictorial zone; the duke holds the commander's staff in his hand). He himself is surrounded by attributes. The duo of horse and ruler is depicted next to a laurel tree (symbol of fame), palm leaves (sign of victory), ivy tendrils (allusion to constancy) as if under an arbour.

Horse and rider

Hans von Marées (1837–1887)
Chariot Drawn by Two Horses (Biga)
c. 1880
Red chalk, smudge marks
38.2 × 41.6 cm
Inv. no. 1913:44 Z

In Marées's best-known red chalk drawing in the Graphische Sammlung, horse and man feature in quite a different relationship from Rubens's equestrian portrait. The picture is a vigorous rendering of a charioteer and his team meeting two standing figures. The vigour is asserted by the artist's emphasis of muscle and body volume of the charioteer, the reined-in horses and the (un)covered figure of the woman in back view, bottom right. The ingenious composition is based on a triangle: our eyes run from the head of the nearest horse via the hands and gaze of the charioteer towards the woman in the foreground, and her gaze and arm gesture guide them back to the horse and charioteer group. The picture brings together elements of Marées's early and late styles to form an impressive whole. Notable features are the quick, busy line work, the overlappings and foreshortening and the broad areas of hatching.

Kurt Schwitters (1887–1948)
Untitled '(Sheba)–to the Nero of Art' *c.* 1932
Collage, 14.7 × 11 cm
Inv. no. 1994:14

This typical Schwitters Merz picture bears witness to a wholly personal style, in which he assembles and overlays various scraps and bits of refuse into a collage. The various levels of the picture are also multiple evidence of an art underestimated even by his fellow artists and wholly incomprehensible to the average person, though accepted by the Berlin avant-garde. It is an articulated arrangement employing a formal idiom of its own, with spatial implications created by the overlapping pieces of paper. Schwitters dedicated it to Franz Roh, the 'Nero' who helped it into the limelight by branding it 'degenerate'. This defiant dedication renders the work especially meaningful in the context of the Pinakothek der Moderne and brings out unintentionally the significant 'multi-layeredness' of the work—'because this [the Museum] would never have been built without the defence of contemporary art' (Hanne Weskott).

Personal styles

Brice Marden (1938)
From Untitled Workbook 1986
Brown ink, 50 × 75 cm
Inv. no. GV 676 Z, on loan from PIN.
Friends of the Pinakothek der Moderne

Brice Marden is one of those artists, those mystics, who are constantly putting themselves to the test. Over the years he has continued to subject his work to the process of searching, improving, destroying, reshaping. This drawing from his *Untitled Workbook* is characteristic of this process in three ways: it is, unusually, quite large; it is significant for a calligraphic art that defines and implements the term 'energy' as energy line; and it marks only a modification—that of a meditative painting approach in the form of a transparent linear style—within a richly varied spectrum of expression and self-discovery. Marden's delicate 'calligraphy picture' rhythmicised with shrub-like organisms declares script and picture to be literally individual, transformable sign power. Willem de Kooning is supposed to have said once: 'You have the form of expression you want, then you lose it and then finally get it back again. You have to change to stay the same.' These words can also be applied to Brice Marden's work.

Architecture: Architekturmuseum der Technischen Universität München

Carl von Fischer (1782–1820)
Design for an opera house in Vienna, cross-section 1803
Pen and watercolour, 62 × 97 cm
Inv. no. 1976/3.4

The 270 drawings of Carl von Fischer's estate are a distinguished visiting card for the Architekturmuseum. This pen and watercolour drawing is not simply a page from a six-part set of drawings for a theatre. The drawing itself, which Fischer did as a student, constitutes a high point in the history of architectural drawings. The cross-section emphasises—like an optical illusion—the impression of space, offering a glimpse inside an apparently real model. The effect is the result of the finely graded rendering of light and shade in the Neoclassical interior of the opera house, evidence of the artist's mastery of watercolours. Various architectural features, such as the design of the roof truss, can be made out as easily as the different materials used and decorative details, such as the frieze and the capitals.

FRANCISCUS II ROM: IMP:

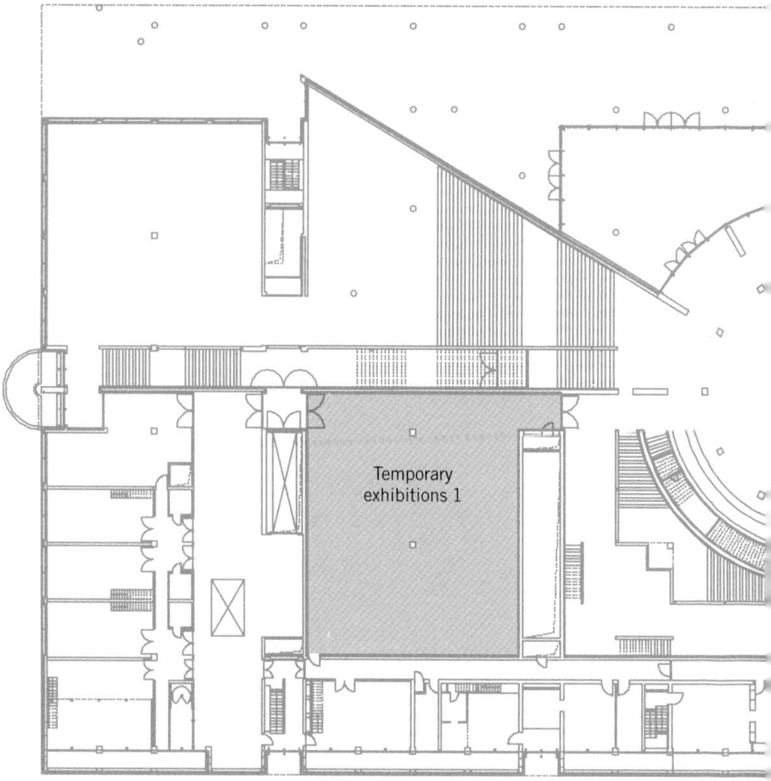

Like the works on paper in the Graphische Sammlung, the drawings in the Architekturmuseum may be exposed to the light for only a few months at a time, requiring that the Museum's treasures be exhibited in rotation. Winfried Nerdinger, director of the Museum, chose not to put highlights on display for the opening: '… that would have been just something additive. We should prefer to develop a central theme based on design and space in 20th-century architecture.'

Bearing this in mind, our catalogue offers a considered selection. Works are presented that the Museum will be focusing on in future. Reasonably enough, the Architekturmuseum opens its department in the Pinakothek der Moderne with exhibits depicting a Munich building that was itself conceived as an exhibition venue, namely August von Voit's Glass Palace of 1854.

Nerdinger refers to the works of Carl von Fischer as the core and genesis of the Architekturmuseum. Not only was he the first Bavarian university reader in architecture; in 1868 his drawings were transferred in toto, on the orders of King Ludwig II, from the Akademie der Bildenden Künste (Academy of Fine Arts) to the 'Neue Polytechnische Schule' (New Polytechnical School), as the Technische Universität München was then known.

The designation Architekturmuseum was given to the collection in 1989. By then it had greatly benefited from an accumulation of drawings, models

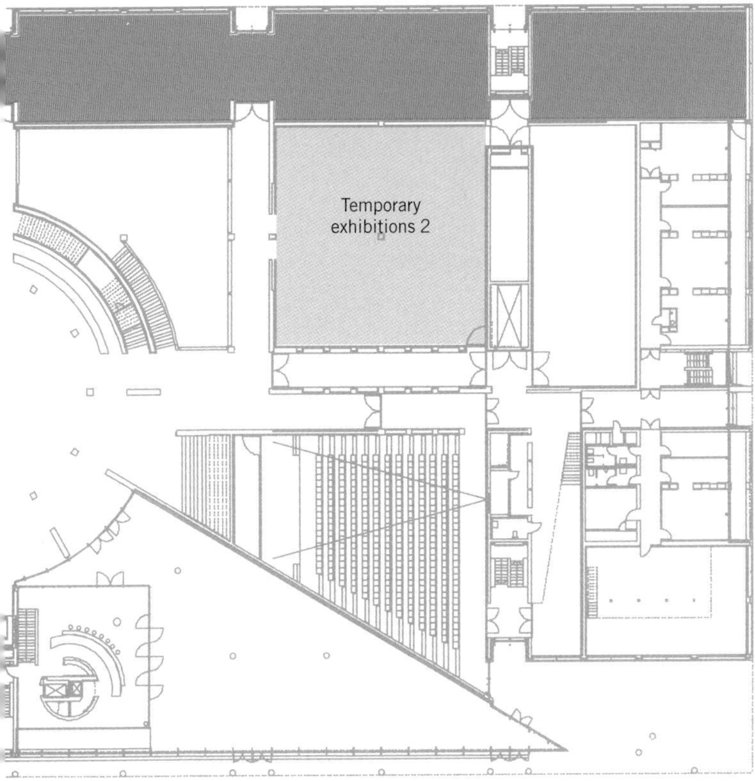

and plaster casts, in addition to works from the private royal collections, which were intended for students to imitate and learn from. Numerous gifts, purchases and archives have also augmented the collection.

After the First World War, 'design, function and construction technology' dominated architectural studies. The historical items vanished from the public eye, and after the Second World War were finally consigned to storage. Collecting continued over the years. Thanks to collaboration with Munich's Stadtmuseum (Municipal Museum), in 1977 the architectural collection was at last allowed access to proper exhibition facilities, which it had lacked at the Technische Universität for want of suitable exhibition rooms and financing.

However, a truly satisfactory solution came only with the move into the purpose-built exhibition space at the Pinakothek der Moderne. The sizeable 'showcase' for the special collection of some 350,000 drawings, 100,000 photographs and 500 models also has a transitional role. Its 424 m^2 of exhibition space on the ground floor of the Pinakothek der Moderne forms a bridge between the various art genres in the building. This means visitors get an overview of concepts of urban living ranging from building plans and models to interior furnishings (design objects in the Neue Sammlung).

Hans Heiss
Centring Model of a Reticulated Gothic Vault 1659
Wood, 46 × 59 × 16.5 cm
Inv. no. 1996/M 350

The wooden masterpiece of a Gothic reticulated vault by Hans Heiss was, along with drawings, part of his examination to qualify as a Nuremberg master stonemason. Such models were not scale models such as we know them today. They were intended to reproduce the statics of the rib system created by the ground plan and vaulting. The point was to get across the construction and lines of force of the design. Thus the model shows not only the rising arches—the ground plan is also incised on the base. Such handcrafted works, of which Hans Heiss's centring model is one of the oldest surviving examples, remained an integral part of an architect's training in southern Germany until well into the 18th century.

Johann Georg Dientzenhofer
(1665–1726)
Longitudinal Section and Half Ground Plan of the Abbey Church at Banz *c.* 1710
Pen and grey wash, 48.5 × 72.6 cm
Inv. no. 2253 C

Planning and construction work on the Benedictine church (from 1710) and abbey at Banz lasted over 80 years. Work began in 1698 under Johann Leonhard Dientzenhofer with the construction of the conventual building. The present drawing, dating from *c.* 1710, is by his brother, and belongs among the documents of the design and implementation period. It is an important example of Baroque architectural draughtsmanship. It acts as a source of information for builders and craftsmen. The pen and grey wash drawing shows a ground plan, an elevation and an orthogonal section, which was common practice at the time. The interior fittings and decorative details of the Benedictine church are not included in the drawing.

August von Voit (1801–1870)
Glass Palace, Munich 1854
Engraving by J. G. Poppel and G. M. Kurz, watercolour
24.4 × 34 cm
Inv. no. S 10/1/6.9.5

After the success of the first World Fair, the Great Exhibition in London in 1851, German industrialists decided they, too, needed a showcase, and by 1854 it was ready. Designed by August von Voit and the engineer Ludwig Werder, the iron and glass structure was modelled on London's Crystal Palace, with some adjustments having been made to it. The number of components was reduced and the statics of the design improved. The new building, which continued to accommodate exhibitions until it burnt down in 1931, was revolutionary for a number of reasons: its design—the thin, skeletal supports and load-bearing frame made of iron and steel revolutionised current notions of mass and structure; the speed with which it was erected was sensational; its appearance—the

combination of a frame structure and transparent façade—meant the design of the Glass Palace could be grasped from the exterior. Inside, the building with its basilican 'transept' and 234-metre-long 'nave' was highly impressive, a breathtaking arena of light and space.

Gottfried Semper (1803–1879)
Design for a Wagner Festival Theatre in Munich 1866
Pen and grey wash, 65.5 × 99.5 cm
Inv. no. 1970/127

If King Ludwig II had had his way, Semper would have built a festival theatre for Richard Wagner on the banks of the Isar in Munich, with a grand façade facing the river. In its design the project represented a high point in the history of 19th-century theatre building. The plain drawing from a set of 58 shows that Semper, though undoubtedly one of the greatest German architects of his day, was not as gifted as an architectural draughtsman. Placing great emphasis on objectivity, he did without coloured washes, thereby reducing his designs to monochrome drawings in earthy colours. Thus the massively monumental stone-built structure comes across as a thin wraith of a line drawing. In the end the festival theatre project for which the fervent Wagnerian Ludwig II yearned failed to come off in Munich.

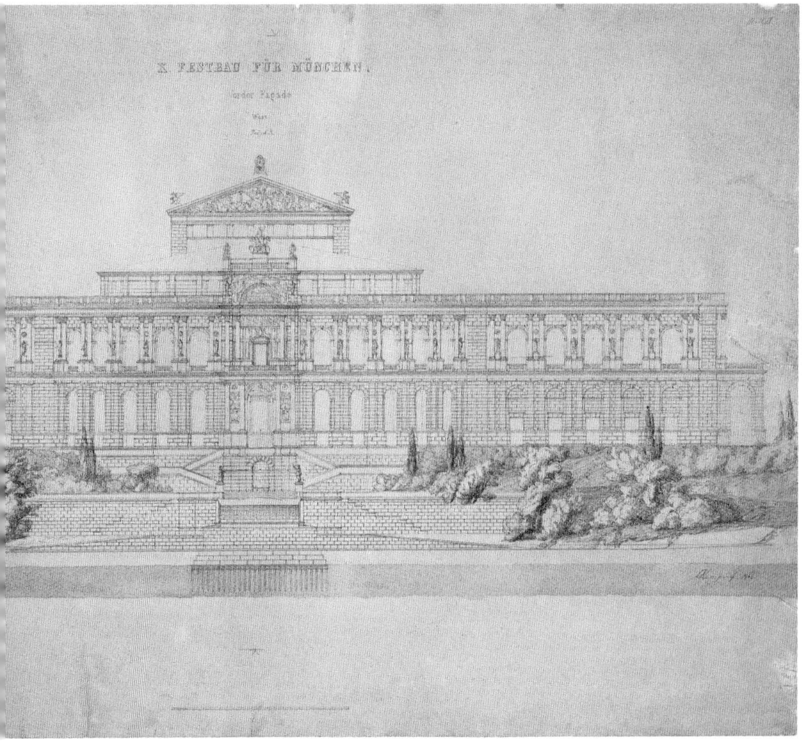

Bruno Taut (1880–1938) and
Franz Hoffmann (1884–1951)
Taut & Hoffmann
Monument of Iron at the International Building Trades Exhibition, Leipzig, 1913 *c.* 1912/13
Nickel-plated steel, lead, nickel-plated copper, iron, 1:275 scale model
11.7 × 12 × 10.9 cm
Inv. no. 2000/M 333

The model is small, a decorative object. Bruno Taut's real 'Monument of Iron' was 30 metres high—an exhibition pavilion for two German industrial associations, the steelmakers, and the bridge-builders and railway manufacturers. It was *the* attraction at the Leipzig Building Trades Exhibition in 1913. Shaped rather like an octagonal ziggurat, the full-height windows from floor to ceiling made the structure look rather like a cathedral. Crowning the four storeys soaring dynamically skywards on steel girders was a golden ball, which on the real building measured nine metres in diameter. The choice and technical application of a steel profile for a showpiece building was significant. Taut's intention was to demonstrate the qualities of iron both internally and externally, which was reiterated by a kinematographic display in the upper central area. The building created a great impression in its dramatic appearance and simplicity of detail, thus promoting a new modern architecture.

Erich Mendelsohn (1887–1953) and
Hans Schwippert (1899–1973)
Krasnoye Snamya Knitwear and Hosiery Factory, Leningrad
(present-day St Petersburg) 1925
Black pastel on transparent paper, mounted on card
28.8 × 42.3 cm
Inv. no. D 70/1/4.0

The buildings of the Krasnoye Snamya (Red Flag) knitwear and hosiery factory resemble a sheltering harbour for anchored vessels. Mendelsohn's L-shaped factory was one of the first modern industrial buildings in St Petersburg, with efficiency of production operations being the key consideration in the design. Despite these constraints Mendelsohn turned out an exciting, dynamic design that further boosted his reputation as an internationally acknowledged architect and outstanding representative of International Modernism. The dynamism of his formal structural idiom derives from contrasting, strictly horizontally and vertically articulated cuboid blocks with the soaring towers of the dyeing and bleaching building—chimneys whose suction effect provided natural ventilation—and the rounded parts of the exposed power station structure. Construction of the vigorous but light-filled design was effected in reinforced concrete, which he used as a design feature along with brick walls.

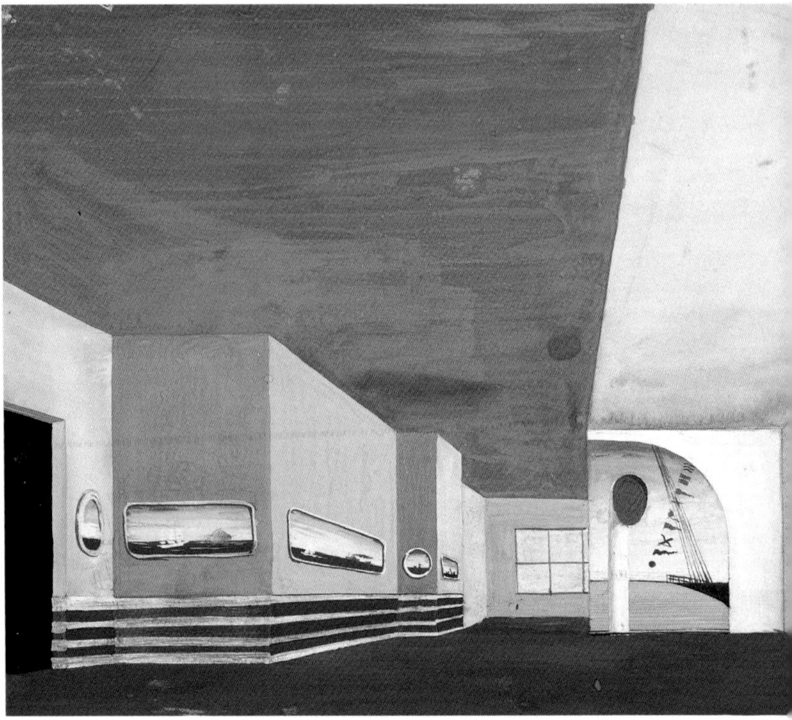

Erik Gunnar Asplund (1885–1940)
Pavilion for the Stockholm Exhibition, 1930 *c.* 1929/30
Pen and gouache, 24.5 × 42.7 cm
Inv. no. 2001/10/6

Swedish architect Erik Asplund is considered one of the most important representatives of Scandinavian functionalism. His exhibition buildings deliberately employed the effect of glass and steel, devoid of any stone monumentality or palatial grandeur. The Stockholm Exhibition designed by Asplund and Gregor Paulsson (1930) presented an exhibition space appropriate to its public and function. The summer halls, kiosks and brightly coloured rows of marquees along a riverside promenade reflected a cheerful, open quality. The drawing conveys the design concept of a modern open-air market with halls and pavilions built of lightweight steel structures and large glass surfaces. Many 'steamship' motifs figure, as representatives of International Modernism particularly liked them as an expression of the technical era. The centrepiece of the exhibition was an 80-metre-long 'advertising mast bearing inscriptions, with an adjacent press pavilion'.

Hans Schwippert (1899–1973)
Design for the Assembly Chamber of the Federal Parliament in Bonn 1948
Tracing of a pen drawing, green, blue and yellow pencil, collaged with orange paper 29 × 21 cm
Inv. no. D70/5/8.5

'I wanted a public building, an architecture for people to meet and talk in. My wish was that the country

should see Parliament at work.' This was Schwippert's comment on his commission to extend and convert the Pädagogische Akademie into a parliament building in 1948. In his assembly chamber, the architect opted for a circular arrangement of seating for MPs, to reflect architecturally the fledgling democratic Federal Republic. Unfortunately, the first federal chancellor, Konrad Adenauer, disliked Schwippert's design. He was also against the full-height glass wall opening on to the Rhine embankment, on the grounds that the light would be 'disagreeable and disruptive'. It was only 40 years later that the notion of a circular chamber for Parliament was revisited by Günter Behnisch in his design for the new assembly chamber.

Günter Behnisch (1922) and Frei Otto (1925)
Behnisch & Partner, Fritz Auer, Winfried Büxel, Carlo Weber, Erhard Tränkner and Jürgen Joedicke, Günther Grzimek, Frei Otto, Fritz Leonhardt, Leonhardt and Andrä, Heinz Isler
Olympiapark, Munich, Original Copy of the Original Competition Model
1967
Paperboard, wood, nylon stretch hose, needles, 1:1000 scale model
85 × 90 × 9 cm
On permanent loan from a private collection

The Architekturmuseum keeps a possessive eye on the celebrated 'Stocking Model' made by Stuttgart architects Behnisch & Partner. The idea of a lightweight, tent-roof design spanning a sports landscape in this competition model for Munich's Olympiapark caused a stir. It was an outstanding solution to the themes of the competition—Olympics in a verdant setting, cheerful and cosmopolitan. To demonstrate the transparent roof design, a nylon stocking was used, whose fine, elastic mesh drawn over supports and tautened by needles automatically adopted the desired suspension effect of the roof. Of course it was a long road from a stocking to a 34,500-m^2-roof surface covered with acrylic glass surfaces on 12 anchored steel pylons. Nonetheless, the design was realised, the Olympic sports venues were 'carved' into the landscape and covered with an open, transparent roof. It was an architectural symbol of the new, democratic, cosmopolitan Germany.

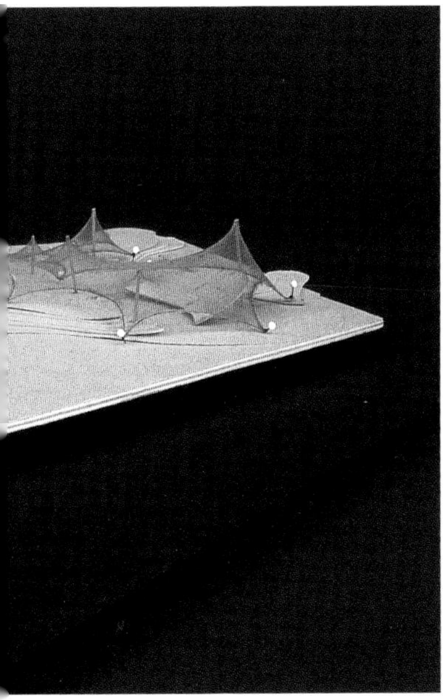

It looks light, straightforward, transparent. This house in Beverly Hills by architect Helmut C. Schulitz is a complex example, in aesthetic, architectural and technical terms, of what can be accomplished with industrially pre-fabricated (steel) components in domestic architecture. The aim of the project was to develop an open system for low, compact domestic buildings using existing, mass-produced girders and façade/extension components. This house acted as an experimental building for the TEST project. The site was difficult, given the steep slope and small volume of the home. During implementation, it was shown that the steel frame could be erected within two days. Schulitz's house, staggered down the slope on three levels, demonstrates that even by using industrially pre-fabricated building components immense variety can be achieved, both in appearance and in use.

Helmut C. Schulitz (1936)
House in Beverly Hills 1976
Wood, paperboard, plastic, aluminium, paint, 1:100 scale model
38 × 53 × 38 cm
On permanent loan from a private collection

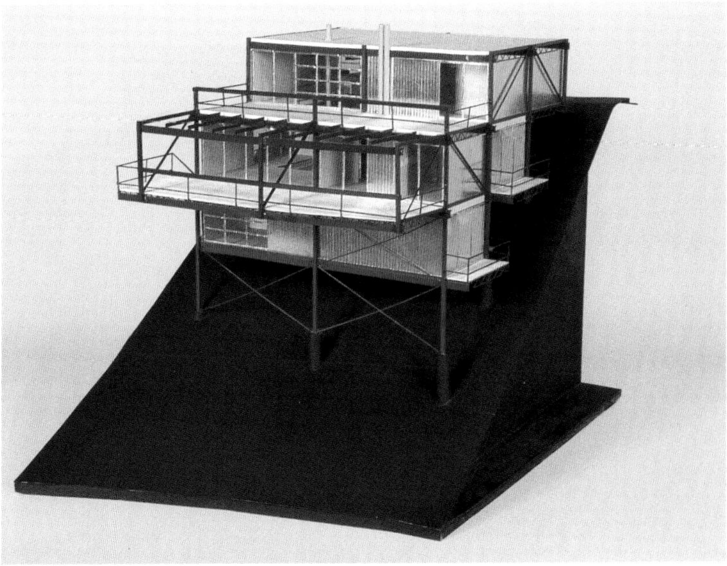

Thomas Herzog (1941) and
Hanns Jörg Schrade (1951) with
Roland Schneider (1956)
IEZ Natterer GmbH, Ing.-Büro
Bertsche, Ing.-Büro kgs Kessel
EXPO roof–Symbolic structure for the World Fair in Hanover, 2000
1999/2000
Wood, 1:25 scale model
84 × 84 × 64 cm
On permanent loan from the architects

The actual structure is over 20 metres high. Ten wooden umbrellas, each measuring 40 × 40 metres along the side, are grouped together to form an architectural, sculptural effect of light, floating butterfly wings, arranged over a carpet of islands and water surfaces. Each umbrella consists of four concave surfaces, four projecting girders of a steel pyramid and a tower of tree trunks. A translucent membrane allows the giant wooden roof to withstand wind and weather. This was a symbolic structure for the 2000 EXPO in Hanover. It was the largest wooden roof world-wide, whose utterly novel design did elegant and imposing justice to the motto 'Man—Nature—Technology'. Herzog's impressive wooden structure is an aesthetic demonstration of how versatile solid wood can be as a construction material and how it can be shaped. Notable was the use of wooden stacked boards on such a grand scale—on the main diagonal, the roof is at least 28 metres long—and the fact that all components of the roof are 100 per cent recyclable.

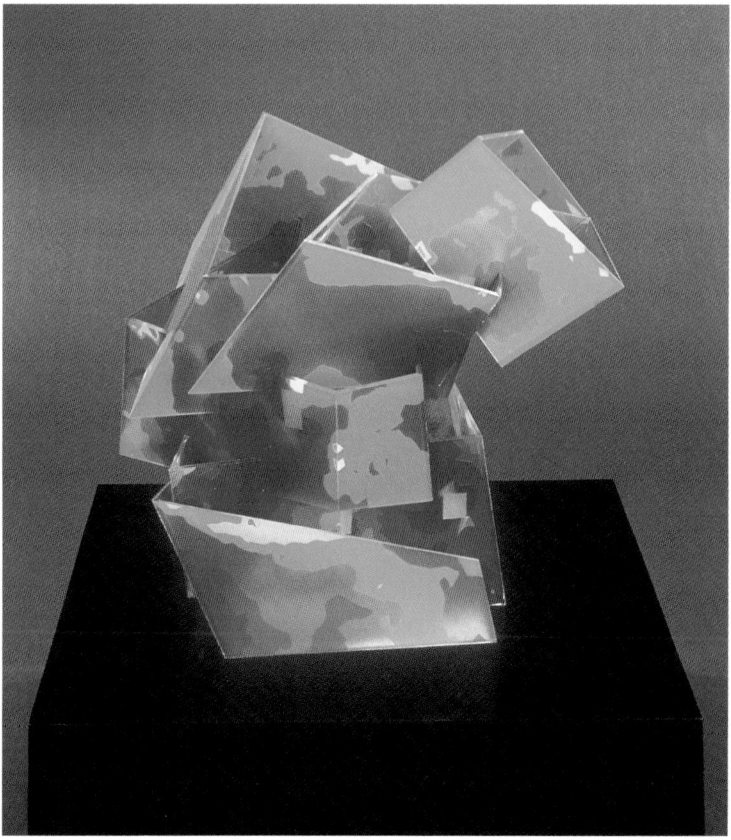

Cecil Balmond (1943)
Ove Arup & Partners and
Daniel Libeskind (1946)
The Spiral–Extension of the Victoria & Albert Museum in London 2002
Plastic, coloured lighting
1:150 scale model
45 × 33.5 × 54.5 cm
Inv. no. 2002/M 617

This extension of London's Victoria & Albert Museum, currently planned to be erected in a courtyard of the historic building of the Museum, is an absolute novelty in architectural history. The sensational aspects of this unique addition, presented here as a model, are its load-bearing, windowless construction and the covering of the interlocking, box-like structure. The design is a composition of self-supporting, projecting walls, with no further supports, over 50 metres high. The impressive dynamics of the design are attributable to it being not a classic logarithm but a 'chaotic' spiral. This produces displacements within individual floors—and yet the optimal load-distribution characteristics mean the interior is completely free of supports. The complexity of the inner structure is taken into account in the design of the façade. The patterning of the tiles is based on a mathematical principle that generates ever-new patterns. The link between this futuristic architecture and the adjacent historic building is highlighted in the choice of terracotta tiles for the mosaic on the façade.

Design: Die Neue Sammlung, Staatliches Museum für angewandte Kunst

Adolphe Jean-Marie Mouron Cassandre (1901–1968)
Poster for *L'Atlantique* liner 1931
Colour lithograph
99.5 × 61.5 cm
Commissioned by Compagnie de Navigation Sud-Atlantique, printed by Alliance Graphique Loupot-Cassandre, Paris

The steaming tugboat looks tiny against the black and blue bows of an ocean-going vessel. The geometricised steel wall of the liner behind the little ship looms breathtakingly, threateningly. Cassandre's lithograph for a French shipping company is an amazing collector's item, an advertising poster for the machine age. The work of this distinguished 20th-century poster artist is rich in extraordinarily suggestive effects both aesthetically and compositionally, achieved by maximum simplification of the subject matter. The choice of a poster as a frontispiece for the Neue Sammlung was indeed deliberate. Even if there are no artist-designed posters in the Pinakothek der Moderne, this essential area of commercial design should not be overlooked. Posters were the means by which products were introduced and advertised to the public. For the visitor, posters also act as a link with other departments of the Pinakothek, especially the Graphische Sammlung.

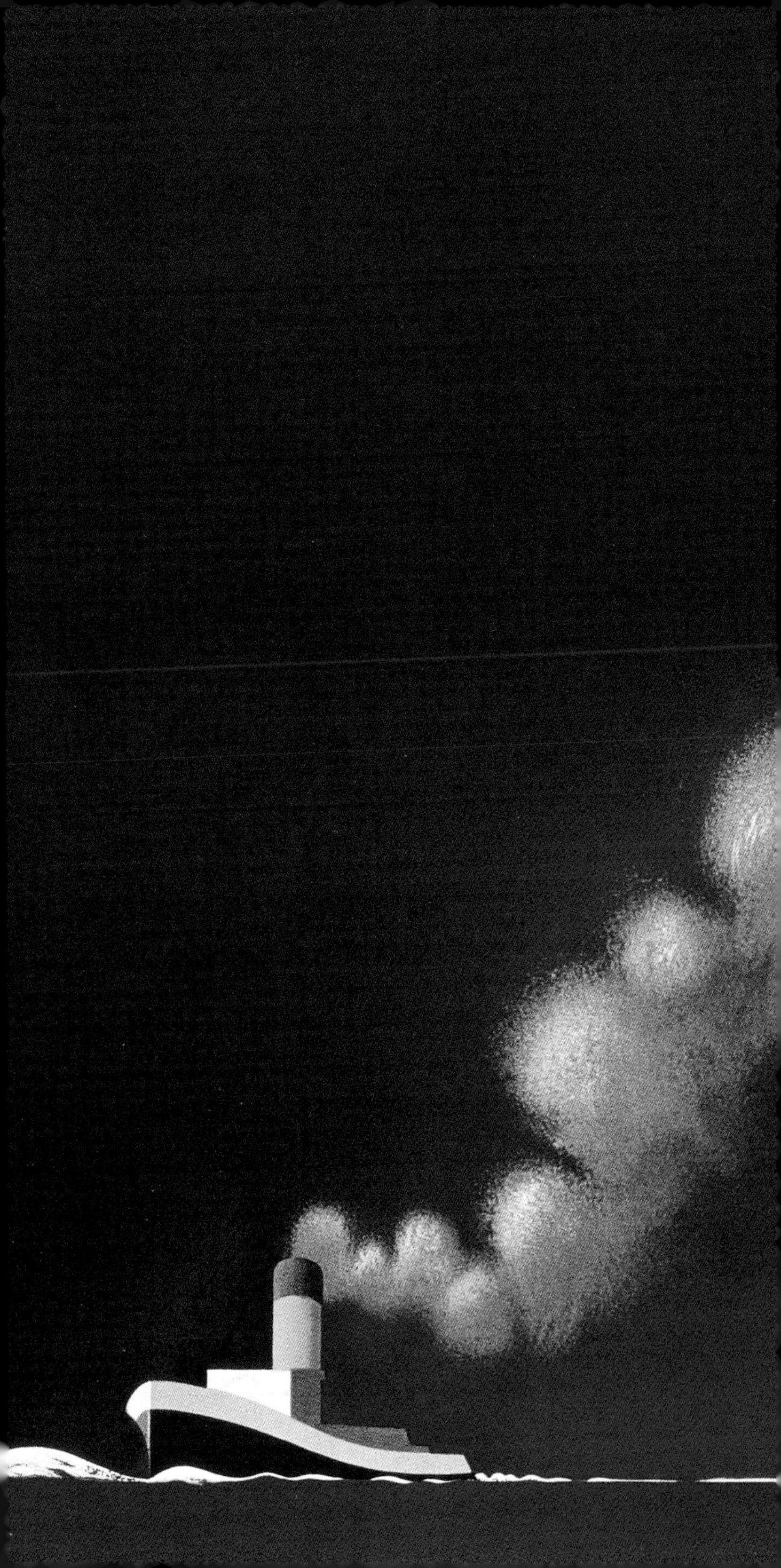

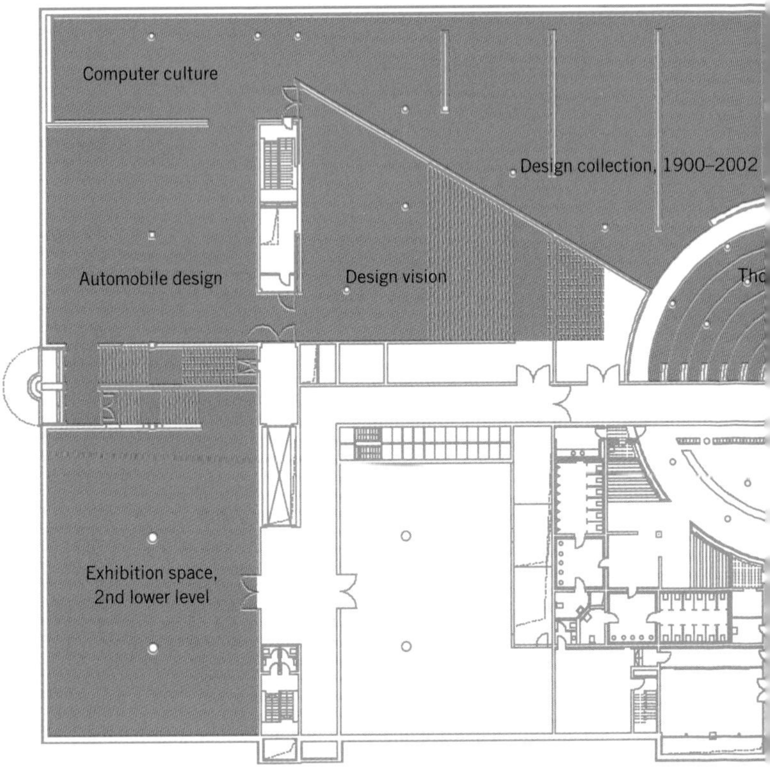

'The Deutsche Werkbund was established in 1907. We have been collecting ever since. That means that the entire 20th century, i.e. all early and important developments, is represented in Munich' (Florian Hufnagl, Acting Director of the Neue Sammlung). Until now, there has been no room for a permanent public display of the Neue Sammlung's holdings, examples of mass and industrially produced objects of everyday use, kept at the Staatliches Museum für angewandte Kunst. Initially 2,000 objects formed the basis of the collection. The number has now risen to 60,000 objects. 'Temporary accommodation' was therefore the watchword—at first in an annexe of the Bayerisches Nationalmuseum (Bavarian National Museum)—and remained a permanent fact of life throughout the collection's history, right from the official foundation in 1925. Plans for a new building came and went, whether because of enforced closure during the Nazi period, when the 'condemned objects' were sold off or dumped, or after 1945. Only with the building of the Pinakothek der Moderne (and the Neues Museum in Nuremberg) has a home finally been found for a permanent exhibition of one of the world's leading museums of modern design and applied art. The total display space available is 2,587 m^2. A particularly attractive feature—wholly in keeping with the design theme—is the design of the display itself. At the end of the staircase leading down to the splendours of the Neue Sammlung is an imposing jig. The impressive eye-catcher acts as a 'contents page with attitude' for visitors, showing what design art, past and present, is on

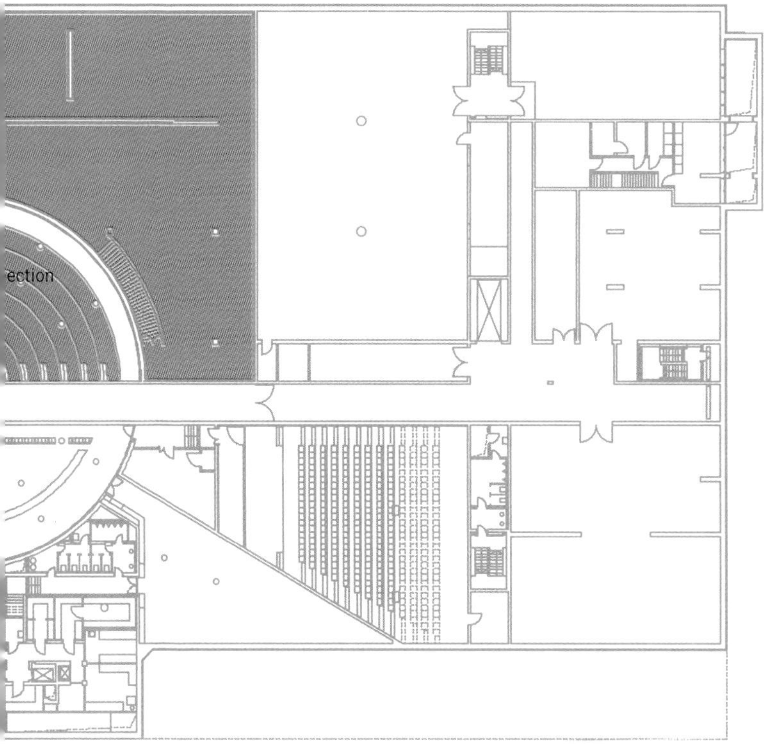

view. Examples here include Toshiyuki Kita's TV with a flat LCD screen, or a 1960s Pop couch in the shape of a kissing mouth. Down below, the accent is on streamlining and aerodynamics—cars and motorcycles as a special area. A computer culture room demonstrates how rapidly the digital revolution and the demand for user-friendliness has changed computer design to ever slenderer laptops and screens. Three special room features should definitely be noted: the long glass showcase exhibiting the ins and outs of design history in a timeline; the Thonet Room, where at least 50 types of chair adorn the tiers of the amphitheatre in various arrangements; and two showcases at the end of the tour, which rotate on the principle of a Ferris wheel and present design objects ranging from the brightly coloured vase stand to competition shoes for speed-skating and Shimano System bicycles. The Neue Sammlung bears impressive testimony to Florian Hufnagl's primary concern: 'It's the vision that matters to me, because design is not just a product but an idea as well.' This idea is one of two things our selection of representative objects here aims to convey. The other idea is that design thrives on contrast.

Chair reform: Prototypes of modern, mass-produced furniture and outré decoration

Michael Thonet (1796–1862)
Chair no. 14 1859
Beech, bent solid, stained brown
89 × 42.5 × 53 cm
Made by Gebr. Thonet, Vienna
Inv. no. 476/96

Thonet's chair model no. 14 is the 'chair of chairs'. Popularly associated with Viennese coffee houses, it is a utilitarian chair. It was developed in 1859 and until 1930 remained the best-selling piece of furniture in the world, with total sales of around 50 million. The novelty of this mass-produced chair was its bentwood technique, which enabled solid wood to be bent into shape under pressure at a steam temperature above boiling point. An additional novelty was the marketing strategy. Good value, made partly by hand and partly industrially, the model could be ordered as a kit of parts (6 wooden parts, 10 screws, two nuts). Unlike the normal heavy German furniture of the late Victorian period, this meant it could be supplied in large quantities all over the world, as individual parts could be stacked and assembled without difficulty. At least 36 disassembled kits could fit into a crate measuring 1 m^2.

Chair reform: Prototypes of modern, mass-produced furniture and outré decoration

Alessandro Mendini (1931)
Poltrona di Proust armchair, from the Bau.Haus I collection 1978
Wood, paint, upholstery material
107 × 105 × 90 cm
Made by Studio Alchimia, Milan
Inv. no. 208/2000

Another item in the Neue Sammlung's huge jig is Mendini's Poltrona di Proust. The 70-year-old Milanese architect, designer and founder of 'counter-design' is one thing for certain—an artist who falls between all available stools, as it were. The Poltrona is a prime example of his artistic philosophy: the material is covered with hand-painted decoration, which is in fact a close-up of dots from a *pointilliste* painting by Paul Signac, whom the French writer Marcel Proust greatly admired. Thus this 'redesign' associates the chair with Proust. In researching Signac, Mendini came across a neo-Baroque armchair, which accounts for the shape of the Poltrona. The Proust chair suggests two propositions: design takes place in the context of existing patterns, i.e. ideas. These can be conveyed only via external features, where they can be exaggerated and stylised to the point of absurdity.

Streamlining:
Cars and radios

Hans Ledwinka (1878–1967)
Tatra 87 1937 (built 1938)
Metal, lacquer
L. 474 cm, w. 167 cm, h. 150 cm
Made by Tatra Works, Koprivnice, Czechoslovakia
Inv. no. 585/93

The message of this avant-garde vehicle by the Czech firm Tatra was 'streamline'! As a style streamlining combined a hint of America with confidence in the future economy. From an aerodynamic point of view the ideal design of a moving object is the one with the least air resistance, mostly tear-shaped. The concept was given concrete form in the Tatra 87 by Austrian designer Hans Ledwinka. It then went into production with a completely systematic aerodynamic body. A particularly spectacular feature of the all-metal body with the short front bonnet was considered to be the elongated rear end with a fin. This high styling was impressive as an additional novelty and promoted sales. It was particularly notable in that the fin was an unbroken line. Inside, the rear window of the Tatra 87 separates the passengers from the engine compartment. Ventilation slits in the rear bonnet allowed the driver a rear view.

Streamlining:
Cars and radios

Walter Dorwin Teague (1883–1960)
Bluebird radio 1934
Glass panes vapour-plated blue, wood, varnished black
H. 38 cm, diam. 36 cm
Made by Sparton Corporation, Jackson, Michigan
Inv. no. 925/86

When you see this astonishing 1930s Teague radio, it comes as no surprise to learn that Walter Dorwin Teague, an outstanding American industrial designer and the principal exponent of streamlining, originally came from the advertising industry. Teague's first advertising commission came from Kodak. To set the product in its proper context, the Bluebird literally 'reflects' the following notion: at the receiving end we see a flight of three lines or streams of information flowing from the membrane of the remarkable circular core of the transmitter. In the interest of its geometrical good looks, Teague hid the technology in a little wooden box behind the blue-vaporised glass panes.

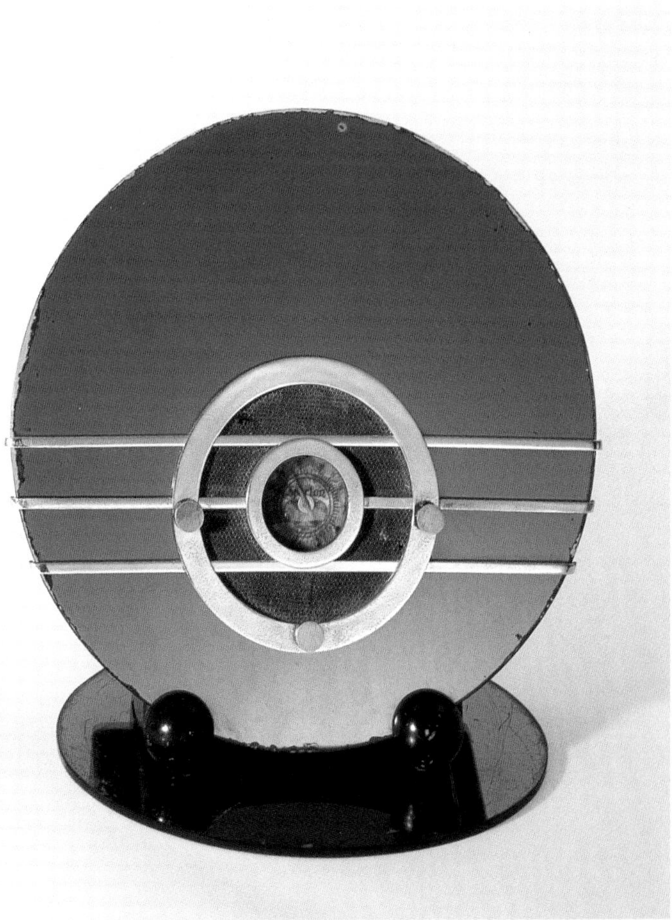

Germany and France:
Art that makes itself useful—Kitchen utensils

Peter Behrens (1868–1940)
Electric Kettles 1909
Brass, nickel and copper-plated brass
H. 19.5–21.5 cm, w. 18.5–22.5 cm, d. 14.5–17.5 cm
Made by AEG, Berlin
Inv. nos. 658/2000, 658/2001, 655/2001, 641/2000

The task was to take three different basic shapes (a depressed oval, an octagon and a cylinder shape), three different sizes (0,75 l, 1,25 l, 1,75 l l.) and three different metal surfaces and design a mass product in 80 different combinations while retaining the minimum number of formal features. This is what the influential designer Peter Behrens did in 1909. Behrens had sole responsibility for advertising, products and construction of a turbine factory of AEG. His electric kettles bear testimony to an unparalleled designer style that moved away from expensive handmade one-offs towards electrical appliances that were well-designed but still good value for ordinary people. Kettles were among the absolute innovations of industrial design in the early 20th century, like turbines and ventilators.

Germany and France:
Art that makes itself useful—Kitchen utensils

Robert Mallet-Stevens (1886–1945)
Tea and Coffee Service *c.* 1930
Silver, beaten and polished, partly gilt inside, macassar ebony
13.4 × 34.5 × 10.8 (including tray)
Commissioned by La Maison Desny, Paris
Inv. no. 53/91

The history of modernist de luxe Art Deco silverware is inconceivable without Robert Mallet-Stevens. In France an exquisite, individual furnishing style flourished, despite the First World War. The metropolis of Paris was the guarantee for both a long tradition of exquisite craftwork and soon competitiveness as well. Mallet-Stevens's tea and coffee service in the Neue Sammlung is a work commissioned by La Maison Desny, a company that produced limited-edition interior furnishings. The service is notable for its severe geometrical purism and a tendency towards abstraction, indicating the influence of the Dutch De Stijl movement.

Form follows function:
Office furnishings

Otto Wagner (1841–1918)
Writing Desk and Stool for Postal Savings Bank, Vienna *c.* 1904
Beech, stained dark brown, aluminium
Desk: 109 × 107 × 66 cm
Stool: 47 × 42 × 42 cm
Made by Gebr. Thonet, Vienna
Inv. nos. 133/95, 134/95

Architect Otto Wagner's Postsparkasse office in Vienna as a total design counts as one of the most significant works of early modernism in Austria. As coolly functional as the building, Wagner's furniture is distributed round the open hall, which is an iron girder structure with a glass roof. Its interior is designed in accordance with the principle that 'nothing that cannot be used is beautiful': function and design form a visible unity. With logical consistency aluminium cladding is used not only on the columns of the great building but also on the feet of the writing table. The stool is another example of bentwood furniture. Wagner commissioned some of the furniture from Thonet.

Form follows function:
Office furnishings

Giovanni Sacchi (1913)
Wooden Model of the Lexikon 80 Typewriter after a Design by Marcello Nizzoli, 1948
Yew wood, 18 × 36.8 × 34 cm
Made by Giovanni Sacchi, Milan
Inv. no. 201/2001

Models are particularly enlightening for understanding the design process, from prototype to the end product. They constitute a compact statement of the design, spatial implications and feasibility of the designer's idea. Giovanni Sacchi's wooden model for the Lexikon 80 typewriter was thus not a simple, apparently clumsy base frame but the first opportunity to take stock of the design before the real thing went into production. In an interview, Sacchi, who was working for the Italian graphic artist and industrial designer Nizzoli, said that if he were to collect all the prototypes he had made in preparation of the finished products, he could set up a museum. This sample item at the Pinakothek der Moderne at least provides some idea of what we're missing.

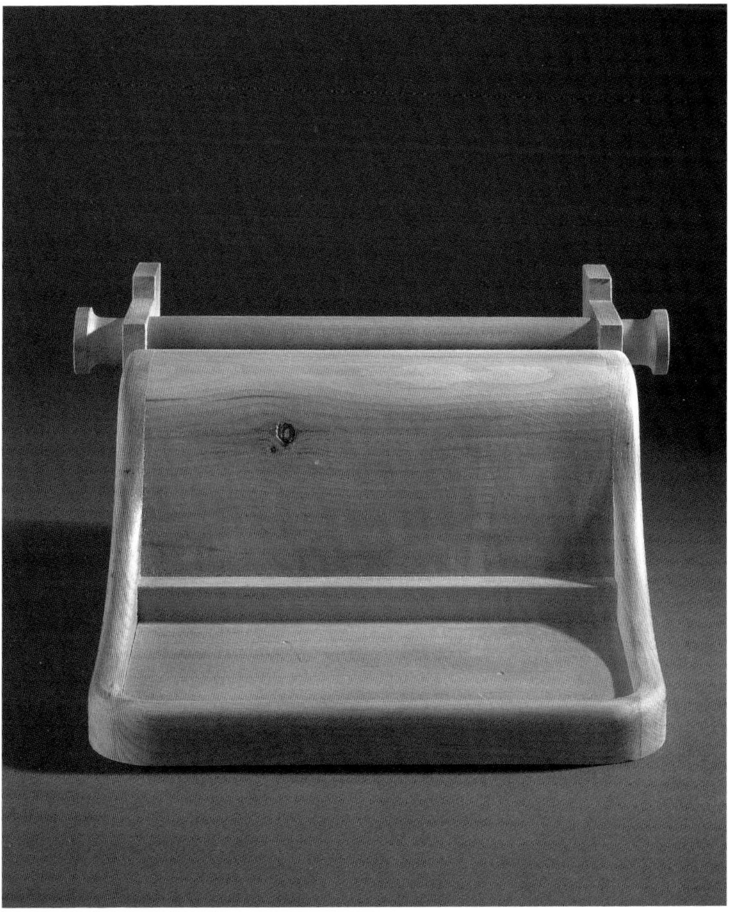

Designer styles in a Bauhaus context

Alma Buscher (1899–1944)
Ship Building Blocks 1923
Wood, paint, various block sizes
(e.g. hull, l. 25.5 cm)
Made by the Bauhaus, Weimar
Inv. no. 377/26

Teaching craftwork was demanded as part of the educational concept of the Bauhaus. 'Art is above method. It cannot be taught, whereas craftwork can' (Walter Gropius). The craft aspect is particularly evident in Alma Buscher's building blocks. It reflects both the technical considerations of the designer (production in the Weimar joinery shop) and children's needs as a kit of parts to make various objects. It contains a wooden hull, sails, rectangles, triangles, cubes and slender bases in simple, harmonious designs and gay colours. The aim is not to confront children with complicated mechanisms but to allow them to play creatively and without difficulty.

Marcel Breuer (1902–1981)
ti 113 Wardrobe 1926/27
Wood, white and red paint
175.5 × 185 × 69 cm
Made by the Bauhaus, Dessau
Inv. no. 16/78-1

It is simple, finished in coloured varnish and emphasises the frame and compact assembly of the cupboard units from functional blocks. Breuer's ti 113 ranks with the clear elegance of his modern interiors from the late 1920s. Made in the Dessau building period, the cupboard is representative of his entire oeuvre. Breuer's room furnishings were intended as plain, combinable units, forming useful surfaces. The unpretentious ti 113 was made for a contemporary but almost rigid lifestyle. The furniture was designed for art historian Ludwig Grothe, and was just part of a complete interior furnishing commission for him. Interestingly, according to Bauhaus brochures, the ti 113 was actually a ladies' cupboard, with a hat compartment, a flap door in the centre and right sections and rails for dresses of varying lengths.

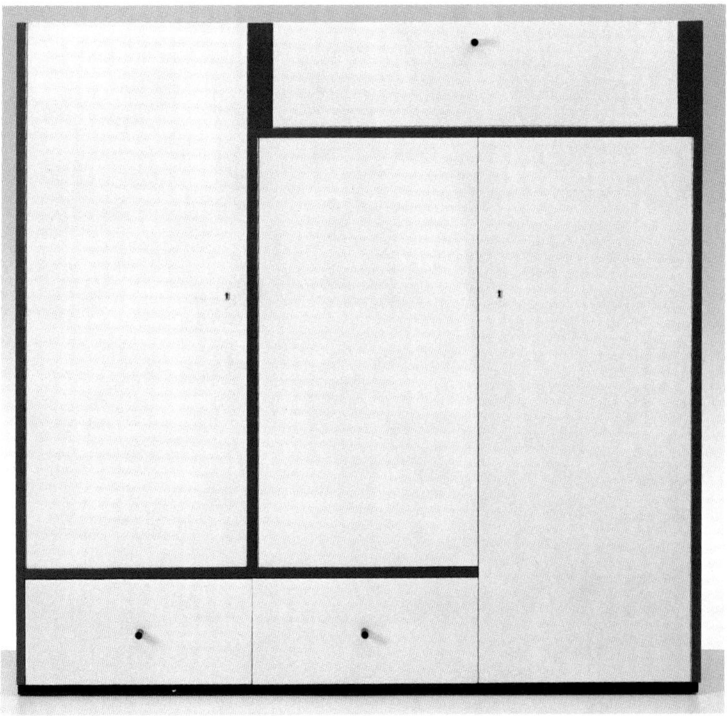

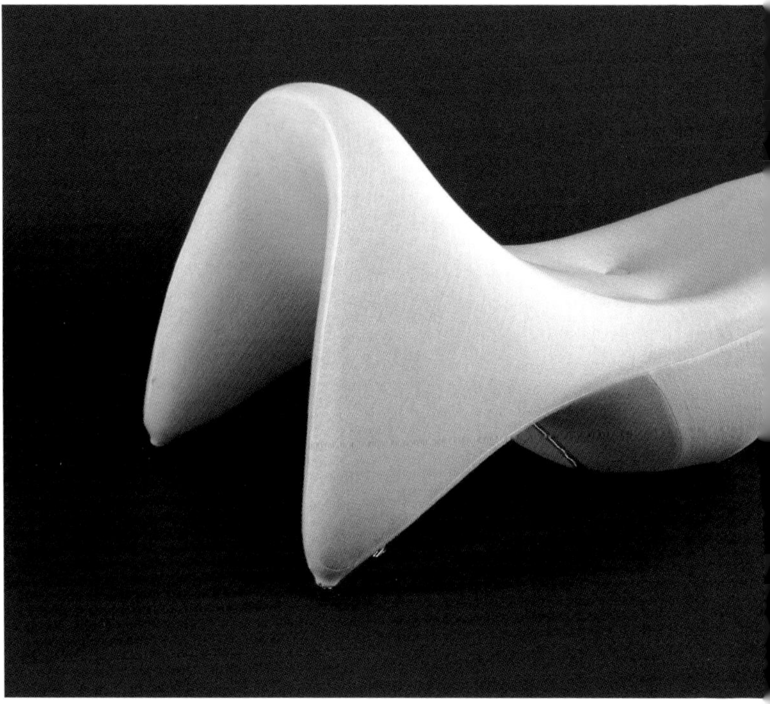

Hi-tech games: Chairs TVs

Luigi Colani (1928)
TV Relax Seat and Reclining Chair
1965
Foam (PU), stretch cover, white or red
H. 70 cm, w. 96 cm, l. 2,000 cm
Made by Kusch + Co., Hallenberg
Inv. no. 430/2001

Luigi Colani studied at the Berlin Academy of Art and aerodynamics at the Sorbonne in Paris. He notched up his first commercial success with shoes for Christian Dior while still a student. A multi-talented designer, he worked for firms such as Alpha Romeo, BMW, Sony, Seiko and Canon, designing a wide range of objects such as air and road vehicles, cameras and chairs with aerodynamically swept-back lines, resembling women crossing their legs. The TV Relax reclining chair from the 'Sea Collection' was produced only in small quantities. The verve and line of Colani's aerodynamic design in this modern chaise longue evoke an 'interior landscape'. The supporting parts vanish in and behind the sculptural form. The 1960s reclining chair heralds lightness and the functional aspect of relaxation.

Hi-tech games: Chairs and TVs

Toshiyuki Kita (1942)
Aquos LCD TV (LC-20 C2E model)
2000
Plastic (PC, ABS), silver coloured, grey
H. 55.6 cm, w. 47.7 cm, d. 22.9 cm
Made by Sharp Corporation, Osaka
Inv. no. 760/2001

When you admire the Japanese-Italian designer's TV set in the jig, your first impression is that it is a hi-tech computer monitor. Toshiyuki Kita's high-performance TV is conspicuously

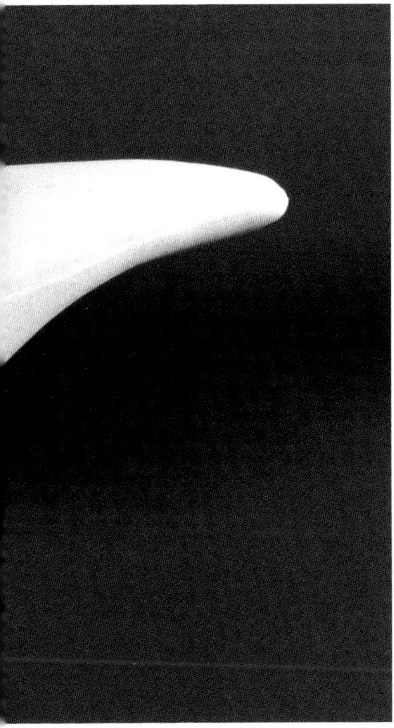

flat—you hardly notice the operating buttons on the plastic strip below. Both here and there, the weight of the screen is reduced while the appliance's capacity grows. The Aquos series, to which this TV belongs, features undulating, organically shaped surfaces. Kita's TV combines the decorative style of old Japanese ceramics with functional aspects. This is no heavy, unwieldy TV box demanding space. The outstanding feature of the design is its space-saving quality and its portability.

Bibliography

The following publications were consulted (among others) in the preparation of the present volume:

Art

Baumstark, Reinhold, Carla Schulz-Hoffmann, Michael Semff, Winfried Nerdinger and Florian Hufnagl (eds.). *Pinakothek der Moderne: Kunst, Grafik, Architektur, Design.* Munich and Cologne, 2002.

Francis Bacon. Exh. cat. Staatsgalerie, Stuttgart. London, 1985.

Franz, Erich (ed.). *Franz Marc: Kräfte der Natur—Werke 1912–1915.* Exh. cat. Staatsgalerie moderner Kunst, Munich. Ostfildern-Ruit, 1993.

Garnerus, Hartwig. *Die Sammlung Theo Wormland.* Exh. cat. Haus der Kunst, Munich. Munich, 1983.

Grisebach, Lucius. *Ernst Ludwig Kirchner: 1880–1938.* Exh. cat. Nationalgalerie, Berlin. Berlin, 1980.

Hofmann, Werner (ed.). *Konrad Klapheck: Retrospektive 1955–1985.* Exh. cat. Hamburg Kunsthalle, Hamburg. Munich, 1985.

Lauter, Rolf (ed.). *Jeff Wall: Figures & Places—Ausgewählte Werke von 1978 bis 2000.* Munich et al., 2001.

Leymarie, Jean. *Georges Braque.* Exh. cat. Kunsthalle der Hypo-Kulturstiftung, Munich. Munich, 1988.

Maur, Karin von. *Salvador Dalí 1904–1989.* Exh. cat. Staatsgalerie, Stuttgart. Stuttgart, 1989.

Pinakothek der Moderne: Eine Vision. Munich, 1995.

Rubin, William, Wieland Schmied and Jean Claire (eds.). *Giorgio de Chirico: Der Metaphysiker.* Exh. cat. Haus der Kunst, Munich. Munich, 1982.

Schmied, Wieland. *René Magritte.* Exh. cat. Kunsthalle der Hypo-Kulturstiftung, Munich. Munich, 1987.

Schulz-Hoffmann, Carla (ed.). *Pinakothek der Moderne: Malerei, Skulptur, Neue Medien.* Cologne, 2002.

Schulz-Hoffmann, Carla, and Doris Guth. *Georg Baselitz.* Staatsgalerie moderner Kunst, Munich. Ostfildern-Ruit, 1993.

Schulz-Hoffmann, Carla, and Peter-Klaus Schuster. *Deutsche Kunst seit 1960: Sammlung Prinz Franz von Bayern.* Exh. cat. Bayerische Staatsgemäldesammlungen and Staatsgalerie moderner Kunst, Munich. Munich, 1985.

Schulz-Hoffmann, Carla, and Judith C. Weiss (eds.). *Max Beckmann Retrospektive.* Exh. cat. Haus der Kunst, Munich. Munich, 1984.

Schuster, Peter-Klaus, Christoph Vitali and Barbara Butts (eds.). *Lovis Corinth.* Exh. cat. Haus der Kunst, Munich. Munich, 1996.

Spies, Werner (ed.). *Max Ernst: Retrospektive zum 100. Geburtstag.* Exh. cat. Tate Gallery, London. Munich, 1991.

Prints and Drawings

Baumstark, Reinhold, Carla Schulz-Hoffmann, Michael Semff, Winfried Nerdinger and Florian Hufnagl (eds.). *Pinakothek der Moderne: Kunst, Grafik, Architektur, Design.* Munich and Cologne, 2002.

Falk, Tilman (ed.). *Staatliche Graphische Sammlung München: Dialog über Jahrhunderte—Erwerbungen und Stiftungen 1990–2000.* Munich, 2000.

Hans von Marées: Drawings—The museum's own collection. Exh. cat. Staatliche Graphische Sammlung, Munich. Munich, 1987.

Holler, Wolfgang. *Zeichenkunst der Gegenwart: Sammlung Prinz von Bayern.* Exh. cat. Staatliche Graphische Sammlung, Munich. Munich, 1988.

Klee, Winter, Kirchner: 1927–1934. Exh. cat. Westfälisches Landesmuseum für Kunst- und Kulturgeschichte, Münster. Munich, 2001.

'Neuerwerbungsbericht 1960'. *Münchner Jahrbuch der bildenden Kunst.* Staatliche Graphische Sammlung. XII, 1961, p. 257.

'Neuerwerbungsbericht 1978/79'. *Münchner Jahrbuch der bildenden Kunst.* Staatliche Graphische Sammlung. XXXI, 1980, p. 276.

Pinakothek der Moderne: Eine Vision. Munich, 1995.

Schuster, Peter-Klaus (ed.). *Franz Marc: Postcards to Prince Jussuf.* Munich, 1988.

Schwarz, Michael, and Michael Semmf (eds.). *Brice Marden: Work Books 1964–1995.* Exh. cat. Staatliche Graphische Sammlung, Munich. Munich, 1997/98.

10 Meisterzeichnungen: Neuzugänge der Graphischen Sammlung. Staatliche Graphische Sammlung, Munich. Munich, 1996.

Zeichnungen aus der Sammlung des Kurfürsten Carl Theodor. Exh. cat. celebrating 225th anniversary of the Staatliche Graphische Sammlung, Munich. Munich, 1983.

Architecture

Archifant. Architekturmuseum. 16 July 2002–03.

Baumstark, Reinhold, Carla Schulz-Hoffmann, Michael Semff, Winfried Nerdinger and Florian Hufnagl (eds.). *Pinakothek der Moderne: Kunst, Grafik, Architektur, Design.* Munich and Cologne, 2002.

Behne, Adolf. *Architekturkritik in der Zeit über die Zeit hinaus: Texte 1913–1948.* Basle, 1994.

Herzog, Thomas (ed.). *Expodach: Symbolbauwerk zur Weltausstellung—Hannover 2000.* Munich, 2000.

Nerdinger, Winfried (ed.). *Die Architekturzeichnung: Vom Barocken Idealplan zur Axonometrie—Zeichnungen aus der Architektursammlung der Technischen Universität München.* Munich, 1985.

Nerdinger, Winfried (ed.). *Bruno Taut: 1880–1838.* Stuttgart and Munich, 2001.

Nerdinger, Winfried (ed.). *Konstruktion und Raum in der Architektur des 20. Jahrhunderts: Exemplarische Beispiele aus der Sammlung des Architekturmuseums der Technischen Universität München.* Munich, 2002.

Nerdinger, Winfried (ed.). *Zwischen Glaspalast und Maximilianeum: Architektur in Bayern zur Zeit Maximilians II. 1848–1864.* Exh. cat. Architekturmuseum der Technischen Universität München and Stadtmuseum, Munich. Munich, 1997.

Pinakothek der Moderne: Eine Vision. Munich, 1995.

Schmidt, Johann-Karl, and Ursula Zeller. *Behnisch und Partner: Bauten 1952–92.* Galerie der Stadt Stuttgart. Stuttgart, 1992.

Design

Baumstark, Reinhold, Carla Schulz-Hoffmann, Michael Semff, Winfried Nerdinger and Florian Hufnagl (eds.). *Pinakothek der Moderne: Kunst, Grafik, Architektur, Design.* Munich and Cologne, 2002.

Droste, Magdalena, and Manfred Ludewig. *Marcel Breuer: Design.* Cologne, 1992.

Hufnagl, Florian (ed.). *Einblicke, Ausblicke: Für ein Museum von Morgen.* Die Neue Sammlung, Staatliches Museum für angewandte Kunst. Stuttgart, 1996.

Hufnagl, Florian (ed.). *Reiselust: Internationale Reiseplakate von der Jahrhundertwende bis heute.* Die Neue Sammlung, Munich. Munich, 1995.

Pinakothek der Moderne: Eine Vision. Munich, 1995.

Vegesack, Alexander von. *Das Thonet Buch.* Munich, 1987.

Wick, Rainer. *Bauhauspädagogik.* Cologne, 1982.

Stephan Braunfels's Architecture

Bauer, Reinhard. *Maxvorstadt, zwischen Münchens Altstadt und Schwabing: Das Stadtteilbuch.* Munich, 1995.

Bauer, Richard, and Eva Graf. *Stadt im Überblick: München im Luftbild 1890–1935.* Munich, 1986.

Pinakothek der Moderne: Eine Vision. Munich, 1995.

Ude, Christian (ed.). *Münchner Projekte: Die Zukunft einer Stadt.* Munich, 1993.

wettbewerb aktuell 12 (1987).

wettbewerb aktuell 7 (1992).

Quotations

Chronicle of the Pinakothek der Moderne by Simone Dattenberger in *Münchner Merkur,* no. 213, 14/15 Sept. 2002.

Stephan Braunfels, from *Archifant, Architekturmuseum,* 16 July 2002–03; *Pinakothek der Moderne: Eine Vision.* Munich, 1995.

Carla Schulz-Hoffmann, from *Münchner Merkur,* no. 207, 7/8 Sept. 2002.

Michael Semff, from *Münchner Merkur,* no. 195, 24/25 Aug. 2002.

Winfried Nerdinger, from *Münchner Merkur,* no. 201, 31 Aug./1 Sept. 2002.

Florian Hufnagl, from *Münchner Merkur,* no. 204, 4 Aug. 2002.

Index